D0950470

LAUREN DANE

BROKEN
OPEN

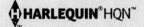
HARLEQUIN® HQN™

Recycling programs
for this product may
not exist in your area.

ISBN-13: 978-0-373-77935-2

Broken Open

Copyright © 2014 by Lauren Dane

HARLEQUIN®
www.Harlequin.com

Printed in U.S.A.

This one goes out to the boy who bought me a rum and Coke
in Paris and let me rant at him for hours
after an upsetting phone call.
Thank you for always having my back and feeding me liquor.

CHAPTER ONE

Before: December

HER WORKDAY OVER, Tuesday Eastwood turned the display lights up before locking her front doors. That's when she realized how cold it was and flipped her collar against the wind with one hand while hurrying to where she'd parked her car.

As she paused to cross at the corner and look both ways, she caught sight of Ezra Hurley. It wasn't one of those moments when you caught sight of a person and then realized who it was once they got closer.

No, she knew it was Ezra because for some befuddling reason she was hyperaware of him. He looked *good* as he waited for traffic, a grin on his face.

In the entirety of her life no one had ever made her belly feel the same quivery, excited swoop when she looked at him. At the rugged, masculine lines of his features. Like his brothers, yes, he was attractive. But he wore it differently than the other three brothers did.

Ezra Hurley was a Capital M *Man.* In that riding horses, baling hay, hands in the dirt, well-worn jeans way. Well-worn jeans that currently cradled a rear end that a sculptor would drool over. The kind of being who seemed to emanate utter capability.

How or why that was so hot to her Tuesday didn't know. But it was.

Even in a wool cap and a peacoat he radiated that something special he tossed around like catnip. In addition to being a rancher, he was a rock star. A one-time hard-living, jet-setting, arena-filling rock star fallen to earth, crashing and burning.

The flames had left him imperfect. But no less compelling.

"Hey, Tuesday." He reached the spot where she'd been rooted as she thought about him naked.

"Ezra. What brings you out tonight?"

"Errands. I was just planning to grab some dinner and head back home." He paused for just a moment. "What are you up to right now? Want to have dinner with me?"

She nodded even though she knew it was a bad idea. Ezra wasn't just a gorgeous rancher–hugely successful musician with a butt any sane woman would want to take a bite of.

He was also the oldest brother of Tuesday's best friend Natalie's boyfriend. It sounded convoluted, sure, but it meant trouble if anything bad happened between Natalie and Paddy, Ezra's brother.

Tuesday told herself it was just dinner. No big deal. She and Natalie were close as sisters anyway. She was supposed to be getting to know the people in Nat's life now.

She slipped her hand around the crook of his arm and didn't make good choices at all. "I'm starving."

He led her just up the block to one of her favorite cafés.

The hostess nearly walked into a post showing

them to their table because she couldn't tear her gaze from Ezra.

"You were very sweet to her," Tuesday murmured when the poor girl stumbled away after he'd thanked her.

He ducked his head a moment before he stepped close. "Let me help you."

The backs of his fingers slid against the skin of her neck as he pulled her collar away and took the coat off.

She closed her eyes a moment as a full-body shiver of delight rolled through her.

"Thank you."

He hung hers up and got rid of his as she settled at the table. Flashing her a smile, he sat across from her as he unwound his scarf.

"I like the beard," she managed to say and surprised herself by not sounding breathy or wheezy even though he seemed to suck all the oxygen from the air around her.

There was a spot she couldn't seem to stop glancing at. Just below his ear at the curve of his jaw. She licked her lips rather than get up and kiss him there.

She gripped the table instead, grateful it kept her out of licking distance.

Then he stroked fingertips over the beard—a nervous habit—and she might have lost consciousness for just a brief moment.

"Yeah? I've had one on and off. Wintertime is good for it."

Tuesday felt much the same way about her legs.

"It suits you." And framed his mouth. He had a great mouth.

She deliberately looked away from him, down at her menu even though she knew exactly what she was going to order.

She'd met Ezra Hurley back in September. Her best friend's boyfriend had three brothers, all gorgeous and successful with immense personal charisma. Ezra was the last of the four she'd met but once he'd walked into the room he was all she'd seen.

She'd seen him several times since as Natalie had got closer to Paddy and they'd been pulled into the Hurley family.

Each time it had been that same shock of connection between them.

They made small talk that wasn't uncomfortable or awkward in any way until their food came.

"Did you have a good Christmas?"

"I did, actually. Got my fill of nieces and nephews. Played a lot of video games. Kids are a great way to avoid shopping trips."

"You don't like to shop?"

"With my mother and sister and all my sisters-in-law? At Christmas? No. I stayed back, drank mulled wine and played video games until the kids got sick of me and then I watched movies and enjoyed the silence."

"I have nieces, both under ten so I know the feeling."

Ezra was like a cat. Tuesday wanted his attention, but she was sort of a cat, too. Each of them brushed up against the other, naturally sort of aloof but totally digging on what the other had.

"I can't imagine what you must be thinking right now." His mouth quirked up and she swallowed hard.

"Do you really want to know?"

He nodded.

"I was just thinking about how you and I are like cats."

He cocked his head, thinking. "Aloof yet demanding?"

She grinned. "Someone has cats."

"I'm not sure if they have me or if I have them."

"That's a yes."

He tore apart a piece of bread and she had to bite the inside of her lip to pry her gaze away from his hands.

She had a thing about hands and his were gorgeous and strong. Rough. *Big.*

"How's business? I imagine things are pretty busy during this time of year."

Tuesday owned and ran a custom framing business in downtown Hood River, Oregon. It wasn't where she'd expected to end up but after her life had gone off the rails, it was this town on the Columbia River and her best friend Natalie, who'd finally given her a place to land.

"The holidays are a good time. It's also great for my custom jewelry." Which was good because she had a huge family and birthdays alone killed her budget. "How goes ranching?"

He looked across the table at her as the server took their food away. "I was thinking of dessert. You in?"

She nodded. "Definitely. They have poached pears here that I love."

He grinned. "That so? Those are Hurley pears— did you know that?"

Sweet Hollow Ranch wasn't only the name of the

band Ezra had founded with his brothers when they were still in their teens. It was the place the Hurleys lived. The land they worked.

And apparently the source of the dessert she was about to order.

"I didn't know. That's pretty nifty."

"I think so, too. If you order the pears, I'll order the cheese plate. We can share. If that's okay with you."

"More than okay. Sounds perfect."

They lingered over their coffee until most people had cleared out and the café got near closing time. He paid up and they gathered their things to clear out.

"I hadn't realized we'd been here so long."

He stood and helped her into her coat. "That's the sign of a good dinner. When you have a great conversation and time gets away from you."

He opened the door for her and even though it was freezing, she got to look at him some more.

His work boots crunched ice as they headed back to her car along the slippery sidewalk.

She couldn't recall any time in recent memory where she'd whiled away three hours over dinner and with someone she'd only met a few times.

Something in him called to her. The shape of his eyes, the history in them, she supposed, a little dark and twisty. His lips, well, the bottom one had to be pillow soft. She'd thought about that issue in great detail. He had the hottest mouth she'd laid eyes on in a long time.

Because she'd been thinking about his mouth she might have been distracted enough that she missed the dip in the sidewalk and started to slip. Not that any such thing needed to be admitted. It was cold and icy after all. Anyone could slip. Who could be expected not to think about Ezra's bottom lip?

"Whoa." He wrapped an arm around her waist and helped her back to her feet, standing very close to her as he did. He was so strong. The energy seemed to hum from him, bringing a shiver she couldn't blame on the cold.

"Are you okay?"

His voice did things to her. A little sandpapery, but wrapped in caramel. It shouldn't have even been possible to be both at the same time but it was. Every once in a while there'd be a burr and it snagged her attention—the pull—which was disconcerting and yet, it was really delicious, too.

He did things to her head. He looked good and he oozed so much raw sensuality it made her tingly. He was handsome, yes, but there was something about him, something elemental that she found herself fascinated by.

And now that she'd had him all to herself like this, she had to admit she wanted more.

"That was close. Thanks for the save."

He paused, still standing near enough that she could smell him. He had really good cologne. Spicy and sexy.

Don't sniff him. Don't sniff him. Don't sniff him.

The moment stretched between them like a physical thing until he finally stepped back and turned, resuming their walk to her car.

She unlocked her driver's-side door, using that time to get herself in order before she leaped on him.

She turned back to face him. "Thanks again for

dinner. Oh, and for preventing a broken bone when I nearly slipped."

His mouth did a thing and it was impossible to look away.

Mainly because it was perfection. Fringed by a minky pelt of a beard she wanted to get all up in. It was messing with her thinking. Like a magical item. Beard of confusion, ha!

But the thing? She'd noticed over dinner that sometimes as she talked, he'd look at her mouth and then he'd lick over his bottom lip as if he was thinking about tasting her. That sweep of his tongue was like a physical stroke against her skin.

Yes, she liked the thing a lot.

She shivered, this time from the cold. He popped open the three buttons lining the front of his wool peacoat and opened it, inviting her.

There was nothing else to be done but take those steps into the warm circle of his embrace, sliding her arms around his waist.

Tuesday tipped her head back to see him better, stilling as their gazes locked a moment before his attention shifted to her mouth. And he did that thing again.

She sucked in a breath this time.

He heard. She knew it because his pupils got very big.

Everything got very far off. Sounds all around them died away until only Ezra and Tuesday remained.

And then his mouth was on hers, the arms holding the coat around her tightened as he pulled her to him.

Snug.

Body to body until there was no mistaking how interested he was in her.

Musician wasn't the only word Ezra could apply *gifted* to.

Oh. Well. Yes, please.

A breathy groan of appreciation came from her and he seemed to lick it from her lips.

It was too much. So much her heart pounded and she fought the desire to run from him.

She hadn't felt anything this powerful with a man since Eric died.

Maybe not even then.

She shoved that far away.

Despite it being too much she wanted more. Throbbed with an overwhelming need to roll around in everything Ezra brought to the table.

Her teeth grazed his bottom lip and she loved the way his beard felt as she did it. She licked over it, squirming to get a little closer.

"Fuckyeah," he muttered right before his tongue slid into her mouth and his taste burst over her.

Vanilla and a touch of brandy from the pears they'd shared after dinner. A little hint of coffee and whatever superendorphin he made with all that hotness.

He kept on, his weight holding her in place against the car.

Inside his coat, the heat of him burned her. But she wasn't sweating from that.

Her heart thundered in her head.

Finally he pulled back a little, sucking in a breath. His gaze was on hers, open. There was pain there with desire and appreciation. Vulnerability.

Please don't apologize or say I should forget it.

After long moments of silence, no apologies or panicked expectation management issued from him and she breathed a little easier even as his taste still lived on her mouth.

Those deep brown eyes shifted his attention to her lips and then back to her gaze.

A smile hinted at the corners of his mouth. "Was that my bounty for saving you from a fall?"

She pursed her lips a moment, enjoying the flirting, and then smiled back. "Maybe."

"I'm always willing to take payment for services or goods via your mouth."

She swallowed. Excited and nervous. Flattered. Turned on. "So I guess I'm rooting for a long, icy winter then, huh?"

He snorted a laugh, letting go and stepping back. The cold reasserted itself with a slap, which made it a little easier to think again.

"Thanks for making my day a hell of a lot better, Tuesday Eastwood." He opened her door.

"Yes. What you said."

He kissed her again quickly. "I'll be seeing you around. You coming to the shows next week?"

Sweet Hollow Ranch, the band Ezra and his brothers created, was set to drop an album and do a short winter and spring tour.

Ezra still wrote, recorded and produced the band's material, but he'd left touring behind once he'd got out of rehab and taken stock of his life.

And now, for the first time in years, Ezra was set to be back onstage with them at a few small fan club secret shows to try out new material before they left for the full tour.

She imagined he was probably excited and nervous about it at the same time. He seemed so capable, though; she bet he wasn't too worried about it.

"We'll definitely be at the shows. Nat and I are driving in together so I'll see you then." She got in her car and he closed the door. Two knuckle raps on the roof and he moved away so she could pull the car out and head home.

He watched her until she turned the corner but she felt his mouth on her skin for hours.

CHAPTER TWO

Now: May

EZRA KNEW WHEN Tuesday had arrived backstage. Every time she was near, an arc of electricity shot up his spine as his hyperawareness seemed to draw them closer to one another. He turned to watch her move through the crowd, that fucking magnificent head of curls setting her apart.

Natalie, Tuesday's best friend and Ezra's brother Paddy's girlfriend, was at her side. The two of them made a picture. Both beautiful in totally different ways. Both fierce and a little wounded.

Maybe a lot wounded. The closer he got with his brother's girlfriend, the more he admired just what she'd overcome. He was uniquely positioned to understand wounded and to not judge it, either.

Natalie squeezed Tuesday's hand before she came over to Ezra. "Ezra, you're looking very handsome tonight." She kissed his cheek and gave him a hug.

"Thank you, sweetheart. I'm glad to see you here. Glad you and Paddy patched things up."

Behind Natalie, his sister-in-law, Mary, had waylaid Tuesday so he forced himself to be patient.

"I hear you were a pretty big part of that finally

happening. He probably won't admit it, but Paddy was so lost without your guidance."

Paddy hadn't just said a bunch of stupid, hurtful stuff to Natalie, he'd said a lot to Ezra as well and then didn't contact either one of them as he spiraled closer to the edge.

Luckily, his brother wasn't as dumb as he was pretty and he'd got his shit straight and made up with Ezra and Natalie both.

"Sometimes you just need to hear someone tell you what you already know."

"You're very wise. It must be why you look at my best friend the way you do."

He scoffed and then made a shooing motion at her. "Go on. Paddy is killing himself not rushing over here."

She gave him one last quick kiss on the cheek and glided over to where Paddy waited—his smile was one all for Natalie.

Finally his patience was rewarded when Tuesday freed herself and resumed her trip over to where he stood, her lips curved up into a sexy smile.

All the spit in his mouth dried at the sight of her once she cleared the crowd. She wore a very short dress that was bright pink and orange and he wasn't sure it was supposed to work, but on her it did. Her shoulders and part of her neck and chest were exposed and the material seemed to wrap around her neck.

He held out a hand her way and she took it. Damn, every single time he touched her it was like a shot of adrenaline. Flipping his hold so he could place a kiss on the heart of her palm and then over her wrist.

"You smell good," he murmured. God help him,

she did. Spicy and sexy and just a little dark. It called to him, like to like.

She stood close enough to hear and her mouth tipped up into another smile.

There was so much chemistry between them it made him a little dizzy. Dizzy enough that he knew the risks and he stood there anyway, planning on kissing every part of her as soon as he could.

Tuesday was his brother's girlfriend's best friend. So close they may as well have been sisters. She lived not only in Hood River but she also lived with Natalie. If something went wrong it could be uncomfortable forever.

And yet he couldn't stop himself when she was in his view. Or his thoughts. Which were pretty frequent. Especially after that kiss in December and the follow-up just the week before.

But if he was totally honest with himself, ever since the first time he'd met her back in the fall.

Tuesday Eastwood was vibrant and sensual and she wore her confidence and intelligence boldly. He found that so attractive he went half-hard just at the sight of her.

"Thank you. I'm excited to see you play tonight."

He looked down to the glittery heels, the pretty painted toes, and then up shapely ankles and calves to toned thighs. Another thing about Tuesday that he dug so much was her love of the outdoors. He worked with his body and it enabled him to burn off all that excess energy...most of it. But he loved to horseback ride and ATV and had been pleased to discover she did, too, when they'd all gone out for rides. She was gorgeous and strong and he wanted some of what she had.

Ezra stood so they were face-to-face. Her sky-high heels brought her level to him, nose-to-nose.

His inner voice screamed caution but he ignored it because it felt so good to want her.

"Thanks. You look fantastic."

"I figured you'd be bringing all this—" she paused to wave a hand his way "—hotness rock star business. Had to up my game."

"Consider it upped. By the way, I'll be escorting you home this evening. I hope you don't mind."

"Paddy asked you to take me so he could sweep Nat off?" Her smile told Ezra she wasn't bothered in the least. "I'll skip the part where I pretend I'm not totally all right with that plan."

"He hasn't asked yet. But he will. I saw the way he looked at her just now. Which is fine with me, as I'd like to have you all to myself."

Techs came through to talk with each brother. With the fame came more money and they could afford to hire people to help keep the instruments they played in working order. And then they'd been able to afford a tech for each member of the band. The tech currently making no attempt to hide the way he looked Ezra over was Ira and he'd been with Sweet Hollow Ranch for a decade.

Having someone who knew his schedule and preferences made it less stressful to be returning to an arena stage for the first time since rehab.

The room got louder and louder as more and more people arrived backstage. The chaos of it jangled his nerves and fucked with his head.

He slid his thumb over her bottom lip. "I need to head to my dressing room for a while."

She reached out, her fingertips brushing against the bone at his wrist as she kissed his thumb. "Go on. You're going to kick ass."

Ezra stepped close again, sliding his arm around her waist. It didn't matter that there were a dozen reasons why pursuing her would be a bad idea. He wanted her, she wanted him, they were both adults and damn it, he didn't want to stop.

He certainly was powerless against it when she moved even closer to him, tipping her head a little, exposing her neck.

He bent his head, breathing her in, brushing his lips over her skin.

"I'll be here when you're done."

"I'm holding you to that." He stepped back and caught up with Ira to talk about his guitars, but her scent lived in him.

Ira gave him a once-over and Ezra pretended not to see it. Ira had been giving him the once-over before shows for years. At least now Ezra wasn't so high he couldn't even stay conscious onstage.

Ezra had his head on straight now. He could be trusted and relied on. No one looked at him with pity-laden expressions tinged with varying shades of disgust. It had been a fight that he wasn't sure he'd win at times, but there he stood, with all that devastation in his past, with great hope for his future.

Satisfied Ezra was all right, Ira relaxed and gave him the rundown before leaving him alone in his dressing room. Even though Paddy was the leader of Sweet Hollow Ranch, it was Ezra who was the founder. The true leader everyone, including Paddy, turned to.

That trust never ceased to amaze Ezra. They shouldn't trust him. Not after heroin. But they did and he would white-knuckle it through every damned day to never disappoint the people counting on him again.

Once he'd finished his shot of wheatgrass juice, he sat back on the couch and put his feet up. With a long, slow exhalation, he leaned back, closing his eyes.

The last time Ezra'd been on a stage this big he'd had a public meltdown that had led him to a stint in rehab. The small club dates they'd played at the start of their tour had been thrilling. It had fed that thirst in him that only playing live could seem to quench.

He'd worried back then that he'd lost his performing mojo. But when he'd walked onstage it had leaped into him as easily as it had the last time he was on stage. Easy, like it had never gone. He'd been *the* Ezra Hurley once more and it had reawakened something inside.

He had something to prove. Not just to his brothers and the fans, but to himself.

TUESDAY'S SKIN STILL tingled where he'd brushed his lips against her neck. It had been so…wow.

She watched his retreating back. Took in the stretch of the soft fabric of his T-shirt at the width of his powerful shoulders. Down to the narrower waist. His brothers were in denim but Ezra chose worn brown leather pants. And cowboy boots with superpointy toes.

His hair was a little more tousled than usual and she noted the tattoos she could see on his arms. Once she saw him all sweaty after they'd gone out ATVing and that was a memory she'd cherish forever. But this? Well now. Rock star Ezra just earned a place next to sweaty, muddy Ezra in her fantasy bank.

Also, he had a fantastic ass.

And he walked like a man who had a big dick.

Natalie sidled up next to her as they both watched him until he was out of sight. "He really works a pair of leather pants," Natalie said in an undertone.

"Indeed. He has big-cock walk, too, don't you think?"

Natalie snorted a laugh. "I can never unhear that!"

"Am I lying?"

"Hell no. What's true is true."

They turned to face one another, grinning. "So things are okay with Paddy?"

Her friend had a huge heart and she was deeply in love with Ezra's brother Paddy. They'd just had a rough patch and had come back together, working hard to get past it, just like Tuesday had known they needed to.

"Yeah. We're good. What's going on with Ezra?"

Which was what Tuesday had been wondering. So she decided it was easier to think on this as a fun, casual thing.

"He wants what I got, duh. Also, I want what he's got so there's a nice synchronicity there."

Mary, Damien Hurley's wife and a new friend, came over to where they stood. "Not going to lie, I am so relieved to be sleeping in my own bed tonight."

They'd been out on tour for three months, which was short, Tuesday knew, owing to the fact that Mary was due to deliver a brand-new Hurley in six weeks. The tour officially ended the next night but Portland was close enough to Hood River that everyone was headed home instead of to yet another hotel.

The gong sounded that indicated it was time to head to the stage. How weird was it that this stuff was totally normal in her life all of a sudden?

Paddy approached, smiling at Tuesday. Tuesday hoped she managed an I-forgive-you-but-if-you-hurt-my-best-friend-I-will-maim-you smile in return.

He got it, nodding again and hugging her briefly before he took Natalie's hand and they walked toward the stage. At the end of the hall, Ezra came out of his dressing room looking fine as hell. A little more tousled. But focused and relaxed.

As if she'd said this out loud, he turned, his gaze locking with hers until she felt the tug between them. He waited until she reached him and fell in beside her. Neither of them spoke. She got the feeling he needed the silence.

At the stage, the brothers moved off, speaking to one another intensely for long moments before breaking apart. Damien went out, followed by Vaughan and then Paddy. Ezra stood beside Tuesday, throwing off crazy amounts of charisma and sex appeal.

"Aren't you going to wish me good luck?" he asked, a teasing smile on his face. But she saw a tiny bit of doubt and it shouldn't have been there.

"No. You know why?" She moved a little closer. "You don't need luck. You're Ezra Hurley. *You wrote this book.*"

He relaxed, taking her hand to kiss her knuckles briefly before he stepped forward, grabbed the guitar Ira held out and slung it on as he hit the stage and started to play.

ONCE HE LEFT the wings, everything changed. He unleashed his energy, powering through, taking the roar of the crowd, the singing to his lyrics, the applause and the interplay between him and his brothers and feasting on it.

Though the other three had been out together a whole tour, Ezra fit in exactly where he always did. They might have been more used to doing this every night, but he was fresher, so it balanced things out.

For those hours, it was Hurleys Against The World once again and everything was absolutely perfect.

At the first encore break they came offstage and he hit the john, rinsing off his face and neck, changing his shirt.

As he approached the stage Tuesday waited. The look on her face was all about him and it sent a slice of longing down his spine.

He'd wait, though. Just as she did, letting him keep his head in the music. Seemingly assured he'd give her the proper attention when the time came.

That sort of confidence was hot.

He grinned her way as he took his guitar back from Ira and they went out once more.

Three encores later and it was time to go home.

AFTER A SHOW was even louder and more chaotic than it was before the show. When Ezra came offstage, he ended up at Tuesday's side as they all headed back to the greenroom.

The energy seemed to spiral through him and he needed to clean up and get himself together.

He leaned in toward Tuesday once they got to the greenroom. "I'm going to shower and change. Okay with you?"

She nodded. "Of course. I'll be here when you're finished." Her mouth, *good sweet Christ,* he wanted to lean in and kiss it. So much his hands shook a little.

Tuesday tipped her chin at him. "Go on then. You won't break me."

He halted, stunned. "What?"

"You were looking at my mouth like you wanted it. So take it."

In two steps he'd slid his arm around her waist as he met her body, his mouth sliding over hers, over lips that opened on a sigh as she gave over to him.

He sucked her bottom lip, grazing it with his teeth. Her fingers dug into the front of his T-shirt, holding him to her.

Need clawed at him, sharp and insistent. He wanted to back her up to the wall and fuck her right then and there.

With a groan, he stepped back right as a bunch of people came into the room.

"We'll continue this conversation when I'm cleaned up." He licked over his lips and tasted her again.

She breathed out slowly, one corner of her mouth tipped up into a smile.

But he got waylaid before he could reach the door, as his brothers surrounded him, slapping his back and hugging him.

His energy mingled with theirs and it was okay. *This* was okay to want. This was part of how it was between the Hurley boys and it was good and elemental and he needed to hold on to that.

But it sure didn't hurt to hear Paddy nearly shout, "Best fucking show in *years,* man. Ez, you fucking ran that shit out there tonight. Well done." Paddy grinned at his brother and Ezra gave him one right back.

There was a flurry of hugs from Mary and Natalie and their other friends who'd come to the show.

Tuesday got tugged away to meet someone so he watched her move as he drank some tea and listened to Vaughan and Damien.

Mary patted his arm, following his gaze. "Looks like we interrupted something when we came in here."

Ezra shrugged. It would happen. He'd been sure from that first time he'd kissed her downtown and then, just three weeks earlier, in the darkness between the grape arbor at her house and the wall.

They'd been heading toward a naked collision for months now. He smiled at his sister-in-law. "No worries, sweetheart."

He managed to escape to his dressing room nearly an hour later and by the time the water hit his skin, he was ready to run a marathon or fuck.

No marathon that night. Maybe fucking—they certainly had chemistry. Maybe not. Yes. It would happen, though. Ezra found the slow pace, this long seduction of Tuesday and Ezra to not only be sexy, but it gave him the time to work through the way he felt about her. All that desire was seriously hot but the want…he needed to find a way to handle it so he could enjoy it and stop being wary.

It made him feel alive on a whole new level.

CHAPTER THREE

"So." Ezra paused at his car, a sleek, sexy, low-slung Porsche. He backed her to the door and her arms slid around his neck as he stepped close for a kiss.

"So?" she breathed as he pulled back after smooching the wits right from her head.

"Nothing really. I just wanted to kiss you again before you got into the car."

Tuesday laughed, delighted. Sometimes he came off so serious and broody that when he cracked a joke and exposed his dry sense of humor it always felt like a delicious secret.

"All right then."

She got in, bending to unstrap her shoes and slide them off.

When she straightened, she found him staring.

"You have great legs," he said in that snarly voice of his and she smiled, leaning back into the buttery-soft leather seats.

He drove with the same sort of intensity he did everything else she'd seen him do. Though their show had ended nearly two hours earlier, the surface streets around the venue were still busy. He seemed to be doing some sort of complicated geometry so she looked out the window as he wended and wove his way to the freeway.

Once they'd got away from the crowded streets he relaxed a little. Enough that she felt she could speak again.

"You were on point tonight."

He smiled, keeping his attention on the road. "Yeah?"

"I saw you once. I mean before. When you were still touring. In Louisville. I was there visiting my family."

"It's crazy to me that we both have family within a forty-mile radius of one another in Kentucky." Wariness edged his words. She talked about family but she bet he thought about his addiction.

"It was early," she said because it was important he know she saw him at his best. Preheroin. "I think maybe right after *Ten To Midnight* came out. Anyway, that's a long way to say I saw you play before so I have a comparison to make. You were good at the club shows last December. You were like that times a thousand. Tonight, Ezra Hurley was a *rock star.*"

And it was hot. So hot she'd nearly melted just watching him move. The Ezra he'd been out there, utterly self-assured, sexy, in charge, made her shiver. When he played and wasn't singing, he'd worn a smirk like he was thinking of something really dirty.

Best of all, he'd owned it, putting it on like a shirt that fit perfectly. All that hot, in-charge stuff had rolled off him in rushing waves. Tuesday wondered what he did with all that energy when he wasn't onstage. Except for those brief moments when he turned it on her and she nearly drowned in it, he was pretty chill.

From a distance.

There was a darkness to Ezra. Something the darkness that lived in her seemed to respond to. A bone-deep grief he didn't use as a shield—in fact he tried to downplay it. But it was there and she bet it was part of what motivated him to succeed now.

She shivered at the idea of being the focus of that sort of attention. She had a very strong feeling Ezra didn't hold back in bed. At all.

She also had a very strong feeling she'd know. Soon.

She'd never been so attracted to another person. Not in the whole of her life, which also made her uncomfortable and feeling as if she was being disloyal to Eric even though he'd been dead four years. It wasn't like she'd achieved expert-level widow status or anything. Nope, she had zero idea of how to begin to think about it.

Thank goodness Ezra spoke to pull her out of that particular self-punishing reverie. "It felt right. Tonight I mean. There's a rhythm onstage. It's different than anything else you do as a band. I've been off tour for years now. Enough that my brothers have a timing that's apart from me at this point.

"In the studio, well, that's one thing. Out on the road they're working with tour musicians, who are really good, no lie, but it's about the three of them. The club shows were more like jamming in the studio. Tonight, that unit of three opened up and I fit where I had belonged at one time when there were four of us in Sweet Hollow Ranch."

She wondered if it was hard to see that they'd moved on without him. Or if he was tempted to go back out on tour after tonight's performance. But she didn't know him well enough to delve deeper. Not without knowing if she'd make it worse.

She liked Ezra a lot and she didn't want to screw things up, but she wanted to know him better.

"Do you find yourself, you know, wishing you'd be able to go back out on tour? I mean… I don't know what I mean. I mean, I do, but in my head it sounded better than it does out loud."

He snorted. "It's fine. I'm not sure how to feel about it. Not yet. Not entirely." He paused and she left it, hoping he'd elaborate but knowing he might not.

"The album just dropped. Mary and Damien are about to have a baby and of course they'll want to be home, close to family. Paddy and Natalie are going to be intertwined for a while—it's not like he'll be willing to leave her behind. It's time to put our lives first. Take care of what's important."

Tuesday didn't miss the way he referred to the band as *we*.

"We should have done it for Vaughan," he muttered.

"Do you want to elaborate?"

"You're not just going to insist I share?"

She waved a hand. "Who am I to do that? I say things out loud sometimes that I may not mean to. Or maybe I do, but I'm just tossing it out to talk about it later."

"I suppose with Vaughan it's more a tossing the idea out there and maybe we can chew over it later."

"Okay."

Things settled into an easy silence for a while. Tuesday liked quiet. She grew up in an insanely loud house. Always alive with kids, family and friends.

It meant she cherished silence and guarded her life zealously, keeping the number of people who didn't appreciate the same to a bare minimum.

Except her family. They were loud and crazy and there was no changing that.

"So tell me what you're thinking right now," Ezra coaxed in his supersexy voice.

"You really want to know?"

"I'm a grown man, Tuesday. I say what I mean."

Okay then. Why was that so hot? Why did he make her itchy and sweaty and a little lonely after they parted?

"I was thinking about quiet. About how I like it and how we'd been sharing a nice quiet moment. I wish more people liked it."

"Quiet amplifies loneliness for some people. Maybe for most people."

"There's nothing wrong with being lonely sometimes."

He hummed. A sound of agreement and approval and it, too, was hot. God, everything about him was hot. How did that even happen? How did one person come with so much on every damned level? What sort of cosmic Scooby Snack was Ezra Hurley anyway?

"I didn't come to appreciate silence until I was in rehab."

TUESDAY SETTLED INTO the seat, looking out the window as he spoke. Ezra had a gut feeling it was because she knew he'd prefer she not watch him as he revealed himself.

He didn't know why he was sharing this stuff. Other than he liked her. He liked being with her and the slow getting to know one another thing was new. And slightly disconcerting because she was such a stupid choice for him to make and he was going to make it anyway.

"They sent me to this place in the middle of no-where. Just trees and fresh air and mountains in the distance." He'd gone straight into their detox unit for the first week. "Rehab is loud. I mean, and look, I *know* how lucky I was that the place I went was as great as it was. But there's a lot of crying in rehab." Puking, too. He hated that part worse than all the crying.

"The rehab was on acres of land and the main house and the outer cabins were fenced off. It was, I remember even now, a three-mile circuit and I'd walk it like four times a day just to go be alone."

"Did you feel lonely?"

"Yes." He'd alienated everyone who'd ever mattered to him. He'd fallen so low and had hurt so many people the loneliness had nearly drowned him.

"When it's quiet you can't avoid it." Her words, the tone in her voice, told him she knew this firsthand.

"No. No matter how much it hurts. No matter how much of it is your own fault." He shook it off. "Anyway, I had to find better ways to process all my shit. What I'd been doing was killing me." It wasn't in a group when he'd first been able to say he was a fuck-ing heroin addict out loud. It was under a tree, by him-self at that fence line. It had been Ezra who needed to say it. Needed to hear it. Needed to believe it.

Her head moved in a slow nod. "I do think some-times that it's when I'm avoiding being alone that I need it most. I can't lie to myself with the same ease I can to other people."

"It's pretty badass to be so—what do you call it? Self-aware?"

"Ha!" She laughed. "My mother is a hippie disguised as an engineer. She made us keep dream journals when we were growing up. She's really into speaking the truth and shaming the devil."

"Is it as annoying as I'm imagining it to be or am I seeing it wrong?"

She started to giggle. First a tiny burst and another and one more until she'd erupted into a full-on fit and he couldn't really do anything but smile.

And want more.

"It's *totally* annoying. She's all woo-woo and hippie-dippy *and* she's an engineer, too. So imagine organized woo-woo. Anyway, she still goes once a year to a holistic healing retreat where they do yoga for fun and eat loaves of mung beans or whatever. Makes her happy, which is the point of such things. Essentially, I was raised to face the unpleasant stuff. Because that's what you're supposed to do."

He'd bet her mom was pretty fantastic. "You mentioned your dad is a roofer?"

"You were telling me about rehab and silence. Then it's my turn."

He sighed. "I guess I used the chaos and the noise to keep from confronting my shit. And then I had so much noise and nothing but time so I found some silence and it wasn't until then that I could really do the work."

"Talk about self-aware."

"Therapy."

"Ah. Well."

"I see you know what I mean." The moment he said it he wished he could recall the words immediately.

"I'm sorry. I forgot. It was careless."

She blew out a breath. "It's all right. I promise. In this case, though, I had therapy when I was a kid. Before I knew Eric even existed. I was nine. There was an accident on a field trip. Our van flipped and ended up in a river."

Her voice had gone faraway.

"Two of my classmates and one of my teachers died. I'd been motion sick and the window had been open so I wouldn't throw up. It's how I got out so fast. Anyway, my parents made me go to a psychologist to deal with the nightmares and the grief counseling stuff. Wow, I've made this rather heavy. I'm sorry to be a buzzkill."

Buzzkill his ass. She was incredible. He made a disapproving sound as he pulled up the drive to the large Victorian Tuesday shared with Natalie. The motion sensor lights flooded the front of the house, exposing pretty front gardens and a porch with furniture that invited you to sit.

He keyed the car off and turned to her. "So we both found our silence it looks like."

She nodded. A shadow across her features meant he couldn't see her expression very well. "And owned our loneliness, huh?"

Maybe so, but he didn't have to be alone right then and neither did she.

He ignored her rhetorical question. "Let me walk you in. Make sure everything is all right."

"Is this a pity good-night hand squeeze for the widow?"

Holding back an annoyed snarl, he got out and circled to her side, opening the door and helping her to her feet.

He moved in close. "Is that what you want from me, Tuesday? Pity? I can give you pity at a coffee shop in broad daylight. I can send you a book about grief but I'm betting you've written one of your own."

Her gaze flicked up, snagging on his. Defiant. Good. He didn't want her afraid or cowed; he wanted her to know who he was and want him anyway.

She licked her lips and then shrugged. "I want you to touch me and never make me think you feel sorry for me. People die, Ezra. It happened. It happened when I was nine and it happened four years ago. I'll die. You'll die. It's what we're born to do. I don't need your pity. I need your dick."

He barked a laugh, surprised. She clearly didn't want to go into it any deeper right then so he let it go because he knew what that felt like. "I think I can manage that."

"All right then." She linked her arm through his and walked, her heels dangling from a fingertip as they headed up her front porch steps.

Ezra was sure the house was fine; they had good locks and security. It wasn't really that he *had* to walk her in, or that he was concerned for her safety. Sharon Hurley's sons might have been an unruly handful at school, but they always opened doors for people; they said *please, thank you, sir* and *ma'am;* and they walked their dates to the door. Hurleys had a protective streak when it came to people they considered theirs.

Theirs. She was his brother's girlfriend's best friend. And he considered Tuesday a friend. So that's what it was. Nothing more.

Ezra paused at that for a moment but let it pass.

He wanted to be with her. Alone in a place he could lay her out and enjoy her awhile. Natalie would be with Paddy so they'd have the house all to themselves where they'd be far less likely to be interrupted by someone whose last name ended in a *Y*.

Tuesday turned to him as he heard the snick of a lamp turning on. The main living area warmed with a golden glow. He'd been there before with Natalie, but this was the first time he'd been inside, alone with Tuesday. It was a nice enough place but he wasn't there to look at the furniture.

"The smile on your face?" One of her brows slid up. "Should I be delighted or worried?"

"All my smiles when it comes to you are ones that should delight you."

"Wow. That's a really bold statement, Ezra."

"I'm full of bold statements, beauty."

She hummed as she dropped the shoes and then headed to him, not stopping until one of her hands rested on his chest. "I think I'm going to like finding out. Come upstairs. I'll show you my side of the house."

CHAPTER FOUR

SHE TOOK HIS hand and led him through the house and kitchen. "Nat and I each occupy half the upstairs. My entry is back here."

Her stairs led up a spiral case that was mainly windows. Even better, he realized as he looked up and up, the highest panes were stained glass.

"Is that as pretty as I think it could be when the light hits it just right?"

She indicated the area with a wave of her hand. "Yes. It lights this whole space with blues and reds. Those panels were the original. The people who sold the house to Natalie had taken them out and replaced them with clear glass. We found the stained glass in the shed out back. Not even a hairline crack. It's amazing but they were in perfect condition."

Once they walked a few steps in, he slid into what was, without a doubt, Tuesday's innermost world. Though the elegance and classic lines weren't a surprise, he found this space—her private space—unexpectedly soft.

The furniture in her realm was more formal, in curves and swoops. He didn't know what the style was called, but he liked it. Decorative moldings and a chair rail defined the walls without overtaking the space. Soft blues and yellows complemented a seat-ing area with a small love seat and table. Bookshelves had been built along one wall, framing the window where a chaise sat with a throw tossed on the back and an e-reader on the side table.

The imagined peace one would feel just lying there reading on a lazy afternoon tugged at him, made him hungry for it. It had been way too long since being lazy had been a luxury he'd allowed himself.

"Reading nook?"

She nodded. "When I came up here the first time, this part of the house had been empty. Natalie didn't have enough furniture to fill it up and she'd really only been living in her half of the upstairs. Anyway. I got up here and it was afternoon. The light slanted across the floors just right and I knew this was a place I should be. I read a lot. I like reading in bed but sometimes I want to sit in my window over there, cover my legs with a blanket and read while it rains."

"I have a library at my house. It's part of my home studio and practice space. But I'm with you—I like reading in bed."

She cocked her head. "I have to admit, I so rarely see you still, I might be totally surprised to come upon you caught up in a book."

"When I was in first grade, I still couldn't read and my parents were dealing with the school back and forth. They said I wasn't very smart and you've met my mother so you can imagine how well that went over. Anyway, finally my mom said, can he read something else? Something he picks? They agreed. Probably to get her to shut up and leave, but it works for her brilliantly."

Tuesday's laugh brought him a step closer.

"Let me guess how that ended. When *you* got to choose you loved reading. You just didn't like anyone else making your choices."

"It's a flaw. I admit it." He looked at her, letting her see what he was thinking. "I like being in control."

She blinked a few times.

"Is this a sex reference? I'm sorry. Is it unsexy to have to ask? I probably shouldn't have even asked."

"Beauty, you have plenty of sexy. That's not a worry. It's a general comment that also happens to apply to sex."

Watching this normally superconfident woman get a little flustered when it came to this—when he sure as hell felt a little flustered himself—filled him with tenderness he rarely felt for anyone outside his family.

She shrugged. "I suppose then, we'll have to go along and see if your need to control and my need to lick you all over are compatible."

TUESDAY KNEW SHE sounded a lot more confident than she felt. Sex with him? Yes. Yes and yes again. Control, though? What did that mean? Like something creepy? Or something hot? Sometimes people inexplicably found stuff like cell phone tracking and that sort of control to be superhot. She was not one of them.

She didn't need a dad. Or a protector. Or a white knight. Or a stalker.

"That's some conversation you're having in your head, given the look on your face." He fought a smile and she was charmed.

Ezra was out of her league. This pull between them had the potential to be overwhelming and end horribly.

But it felt so good she let herself do it anyway.

She was used to confident men, yes. Smart, too. But Ezra wasn't just some dude she planned to fuck awhile.

"I was just weighing what you might mean by control."

The gaze he raked over her was nearly physical. One of his brows went up and one corner of his mouth dented with a freaking dimple. A dimple. He was so ridiculously alluring at that moment, tousled, big and hearty.

Tuesday loved a big man. Some people liked brown eyes; she liked tall men with broad shoulders. The material of his shirt stretched over so much taut skin and work-strong muscle she couldn't have stopped looking if she'd tried. Which she had no plans to do. If something broke, he'd know how to fix it. If something was heavy, he'd carry it.

More than being physically big, Ezra was big with his presence, as well. He seemed to radiate with energy and intensity.

It made her greedy because Ezra Hurley was like chocolate volcano cake. You knew it had the most calories on the menu and that it would be a gooey mess but you ordered it anyway because gooey, messy and high in calories usually meant a good time.

She was going to gorge herself on this man and she was going to do it without apology or second-guessing because she wanted him. She wanted him and he wanted her and this thing they shared was so hot and compelling and sexy that it made her drunk on his testosterone.

She groaned. "You have a really big dick, don't you?"

He did a double take once he truly heard her question and it was so funny she nearly forgot she'd actually blurted out that thing about his dick.

See? *Drunk.* Like an amateur. She wasn't an amateur, damn it! "Um." She put her hands over her face, the skin hot against her palms.

"I didn't actually mean to say that out loud."

He stepped close enough to slide his arms around her waist. Now that she had her heels off, he was much taller and she had to look up a bit but he was smiling.

"Well, if you're going to ask such a question at least your assumption that my cock is big is a good way to go about it. But you can just see for yourself. If you're curious and all."

She mirrored the way he held her. Though her hold on his waist was moot once he pulled her closer, arranging her the way he pleased before he turned his attention back to her face.

And then she sort of got the whole control thing in the way he'd meant it.

Ezra was *in charge* and she liked it just fine.

Ezra touched her like he meant it. The brief bite as his fingertips pressed into her upper arms as he shifted her did all sorts of things to her hormones. Rough, yes. But more because he wanted her so much, he *had* to have her.

He wasn't just there. He was *utterly* present and focused on her.

Thrilling. Flattering. Dizzying.

He bent and she tipped her face up to meet his kiss. He was a master class–level kisser as he gave a long, slow perusal of her mouth. Exploring her, tasting each part as if she were delicious. A lick against her top lip. A lave with the flat of his tongue over the curve of her bottom lip. He tangled his tongue with hers. A quick flick here, a nibble there.

Ezra Hurley pretty much kissed all the reasons not to fuck him that night right out of her head. Which was fine and all, since really, her reasons had been thin and dumb and he was so warm and hard and pressing that part of him she'd just asked about to her belly.

Yeah, big.

When he broke the kiss she licked her lips to get one last bit of his taste. "You haven't seen my bedroom yet."

His smile made her clit throb. Like actual pulsing and she knew she had to take note and relay that info to Natalie because that was the sort of thing you totally told your best friend.

"I haven't. You're a terrible hostess."

For a man with such darkness in his eyes, he also had a wonderful sense of humor.

"I didn't even offer you any juice or a snack."

"I'd rather see you naked."

"Well. I approve of your priorities."

She took his hand and led him into her bedroom. This was her intimate space. Natalie often had people in her room, but Tuesday was more hesitant. Sure their close friends had been up here, but she'd never actually had a man in her bedroom since she'd lived in that house. Hell, she hadn't shared her bed with anyone in four years. Not since she'd been married. She supposed she still *was* married. Wasn't she? Death wasn't divorce, right?

That hit her so hard she actually had to sit down on the edge of her bed.

Concern on his face, Ezra knelt to face her. "Tuesday? Are you all right?"

She considered not answering. It was embarrassing and stupid and if she did tell him they totally weren't going to have sex that night.

Then again, he was precisely the kind of man who wouldn't just fuck her if she said, "Never mind, I'm fine, bone me," either.

Tuesday swallowed her hesitance and said, "Something just occurred to me. Hit me a little harder than I'd expected it to."

"Your husband?"

What a weird conversation to be having and yet it was okay to share with him. So she did. "I was just thinking I hadn't had a man up here. Ever."

He sat next to her on the bed, leaning his weight back on an arm as he looked her over. "He died when?"

"Four and a half years ago."

"It's been years since you've been with anyone?" His voice got a little thready and it made her smile, even through the memories.

"Good lord, no."

She loved sex. *Loved* it. When Eric had been alive they'd had it often until he'd started to get sick. Looking back it should have been a clue but she hadn't seen it. Maybe if she had sooner it could have made a difference.

That was definitely not a road she'd be going down.

He'd been waiting for her to keep speaking. Knowing there'd be more. And there was, of course. "I just don't here."

He rumbled in his chest, again, approval and agreement. It was a good, solid sound and she liked it a lot.

"I do what I need to do but I don't bring it here." Said in her head, those words made her feel tough and independent. Out loud they made her sad that she'd lived like that and considered it enough.

"This is a seriously sexy bedroom." He shrugged, not getting worked up at what she'd said. "Their loss."

He wasn't going to push about Eric. About anything. She breathed a little easier.

She swung herself around to straddle his lap. The surprised pleasure on his features thrilled her.

"That was sort of a boner killer, huh?"

"The stuff you say. It just shoots from your mouth. It's awesome." He writhed a little, stroking his totally *not* dead boner against her. Where only a thin layer of cotton and his jeans separated them.

"You might want to know this, about my boner, that is. It takes an awful lot to kill it. And frankly, you're so delicious I'm not sure it can be done when I'm looking at you, much less when you're in my lap, those gorgeous breasts just right in front of me, the heat of your pussy against my cock. With all you bring it'd take a nuclear bomb to kill."

This was happy in a way she hadn't felt in so long. It rushed through her as she soaked it in. She hadn't even realized how starved she'd been for *this*. Not just sex, but *zing*. That connection with someone that lifts them into a totally different category in your life.

Bittersweet pleasure bloomed through her as she

leaned down and buried her face in his neck as she'd been craving for hours. She smiled against the skin right where it met his shoulder and took a deep breath.

His fingers on her sides tightened and she again thought about the size of his hands. Also big there.

He held her, fingers spread against the fabric of her dress, but he seemed to burn through the material to scald her skin.

She pulled back so she could look at him and right away she was smiling because Sharon and Michael Hurley really did make four stellar human beings in the looks, sex appeal and charisma department.

His grin slid from amused into sensual confidence and promise. Like he hit a switch, though she knew it wasn't put on. She'd seen his stage persona and how he acted with other people. She knew this heat between them was totally real.

It was more that all this simmered beneath a surface he worked very hard to keep intact. He drew that away sometimes to let her see to the heart of his emotions and that made her sort of…gooey. It flattered her that he'd share so much intimacy. It was erotic. Simple and so powerful.

She shivered and he reached up to pull her back down to him. Once he was near enough, he stretched up to kiss her chin and then her neck.

He held her as he licked over her collarbone, which she'd never considered exciting but clearly Ezra had some sort of collarbone secret because it *worked*. One of her hands fisted in the coverlet where she'd leaned her weight as he pretty much set off fireworks by kissing her freaking *collarbone*.

SHE LET OUT a moan that echoed through her body straight up his cock, which was already hard to the point of pain.

He slid a palm up her back to where her dress was tied and paused a moment to be sure she was still with him. That's when she undulated, grinding herself against his dick. Close enough he felt the heat of her.

She sat up above him so he moved to sit, as well, holding her in his lap as they perched on the edge of her bed.

Two or three seconds and he peeled the dress away from the most incredible breasts he'd ever seen. And—not that he'd ever say it out loud in the same state as Tuesday—he'd seen enough breasts to be somewhat of an expert.

So he couldn't be blamed for being focused on the tight, dark nipples capping some seriously fine C cups through the sheer peach-colored material of a bra that also fastened around her neck. Clever.

"That was unexpected. But I like it." He bent his head to press his lips to the left curve of her cleavage before he popped the back open and got rid of the bra. "I like this even more."

He took her breasts in his hands and she sucked in a breath, her hands braced on his shoulders as she arched her back.

"Can't lie—I like that, too," she gasped out as he tugged on her nipples.

He needed more. More access. More *everything*.

He half stood, bringing her with him and spun, dropping her on her back on her bed before settling between her thighs.

That's when he finally noticed the dragonfly tattooed on her belly, just beneath and between her breasts. An art nouveau design with an Alphonse Mucha flair in delicate, simple lines.

"Beautiful." He licked over it and up the bottom swell of her left breast. Her fingers slid into his hair, holding him in place.

He delighted in her responses. The way her skin, nearly bronze in the low light, pebbled up as he licked over it. The sounds she made would never let him misunderstand what she liked and expected. A soft, ragged moan of pleasure, an impatient huff, a pleading sigh. She tugged a little harder than necessary when he did something she didn't like and arched into him when he hit a good spot.

There was something so fearless and fierce about her, about the way she liked what she liked and demanded it. It was a sort of full-tilt sensual experience, but it was real and raw and made him hot all over. It fed that gnawing hunger that drove him so hard he was dizzy with it.

Everything about her pressed against him in the best sort of way. The air smelled of her, of that unique warm, spicy floral scent she wore. Of her sex. Of her skin. He came to attention when he realized he'd be leaving his scent all over her things. Yes, he liked that a lot.

Her body spread out on her bed excited his senses as he took her in. She was tall. Powerful. He loved all the juxtaposition she came with. Athletic but not so much she didn't still have the swell at her hips, the curves and feminine abundance that made his mouth water. She might dress up and wear heels, but her hands were those of a woman who used them to work.

He'd seen the jewelry she made and the work she'd framed. Tuesday was a woman who loved creating beautiful things and he could totally relate. She was bold and strong and vibrant even as she was also cool and elegant and soft.

Confident in a way most of the women he'd been with in the past couldn't get near. And yet vulnerable. The whole of her was everything he craved and worried about at the same time.

She'd taken off her little tortoiseshell glasses and left them on the table so now he could see the smattering of freckles on her cheeks and just how long her lashes really were.

He'd seriously never seen anything like her hair. It was magnificent, an inky dark mass of gorgeous curls. It looked even better spread out around her head as she lay in bed.

Her eyes slowly opened at she stared up at him. There was no sense of urgency. This was playing out how it should, which made him a little nervous, but it wasn't outweighed by the need racing through him to have her.

He hissed as she slid her hand up inside his shirt, over the skin of his back, her fingertips digging into the muscle, urging.

She tipped her neck as he kissed down it and then down her body until he backed off the bed enough to stand. "I need that dress off. I want to see all of you."

Quickly, she was up and on her knees, her dress whipped off and tossed to a nearby chair, remaining in nothing more than a whisper-thin pair of panties in that same sheer material as the bra.

He was *so* fortunate.

Ezra tipped his chin at her. "Ali."

She shimmied from her underpants and continued to kneel there, facing him, utterly and gloriously naked.

He took a long look at her. "Beauty, you slay me."

He yanked his shirt off and she sighed happily.

"You should take your shirt off onstage. Or maybe not." She frowned briefly. "But in front of me you should whenever you like. Or whenever I like. Whichever."

His hands moved to the buttons on his jeans and her gaze never left them. All in all, when he finally—carefully—got out of them and his boxers it was really clear how much he enjoyed her gaze on him.

And that nearly painful erection nearly lost all its vigor when a thought occurred to him. "Please tell me you have condoms."

She froze. "Shit. Hang on." She scrambled from the bed and headed into her bathroom but shortly returned with some little packets he recognized as his brand. "I do. Should I give you one for your wallet?" She winked.

Laughing, he grabbed her as she walked by and sent them both to the mattress.

"I wasn't going out looking to get laid."

She reached between them, wrapping her fist around him and giving his cock a few slow thrusts and sending his thoughts into disarray. "Yeah? Seems to me, Ezra, that you and I have been headed right here since the first time I met you."

Damn, when she was so bold and demanding it sent a wave of desire through him, hot and fast like a wildfire. He wanted inside her and right that very moment.

Instead, he forced himself to slow down and enjoy.

"Yes. That much is true." But he hadn't known for sure that she'd be there and maybe he'd been a little nervous and all his attention had been on the show. He'd forgotten until that moment. He wasn't good at the *hey, I might get laid later better take a rubber* game anymore. "But I wasn't going to take anything as a given anyway."

He took her mouth again, starting off sweet, playful even. But within a minute or two things had deepened and he was so hard that even if he had got in her right then he'd have come too soon.

That wasn't on his to-do list.

He eased down her body, licking the place where thigh met torso. She made a deep sound, a sort of gasp and moan all at once.

He loved that she'd left the lights on so he could look his fill. He spread her open and did just that. She didn't try to close her legs against him or shy away. Instead she watched him look at her, pleased.

He took a lick and the sound she made in response was a lot like what he did when he tasted something delicious. He understood it because he wanted to make that same sound at the salty sweet of her on his tongue.

He built her climax slowly, tasting her, getting his fill of her. When she rolled her hips, urging him and he wasn't ready just yet, he pressed her hips to the mattress and her body responded just as loudly as her moan.

Oh hell yes. She liked it as much as he did.

He wasn't going to rush along when it came to the first orgasm he ever gave her, after all. Ezra wanted her to have his touch burned into her brain, wanted to make her come so hard he pushed every other memory of every other man away.

Deep down he could be petty and admit it was daunting to think about competing with the memory of a dead man. Ezra wanted Tuesday thinking about *him*.

Her body seduced him as he touched and kissed, nibbled and licked. All he felt, tasted and heard was her. Even the breath he gulped in was laced with her scent.

Something about her drove him to please, to preen and show off, and when he finally knew she was ready, he kept his pace relentless, pushing her hard and fast as he slid two fingers deep.

With a hoarse cry, she arched, and the hands that'd been on his shoulders shifted, her nails digging in, urging him on. He kept going, gentling little by little until he finally pressed a kiss to her belly and moved back up her body.

"Now that the edge has been taken off, I have a few more things to show you."

Her smile was lazy and pleased. "Can't wait."

He bent, licking across a nipple when a ruckus loud enough to hear easily from Tuesday's room sounded downstairs.

Alarmed, Ezra moved to stand quickly and quietly. "You stay here. Call 911 if necessary."

"No!" Before he'd even realized it, she was next to him in a robe.

Downstairs someone yelled Tuesday's name. At least he could thank his lucky stars he didn't have to argue with Tuesday about staying out of the way of a freaking prowler.

"Shit, that's Nat."

Before he could tell her to hold up, Tuesday rushed out. With a curse, he found his pants and got them on. He snatched up a shirt on his way out and got it on right as he entered the kitchen.

Natalie looked to Tuesday with a smirk but it was a fast thing, soon replaced by worry. Tuesday had ignored it, so Ezra would let *her* deal with Natalie on this topic. It wasn't that he expected it not to get out if he and Tuesday finally hooked up. His family was nosy and interfering. But *he* didn't even know what it was between him and Tuesday yet, so it wasn't something he could explain.

Natalie's expression made his gut tighten and luckily before he could demand to know what was wrong she started to fill him in. "I tried calling your phone and Paddy tried Ezra. I'm sorry to bug you."

Paddy came in from the living room. "Is he here?" He stopped short when he saw Ezra. "Thank God."

Seeing his brother so worried beat at him. Ezra stepped in and took control. He touched Paddy's shoulder. "Patrick, you're freaking me out. Tell me what's going on."

"It's Maddie."

Maddie was Vaughan's oldest daughter, one of their two nieces.

Ezra's heart pounded. "What about her?"

"Appendix. Vaughan stopped by Kelly's place on his way home from the arena, but they had just decided to take her to the emergency room because of her fever. He called Mom from there. Apparently if they'd waited even half an hour more it would have been really bad and burst. They're operating on her right now."

"Jesus." Ezra simply went into protective big brother mode as he took over from Paddy. "Let me get with Mom to see what the status is."

Ezra got on the phone with his parents and within minutes he'd managed to settle everyone down. His parents had recently arrived at the hospital where they met Vaughan and Kelly, Vaughan's ex-wife and the mother of his children.

Ezra explained everything to Paddy, Natalie and Tuesday once he'd hung up. "Dad says the hospital won't let anyone else in where they're waiting along with Vaughan and Kelly. Kensey is sleeping over at a friend's house already so at least that one thing is taken care of, by the way." Kensey was Maddie's little sister. "Someone will call when Maddie's out of surgery and they hear from the doctor. He said not to come down there right now."

"I feel helpless." Paddy paced as Natalie put the kettle on for some tea.

Tuesday spoke quietly from where she'd been pulling mugs down from a cabinet. "One thing you might do is make your parents and Vaughan a reservation at a hotel near the hospital. After you've been at the hospital all day you need a place to retreat. To shower and nap and just let go when no one else is watching."

Ezra wasn't sure how to feel about the raw pain in her tone. She clearly didn't want to go into it, and at the same time, she didn't hide it.

"That's a great idea." And it was. His parents would rest if it was convenient to the hospital and the room was paid for and would go to waste otherwise. And if they did, they'd spot Vaughan back and forth.

"Let me do it. Give me something to do before I go crazy." Paddy headed into the living room as he scrolled through his phone.

"I'll be right back," Ezra told Tuesday.

She nodded, reaching out to squeeze his hand as he passed by.

He needed to check in with Damien, too. It was past three at that point so he and Mary would be sleeping. But Ezra knew they'd be upset if he didn't tell them. And it would be easier to get Damien to stay with his wife until morning if Ezra handled him just right.

Then everyone would be dealt with for at least the next twelve hours or so.

CHAPTER FIVE

TUESDAY WATCHED EZRA follow his brother and turned away with a sigh. Natalie was right there and she would be insufferable until Tuesday shared. Which was a best friend's right after all and she'd do the same in Nat's place.

"Not yet. You came in right as condoms were procured." Tuesday leaned in close to Natalie. "He could be a gold medalist, world champion in oral sex, however."

Natalie groaned. "I'm so sorry. We tried to call you and then him and we just didn't want to let it wait."

"Of course you came over and that's what you were supposed to do. If you hadn't, he'd never have forgiven himself."

Tuesday got the feeling no one was harder on Ezra than Ezra himself.

Tuesday had noted the way Ezra had eased into control and Paddy calmed down. The Hurleys were very close-knit and those girls were adored by one and all. They'd needed him, he'd responded and had helped and everyone felt better.

It made her happy to see Ezra step in to protect his family the way he did.

Natalie nodded, agreeing. "Still, it sucks. We'd just started to fall asleep when we got the call. That little girl is such a sweetheart. Vaughan must be beside himself."

"They got to it before her appendix burst. It could have been so much worse. At least Vaughan was there when it happened." The youngest Hurley brother appeared to be a great father so Tuesday imagined he'd have been out of his mind with worry if he'd been across the country on tour still. He'd be worried then, too, of course, but at least he was close by and that was a blessing.

"We'll talk about that later." Natalie looked toward the living room, where the brothers both had phones pressed to their ears. "So. A *champion,* huh?" Natalie asked carefully as she bumped her hip to Tuesday's.

One of the things Tuesday loved most about her best friend was the way Natalie knew when to push and when to back off. After Eric had died, Tuesday had drifted awhile.

Unable to face the home she'd made with Eric, Tuesday'd gone off to visit people and sleep in guest rooms. It had been Natalie who'd finally got through to her and told her to start living again. Natalie who pushed and coaxed and cajoled her back to the work of the living once more.

Ezra's rumble sounded from the other room and it made Tuesday smile.

"Yes."

"And it was okay, so that's good."

Natalie had meant being with a man in their home—in Tuesday's bed.

A hotel room was private and impersonal and it wasn't yours for longer than a little while, which telegraphed the attitude she wanted to project. She had *lovers* and not boyfriends.

She wasn't sure when she'd be ready to be *with* someone again and so it had felt to her that the safest thing was to not do it until she knew it was time.

Ezra, though, trod all over that distance. She let him. She even liked it. But she feared it, too, and it had awakened all sorts of stuff inside. Stuff she didn't have the time or the luxury to examine right at the moment.

"It was way better than okay." Tuesday looked down at herself. "I'm going to run up and get dressed. I'll be right back. Keep an eye on the tea."

"I will but don't think this discussion is over."

"As if I'd ever think otherwise. You're bossy and nosy. But I expect you have some stuff to talk to me about, too. I need a Paddy update."

Natalie's features softened with love and it made Tuesday so happy to see it. "Deal."

Her best friend's joy was genuine. Even if tinged with worry. Tuesday kissed Natalie's cheek. "Good. Be right back."

Tuesday dashed up to her room to change. At first she tried to ignore the way the room smelled like him. Like sex and sin and hot, hot man. She'd made herself a promise not to think about what anything meant until they'd got past this situation with Maddie's surgery and it all rushed in anyway.

But then it hit her.

She stood in her doorway, her hand on the light switch, and realized the step she'd taken by letting him up there and between her thighs was way bigger than she'd intended to make. Tuesday wasn't sure what she thought before she'd led him up to her bed. Well, okay, she'd been thinking about riding him like a horse. But…

A man like Ezra marked a place with his presence. He filled up a room just by standing in it. But on top of that he emanated so much charisma and energy; a dark, wounded heart wrapped in so much talent it was a little intimidating.

He'd swept her up. She got caught in whatever it was between them. So powerful. He made her feel things more than just momentary pleasure. But he didn't appear to be looking for anything long-term. Like her. Right? Was that even still the case?

Tuesday shook her head to stop that train of thought as she flicked off the light. There were other things to focus on.

PADDY WAITED UNTIL Ezra had tucked the phone back into his pocket before he got close enough to speak quietly.

"Hotel reservations made."

"Good deal. I just spoke to Vaughan. Maddie is out of surgery and in recovery now. She's stable and if all goes well they'll let her go home tomorrow. I told him you were making hotel reservations."

Paddy's brow rose with appreciation. "Bravo. You cleverly made him think that he needed to be sure Mom and Dad got rest so he'd need to go with them. And it gave me something to do, as well."

As if Ezra'd ever let on just how much he tended to manage them all. He just gave Paddy a bland look until his brother rolled his eyes and relaxed a little.

"Why don't you call Mom and let her know about

the room and then text Vaughan the details?" It would give Paddy something else to do, which would keep him busy, not feeling helpless.

Paddy nodded. "I just remembered, I called Damien but got his voice mail. Can you try again?"

"Handled. I called on the house phone. It woke him up. I told him there was nothing to be done so he needed to keep Mary in bed. I'll call him now and fill him in on what Vaughan told me."

Within ten minutes Ezra had got it all taken care of. All bases covered. Pregnant sister-in-law sleeping, all brothers accounted for and okay. His parents were headed to the hotel with Vaughan once they'd wrapped things up at the hospital.

Ezra had heard in Vaughan's tone that his brother had a lot going on. More than just the immediate situation. Ezra planned to head to the hospital around noon so he could speak with Vaughn a little then.

"I'm sorry." Paddy looked out the front windows. "For coming here and interrupting I mean."

At first Ezra had no idea what his brother was apologizing for. He scanned his memory until he realized Paddy meant sex.

"Shit happens, Patrick." He kept reminding himself of that because he was going to be nauseated all day from blue balls. He was trying not to even glance back into the kitchen because if she still had that scarlet robe on all silky next to her skin he was going to weep.

"But you guys...well finally, right?" Paddy waggled his brows.

Ezra's laugh may have sounded a little less than amused. "Don't worry about it. She and I know where the other lives. We'll pick it up again once this is all behind us."

"Shit. Now I'm *really* sorry."

Ezra snorted, slapping his brother on the back. "I'll let you make it up to me. Come on. We'll fill Nat and Tuesday in and then I'm going home for a while to sleep before I head down to the hospital."

"Should we cancel the show?" Paddy looked at his watch. "Tonight, I guess it is already."

"I left it up to Vaughan. I'll call Jeremy in a few hours to let him know what's up. Vaughan says if she's stable and fine, he thinks we should do it. He said we can play tonight and then he'll head straight to the hospital from the arena." And if he was smart, he'd be working on figuring out how to win Kelly back and get this new guy out of the picture.

When he and Paddy got back to the kitchen, Tuesday had changed into jeans and a T-shirt but she still looked sexy and gorgeous and his dick hurt at the memory of how she'd looked less than an hour before.

Ezra filled them in. Paddy sweet-talked Natalie into going home with him and Ezra wasn't sure what to do with his disappointment at the idea of his own empty bed. He liked his bed. He liked sleeping alone, in the middle of his gargantuan mattress. But he bet Tuesday was warm and soft in the mornings. That might be worth sharing his mattress for.

Paddy and Natalie left and Ezra turned his attention to Tuesday, moving to her. "I'm sorry we got interrupted."

"Well, all things considered, it's all right. For me anyway." She grinned a moment. "You? Well, I can help you out."

He groaned at that. Her hands or mouth on him, quick and hard so he could get off. Yeah, that'd be fantastic, as it happened. And yet, not what he wanted. Not his first time with her.

He pulled her close, kissing her for a while until he felt a little better. "Are you coming tonight?"

She nodded. "Nat and I are driving out together with Mary."

"You and me." And like someone else spoke from his lips: "Come back to my house after the show. We'll start over and do it far better this time around."

He liked the smile he got.

"All right. Go home and rest awhile. I'll see you tonight. I'm glad Maddie's okay."

He hugged her once more at her door before he headed out to the porch. He stepped away, pausing. "See you tonight, Tuesday."

EZRA DROVE HOME with the windows rolled down. A thousand things he needed to do raced through his head. He went through them all one by one, assigning them some measure of importance and by the time he pulled into his garage, he'd tidied his thoughts.

Loopy, his sweet, silly Lab, woke up when Ezra came in from the garage. She looked slightly guilty, which meant she'd been on his bed until she heard the garage door open. "I got your number."

That he said it while scratching her behind her ear meant her guilty face faded, replaced by her normal happy-go-lucky goofiness. She groaned when he moved to her chin, which sent Goldfish and Peanut into the room as fast as their paws could take them.

He tried to move, but was unable to avoid the pain

of kitten claws in his jeans as they climbed him like a tree.

"You were in my bed, too, weren't you?" He took a cat under each of his arms and headed toward his room.

Ezra's house had been the last to get finished because he'd had the first one torn down and a new one rebuilt when he'd got out of rehab. This place was his home. His refuge from the insanity of the world outside.

A cedar-log home, it was open and bright. The central core of the house soared up to the bare-beamed ceiling with a gallery at the second floor.

The master was on the first floor at the rear of the house, behind beautifully carved oak double doors. Doors he usually left open as they were now. He dropped the cats carefully as he headed toward his bathroom.

"Sorry, kids, but Dad needs to be alone." He shut the bathroom door and knew they'd be getting back on his bed the minute he was out of sight.

When he'd come back from tossing his dirty clothes, the water was hot and he stepped under the spray with a sigh. He didn't need to shower then. He could just sleep, clean up before he headed to the hospital with his stuff in the trunk and get ready at the arena.

But a riot of energy coursed through him. It wasn't about getting clean. He needed to jerk off so he could fucking sleep.

He worked soap into his palms, turning the bar over and over until his hands were nice and slick. Head back, he let the water hit him from all three directions as he trailed slippery hands over his nipples, tugging the bar through the left one. It wasn't like he had to do much to get close again.

The memory of how she'd been just a few hours before came easily. Tuesday Eastwood was alluring. Sexy. Smart and funny. She was beautiful and vibrant and so totally in charge of her shit.

Her taste was on his mouth as he licked over his bottom lip. Right before he wrapped a fist around his cock and pumped slowly.

Fuckyeah.

He imagined her back arching as he slowly pressed into her body. She'd wrap her legs around his waist… if he took her missionary. Maybe he'd thrust a few times and roll her over and start again.

Yeah, that worked.

She had a great back, a fantastic ass; he'd look his fill as he got closer and closer. From that angle he could take her in slow, deep thrusts.

He drew close but he didn't want to let go of that image. *Tried* to slow down but the time he'd spent with her earlier that night had pushed him too far.

All the adrenaline and sexual energy he'd been pumping out for hours and hours built up in the balls of his feet and barreled up his legs, lodging in his gut.

He thought about her. Remembered her voice. Remembered the sounds she'd made as he'd driven her to climax. Licked his lips to get one last whisper of her scent and taste as he came so hard he had to slap a hand against the tile to keep from falling over.

When he crawled into bed—yes, around two cats and a dog—it was four already. He'd wake up at nine and check in with Vaughan and depending on what his brother said, he'd head to the hospital after that.

There wasn't anything else he could do right then so he let himself fall into sleep.

CHAPTER SIX

TUESDAY WAS AT her worktable when Natalie came into the shop the next morning just before eight. She looked up, switching off her work light. "Hey. I just put on a new pot of coffee. It should be done in a few minutes. Any word on Maddie?"

"I'd say I couldn't believe you're here, but that's a lie. I wish you weren't but I knew you would be. Anyway." Natalie held up a hand to stop Tuesday from arguing. References to Tuesday's chronic insomnia weren't new. "Maddie's awake and in good spirits according to Paddy. He, Ezra and Damien are heading to the hospital and will meet us at the arena later. Mary is riding with us but I can tell you she's currently in her kitchen cooking for everyone at the hospital. I'm going to guess she'll want to go early so we can all eat together and then go to the show. Would that work for you?"

It had been a little odd to see Natalie make a friendship with Mary. She was part of Natalie's life in a way Tuesday couldn't be. Which was so good for her to have that sort of support within the Hurley family ranks. But there were times it smarted just a little.

It was also undeniable that Mary was a lovely person who cared about her family and Tuesday liked the Hurleys very much.

"Sounds like a good idea. I'm sure it'll make Mary feel better. It'll give everyone a chance to rest and eat after the stress of the hospital. Also, I can't lie—I want to peep at this Kelly character." Tuesday put her tools aside and came around to where Natalie had dropped into a chair near the counter.

The coffeemaker beeped. "Hold that thought. Coffee's ready."

Tuesday poured them both a mug and brought them over with some sugar.

"Just let me know when you want to leave. I managed to finish two pieces this morning and a customer picked up some frames a while back. So I'm good to close up whenever."

Tuesday had finally accepted Nat's invitation to visit the small town her best friend had moved to because she needed an anchor or she was worried she'd float away. Or to be fair it was more like she was beginning to *not* be worried about floating away and that brought her to the person she knew would see just how messed up Tuesday was and how much she needed to have someone refuse to let her spin bullshit anymore about being fine.

She hadn't been fine then. Though she'd got better since, when she'd first slept in Natalie's guest room and let herself accept that it could be her reality, that she could move to Hood River. It had been a step back into a life she actually *lived* instead of something that happened while she hid from it.

She knew how to frame things. Did a lovely job with it because she had a knack for what looked right for each person and back in high school she'd worked for a frame place at the mall so she had the skill set.

Her custom work and the other pieces she sold on consignment of preframed art brought in enough to pay her half of the mortgage.

But what she really truly wanted to do was make jewelry full-time. Big, chunky pieces of a wide variety of shades, shapes and textures. She had a stall at a local farmers' market and had been slowly building a customer base that way. She also had heard recently that a big outdoor market in Portland had given her a spot for a stall starting the following month. The exposure was on a far broader scale. She felt more alive and full of hope for the future right then than she had since about a year before Eric had died.

"I've seen a picture of her." Natalie leaned an elbow on the counter, tearing Tuesday from her memories. "Kelly. Did you know she was a model?" Nat wandered off topic. "You know what would be really good with this coffee? A cinnamon roll. Even a cookie. Oatmeal, which is healthy even." Natalie smiled brightly and Tuesday snorted.

"I have almonds and some apples."

"I said *good,* not apples and almonds." She frowned, still managing to look gorgeous. "So for God's sake, tell me about it. Tell me how you feel after last night," Natalie burst out.

"I'm hungry. Come on. Let's lock up and I'll make pancakes."

"Wow, you so don't want to talk about it."

Tuesday put a cloth over the work she'd been doing and slid the tray into a drawer. "I'm still processing it. I feel fine. He's…well, you know." She threw her hands up, frustrated that he was so appealing. "I don't

know. We haven't even actually fucked yet. We barely
know one another."

Natalie washed out the coffee stuff as she spoke
over her shoulder, "You and Ezra *know* each other.
You have since that first meeting. I see the way you
look at each other, the way you circle and get all
flushed. I've been going out with Paddy since July of
last year and in all that time I've never seen Ezra with
a woman. Or talk about a woman. Other than you."

"Pause the lecture." Tuesday turned off the interior
lights except the security ones and then hit the alarm
before returning to gather her things and lock up.

"I'm sure you walked so I'm up here." Natalie
pointed to her car.

Natalie started in again once they got on their way
home. "And you, well you've built a wall around your
heart."

Tuesday held up a hand Natalie couldn't see because she was driving. But her friend would know it
was happening anyway. "I don't want to talk about
this."

"Too bad. I've let you avoid it for way too long."

"Natalie, I can't do this right now. Everything is
fine. We will eventually have sex and I will fill you in
on it and that will be that. We'll do it awhile and it'll
wear off and we'll be those people who fuck every
once in a while when they need it from someone they
can trust to be a good time but not develop feelings."

"Oh god. Seriously? This is how you're going to
play this thing? You and Ezra are *fuckbuddies?* You
bang awhile and then you see each other all the time
and it's totally hunky-dory?"

"I've seen people I've had sex with in town or

around and I don't burst into tears that I never bore their children, Natalie."

"Don't get defensive with me. I know your tricks. When Paddy first came around, you told me to let him in because I didn't have anything to lose. I'm saying that to *you* now. Let this be good. You deserve that. You can't just let that part of you die."

"I'm not some sort of defective goods, Nat."

Natalie parked and they went into the house, heading to the kitchen, where they began to ready for the pancakes Tuesday had promised.

Neither of them spoke as they moved through the kitchen, washing hands, tying on aprons, getting the griddle heating and then mixing up the pancake batter. Natalie was a horrible cook so she gathered ingredients and then cleaned them up when Tuesday finished.

As they did all this, Natalie put out all the items they'd need with just a little too much force because she was pissed off. Normally, this was the place Natalie had stopped when the topic of Tuesday beginning to date again came up.

But things had shifted over the past year or so and it seemed pretty apparent to Tuesday that Natalie was going to push some more.

The problem was that Tuesday could lie to herself better than she could lie to Natalie. Which was also a testament to the friendship they'd had since the first day of college. They'd celebrated so many things together, grieved others, like the unthinkable when, four years prior, Tuesday's husband had been diagnosed with cancer and had died three months later.

Through it all, through grief so deep it was simply

inescapable, through that numb place she'd floated into, it was Natalie who'd grabbed hold and gave her roots. Friendship that saw everything and loved because of it saved her over and over.

So she couldn't lie to Natalie because Natalie understood Tuesday's grief and her avoidance behavior, too.

Once they'd settled at the table with a heaping platter of pancakes between them and two big glasses of orange juice, they began to talk again.

"He's sexy. I like him." Tuesday poured warmed-up boysenberry preserves on her pancakes. "Before you get huffy over there, I know it's more than that. There's this intensity between us that…" That she'd never in the entirety of her life felt with anyone. "I get caught up in it. It's like he gets near and all my parts samba. He's powerful. He takes up oxygen and space. He's big and sexy. So. Sexy. I can't even with how sexy he is."

Tuesday put her face in her hands a moment before she got back to her pancakes. "Anyway, it's not like I don't enjoy sex. He and I are clearly compatible. He's a grown-up. I'm a grown-up. We do our thing and at some point we don't. Stop arguing with me on this right now."

Natalie huffed but held her tongue. For a minute or two.

"I'll stop for now. But you said it was like right as you were putting a condom on so that means he was naked and really I have to know."

Tuesday guffawed. "He is one of the universe's finest creations. I didn't get to study as much as I wanted to because we were busy getting it on. Next time I'm going to make him stand still and just circle him slow so I can take it all in."

"He's so broody and emo and protective. It's scary and hot all at once. Paddy is hard enough to manage. I can't imagine how tough a job it will be to keep Ezra out of trouble."

"Ha. Not my job. He's a big boy." Boy was he ever.

Natalie and Paddy both had a lot of scars and hot buttons, but they both seemed willing to confront them when they came up and deal with working things out, which was how to make a relationship work.

"I guess maybe I'm starting to believe you can want to hit someone in the nose with a newspaper and still love them. And that in a day or a week you won't want to hit them anymore. *So far*. He's sort of vexing so I shouldn't make declarative statements."

Tuesday burst out laughing. Natalie was beautiful in the way only pale blondes who look really great with short hair could manage. She was classically pretty but with an edge you'd miss until you looked a little closer.

The real Natalie, the one only those who were close to her saw, had a bawdy sense of humor. It had been a joke, all those years ago, that had planted the seed of friendship that made them close to that day.

They'd all been so young that first day in the dorms back at college. Their group of friends—1022 they called themselves informally, after the dorm room they all shared way back that first year—forged a friendship that was like a family.

They'd all been strangers, these five women who all seemed very different from one another.

Over the years they'd known one another, Tuesday had learned that Natalie had a great sense of just exactly what Tuesday needed, even if Tuesday herself hadn't. And it was the same for her when it came to Natalie. Their connection was something big and special, a friendship that'd carried them both through some major life storms.

"After we finish up let's get ourselves set and you call Mary to see when she wants to go over there."

Natalie paused. "Wait a minute. I thought you had a hair appointment. You do! You were saying you'd hit the second show up looking fantastic and all done up."

"I do, but I can reschedule." Tuesday patted her hair. "And, we all know I'll look fantastic either way."

"Truth. However." Natalie raised a brow. "You're canceling a hair appointment to be nice to Ezra. You like Ezra." But she sang it and it made Tuesday smirk a little.

"I'm canceling a hair appointment because a little girl and her family need the support and the ability to be together right now. I *am* a nice person, you know."

Natalie snorted. "You are a nice person. Who totally has it for Ezra because you never give up hair appointments."

"Listen, it is hard to find someone who knows what to do with all this." Tuesday waved a hand at her hair. "I gotta take my appointments when I can get them when Nina is at the salon." She'd learned the hard way that she needed a salon that had stylists who knew how to style and treat black women's hair. Tuesday had found Nina, a stylist who worked two days a week at a local salon and that's who touched Tuesday's hair.

Otherwise, she drove up to Olympia and went with her mom to a friend who did hair on the side.

Natalie's grin undercut her attempt to be serious. "I understand. Well, actually I don't, which is sort of sucky but anyway. I do think I need two more pancakes before I call, though. Going to be a full day— it's really in everyone's interest that I have all the fuel I need."

Tuesday snorted. "You're a giver."

"Also—" Natalie paused to eat a little "—I want to wait until I hear back from Paddy. If they cancel the show we'll know soon, but he didn't think they were going to."

"Smart."

"At least tell me if he asked you to come tonight. You're very stingy with details."

Tuesday sighed and shook her head. "I can't remember if you were this nosy with Eric."

"I didn't have to be. Your bedroom was next to mine. I heard how things were going." Natalie winked.

It had been a really long time since they'd shared like this. It felt nice and Tuesday realized she'd missed it. "Yes. He asked me if I was coming tonight. He invited me to his house afterward. Obviously for sex."

"Did you like it? That he's interested?"

"Oh my god. Are you going to keep this up?"

Natalie laughed really hard and then nodded. "You did it to me with Paddy." She sobered and looked at Tuesday. "I know it's not the same. But I also know it's not what you've been doing, either. Are you scared?"

It hurt to breathe for just a moment and panic raced through her system until Natalie took her wrist. "Hey, I'm sorry. I just…it doesn't matter. I'm sorry."

"I know I need to let it happen. Or stop it. Or not think about it. Or maybe think more about it. I guess I don't know what to do and…"

"And you're not used to admitting maybe you don't know what to do. Because you're so fierce and strong and awesome that you don't know how to let yourself be a little weak."

"Please. I fucked around for eighteen months after Eric died. I was nothing but weak. Fluttering around in the breeze." Running from a truth she did not want to accept.

Natalie's softness hardened up immediately. "You stop. Right now. You had less than ninety days to go from learning he had cancer to burying him. So you took a little while to deal. So what? God, you're so hard on yourself. It makes me mad."

"Oh hush. You're so full of shit. *Who* is hard on themselves? Hypocrite."

"Of course I'm a hypocrite. It's like you don't even know me, Tues. But now that I've found true love and all that, I get to condescend to you. Jeez. This is outlined in the papers you signed back at the beginning of our friendship." Natalie snickered and Tuesday tossed her napkin at Nat's head.

Tuesday wasn't totally sure of the words, but she needed to say them the best she could at that moment. "Please don't make this into a big deal. That's what I'm saying. I am trying to take this step by step. It's new, even though we've been heading here for a while now. I am so freaked out that the only way I can get through at this point is to pretend it's not anything."

Natalie came around the table and hugged her. "I'm sorry. You're right. I'm sorry."

"Don't be sorry. I know you're trying to help."

Thank goodness for this. Tuesday hugged Natalie back and then let go. "We got shit to do. So let's quit this foolishness and weeping. You and I are beyond that nonsense."

"Okay. Fine. But I think we should seal this with doughnuts."

"You think we should seal everything with doughnuts."

Natalie straightened. "That's because doughnuts *are* perfect for every occasion."

CHAPTER SEVEN

TUESDAY ENTERED THE ROOM, drawing his attention. She moved like music. A long stride and yet she made it look like dancing instead of ground-eating purpose.

She wore pert cat-eye glasses and when her gaze found his, the big brown eyes behind them warmed as their connection sizzled.

He hadn't even thought of heading to her before he was doing it.

"Hello," she murmured once he'd reached her.

He kissed her, again before even thinking about it. She curled her fingers around his forearm to hold him closer for a bit longer.

"That's better. Hello to you, too."

"You do know how to make a girl feel welcome." Her smile sobered. "How's Maddie?"

"We spoke to the doctor about an hour ago. If all continues the way it is now, they'll discharge her in the morning. She's managed to get Vaughan to promise a whole bunch of stuff once she's home—like a pro." He looked over her shoulder to where Mary smiled up at his father. "I hear you guys came with lunch. Thanks for that."

Tuesday waved a hand and the bracelets on her wrists jingled. "Wasn't me. That was all Mary. I just came along for the ride."

He leaned in very close. "Well, remember you and I have just that very thing on the menu later."

Her fingers tightened on his arm. "I never forget a promise, Ezra Hurley."

Damn she spun him around. Something deep inside him had roused, slowly filling him. It was so good. Hot and sticky.

"Tuesday, it's so good to see you, honey." His mother came over and pulled Tuesday into a hug. He hid his annoyance at having to let her go. His mother winked at him once she broke the hug with Tuesday.

Sharon Hurley was sneakier than any secret agent the country had ever produced. She had a master plan in that head of hers—Ezra knew it. And the thing was, his mother knew *he* knew.

"Nice to see you, too, Ms. Hurley."

"I know I told you to call me Sharon." His mother looked up to Ezra. "Maddie is tired and needs to rest. Kelly has invited us all over to her house to eat all the stuff Mary brought so I'll see you there." Sharon's mouth flattened just a tiny bit. Ezra knew his mother didn't like Vaughan's ex. Never did really.

But he also knew his mother respected the job Kelly had done raising Maddie and Kensey. Yes, Vaughan was involved. Ezra's baby brother was a damned good father and he loved his daughters with all he was. He saw them frequently, as often as he could.

And yet, when he toured, it was Kelly who was there every single day. Kelly who gave up a lucrative career in modeling to stay near and raise the girls near their father. Kelly who dealt with the daily slog that parenting could be.

So his mother would be civil because she, too, loved those little girls and it was in everyone's best interests to pull together.

And, Ezra hoped, because his mom knew her opinion of Kelly wasn't fair. It was set back when Vaughan had first left and didn't tell the whole truth of the situation. Over time it was clear to anyone who bothered to really look that it had been Kelly who'd stepped up from the start and done what needed doing.

After one last hug, his mom headed toward Natalie, and Tuesday turned his way again. "I know this is a family thing. I'm going to head into Portland for a while. Do some stuff. I'll see everyone at the arena later."

He shook his head, not pleased at all with the idea of her going off anywhere. "No, I want you there. Natalie will want you there. If Nat does then Paddy will. My mother—you've met her so you can imagine how often she gets her way—will think I did something to upset you and drive you off. She'll harass me forever about it. Have a heart. Do it for me, Tuesday. Do it for Maddie."

Her eyes widened. "You're diabolical. Maddie's not even going to be there." A smile hinted at the corners of her mouth and he gave in to his.

"But it's *for* her. And you know, it's neighborly, too. You haven't even met her mom yet."

"I'm sure she's superexcited to meet some random friend of her ex-husband's brother's girlfriend. She probably has it on her bucket list."

"You should know I find a dry sense of humor one of the sexiest qualities." He stepped closer. "It's already four-thirty. We stay for a while, then the band has to leave for sound check anyway. Plus, you're driving home with me. Paddy drove in with me so he can ride home with your blonde roommate there." He tipped his chin in Natalie's direction. "Did you actually even throw this idea past her? I doubt it or she'd be pouting all pretty like."

Tuesday shook her head. "I did, and she said all the stuff you did. You're as bad as she is."

"Maybe. But my kind of bad comes with orgasms."

Her smiled bloomed. "True. You do come in handy that way. Though I think I need more research. It's really the only way to be sure."

"You keep saying I'm trouble but it's really you. I'm going to be thinking about the way you felt on my tongue all night long."

"You're going to pay for that."

"I sure as hell hope so."

"We should go. Everyone is leaving now." Her voice had gone breathy and he liked that. A lot.

"Be sure to eat your vegetables today. You'll need your strength later," Ezra told her as he led her out of the waiting room in his family's wake.

Natalie turned, trying to catch Tuesday's eye, but she caught Ezra's instead. He shook his head, waving her off. "I have it. She'll ride with me."

Natalie's brow rose but before she could say anything else, Paddy caught her around the waist and steered her out.

Hurleys against the world. Fuckyeah.

TUESDAY HAD TO suck in a surreptitious breath to calm herself after Ezra got her all hot and bothered.

Again.

He and Nat thought she hadn't seen their little exchange. She had, but because it was also in line with her own plans, she wasn't going to argue. And he did come out and say he liked to be in charge. Tuesday needed to see how that worked and if she liked it or not.

The sex part definitely passed muster. What they'd been able to finish anyway.

He paused at an SUV and she gave him a look. "No sports car today? Did I let you see my boobs too early?"

He laughed and she felt a little more in control.

"I had Damien and Paddy with me. Paddy's boots were a mess. And then we got into a shoving match." He opened the door of his SUV for her. She hopped up.

Honestly. "You got into a physical fight with your brother. Because he had dirty shoes?"

Ezra grunted as they all made their way out of the parking lot.

"You've met my brother. Don't you want to punch him sometimes?"

She snorted. "I want to punch all sorts of people. Pretty much all day long every day. I have five siblings—it's not like I don't know what it's like to want to hit a brother or sister in the face. But I refrain. They do. Usually. Though my two oldest brothers got into a fistfight at Thanksgiving dinner three years ago. So dumb. My dad let them at one another in the backyard while the rest of us ate dinner. My mom didn't speak to my brothers and my dad for weeks."

"Six kids. I have to meet your mother."

Diana Easton would love Ezra Hurley to the stars

and back. Tuesday's mother would simply latch on and Ezra would never know what hit him.

"To be fair, there're two sets of twins in there."

"Jesus. Your parents really like each other then, huh?"

She nodded. "I never knew other people's parents weren't constantly hugging and kissing and laughing until I got old enough to have sleepovers. My parents are straight up in love. They can fight—don't get me wrong. But yes, Greg and Diana are mates in the deepest sense of the word."

They'd given her an example of what a working relationship was. She and Eric hadn't been perfect, but they had been united. Tuesday sometimes felt that loss like a phantom limb.

A phantom relationship.

Something would happen and Tuesday instinctually found herself turning to Eric. The bones of her relationship with him still remained, though the rest of it had faded over time.

But the instant she remembered—that moment in time when reality came back like a punch to the throat—that hurt to her bones.

For a long time there was so much grief she couldn't see past it. Couldn't imagine a time when it didn't make her ache every moment. But it hurt less that day than it had a year before. And it would hurt less next week. And so on.

Ezra cleared his throat. "So tell me about them. Your family."

"Diana—that's my mom—she's an engineer. She works for the state of Washington and claims she'll be retiring in a few years. I don't believe her because she's a person who is constantly in motion. I don't know that she *can* stop working. My dad owns a roofing company. He and my uncle started it when they first moved out to the West Coast after my mom finished school. Anyway, he fell off a roof about nine years ago and broke his back so he had to slow down some. I say some because he still gets out on roofs when he feels a need."

"Sounds like your dad and mine would get along well."

"Does your dad like baseball?"

"Yes, he's a die-hard Red Sox fan. It's like religion to him."

"Red Sox? Okay then, they'll get along just fine. My dad converted the garage into what they call a man cave now, but it's actually a sort of grungy place with his television and his recliner. He eats bags of peanuts and watches all four hundred sports channels. And she pretends she doesn't know how much beer he drinks."

"Your dad sounds kind of awesome."

She laughed. "He is." Her parents were awesome. Full of love and support no matter what her choices had been or where they'd taken her.

"Where are the rest of your siblings? I know you have a sister in San Diego."

"You do?"

"You went there at Thanksgiving. Natalie mentioned it."

Low in her belly, warmth spread.

"Yes, my sister and her family live in San Diego. She and I are the only girls. The boys are two sets of twins. The oldest set both live in Seattle with their wives and kids. My younger brothers, one lives in Atlanta. He's in sports medicine so he works with a lot of professional athletes. The other one lives in San Jose. He's getting married in the fall. Since his boyfriend has a really great job my parents adore him. No rock stars in the bunch but we do okay."

"Doing okay is underrated."

Neither of them spoke for a while.

"It's up there on the right. I'm going to park here at the curb and we'll walk. Otherwise we might get parked in." After he'd done that and keyed the car off, he turned to face her.

"Are you saying you might want to make a quick escape?"

"Stick with me, beauty." He winked and she drew a breath of appreciation. He paused, cocking his head. "What?"

"You."

"Me? What?"

She flapped a hand in his direction. "Everything. You're handsome and charming and sexy and you just put *all that*—the entirety of which you have a considerable amount—into a wink and a quick response."

He blushed and she wanted to groan. *He blushed.* Which of course was charming and sexy.

She pointed at him. "See?"

He laughed then, taking her hand and kissing the inside of her wrist. A warm wave of pleasure slid through her.

"You're so good with your mouth."

He broke away from her wrist for a moment to say, "Wait till you see what I can do with my cock."

"I'm devastated I have to." Which was 100 percent true.

He'd just started to lick up along the sensitive line of her tendon leading to the heel of her palm, which he nibbled on and her whole body throbbed, when Sharon came out the front doors of the very pretty house just ahead and looked around.

"Your mother sees us."

He cursed under his breath but let her hand go reluctantly. "She'll only come over here unless we go in."

"Is she worried we'll go too far and I'll get knocked up?"

He barked a laugh and it made her laugh even harder.

By the time they got to the front steps, Ezra carrying a bunch of presents for both girls, Tuesday had managed to stop giggling, but as he reached out to put a palm at the small of her back to guide her into the house, she realized how much she liked it, that small touch. In it he helped her, he touched her like a lover, he marked her as being with him.

She just had no idea at all where to put it, this intensity he brought to her life with the smallest of touches.

Kensey launched herself at Ezra so Tuesday stepped to the side and grabbed the bags he'd been holding.

"She loves her uncles as much as all the other women in the world do." A gorgeous blonde came into the entry. Perceptive blue-green eyes took Tuesday in, along with the bags and her proximity to Ezra. Then her wariness fell away and she smiled and it was like all that beautiful went sensual and earthy. Welcoming.

Tuesday knew what it meant to feel like an outsider. Here, even in this woman's home she was outnumbered by Hurleys. For that reason, Tuesday really liked Kelly from the very first smile.

Ezra listened intently to Kensey tell him all about her sleepover and how she didn't *even know* her sister had her insides *bursted out* until she got picked up the next day. He made the right noises and asked the right questions and Tuesday liked him even more.

Turning back, she held out her hand. "Hi. I'm Tuesday."

Kelly took it and shook. "Kelly Hurley. Vaughan told me a little about you. He said you make jewelry. I'd love to talk with you about that at some point in the future. But for now, please come on through to the kitchen. There's some sort of unpacking of food. Ross—that's my fiancé—he's just run over to his house for extra chairs."

"Tuesday has some things for you in that bag." Ezra kissed both Kensey's cheeks and put her down.

She peeked inside as Ezra knelt next to her, pulling things out. Each item resulted in a delighted squeal and a dramatic hug with arms thrown wide and then around him.

"I know. Gifted, right? She's never even had a drama class."

Tuesday snorted as she glanced at Kelly, who watched her daughter with Ezra.

"I'm going to get toothache from all that sweetness," Tuesday said as Kensey gave him one last hug before backing off.

"You have whispers like a walrus, Uncle Ezra." Kensey rubbed her cheek.

Tuesday's ovaries may have exploded when Ezra picked her up and nuzzled her while she giggled and patted his head like he was a big dog.

Paddy bounded into the room and Ezra handed Kensey off to another uncle who had plenty of kisses.

"I only have whiskers, is that okay?" Paddy asked her as she steered him like a horse.

He galloped away and Ezra loped after them. But not until he'd taken a look back over his shoulder to check on Tuesday. It was sweet. Tender even.

Tuesday tried to pretend he didn't totally fluster her as she spoke to Kelly again. "Thanks for having me over. Or whatever you're supposed to say in this sort of situation."

Kelly laughed. "Thanks."

Two other little girls ran through with Kensey.

"That's Julie and Holly. Ross's two."

Ezra and Vaughan headed out through the big sliding glass doors to a pretty yard beyond.

Natalie was in the kitchen with Mary and Sharon. It wasn't that Tuesday felt left out. After all, if she had wanted to she could have gone in. Not excluded, either, but they had a thing going and it would have been weird.

"Would you like something to drink?" Kelly led her to a sideboard where a few pitchers of juice, water and tea sat. "I started coffee so it should be done soon if you'd like some of that."

"Tea is great, thanks. Ezra said Maddie is recovering well."

"Maddie's doing great. She wanted to come home

today but her dad managed to get through to her. They have that sort of connection." Kelly's gaze strayed over to where Vaughan and Ezra were huddled at the far end of the backyard. The girls had swarmed out there and were playing on the big play set and both men faced them, keeping an eye on the girls even as they talked. They were clearly up to something.

There was a commotion at the front door and Kelly set her glass down. "That'll be Ross. Excuse me a sec."

Ezra took one careful look back at Tuesday to make sure she was all right. She appeared to have hit it off with Kelly so he caught Vaughan's attention, jerked a chin toward the backyard and headed out.

The girls flew past them both in a hail of giggles and headed to the play set.

"Apparently we got to the hospital today about ten minutes after the fiancé left. *Fiancé*. Jesus, Vaughan, what are you going to do?"

"I don't know. I should let it go. He's good to the girls. They both really like him. They'd make a family together, his part and her part."

That pissed Ezra off. "But that's *your* goddamn part. If you hadn't stopped by here last night another man would have taken your baby to the hospital and sat up most of the night in the waiting room. You okay with that? Maddie calling him Dad, too? Is he going to take pictures before the prom and text them to you? Will she cry on his shoulder when she gets her heart broken the first time? You gonna be one of those guys drowning in regret when he's sixty-five and his kids have kids of their own and he's a stranger to them?

Vaughan, these are your women. *Your* children and *your* woman. Why are you even hesitating?"

Vaughan's anguish was clear on his features. "Do you think I like it? I hate it. But what can I do, Ez? *I* walked away. *I* wanted a divorce and she gave me one and this is what the price of that act is. I made my decision and it fucked up everything. But I can't take it back."

Hearing the misery in his brother's tone tore at Ezra. "Bull. Yes, you screwed up. You were too damned young and you got married. You made stupid choices, but you've paid for them. Do you still love her? Because if you don't, then yes, let her move on. But I see how she looks at you. I saw whose hand she reached for when the doctor came in today. You have a chance, not to undo your mess-ups, but to move past them and be a better man. Claim your family. Be worthy of them."

Kensey called out that both daddy and uncle watch as she went all the way across the monkey bars.

"You rock, baby." Vaughan kept his eyes on Kensey but he spoke to Ezra. "Once upon a time I loved Kelly. I loved her the first time I saw her. I loved her even when I fucked up so badly I broke the thing some other man is about to snatch up. She made these little creatures with me. Maddie and Kensey are the best parts of what Kelly and I were at one time. Do I love her now?" Vaughan shrugged. "I never stopped loving her. But I was stupid and selfish and too blind to see and appreciate what I had in front of me the whole time. I don't know what to do. The tour ends tonight. I'm staying in the same hotel for the next few days. Thanks for the stuff you brought, by the way. Then after we get Maddie home and settled I'll hang out a while and then I'm headed to my condo in Portland for a while. I need to get it together, man. I need to do it and I can't do it at the ranch."

"I know how that is. Let me know what you need. I can get your mail and all that."

"Thanks." Vaughan's gaze slid to where Tuesday and Kelly stood together inside the house. "So what's the story there?"

"I'm taking that one a paragraph at a time."

"The two of you throw off some serious heat."

Ezra nodded. Startling how much.

"She's Paddy's girlfriend's best friend. Don't be a dick or you'll pay and pay."

"She and I are just cruising around one another. Beyond that? I don't know. But she's not insane and I'm not a dick so I think we can handle it."

Sharon opened the back doors. "Time to eat. Come on in, girls. There's even some cake."

They flew off the play set and headed inside, with Ezra and Vaughan in their wake.

"For the longest time I've felt like you needed to be loved by someone. Someone who knew all your secrets and didn't give a shit."

Ezra caught Tuesday's gaze where she stood with Natalie in the kitchen.

"One paragraph at a time," Ezra repeated. "Now, if I were you, I'd angle myself next to Kensey because then you're on Kelly's other side and the fiancé has to sit elsewhere."

Vaughan grinned as he sped his pace to do just that.

Kelly approached with a very good-looking guy,

who was clearly the fiancé everyone pretended Vaughan wasn't upset by.

"Ross, this is Tuesday. She's here with Vaughan's brother Ezra. Tuesday, this is Ross Porter."

They complemented one another. It was pretty easy to see they had an easy affection with one another and the kids.

He shook Tuesday's hand with an open, warm smile and there was nothing to be done but respond in kind. "Nice to meet you. Sorry about the circumstances, though."

"We caught it before it got scary. Maddie heals quickly so that's a good thing."

Tuesday caught Ezra's gaze as he came in with Vaughan. He moved straight to her and she waited, stuck in place by the sight of all that masculinity prowling toward her. Every bit of his attention was on her and it left her breathless.

"Ready for some food?" He slid an arm around her waist.

"Even if Mary did break out the little meatball things on the drive over I'd be open to having nine more."

His grin was nearly boyish.

When they filled their plates in the large kitchen, Tuesday spied Vaughan setting himself up next to Kensey and Kelly. Which would have left Ross at the other end of the table.

She didn't frown. Because Tuesday knew what it meant to fight for someone. There'd been someone else once, between her and Eric. It was all fine and good to make proclamations about what you would or wouldn't do in a situation like that. But the reality had been different.

The world wasn't perfect.

People weren't perfect.

Love wasn't enough. But the right kind of love would be worth a second chance.

Tuesday snapped out of it and spoke to Kelly. "Those meatball things. You need them in your life."

"Yeah?" Kelly put one on her plate and then added another. "Thanks for the tip."

At the table of course, Kelly figured out what Vaughan had done. Tuesday watched the realization hit her face. Kelly's attention flitted to Ross, who had already settled with his daughters. She looked back to Vaughan, pausing.

"So you know she's figured out what Vaughan is up to, right?" Tuesday said in an undertone to Ezra.

"The key is going to be what she does in response. She's smart and she knows Vaughan better than he thinks."

"Just because she moves to where Ross is doesn't mean she wouldn't give Vaughan another chance if he really made an effort."

Ezra nodded. "I agree. In fact, I'm betting she's going to up and move to where Ross is sitting. She's going to be loyal because that's who she is. She made mistakes, but that isn't one of them. It's then how Vaughan takes that and either quits or redoubles his efforts to win her back that'll be key."

Ezra was so much smarter than she'd ever realized. Oh sure, she knew he took care of his brothers and was the caregiver of the family. But he was sort of scary in his ability to manage people and opportunities to help them realize things themselves.

"Because he won't know until he feels it," she murmured. "The loss I mean. How will he use the pain then?"

The intensity in Ezra's gaze when he got very still, staring at her, sent a shiver through her body. "Exactly." And then he smiled. A different sort of smile from the ones she'd seen from him before. This one made her breath catch. This one was intimate on a wholly new level.

He broke the moment with a tip of his chin. Tuesday turned to find Kelly moving herself down to where Ross was, though Kensey stayed next to her grandpa, who was on one side.

Vaughan watched, disappointment on his face.

Tuesday hoped it would be enough.

CHAPTER EIGHT

HE CAME BOUNDING off the stage, veins coursing with adrenaline and ego. A potent mix and one he'd loved the taste of since they performed the very first time at Jimmie Streeter's kegger.

And right there, long and fierce, was Tuesday. Deep red lips curled into a smile that was for him alone and that adrenaline heated.

Need beat at him so hard he couldn't deny the equally hard cock he was sure anyone looking could see. In fact her gaze flicked down and then that smile went feline. When she looked him in the eyes again, there was a challenge there, banked with no small measure of heat.

They all got carried down the stairs and the hall until they'd got a fair bit away from the stage. "Give me five minutes to shower. I mean it. Just five. Then you and I are getting the hell out of here. I don't care if everyone knows why. I mean to have you as soon as I possibly can." He took her upper arms, pulled her in for a blistering kiss and left her at his door, where he peeled his clothes off on his way to the shower.

TUESDAY BLEW OUT a breath as she licked over lips swollen from a kiss that had made her heart pound. This sort of want made her skin feel too tight.

Natalie came out of the greenroom, smiling as she caught sight of Tuesday. "Hey, you."

Tuesday was able to move her legs and walk over in a reasonable impression of a woman who hadn't just nearly come from a kiss.

"Hey, yourself. I've been instructed to wait five minutes and then we're out of here."

"Really, now? Well, he may not want to go in there." Nat motioned toward the greenroom. "There's a whole giant crowd."

Tuesday's hormones subsided for a moment as concern for her friend overruled it. "Are you all right?"

Natalie had grown up in a house with an addict. With lots of addicts from time to time. Being around wild partying made her uncomfortable, though Tuesday knew Nat would do it for Paddy because her man was so social and high energy.

"It's all right. Just mainly Hurleys. Thanks for getting my back earlier. You and I need to hang out. Are you off tomorrow?"

"I am. You?"

"Yes. So let's you and me have dinner and go to a movie? There is so much gossip and stuff to share." Natalie grinned.

"Ha. You got it. Meet you at the house at seven."

Ezra came out, the ends of his hair still dripping.

Natalie leaned in and whispered, "Wow, that's determination. To do the sex with you. Do be sure to make mental notes of all the high points."

"I might need a spiral notebook for that." Tuesday hugged Natalie quickly. "See you tomorrow."

Ezra caught up to them. He had a duffel bag in one hand and slid the other arm around Tuesday's waist. "Nats, always a pleasure to see your pretty face. Beauty, we're not stopping. I'll get us to the doors in less than five minutes if you just follow my lead."

Delighted, Tuesday nodded. "All right then."

"So," HE BEGAN as they sped east toward Hood River, "I really want to be inside you. I may drive a little fast."

She laughed because despite his joke, he was totally controlled as they drove. Yes, fast, she'd noticed he liked to drive fast the night before. But not too fast. He was definitely an attention-to-details type of person and she'd seen quite well the night before that he extended that to sex.

"Because all I can think of is you naked and beneath me, we should talk about something else for a while."

"I think tonight's show ranks in my top three best concerts ever list."

"Really? Okay, first tell me the other two. Because I need to know if I should be flattered or insulted."

"You're pretty impossible. It's charming and you have a big dick so I'll allow it. Pearl Jam, Madison Square Garden. I was twenty-two years old and it was my first time in New York City."

"Excellent choice. Pearl Jam is one of the best live bands out there."

"The other is Sigur Rós. I don't know if you've ever seen them live or not, but they're meant to be heard that way. I saw them in a symphony hall so they had a full orchestra and there were screens behind them. It was a whole experience. Okay, so wait, I need to add Tool to the list. Have you ever seen them live?"

"Not Sigur Rós, though I've heard their music before. But yes to Tool. One of the best parts of this gig is having the opportunity to hear so much live music. Well, all right, I'm totally flattered to be in that company. Even better than when you saw us the first time?"

"Yes. Ezra, you guys were so tight. Every single song you played was perfect. The crowd was great. That little riff you did during 'Revolutionary'? That was clever and Paddy picked it right up and did that thing with his voice and then Damien and Vaughan ended the song with it. Fantastic."

THE FOUR OF them had been in what Vaughan sometimes called the Hurley Bubble. The world fell away and it was just brothers playing music and having a good time. On top of that, Ezra was pretty sure he'd never had a more flawless night playing live. He was truly amazed at his brothers, who'd been on the road for months. They might have been tired but it didn't show in their music.

"Tonight's show is one people are going to rave about for a long time to come." Tuesday shrugged.

Pride eased back into his heart.

At one time, Ezra had had a lot of pride. He'd had so much he'd ignored the damage he was doing and called it what he was entitled to. Heroin had enabled him to keep on saying that long after he'd stopped believing it.

So he'd been prideful and he'd been careless and then everything had been ripped away and he'd had to rebuild. Including his pride. He still struggled at times with what was too much or not enough, but at least he was around to struggle and not in the ground because of an OD.

"It felt exceptional, but it's hard to tell sometimes. You're too close to really see it. You do usually know if it's a bad show. Sometimes you're just off, or someone fucks up over and over and then Paddy flips out or pouts because he's a goddamn artist perfectionist."

He burst out laughing. "I realize that sounds like an insult. And it is. Sometimes. Make-it-Perfect Paddy is a hard-ass. He needs to be. He holds it down out there. They look to him to set a direction. Like a team captain."

"*You're* the captain, though."

He paused. "What do you mean?"

"I mean, Ezra, you're the leader of Sweet Hollow Ranch. You're their foundation. Paddy leads out there on the road. He's a strong force in the band. His voice is there definitely. But you step out there and they *all* look to you. Even your manager talks to you like you're in charge."

"Paddy is the lead singer of the band. He takes the weight of that out there on the road and he has on his own three tours now." It had hurt like hell to let it go. But he hadn't deserved it and he knew it. Letting go meant owning that. So he had. It still hurt to say it but that pain kept him honest.

"He's good at it. You are all incredibly successful. It's sort of stunning to see it from where we've been. I don't know how you all deal with that much energy coming at you at once."

And just like that she'd steered him onto safer ground.

He turned up the long drive leading to the houses up at the ranch.

"You feed on it. It's more tiring than you'd think out there. So it comes at you and it's so full of love and excitement and it's about *you*. To me it's like taking a long drink of cold water after you've been outside in the heat awhile. I just soak it in."

After a while, though, it wore you down. The weight of all that attention, the pressure to be perfect got in the way, tripped you up.

It seemed like it took forever for the garage door to open but at long last, he was standing, hauling her to his body as he helped her from the car.

This was a crush mouths together in a hot tangle of tongues, teeth and lips embrace. He moaned and she sucked the sound in. Through the cotton of his shirt, Tuesday's nails dug into the muscles of his shoulders.

He broke away, panting. "Now. Inside." Grabbing her hand, he led her into the house. Loopy was at the door and lost her mind when she saw Ezra had company. Then the cats streaked in and Ezra had to half fend them off and half pet them so they'd let him get her to his bed.

Tuesday started laughing and then he tripped over a cat, or maybe the dog and they ended up on the floor in the hall just a few steps from his bedroom.

"Shit. Are you all right?" He rolled to the side and Loopy started licking her face. "Sorry. Loop, leave her be."

"I'm fine. You have a dog and two year-old cats. You, Ezra Hurley, are a big old softhearted animal lover."

"Right now I'm thinking about loving them on a

taco shell." He stood, helping her to her feet. "Don't worry, my bedroom has doors to hold back the furry horde."

The night before she'd had on a halter dress that had shown off her shoulders and back. Tonight she wore a low-cut, sleeveless blouse that laced up over her breasts. She added a necklace of thick chunks of orange-and-blue glass, highlighting the beauty of the line of her neck.

Snug black pants and bright blue suede loafers made the outfit. She looked like she'd stepped out of a magazine. Natalie spoke of that from time to time— the way Tuesday had such a great sense of fashion.

Right then, though, he wanted her out of all that.

He hit the light switch in his room and noted the cat-shaped spots on the bedspread.

"Are you allergic to cats or dogs?"

"Nope." She bent and picked up Goldfish, who thought this was rather delightful. He snuggled her and she scratched behind his ear.

"Don't be nice or we'll never get rid of them." He pulled away the blanket he tossed over his bed to protect it from animal hair. "I promise I changed the bedding this morning. I have to use this because they do what they want if I'm not here. Well, even when I am."

"Don't pretend with me. They were just having a lovely nap on your bed and they ran to you when you walked in. These are animals spoiled and loved by their human. I won't tell if you keep me sexually satisfied."

He laughed. "Why are all the women in my life so incorrigible?"

"Do you have a harem then?"

"Not if you don't count Peanut, who is Goldfish's sister. She's the only female in my bed."

He hadn't needed to add that. It just came out of his mouth. At first she was startled and then it was impossible to mistake the pleasure on her face.

"I'll be right back. I'm just going to make sure they've got food and water. They'll happily leave us alone for that." They'd pig out and probably sleep in the kitchen or on the couch they also weren't allowed on.

HE LEFT AND she kissed the top of the cat's head. "He's a great big squishy softhearted dude, isn't he?" she whispered.

At the sound of movement in the kitchen, the cat lost interest in Tuesday and jumped free to stampede out there with the dog and other cat.

She walked over to his windows to take in the view. His house, what she'd seen of it anyway, was beautiful in that rough-hewn, rugged style. Like him, she supposed.

Beyond his bedroom windows were the pear orchards lit by stars still shining bright in a nearly cloudless night.

"Now," he said, startling her as he returned to the room, "we were about to start something."

He kicked the doors closed and just after that, one-handed, he ripped his shirt off, exposing all that tawny skin and hard muscle.

"I said, goddamn." She blew out a breath as she pushed away from the windows to head his way. She'd taken her shoes off and left them in a corner of his room along with her bag so she noticed the softness of the rugs covering the cool hardwood floors.

"I didn't even have to ask you to get within touching distance." One corner of his mouth tipped up. "It's like you heard me begging you in my head. Where I really was begging you."

She leaned in to kiss his shoulder as she reached him, but danced away when he tried to grab her. "Nope. I need to look at you. Last night was too fast. I didn't get to inspect closely."

He rolled his head on his shoulders and stretched, relaxing a little. Still, the energy came off him in waves that seemed to throb.

"You're holding back just for me, aren't you?" She whispered it as she kissed the back of his neck.

"Man who can't admit it's hot to be admired by a gorgeous, sexy woman is a liar or deluded."

She ran her palms over the muscles of his shoulders and down his back. "Or gay."

He snorted. "Concept is the same. Who doesn't want to preen around a little for someone they're interested in?"

He had a fence inked across his back; the main post of it ran down his spine in black and gray. Full-color roses spilled across it, punctuated by shadowed skulls. The entire picture was haunted. Terrible and beautiful. Sad and joyous.

And it really accentuated the width of his shoulders as his body narrowed at his hips. She wanted to rub all over him. So she gave in, pressing herself to his skin, hugging him from behind.

He made one of those rumbling approval sounds

that made her all gooey as he ran his hands over her arms. "You feel good."

She brushed her fingertips over his nipples and flicked the barbell with her nail. Another rumble. He was like a big cat, or a wolf or something. So close to him, she knew he could be dangerous if he wanted to. He was in his prime. Healthy. Strapping.

But he reined it in. Held it together and didn't use that strength to harm.

He was like a tsunami of testosterone and it was breathlessly hot. Which she didn't understand because she wasn't the alpha-male type.

She pushed back and continued to circle. At his side she bent to read the words scrolled over his ribs: *Brotherhood is the very price and condition of man's survival.*

He had those things—what did they call them? Adonis belts! Yes, well he had them and they confused her because they did all sorts of things to her hormones.

Standing in front of him, she slid her fingertips over the funky skull and crossbones on his belly and also the lines of those muscles.

"This doesn't seem sporting."

"Me standing here with my cock about to explode while a gorgeous Amazon circles me and gives me kisses and pets? I'm a patient man, beauty. But my patience when it comes to waiting any longer to get you under me has expired."

"Well, I was actually referring to your body. And these things here." She brushed her thumbs against the line of muscle at each hip bone. "I'm sure they must be prohibited by the Geneva Convention. This is some sort of confusion weapon, right?"

He had a little hair on his chest. Enough to be hot. Especially that line that led down into his pants from his belly button.

"Why are these on?" She ran a finger between hot, hard skin and the waistband of his jeans. "I know what's in there and I'd like to play with it awhile."

He shook his head. "Your turn."

"I'm trying but you won't take your pants off."

"Your tits have made my mouth water all night long in that shirt. Take it off."

She pulled her shirt off and then got rid of her bra.

He stepped into her personal space and stole her breath. "For months I've watched you. Wondered about what was under all your clothes. The reality is way better than even my brain could have imagined."

Taking her breasts in his hands, he tugged her nipples between his thumb and forefinger. She arched into his touch; the sinew and muscle of his shoulders and neck called to her so she let go of pants he was clearly going to rid himself of when he was good and ready. She slid her hands up his belly, over the wall of his chest. Her final destination was his neck but she took her time at his chest because he felt so good. Too good to leave behind so she used her lips on his throat instead.

His pulse beat steady as she kissed him just beneath his jaw, right at the line of his beard as she learned Ezra *really* liked to have fingernails run lightly over his nipples.

He let go and she nearly wept at the loss of sensation. Luckily, he banded an arm around her waist and picked her up, carrying her to his bed. "I want those pants off, beauty. You wearing anything beneath?"

"One thing you should know about me," she said as she slowly unzipped her pants, "is that I always wear underwear with pants. A dress or a skirt? Well, I guess we'll have to take that on a case-by-case basis."

"All right, I'm tucking that away for future reference."

She shimmied from her pants and the coral-pink panties and leaned back on her elbows, staring up at him.

"You now." Like so much now.

He stood there as she watched and when his grin hitched up a little, she sucked in a breath because there was a lot of promise in that mouth of his. She could hardly wait.

He slid his hands over his belly.

Over flat, hard bands of muscle. She caught her bottom lip between her teeth as he moved his hands up to his nipples.

Nipples he pinched.

Her own nipples ached at the phantom of his touch.

Breath held, she continued to watch as he caressed his upper body. The size of his hands as they cupped his neck and up into his hair made her so hot for him.

Ezra was bigger than life. All that smolder beneath the surface was hot, but then he drew the curtain back and exposed the entirety of that to her and she drowned in it. Held on with her fingernails to keep from being lost in everything he threw out.

Then he moved those hands to his pants.

"Are you breathless to know how this movie ends?"

"Ezra, this movie ends with you fucking me."

"At least twice."

He unbuttoned and unzipped and she saw he didn't share the same rules about wearing underwear beneath pants.

Swiftly he was naked and in half a breath he brushed his body against hers and it was…so good. So good as gooseflesh rose. He smelled good. Like soap and hot rock star about to have sex with her. Which was pretty much her favorite scent ever.

Tuesday wrapped her arms around him, reveling in the weight of his body on hers. She loved this, this feeling of being totally surrounded by a partner. Loved the intensity of that sort of connection.

He kissed her.

He was truly gifted in the kissing department. Each time he kissed her it was a wholly new experience. This kiss was hard-edged. He nipped her bottom lip as he growled low and she nearly lost her mind. What even was that and what did she need to do to get him to do it again?

That heated sexual energy he gave off surrounded her, burned against her skin, incited her own desire.

She gave over to the dizzying depths of it, of that sharp need he evoked in her.

Her fingers slid into his hair, so soft. He got a little closer, gave her more of his weight on her. But when she tugged he gave her that growl and he reared up to his knees. "Up the bed all the way. Hands above your head when you get there."

My.

Tuesday hoped she managed to stay sexy as she shimmied back up his bed to where the pillows were.

EZRA WAS TOTALLY convinced he'd never ever seen anything as beautiful as Tuesday in his bed. He wasn't sure which part of her he liked best so he just took her in from the tips of her toes, up long legs, the flare of her hips, that tattoo of hers. He spent enough time on her breasts that he was able to declare those as his favorite part.

The mass of her curls lay dark against his pillows and the look on her face, good god.

She was a fucking goddess.

He did know his favorite trait of hers, as well. She owned her sensuality. The woman he stared at was at home in her skin. She expected to be treated like a queen, which was her due. And that was hotter than fire.

"If a woman could come just from being looked at, I'm pretty sure I'd be screaming your name right now."

He locked his gaze to hers. "You will be soon enough."

One corner of her mouth quirked up and he picked up the challenge that lay in her eyes.

And then she put her arms above her head and he had to pause, gulping in some air.

"Beauty."

He picked up her foot and kissed her ankle and then up to her knee. He put that leg down and picked up the other, repeating.

Then he kissed up each velvety thigh.

"I need to get you nice and ready for the next part of the program," he spoke, his lips against her labia.

SHE WASN'T SURE she had the fortitude for Ezra's kind of ready.

Then he took a lick and blew her mind.

He wasn't slow this time.

No, he used his thumbs to bare her to him and dived in.

She arched, digging her heels into the bed, wanting more and wanting to get away all at once.

He stopped and looked up the line of her body to her face. "You moved your hands."

Looking back on this precise moment later on, Tuesday would see it for the leap off the top of the Empire State Building that it was. But just then it felt so good and so right it didn't matter. Nothing did but getting more from him.

Heat flushed through her system and the snappy comeback she'd been on the verge of giving him died away. *Yes. That.* She wanted more of feeling that with him.

He waited, hovering so close the brush of his breath against her pussy sent waves of shivers through her body as she moved her hands back.

Then he made her come so hard that if he'd had close neighbors she'd have blushed every time she saw them for years to come.

He kissed her hip bone, licking over her skin all the way up to her mouth—after a significant detour at her nipples—to kiss her slow.

Reaching between them, she grabbed his cock and licked her lips. Turnabout was fair play and all that.

He hissed. "No. If you do that I'm going to come before I'm ready. I want in you. There's time for that later."

Like she was going to argue. Ha.

Still, she slid her thumb through the bead of pre-come on the head of his cock before she let go.

"Roll over."

Shivering, she rolled onto her belly.

He ran his hands all over her in long, slow strokes until she was boneless. "You're the most beautiful thing I've ever seen," he murmured as he kissed the back of her neck.

She wasn't so relaxed that a thrill didn't run through her at his words.

But he wasn't done.

"I need you to get that ass up. You can keep your head down."

It was his tone. Or the words. Well, probably the words and the tone and the way he touched her, but *hot damn* did she move quickly.

He hummed low as he leaned past her. From the corner of her eye she saw him grab a condom. Her hands fisted in the blankets as she tried to find some patience.

EZRA LOOKED DOWN at her as he rolled the latex on. The curve of her ass made his mouth water as he angled himself along one cheek, down to her pussy, circling her entrance with the head of his cock before beginning to push in slowly.

She made a low, ragged sound as he got halfway in and that was it. All his control slipped away. He thrust that last bit and she met him, pushing back until he was in as deep as he could be.

Ezra had to pause to hold off as climax dug its claws into his balls. His entire body seemed to vibrate with how much he needed this woman.

So he let go and began to fuck her in earnest. Lingered in that tight, hot embrace. He leaned down to lick over her shoulder before he bit. Not hard enough to leave a mark. Not a permanent one anyway.

This sound she made, well holy shit, he had to dig in and seriously debate with his cock. His cock was ready to go at that sound but Ezra wanted to hear her make it again and again, first.

She pushed back against him again as her body tightened around him so much he nearly saw stars.

"When *I'm* ready." He took her hips in his hands and groaned. She was strong. Hard and soft. Sweet and demanding. All contrasts. He wasn't under any misconceptions. She *allowed* him to take charge; she made the choice to give over, which was exactly how he wanted it. Otherwise it was a sham.

He put a palm at the small of her back and pushed down, keeping her just right. Her body clasped around him again, superheating, and he knew she was drawing close to another climax.

This time they'd go over together.

He leaned forward a little, reaching around with a free hand to slowly circle her clit. He heard a quick intake of breath as she gasped at the contact.

"I don't know if I can," she gasped.

"Pah, you totally can. It's an orgasm, beauty, and given how fucking gorgeous you are when you have one, I know you can have one again."

She groaned, but her body continued to respond as he slowly teased her higher and higher.

He got close, so close his body tightened up with anticipation. She sucked in a breath and came all around him, the heated, tight clasp of her inner muscles sending him hurtling into orgasm right along with her.

He thrust hard, over and over as the slap of skin against skin stroked over the sounds of moans and sighs.

He pulled out carefully, excusing himself to get rid of the condom and when he got back, he smiled at the sight of her in his bed and joined her.

"How about some juice and something to eat?" He stroked an idle fingertip over her shoulder.

"Yes, that sounds perfect."

He leaned in to kiss her before he rolled from the bed and tossed her a robe that had been hanging on the back of his door. "You don't have to wear it. No one is going to see in, but it's a little chilly tonight."

She pulled it on and he pulled on a low-slung pair of sleep pants.

When he opened his bedroom doors, he nearly tripped over his damned dog and the cats, who'd set up camp right outside the door.

She wisely hid a snicker, but carefully stepped around the cats winding through her legs as she walked. It just gave him an excuse to touch her again so he slid an arm around her waist. "Wouldn't want you to fall."

CHAPTER NINE

WOULDN'T WANT YOU TO FALL.

Ezra had said those words to her the week before. She'd been wearing little more than a robe and had sex hair at the time.

He'd meant to warn her not to trip over his animals, but the biggest danger was in falling for the man himself.

He'd dropped her off, walked her to her door and then, he said he'd call.

Which had made her distinctly uncomfortable, and yet, happy. He *had* called. Twice over the week. Things were easy between them. He checked in and was sexy and charming, but he didn't push into her space. It felt a little like he held back. Which was okay, too. Hopefully he'd lose that over time and grow to trust her.

And here he stood in the doorway to her shop, giving her a look that made her parts stand up to attention.

"Hey there." She was with a customer so she kept it at that. "Be with you shortly."

He nodded and strolled to look at the art on the walls.

By the time she had found the right stuff for her customer and had rung it up, it was near closing so

Tuesday flipped the sign and locked up before she turned back to Ezra.

"Hey, yourself. I was in town and I saw the lights on in here. I just went grocery shopping. How about I make you dinner?"

Flattered and pleased, she hoped she kept her cool when she nodded. "Yeah, that sounds like something I'd be up for, thanks. Why don't I just drive up to your place in a bit? I need to go home to change."

He frowned. Just a brief flash of displeasure and she wanted to kiss his lips to entice them to curve back into a smile. "You're really spoiled, aren't you?"

There it was. He grinned. "Come to me when you're ready and if you ask me that question while you're standing in my kitchen, I'll answer it honestly."

She moved to him. "When I'm standing in your kitchen, Ezra, you'll most definitely be spoiled."

He nodded, attempting to be solemn but amusement was clear in his gaze.

"I'll walk you to your car when you're ready." He leaned against the counter. "I'll check my email so take your time and do what you need to."

But it was hard to concentrate with him there. In her shop. His smell was all over the place now, she realized. It made her happy to know the ghost of his presence would still be in the air when she opened up the following morning.

She counted the till and wrote a deposit sheet out and tucked it in the bag. This was one part of business that, while it was easier than in the old days before you could take a picture of a check and consider it deposited, still involved a trip to the bank to drop her day's receipts off.

Only, that day Ezra was at her side as she headed down two blocks and another one over to the bank.

"You do this alone every day?"

"Every day I work, yes. Well, if it's been a slow day and it's mainly my cash drawer and all credit cards and paper receipts I just keep it in my safe. Tourist season is arriving so there are days, in the summer and fall usually, when I have to go twice because it makes me nervous to have all that cash around."

"Tourists pick up a lot of framed art?"

She laughed as she dropped the deposit bag off and they headed to her car.

"I have a pretty nice selection of local artists in my store. I do small enough frames that people can easily tuck them into a car before going home. I have a booth for the market that I staff on weekends from June through September. That has jewelry, too. Used to be like an occasional sale here and there but now it's over half my overall business. I have a part-time employee—she's a good kid. She'll take over the stall here in Hood River so I can staff the one in Portland when my space is finally ready."

They got to her car and he took her keys, unlocking for her. He handed them back and bent to kiss her. "Since you're off the clock and all, I thought I'd grab one because your mouth is a temptation."

He made her insides all fluttery.

"I'll see you in an hour or so."

She headed home, surprised to see Nat there after she'd changed and headed back downstairs.

Tuesday kissed Nat's cheek on her way past. "I was beginning to wonder if I'd dreamed you up."

"I feel terrible for being gone so much."

Tuesday leaned against the doorway. "Why on earth would you feel bad? You're in love, Natalie. Love. You want to be with him. He's been gone for a few months. You two had a big fight for part of that time. Of course that takes some face-to-face so everyone feels better. I don't feel like you're replacing me with Paddy. Frankly, I'm just waiting for him to invite you to move in."

Surprise lit Natalie's features briefly, but then she shrugged. "I think he wants to but he's scared of my answer."

"You'd say no?" Tuesday knew it was only a matter of time. That fight and making up had been a huge step in their relationship.

"I don't know. I love this house. I love sharing it with you."

"I'm not going anywhere. Eric and I had our own home for years and you and I were friends through all that. Don't make me your excuse to say no. I mean, if you need to use me to say what you want to say and are worried how he'd take it, fine. But he loves you. He's going to love you even if you say you're not ready. But you are."

"Do you think so?" Fear and hope all wrapped up in that question, no doubt.

"I do. But I also think you just had a big fight and maybe if you get yourselves back on track first and *then* move in that might be better in the future as you look back, you know? Get past this moment and then once you're stable again you can take a new step."

"I think so, too. Right now it's good. He's starting to finally really be back. He's different when he's working or out on tour."

"Can you deal with that?" Tuesday wasn't sure she could.

"It's not that my buttons get pushed. I thought for a while, even during this tour, that I was uneasy because of all the wild living they do out there. Childhood-issue trigger. Check." Nat made a checkmark motion with a flick of her wrist. "I was okay when he was gone. I missed him, but we talked. When I went out there on the road with him it was fine. It was, to be totally honest with you, the best sex I've ever had. When it went bad it wasn't his lifestyle that tripped us up. It was just that we came at each other wrong." She shrugged.

In some ways that seemed like it might be more difficult. The normal fight stuff was sometimes the scariest.

"Do you trust him, Nat? He *will* hurt you. It's inevitable with someone you love. But you have to trust him to find a way back to you when things are really bad. That's really it. It's easy to love someone when things are good. Love like that fills our reserves, strengthens and hardens against attack.

"But when something bad happens and that love is challenged, that's when trust will either keep you together or tear you apart. You can't expect another person not to hurt you. But you can, *and you should,* expect another person to protect your heart once you've given it to them."

"Sometimes I forget that you were married. And I really can't believe I just said that." Natalie came over and hugged Tuesday. "I'm so sorry. I didn't mean it like that."

Tears pricked the backs of Tuesday's eyes. "It's

okay. For a long time it wasn't. But lately it's been a little easier to look back."

"Because of Ezra?"

Tuesday took a deep breath. "I don't think so. I mean, he's part of it, but I think over the last year or so it's hurt less and less each day. I don't know if I can say this right but for the longest time it was like that part of me had burned out. Like a circuit that was just always going to be dark. It hurt. Every day it hurt when something would happen and I'd reach out to tell him and he wasn't there. He never would be there." She looked up at the ceiling, trying to stem the tide of tears.

"That's fair."

"I need to take this slow, Natalie." Tuesday took her friend's hand a moment. "Ezra...this thing between he and I is superintense. I wouldn't have been ready for him before that first kiss. Hell, Nat I'm not sure I'm ready for him now. So I'm trying to keep it cool. You're excited because you love me and of course you like him and it's in your nature to want happy things for people you care about. I'm not up to too much joking about it right now. I feel fragile."

Tuesday bet Ezra was feeling pretty fragile, too.

Natalie hugged her again, this time holding on a while until they both felt better.

"Enough tears! So what are you up to? That's your *hey-my-boobs-look-great* shirt."

Tuesday had a certain fit of shirt she loved because it had the perfect cut to emphasize her breasts with the right nip at the waist to show off curves but not too clingy.

"Ezra came by the shop to invite me to dinner so I'm on my way up there."

"Get. Out. Damn. I won't push you on feelings but you do need to pony up the sex details. That's all I ask."

"Fine, fine. Deviant. What are *you* up to?"

"I'm on my way up there, too. I had to grab some clean clothes and I thought I'd invite you over to see a movie. Paddy was headed over to Ezra's after he and I got off the phone—they hadn't hung out in a while. Come over after you two eat. Watch a movie and then you can go back to his house and do sex."

"We'll see." She liked to hang out with Nat and Paddy, watching movies in his screening room. "I'll leave it up to Ezra. If he'd rather skip the movie part and head directly into the riding him like a pony stage... I love you, but um, I'll see a movie with you another day if that's the choice I need to make. I do it for America."

"Fair enough." Nat shrugged and they both laughed.

"You want to catch a ride up there with me? I'll drop you at Paddy's on my way to Ezra's."

"Yeah, that works."

When they'd got about halfway to the ranch, Natalie looked up from her phone. "I got an email from the owners of the house. We're good to go on the trip."

"Yay." Tuesday's birthday was approaching and they'd rented a house up in the mountains. There was a big hot tub, and decks wrapping around the entire first and second floor with fantastic views. They'd rented it a few times before and loved to go up on birthdays and the like because it was pretty and quiet and there was no shortage of activities like hiking and kayaking.

"Are you sure it's okay? Asking Paddy to come, I mean."

Their group of friends usually rented the place. All six of them. But this year everyone's schedule had been so crazy with work or family stuff that it had dwindled down from their usual six to two. They'd rescheduled their group thing for later in the summer but Tuesday had figured it would be nice to keep the reservation and take a trip anyway.

"Why not? It's just going to be me and you in that great big house? You'll hate it when there aren't enough people to go out to play with me. You're too nice to say no if I'd do it alone and it's not fun if I have to guilt you into hiking. Especially when you're on vacation."

Natalie tried not to look relieved and Tuesday loved her for it.

"I like hiking well enough. Just not every day."

Tuesday snorted. It was true. When she was up there she liked to spend as much time as she could outside. The house was right on a lake so she'd kayak and if it didn't rain really hard she'd canoe, too.

"Mary and Damien are staying home. They're going up to see her friends and family the following week so Damien wants her to hang out so he can make her rest. She's pretending like she doesn't know he's managing her. They're pretty adorable."

"They are. I'm sure she'll appreciate the quiet, though I bet Sharon likes to pop in."

Natalie laughed. "The whole family dotes on Mary

and it drives her crazy. But it's so sweet she doesn't complain."

And liked it, too, Tuesday wagered. The Hurleys had a lot of love for each other and Mary definitely loved them all right back.

"I was thinking."

Tuesday gave Natalie a quick look. "Uh-oh."

"Shut up. You should invite Ezra to the mountains."

"He's got the ranch to look after. He can't be gone all the time."

"According to Paddy, Ezra rarely takes time off. He might be gone a day or so here and there, but the last vacation he took of more than a single night away was before all the bad stuff went down."

Tuesday wasn't actually surprised at all. She bet Ezra had a hard time letting go enough to take an actual vacation.

"I'll leave it up to him." It was a matter of whether or not she wanted to make the movie and ask him to go away with her or not. He'd say no, or yes, either way.

And what she'd decided, as they finally came around that last bend in the road leading up to Ezra's, was she'd wait and see how he was. She knew it was time, time to take some risks if she wanted more with Ezra.

THE GATES WERE closed as they approached Sweet Hollow Ranch.

"Weird."

"Oh yeah, Bob has been trying to contact me so they've been keeping the gates here locked." Bob was Natalie's father. A total piece of crap and though Nat-

alie had told him repeatedly that she wanted nothing
more to do with him, he kept showing up and causing trouble.

"I hate him." And boy did Tuesday hate him. He
was selfish and awful. He didn't care about anyone
but himself and he'd never be satisfied until he'd bled
Natalie dry of money and attention.

Natalie gave her the code and the gates slowly slid
open.

"She allowed him to sell the house in Whittier
but that was trust money so he can't get to it. So he
moved in with her. I can't imagine what that must be
like for her."

"No." Tuesday bore to the left around a bend
and pulled into Paddy's driveway. She turned to her
friend. "*Do not* get yourself entangled in that mess
again. They'll use you up and toss you away and you
know it. Neither of them has any sense of moderation. They'll wreck you and not even think about it."

"She's old." Part of Natalie's beauty was how big
her heart truly was. Even after all her family had done
to her, Nat would still feel for them.

So it fell to Tuesday to remind her best friend and
protect her from them the best she could. "She's ma-
nipulative, cold, vindictive and abusive. She raised a
shitty kid and *he* tried to raise one, too. But *you* survived. You're better than that. You built a life. Every
time you let them back in they tear you apart. You
can't fix either of them. It's not your job and even
if it was, you couldn't. They're poisonous. I wish I
could say anything else, but baby, your grandmother
and your father are horrible human beings. Move on

because you have so much good ahead and they represent nothing but pain for you."

Natalie leaned over and hugged Tuesday tight. "I needed that. Thank you for being my friend."

"Back at you. I'll see you later. Either for movies or tomorrow."

EZRA CAUGHT SIGHT of Paddy approaching when he and his horse were still a bit away. The alfalfa spread out all around them would be ready for harvest in another month or so. It would be a pretty good year.

He waved at Paddy once he'd reached where Ezra had been looking over a section of the field where they'd had some problems with mold.

"I went by your place but the pig and the dog were gone so I figured you were out there."

Violet had found herself a shady spot to eat bugs and keep an eye on Loopy and everything else nearby. The pig thought she was a dog and Ezra had no inclination to spoil her little fantasy. Who was he to tell her she couldn't think she was a dog?

"Got back from town a few minutes ago and I wanted to come out here and check these rows." Tuesday would be coming over soon and he was on his way back to the house.

"We doing okay? On track for harvest?"

"I think so, yes. We've got about three to five weeks to go until it's ready. I'd been worried because we had snow and frost so late, but it's looking like we'll have a decent profit this year."

"Good. I'm around so I'll be out helping you every day. Damien, too. At least until the baby comes. He

drives Mary crazy with all his hovering so she'll probably kick him out to get some peace and quiet."

Ezra laughed as they walked the horses farther
north. "Probably. Appreciate the help. Since Vaughan
is in Gresham, the extra hands are even more necessary. I do have a big enough crew for harvest, but
if you're around I can chase Dad away from heavy
stuff."

Their father was a rancher. He was in excellent physical shape but he was getting older and he
couldn't do all the stuff he had before. He had trouble
hearing that. So Ezra and his brothers tried to take on
the heaviest parts to keep their dad occupied with important tasks that weren't as physically taxing.

"I'm sorry you have to do all this on your own
when we're out on tour."

Ezra did what he was supposed to be doing. Ranching kept him tired. Used up all the energy burning
through his muscles every moment. He planted things,
they grew and then he harvested and they started the
next cycle.

He made a difference he could see. After destroy-
ing so much and being such a disappointment, it was
Ezra's way to make things right. To reset the balance
he'd destroyed with his addiction.

"Nothing to be sorry about. This is my job and my
life. I made the choice to be here."

"Don't you resent it? Being here when we're out
there?"

"We've talked about this before." And he didn't
want to do it again.

"No, I asked and you blew me off."

Ezra swung off his horse, Paddy following, not

letting go. "Do you think we don't know how much you do and never complain about? You're meant for more than this."

Ezra rested on his heels as he bent to look at a patch where there was growth, but much slower than most of the rest. "I *like* this. I like working the land. I like that we're taking this ranch into the next generation. These things satisfy me."

"That's not the same as making you happy."

"It doesn't have to be. It's not always about that."

"You've already proven yourself. You're clean. Yes, you were a goddamn mess once. But you were a junkie for what, a year and a half, two years? You've been clean longer than that. How long are you going to punish yourself? Didn't you feel it out there on that stage with us? We have a foreman. We can afford to hire more people to do this so you can make music again."

"I make music right now. I produce every damned album, all the singles, oversee the remixes. I'm in a lot of the videos. I write the music." Ezra shrugged. "Yes, I felt it up there onstage. I miss it. But I don't know how to feel about missing it." He didn't want to think about it for a while. He needed some distance. "Touring is a small part of what we do as Sweet Hollow Ranch. I like what I'm doing."

"Is this your forever?"

Ezra stood, brushing his hands on the legs of his jeans. "It's my right now. Which is enough."

Paddy looked like he planned to argue but then decided against it. "All right. Nat and I are watching a movie tonight. We haven't hung out with you and Tuesday in a while. Come early and have dinner with us."

"I have dinner planned and that doesn't include anyone else. After, yeah, we'll wander down to your place."

"We should all have dinner together. Maybe go to Mary and Damien's. I bet she'd like the company."

Part of him wanted to accept. If they had dinner with a group it would keep a more casual tone. He was already antsy after this stupid conversation with his brother. He wasn't good company for a date.

But he shook that off. He wanted to have her all to himself for a while.

"Fuck off, Patrick. Mary is lovely, but I've seen her today."

Paddy shrugged. "Okay then. We'll start screening the first movie at nine, which gives you time to eat and whatever *else* you might be doing with the supergorgeous Tuesday Eastwood."

"Well, enough time is a relative concept when you're discussing a woman like Tuesday. Anyway, it's enough time to eat." And for part one of whatever else they'd be doing when they were alone and naked but he didn't need to share that with Paddy.

They parted ways behind the stables as Violet and Loopy followed Ezra, and Paddy went back toward his place.

His house was quiet but it had started to smell really good from the dinner he'd put in the oven before he headed out to the fields.

"You guys are on notice," he said as Violet trotted happily back into her pen. She went over to be sure

Big Hoss, the first rescue pig Ezra had adopted, was all right. Assured of this, Violet got herself a snack.

"I'll bring her out here to meet you, but only if you can behave and not try to take up all her attention, which I am not willing to share."

She just stared at him. She'd do whatever she wanted; the damned creature was as headstrong as everything else female in his life. He tossed her some apples and she grunted before crunching into them.

Loopy followed him inside and headed to her bed. Ezra pointed her way. "You, too. I know she's pretty and she smells good but she's mine so back off."

The cats pushed through the cat flap on the back door and he repeated his warning, which they ignored while cleaning their paws.

He needed to shower quickly so he checked the chicken and mushrooms, which were coming along nicely and then he jogged to the bathroom.

CHAPTER TEN

SHE LOOKED AT the screen of the phone in her hand. HEYWOOD flashed in capital letters. Tuesday's heart sank.

Tuesday considered letting it go to voice mail. It was best, when it came to her former mother-in-law, to not give her a chance to engage.

But she'd discovered a way to manipulate Tuesday even more was to call her family to see where she might be.

Rather than risk exposing her loved ones to the horror that was Tina Heywood, she answered.

"Hello?"

"You haven't let us know when you'll be arriving next weekend."

The Heywoods held a luncheon once a year and called it a memorial for Eric. But they held it on Tina's birthday. Which was a pretty standard mood for a narcissist like her.

It was really about getting more attention for a woman who could scarcely be bothered to acknowledge the existence of her two oldest children from her first marriage once she'd got remarried and had children with her new husband.

At six and eight, Eric and his brother had their names changed when their biological father died and their stepfather officially adopted them. But over time Eric and his brother were treated more like lodgers than members of the family.

Sammy, Eric's older brother, joined the Navy right after he graduated from high school and was a pilot living in San Diego and then Eric had run to college.

Tina was cutting and could be cruel, even though Eric wanted so much for his mom to love him and accept him. There were times she'd be unbelievably kind and then she'd turn right back around and hurt Eric. It made Tuesday come to hate her over the time she'd been with Eric.

She wore Eric's death around her neck like a fucking trophy and it made Tuesday's skin crawl.

"I'm not going to be there." She'd hoped after Eric died that at least they could have understood what they were missing. That once and for all his mom would admit her son was a better man than she ever gave him credit for.

But they'd been just as horrible as ever. Worse in some ways, badgering her about money and insurance policies. She hadn't returned since.

"What could you possibly be doing that is more important than spending a day dedicated to Eric?"

She held her tongue until the urge to shout superbad stuff at her dead husband's mother wore off a little.

But that didn't mean she was playing games. "I told you after the first time that I wasn't coming back. You ask me every year—I say no every year."

"You never loved my precious boy. You're spoiled and selfish."

"What is this about? Do you want me to send you

a present? Is that it? You don't like me. You've never liked me. I tried for many years until I got to know you and realized it would never happen. So, you have a happy birthday, but I'll be remembering Eric in other ways besides eating cake and watching you open presents."

"Raised wrong. Those parents of yours. Trash. That's why Eric sniffed after you and not a respectable girl."

She *knew* her buttons were being pushed, but Tuesday sat straight up, nearly honking the horn. Raised wrong? Oh. No. "Shall I have my mother give you a call? I know how much you love chatting with her."

Something had happened between Tina and Tuesday's mother at a holiday dinner. Diana wouldn't ever say what it was, but it was bad enough that Di threw a drink in Tina's face and there was a scuffle. Tina tried to punch Tuesday's mom, who stepped to one side, reached out to grab Tina by the hair to shove her out of the way and avoid getting punched. But she'd been wearing a wig and it came free, along with patches of her real hair, too.

And her mom got a free-from-Tina-for-life card and clearly, given the way Tina sputtered at that threat, she was still afraid of Diana.

"I'm not coming. Happy birthday." She hung up and tried to get her breath back and her heart rate to a normal place.

She looked up at Ezra's house, glad she hadn't actually honked when the call came in.

Time to get her shit in order. She had a date for dinner with a handsome man. That was way better than being upset by a woman she didn't even like.

Slipping her phone into a pocket of her bag, she got out and headed to his door. Ready to be happy for a while.

She hadn't even finished raising her hand to knock when he opened the door, smiling.

"Wow, that's some service."

He took her hand and pulled her close as he shut the door at her back. "I have a lot more services to provide when you're ready." He kissed her and she let herself relax into his touch. He tasted good and he smelled like he'd just got out of the shower, which he must have done because his hair was still wet.

"Come through. Dinner will be ready in about twenty minutes or so. It's a chicken-mushroom thing a friend taught me to make a few years ago. It looks and tastes like it was way harder to make."

"Those are the best kinds of recipes to have. I brought some fresh lemon curd cookies. I made them yesterday. They're nearly all gone but I managed to fight Nat off to hold these aside."

She thrust a bag his way and he took it with a smile as they reached his kitchen. "I love lemon curd. After dinner we've been invited to Paddy's to watch movies with him and Nat."

"I just dropped her off at Paddy's. I said probably to a movie but that you might have plans I didn't know about."

"Nice. Leaving an escape."

She laughed, sneaking a piece of cucumber he'd been slicing for a salad. "Well, I love hanging out with my family, but I don't know if I'd want to be with my brother and his girlfriend all the time. I figured if you'd had your fill it would be easy to beg off."

"I told him we'd show up at nine or so. Which means we have time for dinner and whatever else we want to get up to between now and then."

"Oh? Do you have plans for me?"

He hooked a finger in one of her belt loops and brought her to him again. "I do." This wasn't a kiss of greeting, though—what he laid on her mouth was a promise and she liked it.

Loopy barked a greeting as she came in through the doggie door, startling them both apart like they'd been caught in the gym at a seventh-grade dance.

"We talked about this, Loop," Ezra said to the dog, who head butted Tuesday's leg until she gave in and scratched the dog behind the ear.

"Did you now? And what did you talk about? Did she tell you about the birds and the bees?"

He laughed and the dog yipped, clearly pleased to be part of whatever made her human so happy.

He tried so hard to be gruff, but all that was a front. You only had to look at what a sucker this man was for his animals to know he was compassionate and kind.

"I warned them not to run under our feet tonight."

"Or—" still touched by what a sweet, soft center Ezra had, Tuesday gave in and nuzzled his neck for a brief moment before brushing her cheek against his beard as she straightened "—if they make us fall down in the hallway, you can take me right there."

He got very still, his arm around her waist tightened and she fought the urge to offer him whatever it was he wanted whenever it was he wanted it.

"It wasn't a thing to move you to my bed. It's soft there. I didn't want you to get rug burns or whatever."

"What if I like rug burns?"

He sucked in a breath. "Do you?"

She wasn't sure. But it really seemed to make him hot and she believed he'd make her love it. "I don't know. I don't think I've ever had any. But how can I know until I try?"

"That's a good point. I'll keep it in mind."

He ran a fingertip over the hollow of her throat. "Want something to drink?" he asked after he kissed her again.

She nodded.

"Sit and look pretty. I've got this part handled. I'll steam the green beans when I take the chicken out." He turned to the fridge and she hopped up onto a stool. "Juice okay? I have fresh-squeezed orange but also some lemonade. Soda water. Ginger beer."

"Juice is great." She liked to watch him in his kitchen. Big as he was, he still managed to be graceful as he poured them both a glass of juice and then went back to food prep.

"Anything exciting happen to you this week?" he asked as he scooped the cucumbers he'd been slicing into a bowl.

"It's coming up on a busy time of year for me. My focus is pretty much making lots and lots of pieces so I can sell them in the various places the good weather brings. I think I mentioned to you before that I'd finally got a spot I've been on a wait list for two years for. In Portland. I'm hoping it's a good way to build a base for my work. I'm carrying more in the shop, too. Experimenting with inventory." Maybe finally accept that what she wanted was to run a gallery. "Which is a really long way to answer your simple question."

"I asked because I want to know. How did you end up making jewelry? Is that what you did before you moved to Hood River?"

"No. I worked at a design firm in Seattle for several years. When I was married, I mean. I planned events for our clients' rollouts."

"How did jewelry come into it? If you don't mind my asking."

"I used to make jewelry back in college. A hobby. It started out that way because I had no money for gifts. So I'd head up to campus, toss out a blanket on a sunny spot on the grass and sell the earrings and bracelets I'd made. Paid for those presents and even kept me in ramen." She took a deep breath and said it. "And then Eric got sick and I needed to do something with my hands. To keep busy in all the hours spent in doctors' offices, hospitals and hospice." She shrugged. "It kept me busy."

He looked at her across the kitchen island. "I'm sorry you lost him."

Tuesday licked her lips. "Thank you. I'm sorry, too."

"Do you mind talking about it?"

"I'll tell you if I can't. Or don't want to. It's like any other terrible moment in a life. Everyone has them. It was the worst thing I'd ever experienced and it remains that to this day. Eric was part of my life for a long time. To never speak of him means I can't draw on all that life. I choose not to live that way anymore."

"But you did stop talking about him?"

"For about eighteen months after I scattered his ashes I didn't. I never spoke of him."

He nodded. "I get that."

"My friends let me sleep in their guest rooms and I stayed with my siblings and other assorted family while I pretended I was someone else." Someone who hadn't lost a husband.

"Did it work?"

"Does it ever?"

He didn't respond, but he didn't have to.

"After about a year and a half, Natalie asked me to come and stay in her new house with her for a while. And I ended up staying. I'm leaning toward shifting my emphasis and running a gallery. I want to make my jewelry and sell it, and art, in my shop. I may. It's a multiple-year plan." She shrugged, pretending non-chalance, but in reality that had been the first time she'd said it out loud like a definite plan instead of cloud talk.

"I do that," he said as he tipped the green beans into a steamer.

"What?"

"Have multiple-year plans. I like to spread it all out and break it down into component parts."

"It doesn't seem as insurmountable when you break it down." And so that's how she'd taken each day. Task by task, hour by bour.

Their gazes locked as this depth of knowing passed between them. Ezra hadn't lost a spouse, but he'd lost part of himself for a long time. He got her situation in ways very few others ever could. And yet she knew he wasn't ready to see that right then.

He turned his attention back to the food. "Some

days, checking stuff off a list was the high point. Hell, it's still that way sometimes."

While he finished the prep, she set the table and then went to the windows nearest his dining room table.

The cat, Goldfish, she remembered, hopped up onto the windowsill and walked back and forth, tickling her face with his tail until she picked him up. His purrs were loud as he drooled all over her arm.

"Oh shit, sorry. I should have warned you he's a drooler." Ezra handed her a paper towel she wiped her arm with.

"It's okay. I'll wash off." She balled the paper towel and went to wash her hands before she settled at the table with him.

The food was really good and she said as much, complimenting his skills. "Did you once have a chef for a girlfriend or something?" she teased.

He laughed. "No. One of the women who was a counselor at the sober house I lived in after I left rehab. We all had to take turns making dinner. She taught me how to make this and a few other things. It gave me something to do."

She'd been curious, but hesitant to ask too many questions about his experience with heroin and the recovery after he'd crashed and burned so hard.

"How long were you there?"

"I went to detox first. The place I went uses this process where you're pretty much unconscious through the worst parts of withdrawal. They monitor your physical state, keeping you hydrated, watching your vital signs so that by the time the worst of it is burned from your system, you wake up. Then I went for another hundred and twenty days and after that into sober living for five months."

"Wow."

He tore off a piece of bread. "I had to learn how to cope again. I'd built my life around handling things a certain way and I couldn't ever do that again."

"Did you go straight there? From rehab to sober living? Is that how it works?"

"Not for everyone. They gave me the option of sober living once I'd finished rehab. My counselor recommended it. But I'd been out of pocket for four months at that point. Longer if you consider how useless I'd been for a year or so before that. I had shit to do and I was used to just doing it. I thought it would be easy since I no longer had any heroin in my system." He laughed but there was no mirth there.

"They told me my addiction was way more than just a substance but I wasn't going to listen to that bullshit. I kicked. I'd avoid the people I used with, which wasn't hard because my family wasn't going to let any of them near me. I was ready to get on with my life. And I walked into my house and the stress of it all hit me. It hit me as I stood in the powder room I'd been dope sick in. I'd be sleeping in a bed I'd used in. The whole house had echoes of *that* Ezra all through it, right to the studs in the walls. I wanted to use *so badly* right then I locked myself in a closet until it passed. Once I'd got past the craving, I realized I couldn't live in that house. So I jotted down notes about what I wanted, I discussed it with my parents, who agreed to handle the demolition and construction while I was away and I got on a plane that afternoon and headed to sober living. By the time I got back I had a new house I could start over in and the tools to live with the consequences of the decisions I had to make, like leaving the band."

He looked back to her, his gaze coming back from the past where he'd been dwelling a little as he told her the story.

"I guess it's self-indulgent to demolish a house because I'd made bad choices there."

There was enough self-loathing in his tone that she spoke again.

"The day Eric died I stayed at the hospice long enough to fill out all the paperwork. It's weird. He was there and then he wasn't." She shook her head to resist dwelling on that part. "So they made me leave for a while and then I went back into his room to get his things. I sat next to an empty bed with a kitchen trash bag, which pretty much encompassed the entirety of my husband's life by that point. My parents had shown up and my mother drove me back to my house." Her mother had touched her as if Tuesday was going to fly apart any moment. For years she felt like an unexploded bomb, fragile and dangerous.

"She pulled up and I froze with my hand on the door handle. I couldn't get out. I couldn't go in. I couldn't see our bed and smell him in our bathroom. I stayed in a hotel that night and three days later I put the place on the market. I was inside it only once more after he died and that was to pack up to move. I've never seen it again." She didn't even get off the freeway at that exit or go to any of their old restaurants and favorite places. "I know what it means to have to destroy something to keep going forward."

They were both quiet awhile as she remembered

their house with the front garden Eric had created so carefully, mapping out exactly what went where.

"It doesn't gross you out that I was a junkie?"

Not only was the question unexpected, she heard the shame in his words and it cut her to the bone. "I hurt that you suffered so much, but no, I'm not grossed out at all. In case it's escaped your notice when you look in a mirror, you're beautiful, Ezra. You're strong and your heart was forged by fire. It makes you a lion. With some scars, yes, but all warriors have scars."

"I failed a whole lot of people."

"I bet. I also bet you haven't failed anyone since."

"I fail people all the time."

"Why is that? Because you're human? Tell me of your horrible crimes, Ezra." She had no idea why she was doing and saying all this to him. Provoking. Heat banked in his gaze and she kept poking.

No. That was a lie. She knew why.

Because she didn't want him carrying all the weight he should have cast off long before then.

"A man is worth nothing if those he cares about can't trust him."

"Isn't that the truth?"

He sighed, shifting in his seat.

"Look, we can change the subject. All I'm saying is, you're a good man and the people around you know it. You take care of them. You guide them. When you and Paddy weren't talking last month, Nat freaked out. She was worried about Paddy not so much because they'd been apart, but because she knows how much Paddy relies on you. All of them do. It's okay to cut yourself a break from time to time. Now, I'd like more of the green beans, please."

He handed her the bowl, catching her gaze. They remained there, looking straight into one another for long moments until he broke away and pretended he needed to look at his glass just then.

CHAPTER ELEVEN

EZRA PAUSED IN the doorway, watching her play with the cats. Loopy was lying across Tuesday's feet as she danced a string out of reach of two furry, excited felines. Tuesday laughed, talking to them, pausing to include the dog from time to time.

"I warned them not to cockblock me again and look what I happen upon."

She turned to him with a smile. "With this dog around, I bet your feet never get cold."

"True. Then again, I'm always covered in dog hair. Come on." He held out a hand. "I promised Violet I'd bring you to meet her and if I don't she'll get her revenge somehow."

Loopy groaned but moved as Tuesday stepped over her. Ezra took her hand to keep her steady as the cats shot from the room.

"Those cats are very sweet, but wow, all that energy exhausts me."

"They were worse when they were tiny. They climbed up my curtains and they'd get on top of the fridge so if I went to get something in the middle of the night they'd jump on my head. I nearly had a heart attack a time or two."

He took her hand and led her out back and around to where Violet was.

"I never imagined you as the kitten type. Or the pig type, either."

Ha. Neither had he, but there he was. "It all started with Loopy. Vaughan and I were out on a ride. Vaughan's horse got spooked and when we got down to see what was wrong, we found her and her sister as puppies, barely hours old."

His mouth hardened as he remembered how small and helpless both animals had been.

"They'd been tossed in a ditch. At first I wasn't sure if either puppy would survive. But they did. Loopy stayed with me and her sister lives with my foreman. He's just down the road so he brings Loopy's sister with him to work all the time."

Tuesday cocked her head as she looked up at him. "I know your secret."

He made an annoyed sound, but that didn't deter her at all. Which made him like her even more.

"Anyway, I think the people down at the vet clinic in town figured that since I took in a dog I'd probably take in other animals. So they asked me to foster. Big Hoss was the first but he never left." Ezra pointed to the massive black-and-white pig happily munching away on some of the apples and sweet potatoes he'd put in their enclosure earlier.

"Oh my god." She leaned over the fence and he jumped, moving quickly to yank her back from Big Hoss, who hated anyone near his bed or his food. Instead Big gave her a grunt and kept on eating.

Okay then.

"Sometimes pigs can be mean. Just a warning," he said to her, brushing a curl back from her face.

"I like you in one piece. Hoss will cut a bitch in defense of his bed."

She smiled at him. "Protector of all things living, apparently. Thank you. I do know better, but he's so big and adorable and I lost my mind for a moment. I love pigs. I guess I should have told you that."

He laughed, kissing her quickly before setting her back. He couldn't defend against that. At all. It was fucking adorable that she was so exited over his pigs.

Still grinning, Tuesday turned back to the enclosure. "And you're Violet. I've heard all about you from Mary."

At the sound of Mary's name, Violet gave a squeal and trotted over, grunting a little.

Tuesday made an excited little *eeee* as she laughed. "You are indeed a very fine pig. You're both very smart to have come to live with Ezra. I bet he's a big giant softy who gives you apples and all the things you like."

"I beat them with nettles and I'm going to make Big Hoss into bacon." Ezra frowned and Tuesday snorted, rolling her eyes.

"Sure you do." Tuesday looked at him over her shoulder for a moment and then turned back to Violet. "Between you and me, Violet, I love pigs. When I was a little girl I had a necklace with a pig pendant on it. I loved that necklace. I had pig stuffed animals, too. And maybe a few dozen ceramic pigs people bring me back from trips they take. Oh, and some salt and pepper shakers."

Damn, he'd known she was unexpected. Funny. Heartbreaking. Strong. But he was partial to silly. He'd not noticed the salt and pepper shakers but he did remember seeing a red-and-white ceramic pig in her bedroom.

Violet made her little grunts and squeals to Tuesday, who nodded and spoke back to the pig. Violet let off one of her little satisfied squeaks and gave Ezra a look.

"She approves of me, huh?" Tuesday straightened with one last pat to Violet's head.

"She can be vicious if she chooses. If she hadn't liked you, she'd have found a way to make you sorry. She's a vexing female." He watched his pig trot over to get herself some more apples before she settled in for a nap.

"I'm glad not to be a victim of suspicious pig gang activity. I'd have some story to tell about how I lost my eye—probably get me lots of free drinks in bars."

He barked a surprise laugh. "Maybe next time. She loves bad influences. Look how much she digs Mary."

"Can I come back to see them? Really?"

The idea of Tuesday being around more was one he liked a great deal.

"You're welcome to come see these pigs anytime."

She hugged him. It was an impulsive, easy thing and holy shit he liked it. So much he wrapped his arms around her, just soaking it in for long moments before he kissed her forehead and stepped back.

She looked around, peering closer at the corner of his garden. "Do you have a garden, too?" She pointed at the nearby hedgerow.

"I do. Just a little something I do in my spare time."

"Show me."

He took her hand and led, feeling proud and a little embarrassed at once.

TUESDAY PAUSED, sucking in a breath as they got a few steps past the wall of hedges. "Wow. This is what you do in your spare time?" She took it all in, the paths lined with flowering plants, the trees and bushes and plants. It wasn't a huge garden, but it was big enough that as she wandered through she began to see that each area had its own feel, its own sounds even.

"I think this is my favorite." She sat on a little bench under a tree, near a water feature.

He sat next to her. "Really? It's just a thing, this isn't..." Again the man tried to wave away something amazing he'd done.

She took his hand. "This isn't *just* a thing. Ezra, this is like...I don't know how to explain it, but it's a whole different world in here. It's quiet and it feels faraway and serene. It's nice to have a place to escape to when you need to clear your head."

She could totally see bringing her stuff out here and making bracelets all day as she listened to the water and pretended the world was a million miles away.

He rumbled and she smiled.

"No wonder you're so good at sex. God."

He barked a laugh. "What? Is there a link between gardening and sex I didn't know about?"

"No. There's a link between a man who's undeniably good with his hands and his imagination and really good sex. Ask anyone. I'm sure there've been studies even. You should volunteer. Let them study you. For science."

He pushed to stand, heading to a nearby bush and pinching off some dead growth.

"Are you ever still?" She eased toward him, waiting until he unbristled before taking that final step, bringing her to his chest.

"What do you mean?" He kept his tone wary.

"You're very suspicious." He frowned and she wasn't sure why, but she was charmed, drawn closer by how hard he tried to be gruff. She petted his beard and hummed happily.

"You confuse the hell out of me," he mumbled and she grinned.

"I know. I'm vexing, just like your pig. Except I have boobs. But back to you. You're rarely still. I look at you and your life and I see a man who does more in just one part of his life than most humans ever will. And you do it on several levels. It's pretty impressive."

He shook his head, as if that made her statement less true.

"I do what needs doing. I'm not splitting the atom."

"Sure. If what needs doing is this garden. Or all the rescue animals you take in. Or the whole making and recording hit albums thing. Oh, or the running a ranch to be able to say ranching has been in your family another generation. I mean, most people are glad to fall into bed at night and call it a success that they managed to get through the day."

He pushed back and she felt that wall between them get a little wider. She'd touched a nerve and no one liked that. She understood it, but it stung.

"I'm sorry. I wanted to compliment you but I've upset you."

He ran a hand through his hair, frustrated, emotional. He paced a little. "No, it's me. I'm being an asshole. I'm the one who's sorry."

She watched him through eyes that were as perceptive as they were full of shadows. But she held nothing back. She didn't just look at him, Tuesday seemed to *see* him. That gaze wrecked him. She didn't even see the harsh exterior he used to keep people from getting close enough to see into the darkest parts of him. She just waltzed right up to him, nose to nose, and called him out.

It was…humbling.

His gruff exterior didn't hide a thing from her. Tuesday saw right to the bone in a way that only someone else who'd been out on the edge of their own inner darkness could do.

He shook his head and turned on his heel to face her. She'd gone back to the bench, giving him space to process.

"I have a lot of energy and keeping busy means I usually stay out of trouble. At first it was to do something else. Other than use. For about three months it's all I thought about. Using and then about not using. Thinking about not using is a mental and emotional version of being drug sick." He snorted. "You think about not thinking about it, practice not thinking about it so essentially the outline of your addiction becomes a giant mountain you have to hike around every fucking day until you figure out how to get rid of it."

One of her brows rose regally. "So *that* became your obsession. Fuck thinking about heroin and not using heroin and fuck being enslaved to something that had wrecked your life. Your revenge was going to be nuking that mountain you had to dance around every day."

He had to fist his hands to keep rooted to the spot and not stride off.

A shrug this time as she took in his reaction, knew exactly what was happening. "So you're thinking, what the hell does she know about it?"

He sighed. Her honesty made it impossible to walk away and be a coward."

"When Eric died I didn't get busy, I got blank. It's a coping mechanism to trauma. Just like being really busy is a coping mechanism. Hell yes, you're exceptional. You're special and unique. But you're not so freaking special you get a pass from the emotional devastation that's the aftermath of something like addiction. Or me from my bullshit."

He scoffed. "I'd never compare my shit to yours. Heroin didn't *happen* to me, Tuesday. I ran out after it. I used heroin like it was my fucking job."

"It's not my place to give you a pass for what you did. But it seems to me, you're harsher on yourself than anyone you hurt when you were using."

He didn't speak, but she saw everything anyway. Ezra could watch her face and know everything she was thinking. It was fascinating and horrifying. He wanted to run away. Wanted to give her words his back but that would make him a liar and he was done with that.

What could he say to that? You should have known me then? Should have known the Ezra who nearly let his mother shoot up just to get a taste for himself?

But Tuesday wasn't done. "So sure, you made using drugs the center of your life, but when you turned it around, you *truly* did that. When you turned it around, it wasn't your job anymore. Instead of being owned by your addiction, you were *done* with it. You took your life back. You moved past it and you keep busy so you use all your energy in ways that don't land you in rehab. You have a family that relies on you. Trusts you." She looked him over. "I'd tell you that it's been years and they've forgiven you and you've earned their trust back, but I don't know that you'd believe me. And whatever, it's not my job to manage your recovery. I can only tell you what I see from the outside."

"Most of the time people tell me what I want to hear. It's frustrating because I know they're full of shit. Unvarnished truths are rare outside my immediate family."

She shrugged. "I bet. I'm not your fan, Ezra. Though I do like your music a great deal. I'm not here for who you are onstage. Though I'd be a filthy liar if I denied how hot you are out there. I'm here for the real Ezra."

He was on her in two steps, bringing her to her feet as he backed her against the trunk of a nearby tree. His mouth took hers in a kiss she opened to as eagerly as he delivered it.

She broke with a gasp when he covered her breasts with his hands. "You really do like kissing me in gardens, don't you?"

CHAPTER TWELVE

HE KISSED HER EAR. "I really have very little willpower when it comes to you. You look so pretty and the light hits you just right and all I know is that I want you."

"I aim to please," she gasped out.

He stepped back with a pained groan. "Inside. We could be interrupted and God knows I'd never be able to get enough therapy if my mother stumbled into this scene."

She laughed as he took her hand and pulled her behind him as he headed for the house.

They managed to miss tripping on animals this time and he closed the doors in their wake to avoid having a cat jump up into bed while they were in it. He flipped on the bedside lamps because he wanted to see her as she got undressed.

"Off. I need you naked and I'll rip stuff if I do it."

She'd already got rid of her glasses, so it was one easy movement to pull her shirt off and then get back to looking at him.

Truth was, Tuesday wasn't sure there'd ever be a point where she didn't want to stop and stare, open-mouthed at the wonder of his body, so she didn't even try to hide it when he started getting naked.

"You keep looking at me like that and I'm going to

injure myself getting out of my pants." His shirt had been tossed aside, resting against hers in a far corner.

His upper body gleamed in the low light and she sucked in a breath. "I can't seem to not look at you like that. You're so hard and masculine and hot. It drives me crazy."

She stepped to him after she whipped her bra off. "But the last thing I'd want is for a game-ending zipper injury. Let me, then."

He held his arms wide, giving her access, which she quickly capitalized on because, hello, he was amazing and she wanted to lick him up one side and down the other.

"Like the best present under the tree," she said, pulling his zipper down carefully.

His cock sprang free as she parted the front of his jeans.

She looked up at him and he waggled his brows.

His pants were off a few beats later, leaving him totally naked.

"I didn't notice the puma on your calf."

He stalked her to the bed where she fell back and he pulled the rest of her clothing off.

"We only have about forty minutes until we have to be over at Paddy's so I suggest we use our time wisely. This round I mean." He cupped her pussy. "I'll be back to this again later on."

Oh. Well she certainly had no intention of arguing with that.

"Get to it."

He laughed and then before she knew it, he'd rolled her over and slapped her ass three times. Her laughter died as she realized she liked the way the burn wisped away and left a wash of sensation.

He caressed her hips and thighs as he slid his fingers through her from behind. She pressed her face into his blankets and let herself enjoy and feel what he did to her.

And then he was pushing into her pussy, sending all those feel-good chemicals to run riot through her system. She arched to take him deeper. Needed more.

He put a hand between her shoulder blades to hold her in place. She squirmed a little and he lessened his pressure in response. But she *wanted* that pressure.

Frustrated, she moaned into the mattress and he pulled out, rolling her over to peer into her face carefully. "Are you all right?"

"What?" She was all confused. "Why aren't you in me? What are you doing?"

"You sounded upset. If I'm holding you down and you sound upset, I'm going to check in. It sort of comes with the permission to hold someone down."

"I don't want to have a discussion right now! I want you in me. Thank you for checking in. I'm great. Or I was and now I'm not and you're at fault for both those states. I can tell you which one I prefer, but perhaps you can figure it out."

"Why did you make that sound?"

She lowered her lashes a little. "I liked it when you were holding me down harder. You let up a little. It wasn't awful or anything. Just a sound because you were taking care of all other aspects of the situation. Yeah?"

He turned her over and was back inside in half a breath. His hand at her back returned and he pushed until she groaned when he got to the place she liked it best.

"Each." He thrusted. "Time." Again. "We're." He continued his sentence, emphasizing his point with harder and deeper presses into her. "Together and we…we do this, I want to be sure everything is all right with you. If I can't be bothered to take care of the trust you give me, I don't deserve it."

The palm at her back gave a little more weight and she groaned from a place deep in her belly. She wasn't sure how it was she got so freaking turned on by something like that, but she was.

He wasn't rough so much as he was in charge. Which made her tingly—she wasn't about to lie.

And then he reached around and found her clit. She'd been close already, but just that last bit of direct contact was exactly what she'd needed.

He growled and then snarled a curse as she came so hard it surprised her probably as much as it did him. She writhed, tightening around him as orgasm sucked her in and didn't let go. His free hand ended up at her hip, holding her as he fucked into her hard and fast until he came.

"Now I think I can handle a movie with my brother as he moons at Natalie for hours," he murmured as he came back into the room from his bathroom. "Would you like to walk or drive over?"

"A walk sounds nice. I wore sneakers just in case you wanted to do something active. Outside the bedroom anyway. I'm always dressed for that."

He whistled and Loopy trotted out the door. "She likes to walk along. I need to stop by Vaughan's place first. I promised him I'd water his plants and check his mail."

It was adorable the way he stepped up to take care of things so his brother could handle his business in Gresham. She refrained from telling him so, but she thought it just the same.

He took her hand as they started to stroll down the road.

"I meant to ask you earlier but I was sidetracked. Mind you, I'm not ever going to voice it as a complaint to be sidetracked to have an orgasm. Just FYI. Natalie and I have been renting a house up in the mountains every May for the last few years. It's usually a girls' trip for my birthday but this has been such a weird and crazy spring it's just me and Nat. Well, and Paddy. I wondered if you'd like to come up? Four days, and I know you probably have a lot of stuff to do here so I understand if you can't. It's on a lake so there's kayaking and canoeing and some pretty impressive hiking trails if you'd be up for it."

He thought about it. Paddy would be there and there'd be sex and hiking, too. It had been a very long time since he'd done something like that with friends. "Yes, I'd like that."

"Yeah? You can bring Loopy if you like. The owners are dog people and in years past Jenny and Zoe have brought their dog."

"She's an outdoorsy dog. If you don't mind having her along for hikes and the like, she loves it. Though if there was a bear she'd probably try to get it to throw her a ball."

A romantic trip. He hadn't gone on anything even resembling one. But he liked the idea of being out on the trail with her. He hoped she wore those formfitting yoga pants when she went hiking.

"All right. I'll get you all the details." She picked up a stick and Loop nearly lost her mind with excitement. Laughing, Tuesday tossed it and the dog was a blond blur as she ran past them.

"She's never going to leave you alone now. You know that, right?"

Loopy brought her back the stick, which Tuesday threw again and again as they made their way to Vaughan's. His brother had lodged himself in Gresham as Maddie healed after she'd been released from the hospital. He was trying his damnedest to get back in Kelly's and the girls' lives. Ezra hoped like hell it worked out because they all deserved a happy ending.

Tuesday played with the dog while Ezra took care of things inside.

"I admire your positive outlook, Loopy."

Ezra paused at the side of the house, watching her with his dog. How people treated animals said a lot about them. She threw the stick, gently teased the dog about the slobber on it, scratched and generally was kind. He liked it and his damned dog did, too.

Loopy already loved Natalie and Mary, but Tuesday had been in *Ezra's* pack, in their house, so the dog would see her as one of them in ways she didn't with Natalie or even Mary. He sort of felt that way about Tuesday, as well.

Tuesday ran along with Loopy, who barked merrily as they went.

He finally came out of the shadows and called out

to them both. "Loopy, don't get Tuesday tired. I need her later."

Tuesday snorted as she approached. "Everything all right?"

He put an arm around her shoulders and they set off toward Paddy's place. "Just fine." More than fine, as it happened. And he planned to let it keep on in that direction.

TUESDAY HAD JUST finished stretching a canvas when her phone rang, indicating an unknown number. She considered not answering but did anyway.

"Hello?"

"Is this Tuesday?"

"Who's this, please?"

The woman on the other end laughed prettily and it sounded familiar enough to tug at her memory but Tuesday couldn't quite place it.

"I'm sorry. It's Kelly Hurley. I got your number from Ezra earlier today. Is this a good time to talk a little business?"

"I'm a small business owner. It's always time to talk business." Tuesday liked Kelly so it wasn't a hardship to have a chat. "I'm in my shop right now, though, and it's been sort of busy today so I can't guarantee I won't get interrupted."

"Do you take lunch?"

"I do, usually at one or so."

"This has to do with your jewelry. Do you have an inventory at your shop? Let me back up a second. I'd like to take you to lunch to talk about your jewelry and my business and so I'd also like to see your stuff at the same time."

Tuesday warmed. "Oh. Yes. Today?"

"Yes. The girls are at school so I've got the time if you do."

KELLY CAME IN as Tuesday was ringing someone up, but wandered through the small space until she'd found the jewelry and began to look at the pieces out on the display tree.

"Thanks for waiting." Tuesday turned to her once her customer had left.

Kelly's smile was genuine. "No problem." She indicated the cases where the jewelry was displayed. "This is all yours?"

Tuesday nodded, joining Kelly at the cases, circling to the back to unlock them and slide the trays holding the more pricey pieces out.

Kelly pulled a necklace free, examining it carefully, including a look at the price tag.

"Are you going to keep me in suspense forever or tell me what you're here for?"

"Come on." Kelly put the necklace back carefully. "Let's go to lunch and I'll tell you what I have in mind now that I've seen your work."

"Okay. Hang on a few while I get everything locked down."

Soon enough they'd finished ordering their lunches.

"What sort of inventory do you have?"

"It depends. It's cyclical. If I find something I like, a material or I come across some stones or beads I tend to create a number of connected pieces all at once. I just started a stall at a craft market in Portland, though, so I've recently stepped up production to keep pace with sales."

"I co-own two clothing stores with a friend who designs. We're expanding to include more accessories. Jewelry is hard because we want quality stuff but not so expensive most of our customers won't splurge that much. Your stuff is fantastic. It's bold and feminine. I think we could do some business together. I like that you're local, that's important to us as a brand. I like that you're a woman, also important to us."

Tuesday sat back, really, truly excited. "Wow. I hadn't even considered that as what you wanted to talk to me about. I mean I figured you wanted me to make you a piece."

"You do custom work, too, which will be a selling point. We do a trunk show in the fall at our Portland store and feature the designers we carry in the stores. You'd be a perfect addition. I mean, look, it's going to depend on how your stuff moves, but I think it will. What do you say?"

"I say let's talk some details because this sounds like a great idea."

The details, as it turned out, *were* pretty awesome. A fair split of the profits. Her jewelry being sold in two successful clothing boutiques was a dream. Now she just had to hope their customers liked the stuff as much as Kelly did.

"Maddie is doing all right?" Tuesday asked after they'd finished talking business.

"She's doing great. She just started back to school Monday. Both girls are out of their minds with excitement that Vaughn is staying with us right now. They love seeing him every day."

"You can tell me to mind my own business, but do *you* love seeing him every day?"

"It's complicated."

Tuesday laughed, reaching out to pat Kelly's hand. "Girl. I bet. I'm around if you want to talk about it. You don't know me very well, but sometimes that's a good thing."

"I'm so confused right now. To be honest, I couldn't answer you because I don't know. Well, no, that's a lie. I like Vaughan. I mean as a person separate from my ex-husband or as the father of my kids. I've always liked him, since the start. And it hasn't served me well in every circumstance. I have a lot to figure out. Right now I'm just trying to figure out what it is I want."

"Fair enough. I hear that. Believe me."

"So, what's the story with you and Ezra?" They paid for lunch and headed back to the shop.

"I'm where you are, I guess. We're dating. I like him. I like his family. The rest I'm stumbling through right now." He could be so closed off it felt like a slap, but when he did open up, she realized it wasn't about her at all, but the iceberg of shame and guilt that he dragged along with him.

"He's so imposing and gruff. But with my girls he's a great big softy. And the animals."

"He constantly surprises me. Which surprises me in and of itself. I like to think I'm jaded but he…he's refreshing. Unexpected. I like it and I'm trying not to think about it much more beyond that because I don't know."

She used to love not knowing. Used to love learning new things and being surprised by the universe. Until the universe decided cancer qualified as a surprise. Since then, she and surprises had been on uneasy terms.

"Okay. I get it. I'm with you in that boat. I'm just… I loved him so much before. And he walked away and I don't know if it ever really hurt him. Not the way it hurt me."

Tuesday unlocked and flipped the Open sign and they went inside.

"I'm going to take some pictures of your stuff to send to my business partner. Is that all right?"

Tuesday nodded at Kelly as she unlocked the case again, pulling out the pieces Kelly pointed to.

"Vaughan isn't a bad man." Kelly began to speak as she arranged the jewelry and took pictures of it. "He just didn't want a life with me and the girls. It took me a really long time to get over that."

Tuesday heard the fear there in the words. The fear that if Kelly let Vaughan back in, if she gave him another chance, he'd hurt her again.

"I was married once. Eric and I met in college. He lived on my floor in our dorm. He was something special. I pretty much loved him about ten minutes after the first time we had sex."

Tuesday leaned against the counter. "Things were fast with us. We clicked. He had dreadlocks back then. We were nineteen." Tuesday laughed.

"The next year we all decided to move into a big house together. Natalie and me and our other roommates. And Eric. We all went to school together, some of us worked together, we lived in the same house and we were a family. As we neared graduation, Eric asked me to marry him. Or I guess I should say he and I had this talk about life and the future and we decided to get married. He and I had plans. A path and we were on it together. It was a really great time in my life. I'm telling you this stuff so you can understand what I'm going to say next a little better."

Kelly stilled, looking up at Tuesday and abandoning all pretense of taking pictures. She sighed, a hand at her throat and a blush on her cheeks that told Tuesday what she'd suspected.

"I found a letter. Not a love letter," Tuesday amended quickly. "It was a discussion about this thing they'd had while studying in Central America. It was like, *Hey I get it, I'd never say anything to her, I know you love her and I hope it works out.*"

It used to hurt like fire to think back on that moment. The betrayal. The shame. The horror that they'd gone to that woman's damned going-away party just a few weeks after that letter had been written. Eric hadn't wanted to go but Tuesday had pushed.

"I was planning our wedding, getting ready to move away from my hometown to Seattle, where Eric had a job. Boxing stuff up. I confronted him as he walked in the door. He confessed immediately. He begged my forgiveness. He said he loved me and wanted to be with me. He'd chosen me, deliberately every single day of his life since he returned from that program he'd been in over two years before. I went home, because that's what you do. Anyway, my mom was awesome. She said love can start a marriage, but a commitment is what kept it together. Did I think Eric would do it again or did I think if I forgave him I could have a really wonderful life with a man who wasn't perfect but one who loved me? You listen to me, Kelly. Lots of people will say if he or she ever cheated I'd break up with them forever. And maybe you should, given the circumstances. Hell, you *did*. But it's how long ago now?"

"Eight years. I served him with papers eight years ago."

"You're a different person now. Maybe he is, too." Tuesday shrugged. "Maybe not. But you get to think about it if you want to. Screw what anyone else says about it."

"You were glad then? That you gave him another chance?"

Tuesday nodded. "Yes. I never regretted it."

"Thanks for that. I needed to hear it. Can I say something else? Not about men or marriage."

"Sure."

"I wasn't sure what I expected when you said you owned and ran a custom framing shop. But, Tuesday, this is so much more than that. This is a gallery. You should call it that."

"I guess you weren't the only one who needed to hear something today. Thank you."

Kelly hugged her as they walked to the door. "I'm excited about this. I'll have our agreement sent to you so you can have your attorney look it over. In the meantime, I'd like to buy that choker. The blue-and-citrine one."

"Damn, you have good taste."

Tuesday believed in her gut when it came to meeting people. Kelly fit into Tuesday's life a lot like Natalie had. Pretty much instantly. Which Tuesday believed was exactly what was supposed to happen.

CHAPTER THIRTEEN

"I REALLY THINK all four of us and the dog in one vehicle up to the mountains is a bad idea. Paddy is a horrible passenger and an even worse driver."

Tuesday looked at his reflection as he moved around in the room behind her. They were set to leave for the cabin in the mountains within the next hour and he'd jumped her the moment she'd come through his front door that morning, so she needed to get herself back in order.

"Honestly, you two."

"You smell good." He ranged around, always busy, but got increasingly closer until he was close enough to kiss her shoulder.

"Coconut oil. I use it in my hair."

She caught a flash of white in his reflection as he dragged his teeth over her skin where her shoulder met her neck.

"Don't get started on something you cannot finish to my satisfaction, Ezra."

The gaze he flicked to hers was full of amusement. "Your exacting standards, as always, must be met."

"I'm glad we can agree on that." She turned into his arms as he picked her up and put her on the edge of his bathroom counter. "Just tell Paddy and Nat to go up first because we have the dog."

"I'll tell him he's a fucked-up driver and I don't want to have to dig my heels through the floorboard for an hour and a half."

"Or you could say that so the two of you can get your punching out of the way before the trip."

He thought it over and she sighed, smiling. "Go on. Call him or go over there or whatever. I'll finish loading your truck."

He rolled his eyes before dropping a kiss on her forehead. "Yeah, that'll happen. Never. Anyway, *I'll* finish loading the stuff and then we'll drive over to his place on the way out and tell him then."

"I'm perfectly capable of lifting things to put them in the bed of a truck."

She followed him out, catching a cat before he could dig those little claws into Tuesday for an assist up to her arms. Tuesday held the squirming cat so they could get eye to eye. "You, rogue, go use those claws in a tree, not my leg." She kissed the top of a furry head and put him down.

He wound through her legs and then trotted alongside as she grabbed her duffel bag and headed out the front door.

Ezra gave her a look, but she tossed her duffel up to him, satisfied with his *oof* when he caught it.

"Oh, wait, was that heavy? The thing I just tossed to you?"

He fit the bag into some slot, Tetris style. "I'm not disputing your ability. Or your strength. I like to do things for you. It pleases me when you let me."

He was so good at that stuff.

"Whatever. It's not like I suffer watching you bunch and flex."

Paddy and Natalie pulled up as Ezra finished strapping down everything in the back of the truck.

"He's coming over here to suggest we drive separately. Saves me from having to do it," Ezra muttered as he jumped down.

Natalie gave Ezra a hug as she approached with Paddy at her side. "Hey there, sweetheart."

Natalie beamed at him and then winked at Tuesday.

Tuesday tipped her chin. "We'll see you guys up there."

Natalie wasn't surprised at all. Tuesday knew this because they'd discussed this very thing a few days before. Neither woman had a problem driving up together, but they didn't have any issue going separately, either. Especially because Paddy and Ezra could be superfun or work each other's nerves until a scuffle broke out.

"We'll pick up groceries if you get the keys."

"Deal."

Paddy gave Tuesday a peck on the cheek. "Try to keep him in line, okay?" He waved in Ezra's direction.

"Your brother keeps his own lines. He's particular that way."

Paddy grinned. Holy shit, was he gorgeous. "You know him pretty well. We'll see you guys in a few hours."

"Okay, Loopy, you need to go pee now so we don't have to stop in twenty minutes."

The dog looked up at her after Paddy and Nat drove off, her tongue hanging out to the side.

Ezra whistled in a certain way and Loop trotted around the side of the house where there was more grass and did her business.

"So do all women just obey you or what?"

He laughed. "If only. You ready?"

"Let me do my business and grab my purse. The cats are going to be all right?"

"They're going to stay with my parents. My mother said she'd wait until we left and she'd come grab the cats. They'll just follow her up to her place. Mary and Damien are making sure Hoss and Violet are fed so that's okay, too. She brings all manner of treats down here for those pigs. She doesn't think any of us know."

"Well good. Be right back." She jogged into the house to take care of her business. Of course his animals would be taken care of. It had been a silly question but she liked all his little creatures so she wanted to be sure.

She pulled her hair into two puffs that she rather liked. It was low maintenance and she could fluff it out the next day or the day after, but Ezra got a dreamy look on his face when she came back out.

He opened her door and she hopped up. On his side, he opened up, whistled, and Loopy came running around the house and bounded into the truck, settling across the bench seat behind where Ezra and Tuesday sat.

"Someone likes to go for a ride."

Loopy licked her face and settled her chin on the top of Ezra's armrest.

"The hair, I like it."

"A gal needs to switch it up from time to time. Keep it fresh, folically speaking."

He snorted as he drove away from the ranch.

"Well, whatever. It makes me want to bend you over something immediately."

She laughed, delighted and a little tingly. "Your bar for that is already pretty low."

"When it comes to you, beauty, my standards are high and exacting."

She had no doubts about that at all.

He waved, pulling to a stop at his parents' driveway, where his mother had been standing.

"Hello there, Tuesday! Don't you look pretty today? If you and Natalie could make sure Ezra and Paddy don't wander off a cliff or set anything on fire, I'd be grateful." She winked and Tuesday snickered.

"Good afternoon, Sharon." Tuesday waved. She liked Sharon Hurley. The woman was a boss. Smart and strong. She had the type of protective persona that Tuesday's mother also had. It had drawn her to Sharon from the start.

"I'll do my best, but your sons like to do their own thing."

Sharon laughed. "True. Well, keep out of the way of fists if he and Paddy get into a tussle." She gave her oldest a look. "You have a good time, Ezra. Your dad and I ran this place before you started on— everything'll be just fine for the next four days. I have your number if something happens that we can't handle. We won't break the ranch and we'll keep your creatures alive and happy. Now go." She stepped back after patting his hand.

Loopy barked and Sharon guffawed. "You, dearest granddog, will be missed. Have fun chasing squirrels."

Satisfied she'd got some attention from Sharon, Loopy barked one last time and put her chin back on the armrest.

"Love you, Mom." He waved and her teasing grin softened into a mother's smile.

"I love you, too, Ezra. Enjoy yourselves!"

"It seems like we end up on long car rides a lot." He relaxed back into the seat once they'd got on their way.

She leaned back, liking the view from up that high. "I have what Natalie terms an *unnatural* love of road trips."

"There's a story here. Tell me."

"Nah, nothing superexciting like meeting Laurence Fishburne at a rest stop or something equally fantastic. You come from a big family so I bet you guys took a lot of road trips for family vacations as you grew up. We have family in Kentucky and in San Diego so we would drive to both. Usually Kentucky in the summer and down the coast to San Diego at Thanksgiving or Christmas."

In a funny coincidence the Hurleys and Tuesday's family hailed from the same forty-mile radius in Kentucky.

Ezra broke in. "We did that trip to Kentucky every two years or so. That's a long drive. At first we all jammed into an old cargo van but when I was eight or nine they bought this secondhand RV. Not a big one, but way better than that cargo van. Imagine being stuck in an enclosed space with a ten-year-old Damien."

Tuesday shuddered at the thought of a ten-year-old superhyper, always-in-motion Damien trapped in a car for eight hours at a time. "Your mother is my hero. For. Real."

Ezra laughed. "She's a goddamn pain in my ass. But she's pretty amazing."

So odd to be discussing this sort of thing with a woman he wasn't related to. He didn't really chat about his private life with the woman he'd been seeing in Portland. He drove to her place, fucked her for a few hours and drove back.

Seeing. Hmm.

The woman he fucked when they both had time and he needed something hard and rough. And meaningless otherwise.

He hadn't been to Portland since November. There'd really been no one else on his radar in any way since he kissed Tuesday that first time in December.

"We had one of those campers you hitched to the back of the car. They still have one, only theirs now is way swankier."

"Are they all outdoorsy then?"

"My dad loves to camp. He goes all summer and fall. Now he scoops up the grandkids and he and my mom take them all out. He teaches them how to fish and how to orient themselves if they're ever lost. I hope they grow up loving road trips, too. My dad, my two oldest brothers and my sister are all sporty. Competitive. When GJ—he's the oldest of us all, Greg Junior—was in fourth grade someone told him black people couldn't swim. So as it happened, he ended up one of the top swimmers in the state until he finished college. So there you go. Tell an Easton they can't do something and it's irresistible."

"I'm astounded someone actually said that to your brother. Jesus."

She snorted. "I passed by *astounded* by the time I was four or so. Some people are dicks, as my friend

Jenny says. Anyway. We were a superbusy family as I grew up. All of us had activities of all sorts. We were always going to track meets and baseball games or piano recitals. My parents' house is full of trophies and ribbons and all that stuff."

"Piano recitals, huh?"

"That was Shawn. He's really good even today. My parents were big on art. They didn't care how we did it or what we chose, but we all had to take some sort of lesson. Music, dance, art, whatever."

"Yours was jewelry making?"

"No. Actually back then it was ceramics." Still was. She'd been considering building a kiln out behind the house.

"Very cool. I started playing the guitar because my dad bribed me for staying out of trouble. Then they paid for lessons but I didn't need them long. But I was a convert and didn't want to go to school or do anything else but play the guitar. By then Paddy had also got a guitar bribe. My mom wielded our free time like a weapon. If we did well in school and didn't get into fights or trouble, they'd give us time doled out in half an hour increments to play."

"We might be super careful about keeping our mothers apart."

He chuckled. "Have you heard the story about Mary's mom and mine?"

"No! Oh, do tell."

"Mary and Damien had broken up. She'd seen these pictures and they looked really bad. Like Damien had been with an ex while they were in New York. So Damien chased after her to make things right and my mom went with him to help. But Mary's mom is a lot like Sharon and so there was a time when it looked like they were going to have to break up a mom fight in Mary's front yard. Course, now they're thick as thieves and grandchild obsessed."

Tuesday nodded, getting it. "At first glance Diana is sort of earth mothery. It's sort of cute. But she's very intense and detail oriented, too. But she would cut anyone who tried to mess with her family. Once I got sent home from an after-school camp thing because of my hair. My mom, well she and my dad actually, flipped her lid. She went down there and scared them all into backing off."

"Your hair?"

"Yes. It was natural, like it is now. The head teacher there told me it looked messy and that my mother needed to *do something with it*. My mother was all calm as she came in, holding my hand. The woman, she tried to make it seem like it wasn't a big deal. My mother just looked at her like she was a bug. It was awesome."

"I'm still hung up on this hair thing. It was all curly? Like it is now? And they didn't like that? Your hair is fucking beautiful. You're a goddamn goddess and now I want to punch someone in the face for making any child of any type feel bad for something so stupid. Jesus."

Oh.

That was a shot to her solar plexus. She smiled at him, touched and a little tingly, too. People didn't want to punch people on her behalf. Outside family anyway—her brothers had been happy to punch anyone who needed it. But it was different from Ezra.

"Yes, only my mother made sure it was taken care

of. No children ever left the Easton house unless they were cleaned up and put together. I mean, sometimes it was braided or in puffs like I have now. Anyway, they tried to keep me out, my parents hired an attorney and they let me back in. Imagine that."

"I like your mother already."

"I like her, too. She's pretty awesome."

HE EASED INTO the hot tub alongside Tuesday sliding his arm around the edge of the tub at her back. Steam rose into the air and the stars stood out bright overhead.

"Thank you for bringing me up here. It's gorgeous." He leaned his head back, looking up to the sky. "I've been here less than five hours and already I'm more relaxed than I have been in a very long time."

They'd had a big dinner with Natalie and Paddy, who'd sneaked off to their bedroom about half an hour before. Which left Ezra and Tuesday alone with a hot tub and a very dark night all around them.

It was pretty much like Ezra's birthday instead of Tuesday's.

"It's so quiet out here, especially at night. No lights from a nearby city. It's like I forget this is what the sky really looks like. I love to camp but Natalie thinks a hotel without Wi-Fi is roughing it."

Ezra laughed. "You two seem pretty different but it's so clear how much you care about one another."

"Some people are meant to be part of each other's lives. Sure, we're different in some ways. She's adorable and petite and white and blonde. I am none of those things."

He laughed. "Thank God. I like blondes as much as the next guy and she's beautiful. But you? You're *magnificent*. When you're in the room it's impossible for me to look at anyone else for longer than a minute or two. Then my attention shifts back to you."

She turned her head. Her curls, which she'd put up at the top of her head, brushed against the skin of his arm as she did.

"I think it counts for you, too."

"What does?" He brushed a kiss against her forehead.

"People meant to be in your life. Before I'd met you, Natalie would talk about you with Mary or Paddy and I was already thinking about you. And then when you came around the corner at Damien's, you felt right. In my life right then."

Then she laughed and it unfroze his muscles. "I'm sorry, am I freaking you out?" She pushed to the other side of the hot tub to face him.

Her absence was a palpable thing. He liked her moving away from him even less than any wariness at the depth of honesty she dished out on a regular basis. "Don't go all the way over there. I like you right where you were."

She moved back and he relaxed again.

"I'm not freaked out. I was caught off guard." He sighed. "I don't know how to do this."

"I bet you hate not knowing things."

She was teasing, yes, but it was also an honest statement. It was acceptance.

"Not knowing is a form of being out of control. But that's my stuff. It's not about you." She knew how to do this thing way better than he did.

Her features softened. "No pressure. No crazy expectations. Just you and me. We got this."

She entwined her fingers with his under the water and neither spoke for some time, just floating and relaxing.

"Later this week you should come up for a horseback ride."

She turned, the water splashing as she straddled his lap. "Really? I'd love to. What day?"

He laughed. She made him really happy and he got the feeling maybe this was the payoff to a real relationship with someone. This connection and general pleased warmth in their presence. "Well, this was unexpected, but certainly a positive turn. Had I known before that asking you to come and ride horses would end up this way, I'd have asked you a lot more before now."

"I *love* horseback riding. When I was a kid those long car trips to Kentucky were bearable because we'd be able to spend weeks out on horseback once we arrived. You have such beautiful land to ride on, too. It's seriously so much fun and I'm absolutely accepting, even if you think I'm creepy now because I've been trying to figure out a way to get another invite."

"Aw, beauty." He kissed her. He'd known she rode. They'd all gone out as a group a few times and he'd noted she hadn't appeared to be a novice. But he hadn't realized how much she liked it. Now that he did, though, well, clearly he needed to spoil Tuesday a little.

"I feel bad that I haven't asked you before now. I love getting out and riding horses. They love getting out and about. When the weather is nicer I ride out on horseback instead of taking a truck or the ATV. If you want to ride, come on up. Violet and Loopy always come with me."

She laughed. "i bet. Your women like to keep an eye on you."

Loopy was currently curled up in her bed in the room behind them. She'd run and played and chased squirrels and birds and got so much attention she'd passed out after dinner.

"Violet is the disciplinarian. She keeps Loopy in line and out of trouble. It's very sweet."

"Your secret is safe with me."

"Which secret is that?" He could barely remember his own name just at the moment. Her breasts, the shape and size only accentuated by the royal-blue swimsuit top, bobbed at the water line and so close to his face he dipped to kiss her cleavage.

She did that hum, in the back of her throat, though it seemed to vibrate from her belly.

"You try to be gruff and cranky but I know the real Ezra. Behind all that. The man who took in animals when he was needed. The man with cats named by two silly little girls who love their uncle Ezra very much. The man who makes sure the sweet potatoes he gives to the pigs are made the way they like."

He paused, surprised she'd noticed. Embarrassed maybe, but also flattered she saw this as a nice thing.

"Big Hoss likes them boiled so they're soft. It's not a big deal."

She cupped his cheeks. "It *is* a big deal, Ezra." She brushed her lips over his a moment. "It's okay, you know, to be proud that you're a good person."

Nope.

He changed the subject. "Come up to the ranch on Saturday. You're starting your new space at the craft fair in Portland, right? Come over in the late afternoon. We'll go for a ride and then have some dinner afterward." Natalie was throwing a surprise party for Tuesday to celebrate all her recent business successes that following weekend up at Paddy's place. It fell to Ezra to lure her up. He'd take her on a ride first and then they'd still have plenty of time to go to the party afterward.

"Yes. I was supposed to start two weeks ago but then there was something weird with the papers and my licensing and all that stuff so I'll be there bright and early on Saturday morning. I'll close up at two, so I can be up at your place by five."

"All right." He nearly invited her to sleep over but didn't. He told himself he'd see how things went over the rest of the trip first, before taking any more steps.

"You don't need to make dinner, though. Why don't I bring up something? I'm working on my pizza dough skills, so I can bring some dough and we can make pizza."

Mary had apparently worked up some fantastic menu with Natalie, but he figured if she brought up the dough they could make pizza the next time they were together.

"Are you good at everything or what?"

"Ha. No. April, that's my big sister, she's so good at baking. I do all right, but she's got some sort of magic touch. I was totally intimidated by yeast for years so I never made bread until earlier this year when we had pizza when April and her kids and husband were up visiting my parents. I just like being able to make it exactly how I want it. The size I want. The thickness of crust, toppings, all that. It's not that hard and it's really so much tastier when you make it yourself."

He wasn't sure why this in particular pushed him past all his limits, but it did. "I want to fuck you."

Her grin was quick, but sensual, too. "I can make you pizza on Friday, as well."

He stood up, still holding her, his hands cupping her ass as she wrapped her legs around his waist and held on while he got out. Though it was nearly June, it was still cool, especially after dark at that elevation. Steam lifted from her bare skin as he put her down and wrapped a towel around her.

"Go on inside, I don't want you to get cold. I'll turn everything off and put the cover back on."

"You're a very nice man who is about to come really hard." She leaned in, kissed him and sauntered inside.

TUESDAY HUSTLED INTO the house, grateful for the towel she clutched around herself against the cold.

She headed into the bathroom to rinse off, stripping free of the suit, trying not to think too deeply on how much they just exposed to one another out there. Or about how tenderness filled the cells she'd figured were long dead since Eric had died.

Sex was stable ground between them. There were no misunderstandings about it. She wanted it, he wanted it, they had it. He was fantastic in bed. Inventive. Dirty and darkly sexual. He knew where everything was and what to do with it—boy did he—and she never held back physically. Not ever. Because he'd earned that trust.

Feelings were something else. It was a lot harder to share those than her body.

He'd protected her from the cold. He'd invited her to ride horses. He'd been giving and wonderful and it had filled her with contentment.

But he was still scared and held back. Or maybe he was too guilt laden to accept that he had a right to be happy. It was frustrating, but it was who Ezra was. She had to be patient because the longer she knew him the more she believed he was worth it.

He came in as she exited the bathroom wrapped in a robe. The long, leisurely look he took from her toes to the top of her head. A caress of a look that made her knees rubbery.

"I'll be right back. Going to hang these trunks up in the tub and rinse the chlorine off."

"I'll go out with Loopy if you like. So she can get settled for the night."

He stalked to her and did that thing where he hauled her close. It was so physical and dominant but it made her feel cosseted, too, because the look in his eyes was pure appreciation for what he saw.

"You're far too delicious, beauty. I want to gorge on you."

Her breath caught wherever her words had gone to.

He kissed her and stepped back. "Loopy."

The dog obeyed like everyone else seemed to. She looked up at him with that same silly expression they all did, too.

He knelt and got eye to eye with the dog, who licked him and Tuesday stifled an *aww*.

"Tuesday will take you out. Behave and obey her."

Loopy licked him again and Ezra petted her head before he stood to speak to Tuesday. "Thank you."

He headed to the bathroom, closing the door behind himself.

She put on some flip-flops and opened the sliding glass door. "Go on. There are so many bushes and trees out there, Loop. Let's see how many of them you can mark before we go back home."

Loopy gave a muted, but happy bark and trotted out with Tuesday, across the expansive back deck and down into the yard where she sniffed a lot of stuff and finally decided where the perfect spot was.

"Your dad is a big old softy," Tuesday said quietly as the dog returned to her side, ready to go back into the house.

A furry head butt told her Loopy knew this already.

"Come on then. Don't peek for the next hour. Okay, maybe two."

Loopy headed to her bed, which Ezra had set up in the short hallway between the master bedroom and the back porch and mudroom. It was still private, but she wasn't lying and staring up at Ezra and Tuesday getting down.

Two circles and Loopy settled with a happy sigh as Tuesday made sure her water dish was full. Her rawhide was in the bed with her, as it was a sort of comfort object.

As Tuesday started back toward the main part of the bedroom, it hit her that she was beginning to accumulate little factoids about Ezra's animals. And about Ezra, too.

Before she could pretend not to think about it, the bathroom door opened and Ezra came out.

Totally and utterly naked.

"Honestly, Ezra." She shook her head, motioning his way. "How can you constantly be this much? I don't know if my heart can take it."

The smirk on his lips was 100 percent male smug satisfaction.

"You know how hot you are, don't you? You like that you make me all stuttery and silly and breathless."

He tugged the tie at her waist and the robe fell open.

"I like that you want what I have to give you."

Heat flashed through her at his words.

She shimmied enough to let the robe drop, leaving her as naked as he was. "Now, I've had this thing in mind all day. Can you help me out?"

"Mmm, you have trouble written all over you. I need a lot of whatever you're about to lay on me."

She slid a hand over his abdominal muscles, enjoying the heat of his skin, the soft caress of hair as she brushed from his belly button to his nipples, playing with the barbells there.

"Did this hurt?" she asked, before leaning close to drag her teeth across first one nipple and then the other.

He rumbled and she smiled against his skin. By that point he knew she loved it when he made the sound. Sometimes she knew he made it just to tease her, which was hotter than hot. But right then he felt it right down to his toes.

"The piercings?" His voice had gone desire-rough.

She hummed her yes.

"Yes. For a moment and then it's something else. Your body reacts to the pain and releases all that pleasure to counteract. It's how I feel after an hour or two in a tattoo chair. High on body chemicals and pain."

She kissed up his neck. He may have made his own wheatgrass shots and lived a life outdoors and full of physical labor these days, but Ezra did love the rush, the head change.

He put a palm on her chest, between her breasts. "Didn't you feel it when you got ink?"

She nodded. "Parts of it. The drone of the tattoo machine. The vibration of it. It's hypnotic. Sometimes when I meditate and it's very deep and I achieve this sort of total peace. It's a warm wave of pleasure. There are parts of getting a tattoo that are like that. Other parts hurt and you just have to endure it until they move away from that spot."

She dragged her nails down his belly and he sucked in a breath.

"You had a thing on your mind you needed my help with?"

She dropped to her knees and looked up his body with a smile.

"I can definitely help you with this thing."

Grabbing him at the root, she angled him to lick across the head and then around the crown.

He locked his knees and his thigh muscles bulged against her palm where she braced herself for balance. She moaned and he groaned, which made her do it again.

She licked and took him a little deeper each time she pulled back and started again. Over and over.

Tuesday loved this. Loved being all about giving pleasure to her partner. Loved, too, being on display in a sense, being seen and thought of as beautiful and sexy.

This man made her feel like a goddess. That there was no one like her. She took him as deep as she could.

His fingertips dug into her shoulders.

"Fuck yes," he snarled, and this driving desire to please him, to make him feel good filled her.

All her attention focused on him, on the feel of him against her tongue, on the sound of his breath getting more and more ragged the closer she dragged him to orgasm.

With her free hand, she cupped his sac before drawing her nails lightly against all that sensitive skin.

He wrenched himself away. "Wait."

"What? No. Get back here."

The expression on his face made her laugh. She couldn't help it. Like he'd never actually experienced any sass before.

Then he looked her over and sent a shiver through her. "Look at you." He sucked in a breath, shaking his head, a smirk on his lips. "On your knees. Naked. Your mouth is all swollen from sucking my cock. Your nipples are hard and dark. I've done a lot of shitty things in my life—I'm not sure where you came from or what nice thing I must have done when I wasn't paying attention. Even if you do talk back."

He held out a hand. "There is nothing like being in you when I come. Your mouth is fantastic, but I want to be buried deep in your pussy."

Not much to argue with in that statement. She took

his hand and he hauled her to her feet, dancing her back to the bed until she fell to the mattress.

"I wish you could see how sexy you look right now. Your hair spread around your head. Raven-winged curls. Curvy, like the rest of you. You're valleys and peaks." He drew a fingertip over one nipple until she arched into his touch. "You're all velvety smooth skin and toned muscles. You carry so much power in you, beauty."

If he kept that up, she'd orgasm before he even touched her.

Then he dropped to his knees, sliding hers wide to admit him as he kissed up her thigh.

He parted her to his mouth, to his attention, which was nearly as hot as that thing he did with the tip of his tongue and his top lip.

She shuddered as pleasure bounced through her, lighting nerve endings, heating, softening. He made her soft in so many ways, but this—with his mouth like a prayer on her skin, with his hands, so strong, holding her in place—this made her feel supremely female. Soft where he was hard and yet strong, always. She could be that with him like this where there was only raw honesty.

Ezra touched her like a man who knew her intimately, and delighted in everything he encountered. That sort of attention could be near adoration, even when he was sexing her up so relentlessly she was about two minutes away from coming really hard.

She dug her heels into the bed, arching as he increased his pace, licking against her harder and faster.

And then he stopped, kissing her thigh again and then up to her hip, across her belly just below her navel. He scored short, blunt nails up her sides and then over her breasts.

Holy cow!

She didn't even know what to do with how good it felt as he dragged his nails across her nipples. Pleasure and pain all mixed up like he'd talked about with his piercings.

He groaned. "The sound you just made, you're killing me." He reversed his hands, drawing his nails over her breasts again. Her eyes rolled back as she closed them, her hands fisting in the bedding as she arched up to meet his touch.

Then he shifted and his mouth found her pussy again with long, slow licks as he tugged her nipples.

The climax that built this time couldn't be denied. It dug in with sharp claws as he continued to devastate her bit by bit until it finally tore through her. She cried out before she thought better of it but it didn't matter.

He stood and bent to kiss her. "Come with me."

She rolled over as he got on the bed, sitting with his back against the headboard.

As she crawled over, he rolled a condom on and unbelievably, her body seemed to think it was just dandy to get turned on all over again.

She straddled his legs and brushed herself over the line of his cock, undulating until she went to her knees, guiding him right and then sinking down, taking him inside her slowly, enjoying every single inch of him.

When he was fully seated, they both sighed. He pinched her nipple and then tugged. She moaned and he got that smile of his.

"Are you going to come loud again. Hmm?"

It wasn't like dirty talk was exotic or anything. She'd heard it before but it usually just made her sort of impatient and embarrassed for her partner.

But Ezra made her believe it. Made her want every dirty, dark thing he whispered against her skin. Ezra was like a nuclear bomb of sex talk. He just turned her to molten hormones.

"I don't know," she managed to say around a tongue that felt too big for her mouth. How could she keep quiet with him inside her like this? With his hands and mouth on her? She wasn't some kind of fucking warlock who had the power to resist all that and the beard, too. She was only human.

He grinned and nipped her bottom lip. "Not like I'd complain that people knew I did something to you that made you come hard enough to scream."

She made a circle with her hips with his cock still deep inside. "I think scream might be an overstatement. It was a loud groan."

He grabbed her hips, thrusting up, hard and fast until the heat of it spread outward.

"You're so wet right now. I can hear how much you love this. A scream, beauty. My mouth on your pussy as I played with your nipples. You came hard and you screamed."

She nodded, beyond words. So she held on, her hands first on his shoulders and then sliding up into his hair and tugging. He rumbled as their gazes were locked and then let go with one hand, pulling her to his mouth for a kiss with a palm around her throat.

"Make yourself come, beauty."

She let go, moving her hand to obey. Still sensitive, Tuesday kept her touch light but with him it never went slow, even when she thought she was past the ability to come.

"I can feel your inner muscles clench around me when you start to get close. Damn, that's so good. So. So. Good. I'm close, though, so you need to be close, too."

There was no question. No request.

And she didn't want one.

She grabbed her orgasm and let it build up, filling her as he fucked into her body, until sounds started to come from low in her belly as the pleasure of it was nearly too much.

"Yes, yes, yes. Come on, with me," he said.

Then he put a hand over her mouth and her orgasm burst over her as she gasped and groaned. He braced an arm around her waist to pull her closer, his lips against her ear.

"You feel so good around my cock right now. You're so beautiful. You come so fucking pretty. Jesus."

She sighed as she melted into him and he let go of her mouth, kissing her where his hand was.

Then he looked at her closely before setting her down and going to get rid of the condom.

"Now I feel relaxed enough to come again in a while."

She laughed as she got out of bed, putting on panties and a pair of pajamas.

"I can't see why on earth you'd need pajamas. I'm just going to strip you naked again in a few hours."

"Because we're staying with other people and your dog might need to go out in the night. I don't want Nat seeing you naked. Call me selfish. She has her own

Hurley boy. Also I'm quite sure Paddy doesn't want to see my naked butt, either."

"If he did, he'd need to be punched in the mouth a few times."

It shouldn't have thrilled her. It was just a silly, throwaway sentence. But it got to her anyway.

"I'm pretty sure that's your answer to all sorts of issues with your brothers." She pointed to the bright blue scarf she'd left on the chair. "Can you hand me that?"

He sidled up, handing it over. "You gonna let me tie you up with that?"

"Maybe later. It's for my hair. I wear it when I sleep. I mean, okay, so I figured one night I don't need to. But four days, and I'm here with you. And you look like what sex would look like if it was a person instead of a word." He liked her hair as much as she liked his beard so she wanted it to keep looking good while they were in the mountains.

He whistled low. "I look like sex personified. That's a really good one. But, beauty, you've seen yourself, right?"

"Looking like this takes effort, Ezra," she said on her way past. Wearing a smile.

CHAPTER FOURTEEN

EZRA BREATHED DEEP. He and Tuesday had left the house just after dawn and headed out on a hike. Loopy ran past, chasing birds and squirrels, overjoyed at being outside in a new place with Ezra and Tuesday.

They paused in a pretty little meadow long enough to eat their breakfast sandwiches and some fruit and got started again.

It warmed up as they hiked. Enough that he'd tied his sweatshirt around his waist.

Mainly they said nothing as they went. The birds sang all around them. In the distance they could hear the water from a creek running to the east of the trail they were on.

The day before they'd gone out kayaking on the lake down the hill from the house and had a picnic with Paddy and Natalie, who'd chosen to canoe instead. Which had worked out because Loopy could come along that way.

One of the things Ezra liked most about Tuesday was that she never seemed to feel the need to chatter and fill up silence. She was confident in herself and her appeal.

It wasn't taxing to be with her. It wasn't hard. He didn't feel trapped or that his skin was too tight. She never made him want to run in the other direction.

In fact it was the opposite. He wanted to run toward her. If something happened at the ranch he wanted to share it with her. If he was having trouble with something, he found himself reaching for his phone.

The only people he'd ever had that response with were his brothers.

That may have made him want to run away a little. It was big and scary and the way he felt about her was something beyond his experience. He liked it. She fit in his life in a way that seemed pretty effortless.

And, he thought as she headed up an incline and his gaze latched on to her glutes in those formfitting shorts she had on, she dealt well with his temperament and looked fantastic as she did it.

It wasn't love at first sight or anything. Certainly a friendship, as they'd known one another for some time. He liked her and they were good together. They had a rhythm he really liked. She let him be who he was, even when he wasn't sure who the hell he was.

He had reached a place where he could let himself enjoy being with her without questioning it. Too much.

She paused as Loopy approached and sat at her feet. "Do you need a break? I may have some cheese in my backpack for a certain canine as a treat for all the hard hiking you've done this morning."

Loopy heard cheese and stood again, tail wagging wildly. Tuesday straightened, scratching one of Loopy's ears as she did.

"I think that's probably a yes." Ezra grinned at his dog.

"There's a pretty little overlook coming up. We

can sit and look awhile as we eat. I brought snacks for us, too."

"You're prepared."

"I have my moments." She paused, looking him over carefully. "Did you bring any sunblock? You're a little red on the bridge of your nose."

Ezra pulled a ball cap from his back pocket. "Got it. I've been sweating so I'll put more on when we stop and I cool down."

"Too bad it's so cold," she called back over her shoulder as she got started up the trail again, "or we could swim."

Too bad indeed because he bet she looked fantastic in the sunshine, water beaded like diamonds on her skin. Thanks to the hot tub on the deck outside their bedroom, he knew what her skin looked like in the moonlight.

"Next time. We'll leave Paddy and Natalie and all D-O-Gs behind."

"I love that you think just because you spell it, your D-O-G won't know you're talking about abandoning her. She's goofy but totally in tune with her human," Tuesday called back over her shoulder.

Loopy yipped twice and then ran up to trot next to Tuesday after a snuffle back Ezra's way.

"Whatever. I don't feel bad for wanting you naked and all to myself."

She laughed and kept walking.

The beauty of the overlook she'd mentioned hit him as he came around a bend in the trail. The valley spread out below with more mountains across the divide. A lake glittered off in the distance, brilliantly, frigidly blue.

She paused to spread out the sheet on the grass. Loopy lay on a sunny patch, her belly on the cool ground.

Ezra pulled out a lightweight bowl he used to give Loopy water when they were out on an adventure. She watched him, tongue lolling as he poured water.

He petted her as she finally moved to drink. "Good girl." It had taken a while to get her to stop rushing to her food when she'd been a puppy. She'd inhale it and puke it up, or spill water everywhere. But he'd been patient and she was a smart dog and now she had impeccable manners.

He headed to sit with Tuesday and stare out over the incredible view. She handed him an apple and then some cheese he'd seen her dicing that morning.

"This is for her?"

"Yeah. That's how you do it, right? The size of the cubes?"

"Yeah. Yes. Thank you. That was pretty nice of you."

She shrugged. "I like your dog. She was coming out here on this hike, too, so I figured she'd need some protein."

"Don't minimize it. Kindness is important and rarer than it should be sometimes."

"I'll make you a deal, Ezra. I will if you will."

He frowned a moment and then grunted as the pointed comment hit its mark.

"You're welcome," she responded not just to his compliment about the dog, but the reminder, too.

He gave Loopy the cheese and then one of the jerky treats he'd brought along, as well. She did need protein just like humans did.

"Almonds. Hummus. Carrots and some dried apricots." She put out a bunch of little containers and they had a wonderful feast out there where the air was clean and full of nothing but sounds of nature. No planes overhead even.

After she packed the food back, he brought her to the sheet before she could stand up. "Wait a minute. I have a few more things I'd like to get a taste of before we start back."

She met his lips, parting hers to allow the sweep of his tongue. He nipped her bottom lip, meandering into the kiss at his own pace and she let him. The pride of that burned in his belly.

"Now I feel like I can make it back." He rolled off and up to his feet a few minutes later.

She took the hand he'd extended and he pulled her to stand.

In just a few short minutes he'd applied more sunscreen to his nose while she packed up and they were headed back to the house.

"How'd you find this place anyway? What a fantastic location for a house. I'd never want to leave if I lived up here. Well, actually maybe in the winter I'd think differently."

"There's another trail, it heads in pretty much the same trajectory as this one but it's a little farther down the hill." She pointed. "So we were on it and I saw this trail and I wanted to know where it led. And it led to the backyard of the house, which was empty but had a sign out front with the number for the rental agency. We came back for my birthday the next year and we've returned each year since."

He wondered if Eric had been there. Had held her

for the meager hours of sleep she allowed herself in that big bed in the room under the eaves.

"How long now?"

She turned to face him. "He never came up here. I discovered it after. Is it weird for you?"

He lengthened his stride to catch up. "Is what weird?"

"That I was married. That I loved someone else. That he died. I don't know. It's weird to me sometimes."

"It's not weird. It's... I never expected to feel this."

He stopped and she did as well, though she gave him a little space as she watched him. Her features were blank but her eyes told him she was nervous. Hell, he was, too, he supposed.

"I've been alone a long time. You make me less alone. Sometimes that might even be because I can look into your eyes and see ghosts. You loved someone before me. Okay. I don't care about what happened before me. It made you a better person I'm sure. That you were married? Also not weird. But I'm working on how I feel about it. Mainly it happened before I knew you. It happened at a time my life was a hot mess and I had to rebuild myself minute by minute, day by day. Sometimes I think you might know how to do this thing—" he waved a hand between them "—better than I do. Which to be fair isn't hard because I don't know what I'm doing at all. I just know I really like to be around you."

TUESDAY SUCKED IN a breath and then let it out slow. Wow. He was so emotionally vulnerable to her right at that moment and she didn't want to ruin it.

Humbled, she licked her lips and finally spoke. "I like being around you, too. And maybe I don't know how to feel about it, either. Not all the way. Mainly it's that you're charming and sexy, handsome—you're really good in bed and you like doing the same things I do. It's easy to like being around you."

He stepped closer, filling the gap she'd deliberately left in case he felt the need to escape the discussion.

"Is it weird? That he died? Well that part sucks. I'm sorry because if you loved him he had to be a pretty rad dude. And I'm sorry because you lost someone you loved. Sometimes I don't quite know what to do with all this history. Like I want to ask but I don't want to stir you up and hurt you. You're important to me and that happened to me while I wasn't looking. I'm off balance. Hell, I don't know what the fuck I'm doing."

"And you don't like that. Not being in control of every single thing."

"There was a time in my life when I thrived on chaos. I embraced it. And you know how that turned out."

That was it right then. He was scared. She had her own baggage to carry on her back, but Ezra was scared of failing and of ever being what he'd been when he was addicted.

Scared of liking something too much? Needing it too much?

"Unforeseen isn't the same as chaos. So you didn't plan on me. Big deal. You don't plan for what this is." She flapped a hand. "This...draw I feel every time I'm around you. I could deal with it if it was just physical. Fuck you out of my system and then we could be friends because we have chemistry."

She took his hand. "But we have that sort of super-sizzling zingy thing. You know what I mean. We click. You can't plan for that. That's not how this works. Important people come to you when you aren't expecting them."

He slid his palm around the back of her neck. "I find that I need you. I don't know how to need like that anymore. Not healthily anyway." There was so much anguish in his tone,

She tiptoed up and touched her forehead to his. She wanted to tell him it was okay to crave her. But she needed him to understand it on his own first. She kissed him and he wrapped his arms around her, holding her close as they stood quietly for some time while they both remained in their thoughts.

SHE TURNED SO THAT they walked side by side, once again moving back down the trail toward the house. Again, after pushing him and then knowing exactly when to back off. Part of him was in awe of her ability while he still resented that she could be so goddamn sure of herself in the wake of all she'd experienced.

"There you are!" Paddy raised a hand to wave as Ezra and Tuesday came down from the fork in the trailhead that led down to the house.

"Was there doubt?" Ezra checked to be sure the bowls of water and food Loopy ran for were full and tried to get his shit together after that talk he'd just had on the trail.

"We woke up and you were quiet. We figured you were still in bed. Nat went up to see if you wanted coffee and that's when she saw the note that you'd gone out on a hike."

"We've been out since six this morning. Had breakfast and a snack. Gloried in nature."

Paddy looked at Ezra and rolled his eyes. "Looked at Tuesday's butt a lot."

Tuesday raised a brow his way. "Of course he did. Do you think I wore these shorts by accident?" She turned to Ezra. "I'm going in search of coffee. Would you like some?"

Some of the tension left his spine. It was okay between them again.

"Yes, please." And for good measure, he watched her ass as she went up the steps and into the house. Holy shit he was one lucky man.

Still grinning, he turned to Paddy. "Hey. Have you guys eaten yet?"

"I made us toast."

"I'll make waffles for some brunch since it's our last full day up here. Come on."

"Wait. Ez, things are really good between me and Natalie and I wanted to thank you. You said what I needed to hear even when it wasn't easy. Even when I was a dick to you. You pushed me to make things right with her and I did. Thank you. Really."

Ezra nodded. "Anytime. Don't fuck it up. She loves you. She trusts you with her heart."

"I know. Crazy as it is, she does. Makes me so lucky. So. I watched you two as you came around that bend up there and around. I'm not used to seeing you be that open with someone outside the family. This is more than just dating, huh? Makes sense I guess.

You two have been dancing around each other since you first met last November."

"September. I met her in September. I kissed her for the first time in December and I haven't stopped thinking of her since. It's nice. This is what grown-ups do." They'd just shared some deep shit out there on the trail and over the course of this trip and he wasn't ready to start examining it too closely on the front porch with his brother, who was love drunk anyway. "Now, let's see if there's a waffle iron here."

Paddy put a hand on Ezra's forearm as he passed. "You've listened to me moon around about a lot of stuff over the sum of our lives, Ez. You've given me great advice. You've pulled me out of a hundred binds. Hell, you've pulled us *all* out of hundreds of binds. You have three brothers who are ready and able to listen and help. I'm making the offer on behalf of all of us so you don't even need to ask."

Paddy had done a lot of growing up over the past nearly year he'd been with Natalie. Ezra patted his brother's shoulder. "Thanks."

CHAPTER FIFTEEN

"Tuesday, babe, your phone is ringing." Paddy said this as he wandered past, dropping said phone in her lap.

She'd been so wrapped up in how Ezra's forearms looked as he shuffled a deck of cards she hadn't even heard her phone.

But this was a call she couldn't get away with ignoring.

Tuesday slid her finger along the screen, answering. "Sorry about that! I wasn't near my phone when it started ringing."

Her mom wasn't having any excuses. "I expected you to call this morning. We left a message last night."

What could Tuesday say? *I could have called you back but my boyfriend was probably fucking me from behind while he held my wrists and snarled at me about how gorgeous my ass was when you called the first time.*

"I'm sorry."

Her mother accepted the apology and once it had been offered genuinely, she moved on. "I'm calling to see what you want me to make for dinner next weekend."

Oh crap. She'd totally forgotten about her birthday dinner at her parents. She was totally going to hell for that.

"How about butter chicken?" Time-consuming, Tuesday knew, but her mother considered every child's birthday dinner to be worth a great deal of effort and planning. She was a scary machine sometimes.

Her father hooted in the background. "You owe me twenty bucks!"

"I do?" Tuesday asked. "Hang on a second," she told her mother and then looked toward everyone else as she got up. "Excuse me."

Tuesday headed to the kitchen. "I was in a room with several people. I needed to excuse myself." Talking on the phone in the company of other people was one of Tuesday's pet peeves. Which she got from her mother.

"You don't owe me a twenty, sweetie pie. Your mother does. I told her you'd head straight to butter chicken. Your mom figured you'd ask for something easier to make and she'd have to talk you into butter chicken. My baby girl is herself again. She knows how to ask for what she wants. Isn't that what I said, Di?"

"That's exactly what he said. I said of all six of my children you were the one who always tried to put everyone else first. I already have an order in for the chicken. I've got potatoes and cauliflower for aloo gobi and I bought some mango chutney at the farmers' market last weekend. Can you pick up naan on your way up?"

In the span of a six-minute phone call her mother had chastened her for not paying proper attention and then she'd complimented her and also underlined for Tuesday how much her parents loved her.

"You're like the Jedi Lord of mothering. You know that, right?"

Diana laughed, clearly touched. "That's a good one. I'm going to have to add it to the list. Thank you, baby. I sure do love you."

"Love you, too."

"Going to be a full house. GJ and Alana, Shawn and Tisha. All the kids."

Her older brothers and their families lived in Seattle. She saw them frequently as her niece and nephews were all active in after-school activities so Tuesday spent a lot of dutiful auntie time in school gyms and multipurpose rooms along with huddling in the rain watching games of all sorts.

It pleased Tuesday to know they'd all be coming down to help celebrate her birthday.

"Will Natalie be coming? I think it's far beyond time she bring this boy to meet us. Your father was just saying he hoped she didn't plan to make any rash decisions until he'd had the chance to look the boy over."

Nat would be so touched to hear about this conversation. It didn't matter that Patrick Hurley was in his thirties, he'd be a boy to them. And until he passed her father's muster, he'd never be referred to by name.

"I'll ask her. She's here now."

"We'll hang on. Is the boy there?"

Tuesday wisely withheld a giggle. "Yes, Paddy's here with Natalie." She paused and then just leaped forward. "I'm seeing someone. I'm going to ask him

to come along. He may not be able to. I just wanted
to let you know so you made enough food."

Oh my god.

She'd just babbled so badly her mother would totally know everything Tuesday didn't want to address.

"Are you now?"

"I didn't tell you yet because I didn't actually know
what it was until recently." An hour ago. Maybe two
weeks earlier when she'd asked him to the mountains
and he'd said yes. Or before. Maybe. Probably.

It wasn't that Ezra knew. He was freaked the fuck
out. She saw it out on the trail. Scared and ashamed
and guilt laden. And God help her, she wanted him to
let her in. Wanted to soothe him and pet him. Wanted
to poke at him until he saw the truth of what they
were to one another.

She shook her head. It didn't matter. "I wanted to
tell you in person but he's here so when I go out to
ask Natalie, I'll invite everyone."

"All right."

Her mother not homing in on something this poten-
tially juicy? She clearly had other plans. Not knowing was sort of scary.

"I'll call you right back. I promise."

"You'd best."

Tuesday hung up and tucked her phone into a
pocket. Loopy looked up from her place at Ezra's feet.

"Hey, Loop."

"Did Diana yell at you?" Nat teased.

"She called and left a voice mail last night. I meant
to call her today but my schedule wasn't compatible
with hers." Tuesday snickered. "Your presence has
been requested for the official birthday dinner feast

not this coming weekend but the Saturday after. I've also been instructed to inform you *the boy* needs to be brought around for inspection. Greg says you best not be making any hasty decisions until Patrick passes muster."

Paddy raised a brow Natalie's way.

"Greg and Diana are Tuesday's parents. They're sort of like mine, too, in some ways," Nat explained.

Tuesday looked to Ezra. "I don't know what your schedule looks like so it's cool if you're busy, but if you aren't, there's a seat at the table for you. My mom is making butter chicken and aloo gobi. For this alone, you should come. But also, my birthday cake is always double chocolate, chocolate chip cake with chocolate frosting. My dad is the baker. He is sort of genius with roofs and with baking."

She probably should stop speaking.

He smiled at her, slow and easy. To an outsider it was a nice smile. But she saw the pleasure there. The sight of that brought her shoulders down a little as she lost some of the anxiety she'd had.

"I'm not busy on Saturday. Or, well I guess I am now. We staying over? Or should I get a hotel and we pretend we're not sleeping together?"

She and Natalie both burst out laughing. "They're super old-fashioned in some ways. But not that one. Their house will be full already, though. Both my brothers who live in Seattle will be there with their wives and kids. We can get a hotel room and then I won't feel weird."

"Heaven forfend you feel weird." Natalie winked.

"Hush up or I'll tell them you and Paddy need a place to sleep and you'll get the garage with the air bed. You can try to sleep while my dad watches reruns of *Hill Street Blues* and cracks peanuts over your head."

"You are evil. That's all I gotta say." Natalie said this but through a gale of laughter so it wasn't like Tuesday took it seriously.

"I'll be right back. I told them I'd ask and then call again."

"You can call in here," Ezra said.

"If my mother ever thought I was having a phone conversation in a room full of people who were my guests she'd kick my butt. Plus they're going to ask questions about you and I need to answer and not blush. If I do, she'll hear it in my tone."

He got up and stalked to her. She was so surprised she stood rooted to the spot. Ezra caught her around the waist and walked her from the room. Around the corner he backed her against the wall.

"Are you insinuating I make you blush?" he asked in a low tone.

"Only when I have blood in my face to blush with. Right now it's all south of my belly button."

He paused and then laughed, leaning in to kiss her. "All right then. My work here is done." He stepped back. "Make your call. I'm going to work on a few ideas on how to make you blush even more."

"I'd complain about you being incorrigible or whatever, but I can't really find anything to dispute in your statement. So, you go on and get to brainstorming. I'm going to call my mother. By the way, they're going to refer to you, and to Paddy, as *the boy* until you pass inspection. This is the cross anyone dating an Easton has to bear."

She petted his beard a moment, pleased at how it felt and that he stood still and allowed her to pet him the way she did.

"She's going to love you, though. I can tell already."

"Why? Does she have exceptional taste?"

"She does actually. But you're handsome. You work hard. You have fantastic facial hair. You're charming. She loves a pretty, charming man."

He kissed her again and swatted her butt. "I am a charming man, beauty. It's a curse, but someone has to do it."

She called her parents back to let them know three more would be attending the birthday dinner.

"Jim and Brenda say you can sleep over at their place. You can all stay here, too. Just bring a sleeping bag."

It wasn't as if she never had. She'd slept on the couches in the bonus room at her parents' house with her friends dozens of times. But this was different. She liked having him all to herself at the end of the day. Like a delicious secret.

And after a day with them she'd need to escape. She loved her family. They were important to her. But no one could get to her and hammer at all her insecurities like her family.

"Thank them for me. And yes, I'll thank them, too." Jim and Brenda lived three houses down. Their sons were close with the two oldest Easton boys. The Cuthbarts were for all intents and purposes, her family, too. "We'll get a hotel and come back for breakfast Sunday."

"How long have you been seeing this boy?" her father demanded.

"No, Dad, Nat is seeing that boy."

Her mother whooped a laugh, along with her dad once he'd got the joke.

"Nicely done. Now, who is this man you're seeing?" Her father's teasing lilt hardened to steel.

"He's Paddy's brother." All kidding about *that boy* aside, they knew who Natalie was seeing. She was considered part of the family. They'd have looked closely at who Paddy was. What he did. "I met him in September. He runs the family ranch."

"And you said—"

"Enough. Greg, leave it be," her mother interrupted sharply.

"It needs to be discussed, Di."

"I am aware of that."

Tuesday broke in. "If you two can hold off for a moment. I'm right here. On the phone. Stop talking about me like I'm helpless."

This was one of the reasons she liked staying in a hotel when she went up for some big dinner-type thing at her parents' house. They wanted to wrap her in cotton and protect her from all the hurts in the world. Which was their job when she was growing up, she got that. But man it drove her nuts as an adult.

Probably just a little because she felt better when they did it, a reminder that she could always go home and her mom would make her grilled cheese and tomato soup and let her watch sitcom reruns all day until things got better.

Which she'd done for about three months.

They'd gone out to scatter Eric's ashes and something had just sort of given out inside. They saw her at the lowest point of her life. Natalie told her once that seeing Tuesday broken and aimless and not being able to reach her for so long had been a terrible nightmare.

Her annoyance wisped away. They loved her. They never wanted her to go through any of that mess and so she needed to give them some space to feel however they wanted about it.

"I'm sorry. I shouldn't have snapped at you."

"Always had the best manners of all six. Thank you, punkin," her father said.

Her mother broke in. "Your dad and I know you're not helpless. But you're our child and you've had some hurts to swallow. We worry. It's our job to worry. Daddy and I watched you fade and fade to little more than a shadow. You haven't brought us a man, or even talked about one, since Eric. We can talk about it another time. I know you're there with your friends and it's your birthday. We love you, Tuesday Marie."

"I love you, too."

She hung up, leaning against the wall for a few moments, her eyes closed as she mended herself once more.

With a long exhalation, she pushed away and headed back out to the living room where her friends played cards, laughing and trash talking. With a smile, she let herself enjoy the butterflies of a new relationship as she slid herself into the chair next to Ezra.

"When you three are done losing to one another, deal me in again."

"Bold words, beauty." Ezra winked as he shuffled the cards and tossed one her way. "Let's see what you got then."

He'd already seen it.

He grinned as he looked down at his hands and she knew that had been exactly what he was thinking.

CHAPTER SIXTEEN

TUESDAY AND NATALIE settled at their table. "I'm not going to play around with some wussy little single margarita. I need a pitcher," Natalie announced.

Since Nat rarely drank, this was a signal of a really tough week. "Uh-oh. Problems with Mr. Hurley?"

They'd been back from the mountains a few days and both Tuesday and Nat had been playing catch-up at work after their short absence.

They stopped talking long enough to order a pitcher of mango margaritas and their food before returning to their conversation.

Natalie's face got all schmoopy with the starry eyes and softened mouth so Tuesday figured it wasn't a Hurley-related problem.

"No, it's a work thing. Grant time. You know how that goes. I've just spent a lot of time on math today and my brain is broken."

"Gotcha."

Her phone buzzed and she looked down to see Kelly's number. "It's Kelly. She's coming out tomorrow afternoon to pick up some more pieces and wants to know if we want to get lunch with her."

"Oh yeah, definitely."

Tuesday texted back the info and they signed off. "This is so exciting for you."

Chips and salsa were delivered with the drinks so they dived in. "She said something to me. When she came to the shop I mean. I've been thinking about it a lot since then. It's actually something you said first so you can actually say I told you so here."

Nat leaned in, delighted. "Yeah? Do tell. You know how much I love being right."

"She said that the shop wasn't a *shop,* it was a gallery. She said I should call it that."

Natalie's brow rose. "I could lord it over you, but there'll always be time for that as you well know. So what I want to say instead is it's about time you let yourself hear it. And so what do you think now that it's totally clear I was right?"

"I need to point out, Nats, that your last sentence *was* sort of lording it over me."

"So it was. I guess I'm petty enough to do a little I-told-you-so-ing after all."

They both laughed, clinking their margarita glasses together.

"I called the guy who did my signage. He's working on a bid for a new window and over-door design. Easton Gallery. That's what I'm going to call it."

Nat's eyes went wide as she sat back. "Easton? Not Eastwood?"

When Tuesday and Eric had married, they'd decided to create a name fusing their last names—hers, Easton, his, Heywood—to make a whole new name. It had been a way to make a deeper commitment to one another when they were both still treading carefully after their reconciliation. Eric had mixed feelings about his last name as it was, but he wanted them to be proud of him. So his agreement to do it had been a much bigger deal than it seemed from the outside.

But that time was done. The person she'd been then didn't exist anymore. Not in the same way.

"I'm not her anymore. It'll be five years in a month. I've been without him almost as long as I was with him."

"I don't know, Tuesday. I think that's kind of bullshit."

"You what?"

"Don't swivel your head at me. I don't disagree that you should go back to Easton. I don't disagree that you're different than you were six years ago. If you want this to be your next new start, so be it. *Own* it. You get to move on with your life. You get to have a boyfriend instead of a lover. You get to introduce him to your parents and sleep over at his place. All that. You get to think about your future and let yourself accept that Eric is only in it as a memory."

"Wait, so you call me out and say I'm full of shit and then you agree with me about changing my name back?"

"I think you're full of shit to not just call it what it is. Look, you made me accept the truth a whole lot in my life. I'm doing the same for you. Just say you're moving on and that going back to Easton would ease your heartache and let you step away from your past enough to truly enjoy your present and your future."

The thing about a best friend was that they knew you. They saw your flaws, knew your crap, could tell when you're avoiding a topic. They would steal your shoes but let you borrow theirs and a true best friend like Nat would let her avoid the truth until she was ready to face it. As she had for a very long while.

And it looked like Natalie felt right then was that time.

"I've backed off for years. Not going to now. You held on to Eric to protect yourself. He was your shield. You had all the heartache you could process and so he kept you safe as you got stronger. You're ready to step away from being Eric's wife. It will always be part of your history. But you don't need him to protect you anymore."

"This isn't about Ezra, if that's what you're thinking."

"It is so. Not entirely."

"Goddamn you and this truth-tea bullshit."

"Whatever. You can be mad all you want. But I'm right and you know it. You don't need a man to be whole. No. You didn't need a man to be healed from losing Eric. But Ezra's part of this. He's part of why you're taking more steps at long last. That's not weakness. It's merely a reason."

"Where did the nice Natalie go?"

"*Nice* Natalie let you hide because *nice* Natalie loves you and wanted you to get strong before you jumped out into the world again. Baby-step time is over. Get off your ass and gut up. You're a fucking gorgeous woman with a successful small business. You're smart. You have a really pretty best friend you feed so much she would have wasted away without you. In lots of ways." Natalie reached out to squeeze Tuesday's hand briefly and tears sprang to the backs of her eyes at how much her best friend meant to her.

"I am pretty fucking gorgeous." Tuesday patted her hair with a wink.

"Saucy. Now, back to the topic you're still trying to avoid. You're forged by fire, Tuesday. You've spent the last year and a half or so taking baby steps and now you're seeing the difference. It's miles away from where you were three years ago. Even two years ago. I like it. I want to see it. You deserve to have a new chapter that is happy and wonderful. Oh sure, you'll be hurt here and there—that's how it works. But you survived a horrible thing. You're ready for Ezra. And to change your name if you want. And to finally admit you make art."

"I'm going back to Easton and not because I don't love Eric and not because I don't cherish that part of my life but because I need to let it go. To move forward."

Nodding emphatically, Natalie raised her glass. "Damn right. We keep motoring because the future is ours. And Ezra?"

"He's a risk, Nat. He's scared and skittish and there are times I know he's deliberately not calling or seeing me. Times he holds back. There's so much grief in him. Guilt. I may never get through his defenses."

"It's a risk you think you should take." Natalie shrugged. "If you didn't, *you're* the one who'd be holding back. So take the risk and trust yourself. He's different with you. I can see it. Heck, everyone can. I think you guys are good for one another."

Tuesday thought so, too.

"You going over to Paddy's tonight?" Tuesday asked, effectively changing the subject.

Natalie shrugged. "No. I have a lot to do with this

grant stuff and he's dealing with alfalfa apparently. Plus I like my house, darn it. I miss not being in it as much. And you know spending the time up at the house in the mountains last weekend made me miss hanging out with you more, too."

"Well, you have work. I have work. You have Paddy and you love him and you're building something. Eventually you're going to move up there. It's just how it's going to go." Which was wonderful and all, but it made her sad, too.

"Just because I won't be living with you anymore doesn't mean we won't still see each other all the time. I mean, it's sort of fantastic you're dating Ezra so we're all together more than we were before."

"I hang out with you two so stop acting like I dumped you in Bend and left you to walk home."

Natalie threw a chip at her.

"I hate being the third wheel. I guess it's how you felt with me and Eric. Hey! This is what they call the shoe is on the other foot moments. Though that's such a weird saying."

What she hadn't said to Ezra during their conversation in the hot tub was that Eric had been a person she'd known immediately would be part of her life, too. They'd connected right away and were a couple by the third week of that first year of college. And remained that way, despite bumps in the road, until he'd died.

"He was one of my closest friends, too. It worked that we all ended up together a lot. Then you got married and we lived in different places so that took adjustment. This is just another chapter in the Natalie-Tuesday story, dumbass."

"Going to wash your mouth out with soap, blondie."

"You're all talk now that you get laid a lot more frequently. Much less violent than normal."

"I'm a freaking Nobel Peace Prize winner compared to those Hurleys."

They paid the bill and headed out. "I know. Though it's sort of sweet that they all seem to miss Vaughan so much."

Tuesday snorted. "I think Ezra is a little at loose ends with Vaughan in Gresham. He went over there yesterday he said. Saw the girls."

"Is he living with Kelly again? What's her perspective on this?"

"I'm totally asking her tomorrow if I get the chance. He's been there with Maddie as she recovered. Ezra said he'd been missing them after being out on tour and Kelly was good enough to let him stay in her guest room awhile. Ezra says the girls are really happy to have him around. But he got tight-lipped about the situation between Vaughan and Kelly. I said, 'Oh, is that bros before fros?' He got all nervous until I laughed."

Nat giggled. "I wish I could have seen his face when you said it."

"It was on the phone. I haven't seen him since we got home from the mountains. But it's only been a few days and I'm seeing him Saturday night."

"This is me not even saying how cute it is that you miss him if you don't see him for a few days."

"If so you get an F."

Natalie cackled. "I like this. I get to tease you, too. Ha!"

"Joy."

"Don't front. I know you like him. It's cute."

"I am fierce and fantastic, not cute."

"Sure. Whatever you say."

EZRA LET GO of the chin-up bar and landed on his feet with a sweaty grunt. He'd seen her last on Monday as he'd dropped her at her house.

He'd last kissed her then, too. It hadn't even been a week since he'd seen her last and he missed it. He'd got used to her, especially after those days up in the mountains.

Each day without her, the energy had built along with the craving.

The energy he could deal with. There were a lot of things to be done on a ranch so he had lots of opportunities to burn through any excess. But it was the craving that made him panicky.

At the end of the day when he'd not given in and gone to her, he'd been proud that he'd resisted. And then miserable he even considered what this thing was between them marginally close to what he'd lived through as a junkie.

Paddy called out a hello and Loopy tore out of the yard to greet him.

Ezra grabbed a towel to mop his face and neck. "Just over here."

"Ugh, why do you work out? You make me feel bad. Then I have to do it or all the beer and pizza will settle in my belly."

Ezra looked at his brother and rolled his eyes. "I have to lift and haul crap all day long. If I don't keep strong the ranch will eat me alive."

Ezra wasn't exceptionally superstitious but he did believe that he needed to be his healthiest to keep the ranch at its healthiest. There was a synergy between him and the land.

"But you can also sex up a fine lady now. Which seems more fun than pull-ups. Things are okay between you guys, right?"

"Things are fine. She'll be up here tomorrow night."

"Make me some of that shitty wheatgrass you drink and tell me things." Paddy leaned over the fence to pat Violet's head.

"Come in. It's too late for wheatgrass, but I was about to have some dinner and you look hungry."

Paddy grinned. "Score."

They headed inside and Ezra pointed toward the kitchen. "Get something to drink. I'm just going to shower and change."

Paddy was already playing with the cats so Ezra ducked down the hall to clean up.

By the time he came out, Paddy and Damien were in his living room drinking his juice and eating his food. Just a normal Friday, he supposed.

"We left enough for you so don't frown." Damien pointed at a glass.

"You're in my chair."

"I figured you'd be up cooking anyway. But I also figured that since I came over with a huge amount of food that my very pregnant, frustrated, achy and nesting wife prepared, you'd be fine with me sitting here."

"Fuck off. I'm fine eating food your way-too-good-for-you wife makes, though." He grabbed his glass and headed into the kitchen where really good smells hung in the air.

He was a decent enough cook, but Mary was magic and her food was, too. He opened up containers, poking around, grabbing a fork to taste things.

"Don't get your spit in the food." Damien strolled in along with Paddy.

"My kitchen, my spit. Also, I'm not actually sharing this with you two, so you don't need to worry about my spit." He ate directly from the container of cellophane noodle salad with fat, succulent shrimp. "I don't know what you do to keep Mary around, but keep it up."

"I don't know most days, either, dude. She loves me and feeds me and likes my weird family so whatever it is, I'll just try to do a lot of it so she'll overlook my flaws. You've been ducking me for a few days."

"Ducking? In case it's escaped your notice— Hey what's that?" Ezra pointed his fork at whatever Damien was putting on his plate.

Damien finished dishing some up before he replied. "Don't know. It's mushrooms and some sort of Italian ham stuff. It's awesome."

Paddy snatched the container before Ezra could, laughing all the while like a mushroom-stealing jerk.

"Don't you people have women to be with? Why are you at my house drinking all my juice and stealing my chair?"

"You're such a baby." Damien took his food back into the living room, Loopy following hopefully.

"Loop."

She gave him a sad face and he gave her a little

cheese and then of course the cats needed a treat but luckily for his brothers, neither of them were in his chair when he finally made it to the living room.

"My woman told me to take the food and leave her alone for a few hours. Her hips are hurting so she's napping and secretly watching reality television she thinks I don't know anything about. I wish I could help her, make it better. Gestation is hard work. It's tough on her body and I can't do it for her."

"She was looking a little pale when I saw her earlier today. I'm glad she's resting."

"Mom came by to help with some project for the baby's room. I keep telling Mary to hire some whiz-bang designer to do all the work or at the very least let me do it, but she won't have it."

They'd spent several days earlier that month getting the outline of the nursery in place. Mary's friend Daisy had come down to paint a mural and ouitfit the baby's room with bedding and stuff while Damien and his brothers had put together the crib, installed a custom kit for the closet, hung shelves and the like.

It had been a happy time, watching his family continue to grow and fill with people who loved one another.

He'd hung out some with Levi, Daisy's husband, who happily toted around their five-month-old daughter who adored her dad right back. Similar in temperaments, Levi and Ezra had hit it off quickly and that weekend for the very first time the desire to have that, a wife and a kid, to make his own part of the Hurley family had sprouted, growing roots rather quickly.

And after all the time he'd spent with Tuesday recently it had left him a little unsettled. Expectant. She'd become important to him and he wasn't sure he was capable of not fucking up in some way with her. He didn't know what to do with the intensity of feeling she brought his life, either. He knew enough to understand he liked it. A lot. But he wasn't sure if he should.

"Should we tell Nat then? There's still time to get the food for Tuesday's party elsewhere. I don't want Mary running herself down and I know Tuesday wouldn't want it, either."

"Do you now? Know what Tuesday would think? Pay the hell up, Ez. You have this shit going on in your life and Paddy gets to see it and I don't and I feel left out and it's making me grumpy. You're way better at grumpy than I am so cut me a break and share."

Ezra cleared his throat. "We don't share a mind meld, Damien. I know enough to understand she's a good person who cares about her friends so of course she wouldn't want Mary to do too much. Mary doesn't need to be our caterer."

"Ezra, Mary *is* a caterer. It's not just what she did for years, it's also in her nature. She uses food to care about people. Uses food to be sure they keep strong and healthy. She uses food to make people smile and feel loved. My woman lives for stuff like cooking for surprise congratulations parties. Even at eight months pregnant. But I'm going to tell her about this anyway because she'll like knowing you two were concerned over her. She says you and Tuesday are serious about one another. She right?"

"Paddy, stop feeding the cats."

"They're hungry! Look at these faces." Both cats

stood on the back of the couch, leaning down on Paddy's shoulders, rubbing their cheeks against his head.

"They're whores is what they are. And you only make it worse when you reward it."

"Sure. Because you never give them treats or spoil them at all." Paddy sent him a raised brow.

Ezra turned to Damien. "To answer your question, I like Tuesday and she likes me. We're seeing each other." He shrugged, feigning nonchalance. "I don't know why this has to even be a thing."

Paddy interrupted. "Because you've been alone. As long as she's been alone from what I understand. Years and years you isolate yourself and throw all your energy into this ranch."

"How the fuck you think it stays running?"

Paddy flipped him off without even pausing in his shove-food-in-his-piehole process. "Don't get defensive, asshole. I'm just saying you have an actual personal life instead of whatever it was you did before."

"What does that mean?"

Damien ate, his attention on Ezra and Paddy as they volleyed.

"So we really going there?" Paddy looked to Ezra and then to Damien.

"Why is this sounding like an intervention all the sudden? I've done that. Don't have any desire to repeat it."

"Eat it, Ezra. You can't divert my attention from the real subject here. Why is it so hard for you to share with us? Huh? How many times have you listened to us? Or is it okay for you to fix us but not the other way around? You don't think we have anything to offer you?"

He'd only recently learned that Paddy measured himself against his big brother. It had made Ezra proud to have earned that back after he'd done so much to destroy it before. Ezra figured that might be the source of at least part of why his brother was so agitated.

Still, it frustrated him to be accused of trying to hide whatever it was he had with Tuesday.

"Tuesday's more to you than some chick you drive to bang when you get the itch. That's what I meant. I didn't say you had to marry her."

"Take it easy, Paddy." Damien rarely interrupted, but in this case, Paddy snorted.

"He's right. Yes, Patrick, Tuesday is more to me than a woman I only occasionally see for sex when I feel like it and when she feels like accepting my offer. Is that what you wanted to know?"

"No. I want you to be honest. I want you to think we're worth that."

"Okay then. Once every few weeks I used to head to Portland because there's a woman there who I liked fucking. She liked being fucked. She liked it a little rough and that's what I had for her. I never met her friends. I never mentioned her name to you or anyone I know. Everyone got off and no one cared much beyond those hours we spent together. That was all I needed."

"Maybe it was all you allowed yourself to need."

Ezra turned to Damien. "I don't know. Maybe. But whatever it was, why ever I did it, it's not happening anymore. I haven't seen her since late last year. I don't *crave* her. I don't miss her or think about her. Makes me sort of a cock for fucking a woman I didn't really care to know, but I'm guessing she felt the same."

"I think it's interesting you use the word *crave*."

Loopy jumped up with a happy bark as Vaughan came in with his dog Minnie. Minnie was a corgi so Loop was about three times her size, but it didn't seem to get her down.

"The prodigal Hurley returns. Pull up a plate and something to drink. We're poking Ezra about his love life," Paddy said as he got up to refill his plate.

"It's times like these I miss getting drunk, fighting a bunch of assholes in an alley behind a crappy little dive and crashing with a black eye and blood on my shirt in bed as the sun came up. Life was simpler back then."

Everyone got uncomfortably silent at Vaughan's words until Ezra started to laugh. Normally they tended to avoid the subject of his addiction and sobriety. Even after all the therapy. They didn't want to hurt one another, which was a nice thing, he thought most days.

That day it made him laugh and it was the perfect response.

"It's okay to laugh, you know. I'm not going to run out and buy heroin because Vaughan brings up our storied and violent past. But if I do you can blame him in therapy. I will."

He hugged his baby brother on his way back into the living room.

They all settled in once again and felt surprisingly normal considering all the stuff going on for each man in the room.

Paddy wasn't one to let it go, so of course he got back to poking at Ezra. "To catch up, I was remarking on your use of the word *crave*."

"Why? It's a good word."

"It's a good word for me. Or Damien. But you? Well it's a *loaded* word."

Ezra didn't say much for a while.

"Needing something on that level isn't stable ground for a junkie."

Paddy nodded. "Fair enough. Do you see the situations as similar?"

"I know the difference between a woman and drugs." Though he wondered if quitting Tuesday wouldn't actually be harder than kicking junk.

"Stop being such a defensive dick. I might even agree if you were a junkie. But you aren't. You used to be. Now you're just a grumpy asshole who could be getting laid a lot more regularly but would rather punish himself by holding what he *needs* away to prove some sort of point that does not matter. You kicked heroin. Tuesday is not drugs. She's not an addiction. You're not out of control for liking a woman a lot," Damien said, feeding the cats.

"You guys stop feeding the cats from your plates." Damien had hit the mark on several of those comments and Ezra would rather not focus on that right then.

"Whatever."

"I'm going to spoil the fuck out of all your goddamn kids. Know that right now."

Vaughan snorted. "Too late. My girls already have more shit than they need and it's got Hurley written all over it. Kelly's family are assholes, but you people send my kids so much stuff. I had no idea how much stuff until I was at their house on a daily basis."

"Yeah, so what's going on with that?" Ezra leaned forward.

"Nope. I'm here to talk about you. And to pick up mail and some clothes. The girls are up with Mom and Dad having pizza and when that's over, I'm taking them home because they have school and Kelly will punch me in the throat if they're back after nine."

"Are you living there now?"

"In the guest room. But again, first we talk about Ezra and then I'll talk about what's going on in Gresham."

"There's not much more to say. I have what I guess you'd describe as a girlfriend. It's far more serious than anything I've done before and I'm mainly okay with that. It's not like no one knows about it. Hell, Paddy and his girlfriend just spent four days with me and Tuesday. I'm done talking about it. Thank you for being concerned."

Paddy used his middle finger to salute that comment. "I'm more nosy than concerned. I figure you two have it handled. She's got as much dark, tragic backstory as you do but she's strong. She doesn't take your shit, which I like."

Vaughan hooted. "Ha! Do tell."

As his brothers started teasing him about how Tuesday managed his grumpiness without too much effort, Ezra looked around the room and was totally content. It wouldn't be that perfect moment all the time. They'd fight; they always did. But it never failed to click back to this connection and closeness they all shared.

And that was something to count on. Something he did count on all the time. He'd get through this whatever with Tuesday. They had something. A draw to one another she'd said and had been right.

But no matter how that turned out, he always had his family. And that meant everything.

CHAPTER SEVENTEEN

SHE SHOWED UP at his door in her most flattering jeans, a button-down shirt she knew made her boobs look righteous and her boots. When he opened, his gaze lingered on her cleavage—which is why she'd worn the shirt—and then up to her face.

"Hey, come in."

He pulled her into a hug once she'd got inside and it felt like coming home. And then the fear came. She had this thing, this wonderful sense of belonging with someone. It was something she wondered if she'd ever have again with a man. It had been difficult to live without that after Eric died. If Ezra walked away after this...

"You smell good," he murmured into her hair.

She kissed the side of his neck. "You taste good. Happy Saturday, Ezra."

He stepped back after one last kiss and suddenly three furry bodies were there, each demanding attention. Laughing and feeling much better, she knelt to deliver love to everyone else who lived in Ezra's house.

"Okay, guys, leave Tuesday be." Ezra helped her to stand. "You want to head out now to ride?"

It had only been since Monday that she'd seen him last. Four days. It wasn't that long at all. Hell, the week before they'd gone up to the mountains she had only seen him once and it hadn't seemed like a big deal.

But this time, wow, she'd missed him.

"I'm a little embarrassed at how excited I am to go out riding."

He grinned. "Figured as much. I asked one of my hands to get the horses saddled up and ready for us."

He did?

"I might have to thank you in my own special way for being so thoughtful."

"Counting on that, beauty."

He took her hand and they went through the house and out the sliders in the kitchen. Loopy accompanied them and the cats preferred a sunny spot on the kitchen floor for a nap.

"Is Violet coming along?" Tuesday asked as they headed down the steps from the deck to the yard and land beyond.

"She is. Loopy will keep her in line and from digging up any of my plants. She and I had a tangle about that at first." He opened the gate of the pigpen and she came trotting out in all her pale pink glory.

She butted her head against Ezra as she passed and he patted her. She did a turn around Tuesday and then stopped, even with Loopy, ready to go.

"She needs a cowboy hat I think. Do pigs get sunburn?"

Ezra laughed. "She'd eat a cowboy hat and her bristles, the hair? It protects her. She's good."

He took Tuesday's hand again and the four of them headed to the stables.

As promised, the horses were ready when they

arrived. Right down to the same horse she'd ridden before, Peaches.

"I noticed you rode Peaches last time. She's mellow and pretty hard to spook. This saddle is probably better than the last one, though."

She stepped to Peaches and took in the details of the saddle. "Probably better? Ezra. This is like a Rolls-Royce saddle of some type."

And for whatever reason she knew he'd got it for her. The saddle wasn't one just sitting around waiting to be used in some tack room.

He made a sound, like a harrumph but he didn't quite commit to it. She ran her fingertips over the delicate design burned into the leather and that's when she saw the dragonfly near the pommel.

Swallowing hard, she looked away from the saddle to find him watching her intently. "Happy birthday."

Jesus. Her heart beat so fast she felt faint.

"This is a pretty big gift. You know that, right?"

"I have a few dollars in the bank to buy a saddle for a beautiful woman if I want to."

"Savings from not having to buy beer over the last years?"

Surprise scattered over his expression and then he laughed, hugging her. "Exactly. My accountant said kicking heroin and quitting drinking was a great retirement savings."

She sobered a little, tiptoeing up to kiss him. "Thank you, Ezra. This is really lovely." And it was. Thoughtful. He paid attention to what she liked and didn't. Extravagant.

The old Tuesday might have balked at a present like this. But she wasn't that person. And this man, well he wasn't Eric. And thank goodness the Hurleys weren't crazy like the Heywoods.

Briefly she wondered if she should share all this business with her former in-laws but decided against it. She wanted it to keep being a good day.

"I wanted you to know you could come up here to ride anytime you wanted. Even if I'm not here. I figured if you had your own saddle you'd know I really meant it."

She blew out a breath and he hugged her to him again. "Thank you."

"How'd you get such a perfect seat?"

He looked back over his shoulder. "I spend a lot of time looking at your ass. I know it quite well."

He really did. It was like they'd measured her butt themselves.

"Okay then. Well, you have a good memory because it's really comfortable." Her phone buzzed in her pocket. Again. She pulled it out, saw it was yet another text from Tina. Tuesday turned off the notifications and tucked it away.

"Everything okay?"

He was a very perceptive person when it came to how other people were feeling.

She nodded. "Just wanted to turn off the notifications so I won't get a buzz each time a text comes in."

"Good. We can make adjustments to the saddle. It'll take you a while to get used to it. We'll see how Peaches takes it but she seems to be fine. Let me know if she's acting like it's rubbing or fitting her wrong, okay?"

"I've been watching her for cues she's uncomfortable but nothing so far." Tuesday ran her hand over her horse's neck. "She's an awesome horse."

Like all women around Ezra, Peaches was ame-nable and mellow. Though *his* horse wasn't. Randy, which was such a weird horse name, was one of those fiery stallions you read about in books. Muscled and powerful, he was tall and definitely as cocky and ar-rogant as the man on his back.

Once they'd cleared the residential part of the ranch, they let the horses run awhile. Peaches was awesome because she was like, whatever, when Randy ran way faster.

"He's a show-off, Peaches. I think he might have a crush on you. And he should because you're a very pretty horse with really good manners."

It was a gorgeous late-spring day and the sky was heading toward twilight but they had at least an hour or so to stay out and still be safe for the horses.

"How was it then? Your first day?" he asked of her stall.

"It started off slow and I thought, *oh no, I thought this was going to be so awesome and now this sucks.* But after about two hours it picked up and kept super-busy for the rest of the time. I sold all but one piece. Paid for my gas and the cost of the space and materi-als and even gave me a small profit."

"That's fantastic. What are you going to do next weekend when you have to go to your parents' for dinner?"

"I don't need to leave until the very end so I'll go out there in the morning like usual. Believe it or not, Kelly is coming out to close up for me that day."

"*Kelly?* Vaughan's Kelly?"

"The same. I was talking to her over lunch yesterday and she volunteered to take over for me. It's pretty easy. Everything is marked. I think she might want to snag some of the pieces for her store or for herself." Which was so flattering.

"So you and Kelly are friends?"

"Why do you sound so surprised? You're the one who gave her my number to start with."

He nodded. "I did, yep. I knew she was going to talk to you about business stuff and you mentioned it briefly about a jewelry thing with her maybe? I didn't know it had progressed past that."

"She's one of those people I clicked with immediately. A whole lot of you lately. And you're all connected in some way, which is even weirder. Like I need another gorgeous blonde girlfriend. I told her it was super inconvenient that she's so pretty but I liked her anyway. The business thing is that she and her partner are carrying my pieces in both their stores. They're trying out accessories."

"Congratulations. Good for you. And for them because your jewelry is amazing. I've been in her Portland store. The partner is a designer, right?"

"Right. They have a house brand that's all her stuff. But they sell other labels, too. A lot of local people, which is pretty cool. It's great exposure for me and the money is nothing to sneeze at." And it was progress she could see.

Loopy and Violet had their own little rhythm. They'd run along with the horses—out of trampling distance of course—and then pause to sniff things whenever the spirit led them. When they lagged behind too much, Violet nudged the dog with her nose and they trotted to catch up.

"They're like your own camp followers."

"The only groupies I've had in some time."

"Ha!" Well that was just fine and dandy with Tuesday. Natalie and Mary seemed pretty well adjusted and patient with all the groupie stuff. Neither of them liked it one bit, but Natalie said she felt sometimes like *oh well, it comes with the territory.* But Tuesday had to wonder how she'd react if two women just up and asked Ezra to fuck them both right in front of her like what had happened to Natalie over the holidays.

Tuesday leaned toward the idea that she'd probably punch someone. Natalie was dignified and shit. Tuesday was nowhere near *that* dignified. She had a sneaking suspicion she'd have made it worse by punching someone.

A howl sounded in the distance, breaking her away from visions of punching rude people.

Peaches skittered sideways and snorted, clearly distressed and it hit her that she was pretty little on the back of a giant animal and she had to get this under control or it could be bad.

"Ezra," she called out, trying to stay calm.

He reined in and turned his horse in a neat set of very quick movements. Loopy's sweet demeanor changed, her lips drawing back as she bared her teeth in a snarl, which only seemed to make Peaches more nervous.

"Tighten her up just a little. Knees close against her but don't squeeze. Let her know you're there and you're going to guide her where she needs to be to keep safe."

Tuesday really had no idea how she'd execute his very sound advice so she just went all in and hoped for the best.

EZRA WATCHED AS A visibly anxious Tuesday obeyed him to the letter. She spoke soothingly but firmly to Peaches, who reacted, calming. Thankfully, Tuesday was a natural with horses—not everyone was.

Randy shifted to be even closer to Peaches to protect her, as well. Ezra stroked a palm down his neck.

"Good girl. Watch." He gave the order to Loopy, who stood between them and the direction the coyote's howl came from. She'd rip a coyote to shreds if she could, but if it was bigger than her, or got her by surprise, she could be the one ripped to shreds. He wanted all the creatures under his protection safely away.

He turned his attention back to Tuesday, who waited, speaking quietly to Peaches. "You did a good job."

She laughed but he heard the tension in the sound.

"Not really anything to do with me. Your super killer guard dog and those step-by-step instructions you gave me worked. Peaches is also a really smart horse."

He liked the way she continued to reassure Peaches with touches and praise. Not too much, but enough to relax them both. And he really liked that even when she was clearly scared she handled herself well and did what she needed to. How people reacted in a bind said a lot about who they were.

"I'm sorry to cut this short, but if there are coyotes out here it'll just keep spooking the horses. Loopy is a great dog and very well trained but I don't want her running off thinking to protect us. Violet has no defenses at all on her own."

"Of course. We've been out for an hour and a half anyway."

On the way back, he kept even with her, gaze peeled on their surroundings. He'd need to deal with this situation but he wanted to get her safely to his place and the horses inside before he did.

"Why is your horse named Randy? Because it seems to me you have a giant tawny stallion you name him Lucifer or something like that."

"He's a badass. He doesn't need some showy name like Sin Eater or Lucifer. He's so hard-core *because* his name is Randy and he does not even care what you think."

"Sounds to me like Randy might be a little defensive that his human named him Randy and not Sin Eater."

He chuckled. "My mom named him Randy. Her next oldest brother is my uncle Randy. They're close but they fight a lot. One of her favorites is to call him a horse's ass. So when I got the horse, she joked that we should call him Randy. He doesn't care as long as you give him carrots and apples."

"You know, Ezra, you're adorable. I won't tell on you or anything. But you are so soft when it comes to the people and animals in your life."

"I'm ferocious. I'm dark and broody and broken."

"I love that song," she said to the lyrical reference to "Threatened," one of her favorite Sweet Hollow Ranch songs.

"I wrote it after I was back here. There had been

an article about me. About rehab and my addiction. But it was more like, *hey this guy's writing will be even better now that he's gone through all this gritty stuff.* And then a few days later an article responding to that one came out saying I was too broken and now that I was clean my songs would get boring."

She curled her lip. "People are dicks."

He snorted. "Yes. And so I thought, *fuck you,* I'm going to write a whole goddamn album of hits. Heroin didn't make my success."

"And you did." That album had broken all sorts of sales records.

"I don't like to be told I can't do something."

That moment, when he chose to rise above and prove all the doubters wrong had been a huge turning point in his recovery. He'd taken his life back and wasn't going to let anyone make choices for him. And he'd been that way ever since.

"I bet they never did again after that."

She was right.

"I can't lie. Nope they never did."

"You proved yourself. That's important. But people are still dicks and hearing that makes me want to punch that guy in the nose for saying you were broken."

"I'd love to see that."

They got back to the stables and she insisted on helping the stable manager with the horses so he stayed through that part, liking the harmony of physical activity with her. Once they'd finished up, he took her back to his place.

"Look, I need to handle this situation with the coyote. He's going to spook my animals." Or worse.

She nodded. "I understand. What do you need me to do?"

"Stay here. I'll be back in about an hour."

"Nope. I'll come with you. I can help."

"If you think I'd let you come out into any situation you could be harmed you're out of your beautiful mind. I'm going to call my dad to let him know what's happening. He'll call wildlife while I do a check. But I need to take the ATV and a weapon."

Then she flattened her lips. He could tell she wanted to argue but she didn't. Which gave him wood. Jesus, this woman.

He kissed her hard. "It's not that I don't think you're capable. I need all my focus on this thing that threatens my land. Do you understand?"

She smiled a little, her posture relaxing a little. "I do, but thank you for saying it that way. Maybe I'll toodle over to Mary and Damien's. Since Paddy and Nat are out tonight doing something fancy and all."

The party.

"Actually, can you do me a favor?"

"Of course."

"Can you run down and grab some food for the cats? I'm nearly out and they'll kill me and eat me in my sleep if their dishes are empty tonight."

She gave a look at the spot Goldfish stood on top of Peanut, whacking him in the head repeatedly while he chewed on her tail. "Yeah, I can see that."

He wrote down what he needed. She'd have to go to the feed store for it, which would eat up some time, as well.

"Just tell whoever is behind the counter to charge it back to the ranch's account."

She nodded and headed out. He watched until she'd driven out of sight and then called his father while he retrieved his shotgun and shells.

Damien showed up as he was strapping things to the ATV. "Dad called. You're a jerk for not calling one of us to get help."

"You all have stuff happening right now. I sent Tuesday down to the feed store because she wanted to come visit your wife."

"She's over at Paddy's right now anyway. She and Nat would have been bummed to have their surprise ruined. Good call on sending her away. Shitty call not to use the help you're so freely offered. Asshole."

"I'm an asshole because I don't make you come out to maybe kill something? It's not my favorite, either."

"You're an asshole because you don't let us help with the difficult stuff. We're grown men. This is our land, too. It's shitty and stupid for you to do everything all the time."

Ezra sucked in a breath. "Yeah, okay. Fair enough. Let's go."

He keyed his ATV on and they headed out.

CHAPTER EIGHTEEN

TUESDAY PARKED AT the feed store and headed in, only to bump into Michael Hurley. He gave her a hug when he saw her.

"Hello, sweetheart. Fancy seeing you here. I was just talking to the wildlife guy about the coyote thing. Are you all right?" He looked her over carefully.

"I'm fine, thanks. Ezra has good horses and he was there to talk me through it when she got spooked."

"He's magic with animals. He and Damien are out now."

"I'm just here retrieving cat food for Ezra. I think it was his way of getting me out of there without barring me from coming with him."

"That's very possible. Why don't you have them add the cat food to my order? I have the truck and they're loading feed for the chickens and some other stuff up now. The bags are a hundred pounds each. I had four strapping sons to have someone do the heavy lifting once I got old. I'm old. So Ezra and his brothers can unload the feed back at the house."

He winked and she laughed. She saw bits and pieces of Ezra in his dad, or she supposed it was the other way around. They had very like temperaments.

"I'll do that. Thanks. I should have known he didn't want some twenty-pound bag I could fit in my trunk."

He walked over to the huge stack of pet food bags and pointed. "This is it. Don't worry about hauling it up front. They'll just take it out for me. Go ahead and let them know up at the counter. I'll be with you in a few minutes. I have to check on a trap we might be able to use for the coyote. I hate killing them if I don't have to."

She went up to the counter and waited her turn. The woman who looked up after she'd said, "Can I help you?" smiled, pushing glasses up the bridge of her nose.

Tuesday did the same thing and laughed. "I hear you. I need a bag of that cat food over there." She read the name Ezra had written down. "Can you please add that to Sweet Hollow Ranch's account and have it loaded along with the rest of Michael Hurley's stuff tonight?"

The woman looked around Tuesday, checking stock most likely. "Sure can."

She handed Tuesday a receipt and Tuesday thanked her before wandering back to find Michael. He didn't need to escort her back or anything and she knew they had all this business with the coyote to deal with so she didn't want him feeling saddled down with her.

She'd caught sight of Michael standing a little bit away and was heading there until someone hailed her.

"Excuse me."

She turned. "Yes?"

A harried-looking dude came at her. He wasn't just walking her way, but sort of top heavily bobbing at her. She took a step back.

"Who are you and what are you doing in here?"

She looked to her right and left and then back to him. His tone pushed her buttons. "Pardon me?"

"You heard me. What are you doing lurking around?"

"Lurking?"

"It means studying something, getting ready to steal it."

She knew her head whipped that time. "No, actually, that's *casing*. Lurking is more like stealthily hanging around with possibly ill intent. I'm doing neither actually. I just bought some cat food." Not that she'd ever shop in this place again if guys like this asshole worked there.

"Your hands are empty."

"Just what exactly are you saying?"

"I'm saying you're in here and I don't know you personally and I want you to understand we don't stand for any nonsense in our store."

"Please clarify for me. Are you saying I'm nonsense because I didn't immediately confess to your accusation of some sort of nefarious motive?" She paused. "Nefarious means bad or criminal. Since our game includes word definitions now. But since you did use you in a *you people* sense a few times, I'm guessing it's that I'm a black woman in your store and since I'm black I must be thinking on ways to steal chicken wire and nails"

"Playing the race card. You people always do."

And then there was a huge, hot, angry presence at her side for a brief moment and then in between her and feed-store bigot. Or FSB as she now thought of him. "I think you need to go ahead and get Ed out here. I'd like to talk with him about you."

"Mr. Hurley. This woman was causing trouble and

when I confronted her she of course said I was a racist. You know how they are."

Michael vibrated with so much rage that both Tuesday and FSB took a step back. "You will shut your
mouth before my fist does the talking." His voice
was a little unsteady, like he was so pissed he had
trouble speaking.

Tuesday was familiar with that place.

The woman who'd helped Tuesday at the counter
came over. "What's happening here? Gary, what are
you doing?" she demanded of FSB.

"Your employee just stalked my son's girlfriend
through the store and then accused her of casing the
store, all while making it abundantly clear he did so
because she was black. You need to know Sweet Hollow will do our business elsewhere if this is the sort
of behavior practiced here now."

"No, sir. I am horrified and so very sorry," she said
around Michael's body to Tuesday and then back to
FSB. "Gary, please go wait in my office."

FSB leered Tuesday's way and that's when Michael
caught him by the shoulder, picked him up and set
him back a few feet. "You will *not* act like a beast in
her presence. I won't allow it."

Tuesday wanted the ground to open up and swallow her.

She wanted to kick FSB in the taint.

She wanted to kiss Michael right on the mouth but
then realized Sharon was too scary to even try.

The guy stumbled back. "This is taking over our
country. Go back to where you came from!" FSB sort
of mewled it as he scampered off.

"Olympia?"

Laughing, Michael turned around and pulled her to his side, one armed. "I'm so sorry about that."

"*I'm* the one who's sorry." The woman from the counter held out a hand. "I'm Shelley."

"Tuesday."

"This isn't a reflection of who we are. Not as a family-run business and not as people. He's a second cousin and my dad gave him a job. He's been trouble here and there, but this—there's never been anything like this. I just can't apologize enough. I'm so embarrassed."

Tuesday had heard that one before. Apologies were a dime a dozen. Action? Now that told her a lot more than *I'm sorry*. "Now you *do* know. I expect this will be handled appropriately."

Shelley agreed. "Absolutely. Again, I do hope you'll give us a chance to set things right and understand this is not us, but an employee who'll be unemployed by night's end. My dad's going to flip his lid when he hears. I wasn't raised that way."

"You can't control how he was raised or what he was taught. I won't hold you responsible for anyone else's mistakes."

"Thanks. I appreciate it. I need to get my dad and handle this. I'll call your business line later, Mr. Hurley, to let you know what we've done."

"I'll expect that call then, Shelley. Come on, sweetheart. Let me walk you to your car."

When they got there, he opened her door but stopped before she got inside. "Honey, I'm so sorry that happened."

He'd got in between a crazy old racist who'd decided to terrorize her in a fucking feed store. He'd used his power and his size to protect her. That meant a lot.

"You don't need to apologize." Tears stung her eyes, even though it wasn't even as bad as some of the things she experienced on a regular basis. It was difficult not to let it get to her. Especially after the stuff with the Heywoods earlier.

"Aw, sweetheart, come here." He pulled her into his arms and she couldn't seem to stop the tears. Which made her mad but it didn't matter because he was big and strong and truly cared about her and was giving her a hug she needed more than she thought she had.

He waited until she'd stopped crying to hand her a handkerchief.

"If they don't fire him tonight we'll never do business here again. I meant that."

"If you're expecting me to argue you have a long wait. I think the only way to get people to confront this stuff is financially."

"Happens to you a lot?"

"Not usually so in my face. It's usually subtle."

"Which is worse because it's tolerated that way I bet."

She laughed in that it was either a laugh or more tears and she wasn't going to spill any more over any dumb racist jerk. "It's all pretty crappy. But having a crazy old man leap at me in a feed store and accuse me of casing his goods to steal is worse in my book than the shopkeepers who watch every move I make in their store. Overall, though, it comes from the same place. The quiet racist just hides it a little better."

He exhaled and began to pace. "I...I'm sorry. I

BROKEN OPEN

don't know what to do with how mad this makes me. Which is selfish because this is about you. You must think I'm a pretty naive old man for being so shocked by what you see regularly."

"I think you're a fabulous man, who stood up for a near stranger in public. It *is* shocking." She snorted. "I need to get back to the ranch. Ezra and I are supposed to have dinner after he gets back so I'm going to get it all started."

Michael hugged her again. "I'll see you in a bit when I drop the cat food off. You're going to tell Ezra about this."

A statement.

Bossy, just like his oldest.

"It's been a jam-packed day for Ezra. This was handled." And what she didn't want was for him to feel saddled by *her* shit.

"It happened to you. He cares about you. It happened in public. It happened at a business we've patronized for years. You should tell him before I do."

She saw his point. Ezra was his son and he had to know.

She blew out a breath. "Fine."

He kissed her cheek and closed the door after she'd got in.

SHE TRIED CALLING NAT, but got voice mail. Tuesday decided to keep it brief. No reason to get her friend upset. The scene was over now. There was nothing she could do. But she'd hear it from someone so Tuesday wanted to be first.

She got out right as Damien and Ezra came out

from the gear garage where Ezra kept the ATVs and his other stuff.

"Everything okay?" she called out as she approached them.

"Hey, gorgeous, how are you?" Damien gave her a hug.

"It's been a weird evening."

"You're okay here." Ezra moved around his brother to approach, concern on his face, thinking she meant the coyote.

"Well, that's a small part of it. You're going to hear this from your dad so I promised him I'd tell you first."

He put both hands on his hips and she got sort of caught up in all that male beauty for a moment.

"What's going on?" he repeated to get her attention back on the story and not his biceps.

"Just an incident at the feed store." She told them both but kept it simple with not a lot of extra detail.

Ezra's face darkened and the hands he'd had at his hips curled into fists. "And I sent you down there."

"You sent me to get cat food. Anything else that happened wasn't about you at all. I don't know about *your* normal grocery store trips, but mine don't generally end that way. It was some random, crappy thing you *couldn't* have anticipated."

"I'm going down there."

She stepped into his path, a hand on his chest. "It's handled. It's over." She told them about his dad and all the stuff he'd said to Shelley.

Damien gave her a look and she stepped closer to Ezra, touching his arm. Tension radiated from his muscles. A sort of barely leashed violence that sent a thrill through her even as she knew he was really angry.

"Please calm down."

"No one should be treated that way, much less you."

She took his hand, still bound in a fist, and kissed his fingers. Damien stepped back and found something to do.

"This isn't all right."

She snorted. "No kidding." She pressed another kiss to his other fist. "But you can't punch every single racist you see."

"Why the hell not?"

She smiled. He'd relaxed just a tiny bit.

"Because you'd have really sore fists. Because that's what they want. Mainly because jail is dumb and they're not worth it. There'll be more. There's always more. You'll just see it now because you're with me. You're a white man with a black woman. It gets attention." She raised a shoulder.

"I'm a man dating a *gorgeous* black woman. It's probably jealousy."

She shook her head. "Ezra, you need to always remember something. Bigots are ignorant. It's why they're bigots. You start threatening their reality and some of them lose their shit. You just can't go around punching racists because some of them *want* the excuse to do you harm. *That* is my reality. If I don't operate with that reality at the forefront of my mind the consequences can be pretty dire."

He freed one of his hands to shove it through his hair. "Okay. All right. I'm sorry. I'm sorry that while

I knew racism was a problem, I didn't really get what you have to live with every day."

"And you still don't. You can't." She kissed him again. "But you'll see it from a new angle now and I want you to be prepared."

He frowned and she wanted to laugh all the sudden. He was so perplexed when he couldn't control every aspect of something. There was something so sweet about that even though it was annoying, too.

"Well, did my dad get to hit him at least?"

"He reached out and grabbed the guy's collar and shirt." She showed Ezra what she meant. "And then just sort of picked him up and chucked him back a few feet. It was pretty awesome. He was kind of my hero right then."

He hugged her. "Good. You need heroes."

She squeezed him, burrowing into him as much as she could. He rumbled then and it made her smile. As he'd intended most likely.

"Hey, boys and girls! Exciting night, huh?" Paddy and Natalie approached. "Dad just called but we were already on our way over here after Natalie got your voice mail, Tuesday."

Natalie knew Tuesday would hate it if she tried to hug her or make a big deal out of the situation. It did suck, but making a big deal out of it would just draw more attention and make it worse.

Michael Hurley had done what was right and she would not forget it. But she didn't want to dwell on it.

"We just rolled up from the great coyote hunt." Damien came over. "We should all have dinner."

"Yeah, Mary is at my house with some food. That's

why we're here." Paddy looked his brother over carefully.

"I'm a mess. Give me five minutes to tidy up and get some lipstick on and we'll walk over."

Natalie linked her arm through Tuesday's. "I'll come with you because I know you're hoarding that tube of red I gave you for your birthday."

"That's not hoarding, Natalie. You give someone a gift it's theirs to use how they wish. But I have it in my bag and you can use some because you're adorable."

She looked over to Ezra. "We can make the pizza another day. I'll be back in a few."

He stalked over and Natalie scampered away with a squeak when Ezra hauled Tuesday to him and laid a searing-hot kiss on her.

There was so much in that kiss it was all she could do to hold on to his biceps as he devastated her with his mouth. Left her totally bare and broken open. He looked into the heart of all that and he kissed her like there was nothing else in the world he could do. He kissed her like he needed her to survive. Like her taste was the best in all the world.

"I'll be waiting." He set her back and she blinked up at him as she gulped.

"O-okay."

Natalie was at her side again, linking arms. "Lean on me because I bet you got some rubber knees right about now."

Tuesday laughed as they headed inside. Loopy showed up, shadowing her through the house, protecting and defending.

"My bag is in Ezra's room. Hang on."

Natalie paused at the end of the hall leading to

Ezra's room, gaping at the ornate glory of those double doors.

"I know. Wait until you see the rest."

"It smells really good in here. My god, what does he use?" Natalie puttered around Ezra's room, looking around as Tuesday found the lipstick and pulled out her little spray bottle of the oil she used to make her hair happy after a hard day.

"Right? It's some essential oil with bergamot and myrrh and something else." Tuesday pointed to the plain little brown bottle of oil. "I look horrible. Why didn't you tell me?"

"You look like you've been crying but that's mainly because I know you so well. I'm really biting my tongue right now because I know you don't want to do this here and now. You look like someone who had something upsetting happen to her less than an hour ago. Not in a weak way. You're still pretty."

Tuesday pressed a cool, wet washcloth to her eyes and snorted. "Obviously. It takes a lot more than FSB to make me look anything less than fabulous."

Natalie put her head on Tuesday's shoulder briefly. "People are dicks. What's FSB for?"

"I was *just* saying this to Ezra earlier today about people being dicks. FSB is feed-store bigot. I think his name was Gary."

"Whatever his name, he's a lesser."

"You speak true." Tuesday spritzed her hands and rubbed them together before getting her hair back in order.

She caught Nat's eye in the mirror's reflection. "Heywood stuff, too."

Nat's expression darkened. "What are those fuck-nuts up to now?"

Tuesday braced herself and then told Natalie about the phone call she'd got from Tina right after she'd pulled up in Ezra's driveway.

"Why didn't you tell me? That woman. Oh my god. Block her number!"

"I know. I know I should. I guess part of me still feels a responsibility to Eric to be nice. Even though she's awful."

"Fuck her."

"No thanks."

"Stop talking to her. I mean it. Block their number, block her email. Stop letting them cut you up for kicks. You don't owe them anything and I don't even care what Eric might have thought. He's dead, Tuesday, and his family has no right to do this."

Tuesday knew this was true. Felt it. Said the same to Tina even.

She decided not to tell Nat about the reaction she'd got when she'd told them she was changing her name back to Easton. It would just upset her friend and in turn, upset Tuesday.

Enough for the day.

"I should tell Diana about this."

"Yeah? How about you stop letting your grand-mother fuck you over and then we can talk."

"You're vicious."

Tuesday nodded. "Yep. But you're right. I know you are. Which doesn't mean I'm not serious about you cutting your family out like a diseased organ."

Nat held her hands up in surrender. "Ugh. Okay.

Truce. Tomorrow let's go out somewhere. How about we get manicures."

She looked down at her hands. She kept her nails short and usually painted with light colors because she was constantly chipping them as she worked.

"Good call."

Tuesday took the tube of lipstick Natalie handed over. An expensive brand she would never buy for herself but Natalie gifted her with from time to time.

"I'm ferocious. I'm dark and broody and broken," she whispered as she slid it over her bottom lip, leaving a bright red shine in its wake.

"What?" Natalie had been poking her head into Ezra's giant shower arena. He called it a stall. But his damned horse could fit in there. "Jeez, this is as big as my whole bathroom."

"He likes pleasure." She smiled at herself in the mirror when she said it.

"Jeez-a-lou. You can't say stuff like that and not share what you mean."

"I mean sex, Nats. The man is a fucking machine. That giant shower is just a glimpse of just how much Ezra likes to feel good. His bed was custom made so it's like a third bigger than even the biggest king bed." She looked behind her at the closed bedroom door. "He told me he liked all the room to spread me out and lick every part of me."

Natalie fanned her face.

"So, despite the Heywoods and FSB, my life is pretty freaking good, complete with heaping helpings of super-duper hot fucking."

"Yay for happy but the stupid is still there. Makes me want to flip tables and burn things down."

Tuesday laughed as she left the bathroom to grab the extra shirt she'd tucked into her bag. "I brought an extra in case I got dirty when I was out riding." Or to wear home in the morning. "A skittish horse and a dramatic public scene in front of my boyfriend's dad can make a girl sweat."

She pulled her blouse off and changed into the spare, bright blue and sleeveless.

"Feel better?" Natalie asked as she finished up, tossing her stuff back into her bag.

"Yes. Much. But I am so hungry and I didn't even get to tell you about how well things went today at my stall at the market."

Natalie hugged her. "Such a jam-packed day. Come on. We'll have some food and hang out and you'll be around people who love you and want to punch FSB. And we can ogle all that Hurley butt."

"This is a very good point. Come on then. I know you have junk food at Paddy's so you better share some."

Natalie laughed as they dodged cats once they'd headed back outside. "I will always share my secret junk food with you after a hard day."

"True friendship."

"Always and forever."

CHAPTER NINETEEN

ONCE THEY'D GONE inside and he was sure she was out of sight, he gave over to his volcanic rage, storming into his home gym where his bag hung.

"Wait!" Damien caught his arm as Paddy handed him gloves. "She'll see it if you don't use gloves."

Nodding, he put on one and Paddy helped him into the other and then he stepped up and began to pummel the bag so hard sweat broke over his face and down his spine. All his rage that anyone would make her upset, threaten her in any way, even to just look at her wrong and make her feel bad wasn't acceptable.

Each strike vibrated back up into his body, the concussive force battering what felt like a tsunami of rage. *Boom. Boom. Boom.* His fists hit the leather. He wanted to be doing this to the man who'd made Tuesday cry.

He'd seen it in her face when he'd got very close. Her eyes had been a little puffy and red. That someone had done that to her filled him with a murderous need to do something he couldn't. He hadn't felt this way since he'd first started to kick.

A bone-deep ache to do something he simply couldn't be doing. He wanted it. Could taste the way he'd spin on his heel and head to his truck. He'd tear ass over to the store and beat this dick down.

He could taste that violence. The unacceptable, dark violence of crunching bones. It wasn't civil to make those choices. Those choices were always trouble. But he *wanted* to rain his fists and his rage on this piece of shit.

Slowly that haze broke away and he eased back, already feeling the exertion in his shoulders. He wouldn't make stupid choices because he had reasons to make better choices. She was inside his house, putting herself back together because she was a survivor. A badass goddess who hadn't broken after all the stuff she dealt with, but instead had grown stronger. He hated that she had to, but he admired her spirit. Respected it. And fucking got terrified that she was way out of his league.

Finally he could breathe again and he stepped back, head tipped to the ceiling as he dragged in lungfuls of air.

He hadn't been there. But thank goodness his father had. He needed to talk to his dad but not until he burned off some more of this anger.

"Dude," Paddy said. "I think you killed it. Take a rest."

"First, she's out on a ride and her horse got spooked. But she handled it. Then I sent her down to the store because I didn't want to ruin the surprise and instead some jerk accosts and terrorizes her. I didn't protect her either time."

Paddy threw him a bottle of water from the fridge at his back. Ezra drank it slowly, still putting himself back together.

"Jesus. Ezra, you think it's within your powers to what? Control coyotes? You a wizard now?"

Damien interrupted. "How did she handle it on the horse?"

She'd been fantastic. Coolheaded. "She's solid. Capable. She was scared but she listened and handled it. She was fine."

Paddy nodded. "She likes horseback riding so she's not dumb. Sometimes your animal gets spooked. You handle it when it comes up. She did and she did it right. I don't think she's upset over that horse and coyote thing anyway."

Damien helped Ezra get the gloves off. "How you feel? You hit that bag pretty hard."

"I hate that I can't make it better," he said, not worried about his hands.

"Racism?" Damien laughed. "No, Ez, even you can't end racism to keep it from hurting Tuesday." He sobered up. "What happened to her was awful. It makes me want to punch someone, too. But you can't be with her every moment. And it's not like she didn't have to deal with this before you came into her life. I understand that you want to protect her from this stuff. I want to protect Mary. Paddy wants to protect Natalie. It's how this works. But reality sucks sometimes. The truth is, you can't protect people you care about from everything that will hurt them. We'll make sure that joker at the feed store gets fired. But if you make a bigger deal out of it, at some point she's going to feel bad about how *you* feel. She needs to come to you with this on her terms. You get that?"

"When the hell did you get so wise?" Ezra stepped out onto the porch and pulled his shirt off. He grabbed the hose and sluiced water over his upper body and hair. The shock of the cold helped him think clearer.

Damien was right. He needed to let this be about her feelings and how she wanted to handle it.

"Love makes us fools and wise men all at once." Damien bowed when Ezra walked back inside, toweling off.

"Fuckyeah." Paddy threw up the rock-and-roll devil horns and Ezra laughed.

He kept spare shirts out there in the bathroom so he grabbed a clean one, tucking it in. Once his hair was brushed he looked to his brothers.

"I need to talk to Dad."

"He and Mom are going to stop by in an hour, he said. Give us all time to settle. He's upset, too. He said to keep an eye on you because he wanted to punch the man as well and he knew you'd end up in trouble if you went in search of the guy." Paddy shrugged. "Then Natalie listened to her voice mail and heard how upset Tuesday was, even though she tried to sound matter-of-fact about the whole scene."

"Sure, Paddy, that seems like a great idea to get him all riled up again." Damien punched him in the arm.

Paddy shoved him back. "Get off, ballsack." He continued speaking to Ezra. "I'm saying he's got enough to take care of right here. That loser is going to get fired and we'll still be Hurley. Right?"

Ezra nodded, remembering the pain on her features and the sadness in her voice as she laid out what she had to experience as commonplace. He couldn't make this disappear for her. But how he reacted could make things worse. He focused on that.

He heard her voice just then as she came out of the house. Natalie's joined it as they laughed. Paddy and

Ezra both relaxed and then Ezra realized he was having the same exact reactions as Damien and Paddy.

Which *only* meant he liked her and she was his girlfriend. He cared about her like they cared about the women they...loved. It was just in a different place in the continuum, that was all. He could like her and not freak out that he was liking her. This feed store business was handled and he needed to let it go. For the time being anyway.

And then he moved to her because there wasn't anything else in the world he'd rather have done.

HE SLID AN arm around her shoulders and hers went around his waist. As if they always did that in front of everyone. It was exactly what she'd needed. He made her feel safe and special.

"Will the animals be all right?"

"Yes. It's handled." Ezra didn't say what happened but whatever had been done, she knew he'd never be strolling over to dinner if his animals were in danger. "They're safe and so are you."

He held her a little closer and it did make her feel a lot better though her worries and fears for herself weren't anything he could protect her from. No one could.

"By the way, I forgot to say earlier how much I like that shade of red."

"Thanks. That's a new shirt. I like how it's all snug across your shoulders like the cotton is just, *Oh my god how can I not always be laying myself all over Ezra Hurley?* Probably rocks and weeps in your closet when you don't wear it."

He laughed. "You're wearing a new shirt, too." He

dipped, pressing his lips to her ear. "From my angle I can see the edge of your bra. I can tell I'm going to like it."

She smiled in the dark as they headed up the road to Paddy's place but they wended around and ended up approaching from a direction she hadn't before, coming in through the French doors leading into a first floor sitting room Paddy had put three pinball machines in.

"I can really go for a few games of pinball after dinner," she told Ezra as they went down the hall and out into the open kitchen living area.

Full of people all shouting surprise at her.

She skidded to a halt, truly surprised.

"It's not a birthday party but we do have cake. It's a we-are-all-so-proud-and-thrilled-for-all-the-great-stuff-going-on-for-Easton-Galleries-and-her-owner party." Natalie hugged her.

Two of her dearest friends came toward her, pulling Tuesday into a hug. "You're here. You look so pretty." Jenny stood back after a kiss on the cheek. Jenny was a third-grade teacher and lived in Seattle with her wife, Zoe, who was a biologist and the next kiss was from her.

As was a whispered, "Holy crap, that's Ezra? He's like a nuclear testosterone bomb wrapped in velvety smooth hot man skin."

Tuesday looked back over her shoulder at him. He stood just about three feet away talking to Damien. "Right. You should see him naked and sweaty."

They all laughed and she turned to Natalie, hugging her again. "I know you're responsible for all this.

Thank you. I couldn't think of a better way to spend tonight at this point."

"Mary did all the food." Natalie looked around.

"She's at the front door with my parents, Nat," Paddy called out.

"Ezra?"

He came over, his arm wrapping around her shoulders. She leaned into him a little. "This is Zoe Marsden and Jenny Dan. Guys, this is Ezra Hurley."

"Ah, two more of this infamous 1022 you both speak of so often." He shook hands with both women. "Really nice to meet you in person."

"Thanks. You, too. You guys have a pretty spread up here."

"There she is!" Sharon came in with Michael and Mary. Mary mouthed *I'm sorry* when Sharon barreled in and hugged Tuesday.

Michael shrugged. "So I figured, hey, I'll have the time to get past what happened down at the feed store. I'll tell my wife what happened. Rail about it. She'd send me out to chop wood. I'd chop wood until my arms hurt. I'd feel better and we'd come on over. But silly me, I forgot I'm married to a stone-cold viper when it comes to people hurting people she cares about and while I did go out and chop wood, your mother paced the kitchen getting herself all worked up and called down to talk to Shelley, who told us she and her dad had fired Gary and sent him packing. Apparently he's the kind of guy who is always making promises he never bothers to keep anyway. He's bounced around and this is the last of his relations in the West so he'll be heading east this time."

Jenny and Zoe looked confused. "What are you all talking about?"

Which led to a retelling of the story with added outrage.

Tuesday stood at the outer edge of it, glad they all cared so much but exhausted by it all at the same time. There was only so much she could say or feel or do about it.

"Come with me." Ezra eased her from the room, grabbing a platter of sliders on the way. They sneaked quietly out to the front porch where he brushed off the glider so she could sit.

Out there in the dark, they said nothing. He rocked them back and forth slowly as they ate sliders and she rested her head on his shoulder.

They stayed out there until she heard her name a few times.

He stood and she took his hand. "Sorry about my mom. She didn't mean to cause all that in there."

Tuesday blew out a breath. "I know. She just wants to help. It's all right. It was too much for a little while but you pulled me out here with your shoulder and some sliders. I'm better."

"I'm sorry I wasn't with you today down there."

She took his face in her hands. "You don't tear yourself apart with guilt and recriminations enough that you have to start grabbing stuff at random now? He doesn't have a job. I'm done now. I can't hold on to it like that or it'll eat me alive."

He nodded and she smiled.

Natalie opened the front door. "There you are! Cake!"

"Can't miss that."

Ezra led her back into the house, his hand at her back. "First we'll eat cake and then later, back at my place, I'll eat you," he said before they reached the kitchen.

She groaned. "You're a menace."

He stopped her, kissing her quickly. "I am. But I'm really good at eating pussy."

She laughed, hugging him. "So modest, too."

CHAPTER TWENTY

THE FOLLOWING WEDNESDAY as she turned after locking up the gallery, Ezra was standing there with Loopy on a leash. Happiness surged through her at the sight of them both. "Hey."

He hugged her and she hummed her delight at his kiss. "What brings you to town?" She bent to give Loopy some attention and got a few sloppy kisses in thanks.

"Vet appointment. Just a checkup. But you're between the vet and the ranch so we thought you might be up for some company."

"I need to finish up some work tonight. I have supplies for sandwiches, though. I bet we could find something for Loopy."

"I can leave her outside. She'll love your garden."

"She can hang out in it if she wants, but she's welcome in my house." Tuesday knelt in front of Loopy again. "You got between me and a predator. That was pretty brave of you. You're welcome to get dog hair on my sofa any day."

"We'll follow you over after we walk you to your car."

"I didn't drive today. It was so warm and pretty I walked over. It's only fifteen minutes or so."

"Well come on then, ride with us."

NATALIE AND PADDY were in her kitchen when they arrived and Ezra halted her. "Is it awful that I want you all to myself?"

"No. I'm awesome so I'm not surprised," she teased.

He hugged her. "I missed you this week. You could come to my place. Bring your supplies. And a change of clothes. Sleep over. I feel like I haven't seen you in a long time. Obviously I need to get at what you've got under your clothes—that goes without saying. But I promise to give you the space and time to work. And I'll make you breakfast tomorrow."

"Wow, you're like Santa all the sudden. I really can't say no to any of that."

She could have. But she didn't want to. He struggled with pulling her closer, she knew. He'd come to her that day and it didn't feel as though he'd resentfully given in to what he wanted. It felt like he wanted her as much as she him.

They went in and Ezra hung out in the kitchen with Paddy while Loopy followed Natalie and Tuesday upstairs.

"Yes, you can lay on my bed," she said to Loopy as they entered her bedroom. Loopy head butted her and trotted ahead. First she sniffed around and then hopped up to settle on Tuesday's bed, her head on her paws as she watched Tuesday and Natalie.

"You let a dog on your bed? You totally love him. Oh my god." Natalie sat down on the bed next to the dog and Tuesday rolled her eyes as she changed from her work clothes into some capri pants and a T-shirt.

"I'm so glad you're not a drama queen," Tuesday said as she tossed her makeup bag into a duffel.

"I like it. On you I mean."

"Stop."

"Nope. You poked and prodded me for a year over Paddy. You think you get a pass? What sort of best friend would I be then? Deal with it, East…Easton. That takes me back."

"Sometimes I forget I didn't start out as Eastwood."

"Anything else from them or did you do as I suggested and block her number? You know your mother would tell you exactly what I did."

"Well, Diana told Tina Heywood she was a dumb hooker the last time we were all together, so my mother isn't unbiased."

Tuesday zipped her duffel and shouldered it.

Natalie snorted. "She's not unbiased on any subject I've ever encountered. Diana has feelings about everything. But this isn't terry cloth versus other kinds of cotton."

Both women cracked up. Tuesday's mother *hated* terry cloth in that *terry cloth was the mortal enemy of all mankind* way. Diana could rant about it for a good half an hour.

"Anyway, Tina Heywood is human terry cloth as far as Di is concerned. Everyone knows that."

"It's truth. It's not as far as your mom is concerned. Tina Heywood wants you to pay for her own sins with her children."

"She'll never be able to make up for that, though. Don't you see? She is terrible—I'm not denying it. But Eric is gone and she will never, ever be able to make that right. I try to give her extra space when she's a dreadful bitch."

"Yes, but she has another son she's driven away, too. If she wanted to change her ways, why isn't she talking to Sammy?"

Tuesday wasn't sure Sammy would hear it anyway. He'd done what Eric never could, which was to fully let go of their mother and adoptive father and live his life, surrounding himself with people who were positive. He'd come to the memorial but hadn't stayed with the Heywoods; he'd stayed with Tuesday's family instead.

"I told Sammy, by the way. About the Easton thing. He congratulated me and said he knew Eric would want me to move on. He also urged me not to listen to Tina."

Natalie blew out an angry breath. "I will never, ever forgive them for what they did at the memorial."

Tina had cornered her and said, to Tuesday's face, that it was her fault Eric had not gone to the doctor. Said Tuesday had willfully ignored his decline in health to be done with Eric and get the insurance money.

She'd said it within hearing distance of GJ, who'd nearly got into a fistfight with more than one Heywood. The cops had been called and it just made falling away from all that noise easy. For a while anyway.

"They lost Eric and that's the one thing that makes me not say they're utterly worthless "

"Dude, let's not go there. I'm about to spend a lovely evening with Ezra and his menagerie. He's promised me sex and breakfast tomorrow. That is a good thing. I want to think about good things. Come on, Loopy." She made the sound Ezra did, a cross between a smooch and a *tsk,* and must have done a pretty good job because the Lab hopped down and came to Tuesday's side, looking up, waiting.

"You are such a pretty, smart and awesome dog."

Loopy licked Tuesday's nose in thanks, her tail whipping back and forth so hard it made a little breeze.

Natalie stared, blinking. Then she grinned and Tuesday stood again with a groan. "What? Say it now before we go back downstairs."

"You're happy. He makes you happy. You just talked baby talk to a dog and you let her lick you. With her tongue. I don't even know who you are right now. But I like it."

"You act like I walk down main street frowning at kittens and toddlers all day long."

Natalie waved a hand. "Now who's the drama queen? All I'm saying is he makes you happy. Just in general. Not that you cried all day long or kicked puppies before. You say, *Oh no, I can't talk about it!* Like it's a talisman against falling in love. And it's not. Trust me on that. It happens whether you want it or not. It's good on you. It's really good on him."

"We've been seeing each other a month. Slow it down, sister."

"You and he had instant hotness. Plus he kissed you in December. It's now June. So that's much more than a month."

"He kissed me in April, too."

"What?" Nat yelled it and Loopy barked.

"Should we go downstairs when I tell you the details of this thing I haven't told anyone? I'm up here saying so—quietly—because I don't want to say all this in front of a crowd."

"Well I'm sorry! You have withheld him kissing you. Twice!"

"Hush. I told you about all the sex stuff because you're insatiable and a deviant. What's a kiss a few months ago? It was a surprise one!"

"When? I need details before I can be sure I'm not mad."

"You're not mad."

Natalie grinned. "Not really. But you still have to give me details."

So she told Nat about the day Ezra came to the house to talk about Nat and Paddy's fight and how they'd get the feuding couple back together. Oh, and the way Ezra had pinned her to the wall next to the new arbor and kissed the heck out of her until he left her wobbly and with a need on for more of what he delivered with that mouth.

"I *knew* something had happened between you that day! And then how the two of you were at dinner that night we went up to Sharon and Michael's. Did she know?"

"Who knows? She's spooky. Like Diana is spooky. Whatever she knew, it's clear she invited Ezra that night for me."

"So the truth is, you and Ezra have been involved on some level since you first met in September. That's nine months. And you kissed him in December, and then in April. Those were like first dates. Anyway, you can't deny there is something major between you. This is not—" Nat made air quotes "—*I've only dated him a few weeks! Oh no! I don't know him well enough yet.*"

Tuesday sent Loopy downstairs and turned back to Natalie.

"No, it's not. I've *never* felt this way about anyone." Tuesday dropped the duffel and paced back into her bedroom. "Not even Eric."

Once she'd let the words free they seemed to slice through her.

"Why can't it be that loving a person is a totally unique thing? Of course you feel things about him you didn't feel for Eric. He's not Eric. I'm sure you're always going to feel things about Eric that you won't feel about him."

"What if I'm tossing away Eric for something I think is better only it's not and then I'm screwed and alone?"

Natalie shook her head, taking Tuesday's hands and stepping into her path to stop the pacing,

"Tuesday, that way lies madness. I'm not going to let you do this. Stop."

"I can't. I've tried. Sometimes, when he touches me it's like chain lightning all through my body. He's just…" She licked her lips. "He's *so* much, Nat. But, I want it. I want it all even when I feel like I'm drowning in him. He's messed up and afraid to let me in. And I'm messed up. And yet he knows me. He sees it and he wants me despite that. Or maybe because of that. I don't know. And part of me? Part of me doesn't care which. Because, regardless, it's part of me. Sometimes when people who've known me from before I was married are around I feel sort of like they're not only sad that Tuesday is no longer, but they're sad they don't like this one as much."

"You wear a mask with most people. You don't

think I can see it? Not with me, no," Natalie reassured before Tuesday could argue that point. "I've known you pretty much my entire adult life. You're the strongest personality I know. You wear your skin easily. You leave people alone as long as they don't mess with you and you do your thing regardless of what people think.

"But even before Eric died I watched you put on that friendly but polite mask with people. You show them what they want to see, but really to keep them away. The real Tuesday is something only a few people ever get to see. You show that Tuesday to me." Natalie paused, pressing a hand over her heart as she had to blink back tears. "That Tuesday is like the dragonfly on your body. You're incredible. And special and talented and wonderful. Fragile and vulnerable for all that beauty, too. You show that Tuesday to Ezra. You love him, Tuesday. It is different than what you had with Eric because you were different then. Eric was different than Ezra definitely. It doesn't make your love for Eric *less* that you feel the way you do about Ezra. But even if you loved Ezra more or better or whatever, it doesn't matter to Eric. It matters to *you*. So here's my bottom line. I want you to be happy. I want you to be in love and for it to be the very best possible love. I want you to accept that you deserve it."

"You're going to make me cry. And then he'll know and worry."

"He loves you, too. You should see how he looks at you, Tuesday. I don't want you to cry. I want you to dance and joyfully accept this experience. What it'll mean next year? Who knows? We both know how fast life can change. But come back to the world once and for all. You're too special and wonderful not to live as you were born to."

"I'm in love with him." Tuesday closed her eyes.

Downstairs she heard the low bass of a conversation between men. Loopy had gone down already so they'd be expecting Tuesday and Natalie any moment.

Natalie hugged her. "I know. It's awesome. Let it be awesome."

"Mainly I feel nauseated. I've been in love. I've been serious about someone. I've been married and talked about having a family with someone. Love isn't a new territory. But this thing between he and I? It's so intense. Supercharged and sex laden. I can't believe I'm saying this out loud. But I've never in my life come as hard as I have since Ezra entered my life. He just does something to all my parts. To my brain and my heart and all the good stuff boys like, too. He makes me feel like a goddess in bed."

"You can take a look at the man and know that. I mean Paddy does the same thing. It's a Hurley trait I bet. Mary talks about it with Damien and you've seen Michael and Sharon together—he does it for her in a big way."

"I have to go. He's going to wonder where I am."

"We'll talk more soon. I love you, Tuesday. I'm thrilled for you. For us both."

"I love you, too. By the way, borrow that red sundress from my closet for wherever Paddy is planning for you."

Ezra waited for her downstairs. He took her duffel and then the large kit that held all her work tools and supplies for the pieces she needed to work on that night. She didn't argue; they were heavy and he liked to lug stuff around for her.

"See you guys later." She waved and Nat blew her a kiss.

CHAPTER TWENTY-ONE

THEY'D MADE DINNER together in his kitchen. They worked well as a team even though she spoiled the animals as badly as he did, tossing cubes of ham for the omelet he was about to make for them to Goldfish, who loved her best and got quite pissy when Tuesday didn't visit regularly.

They'd eaten it out on his back deck and now she'd ensconced herself at the large worktable in his office, creating a bracelet of some sort.

Music played in the background—and thank goodness she loved music as much as he did—and furry creatures passed through the space from time to time. He puzzled through a spreadsheet for the ranch on the other side of the large room they currently shared.

It worked. Normally it took effort to be around people. He constantly had to measure his responses to those outside his very small circle of family and friends. He didn't need that with her. She didn't need his attention every moment. Though, he thought with a snort, she pretty much had it. She took up his thoughts all day long.

She worked with an intensity he respected because he saw it in himself and his brothers. Adjusting, tightening, loosening, she tinkered until it was right. It fascinated him and made her so beautiful to his gaze.

Even better, she'd changed into her pajamas, which were little more than boy short panties and a T-shirt with a ferret dressed like a ninja on it. All sorts of skin was exposed to his gaze. The strong curve of each calf, the power of her thighs, that breathtaking dip after the swell of her hips and then, the breasts. She had no bra on so the outline of her nipples was visible through the material.

He loved her neck and shoulders. Breathtaking femininity flowed through the harder outline of muscles put there by a woman who enjoyed using her body. Who pushed herself. Her throat, where he knew her pulse beat strong and her scent lingered as if it waited just for him.

Her lips, pursed as she worked on something very detailed, drew his attention next. She'd taken her makeup off and it didn't matter because she was gorgeous either way.

She wore glasses while she worked, but this pair was sturdier than her day-to-day pair. They magnified the lush, dark sweep of her lashes and the dark brown eyes.

He smiled at the scarf she had wrapped around her head, the puff of her curls coming out the top.

This Tuesday was totally relaxed. It warmed him that she'd feel safe enough with him to let her guard down this way.

He worked for a while longer before he allowed himself to look at her again and this time she was looking right back.

"You must like what you see, mister. You sure are looking over my way a lot."

He grinned. "I most definitely like what I see. I'd

give it five stars any day of the week. I'm sorry. I know you're trying to work."

She stood and walked to him. He swiveled his chair to take in the full majesty of the way she moved, her attention totally on him, the left side of her mouth quirked up.

Tuesday climbed into his lap, straddling him and wrapping her arms around his neck. "I can take a break."

"This day keeps getting better and better." He palmed her breasts through her shirt and she pressed into his touch.

"Now I guess I'm interrupting your work."

"Whatever shall I do about that?"

"Maybe I might need a little correction."

She undulated her hips, brushing herself against his cock as she said it and he saw spots for a moment. Probably because all the blood in his brain rushed to his lap.

She leaned her upper body back and whipped her shirt off. He banded an arm around her waist and hauled her close for a kiss.

He made a sound in his chest. Bone-deep pleasure at her taste, at her weight in his lap, at the heat of her skin seeping through his own shirt.

But mostly, as happened every time, it was a sound of appreciation at the way she bared herself to him totally when they had sex. She demanded what she wanted. Took it if it pleased her. Made him deliver it in whatever way she liked.

She thought that it was he who held the power because he liked to hold her wrists or be in charge.

He might have been in charge, but she was the

one who held the power because he'd have done anything for her. Anything. Because she'd given herself so frankly.

He slid his mouth down her throat and gasped at her whispered plea.

He stood, giving her a moment to wrap herself around him before he headed to his room. Animals scattered, excited by movement.

Ezra cursed as a cat nearly got squashed, though fortunately he kept them from sprawling.

He put her down before he dropped her. "Come on."

She took his hand and he led her upstairs, across the landing and then pointed to a ladder. "Up."

No animals up here. Just a reading loft he escaped to.

"Wow." She looked around at the soft couch and chairs, the shelves full of books and the skylight overhead. "This is such a treat. I love this."

"So you said you wanted to see if you liked rug burn." He pushed the sleep pants he'd been wearing down, freeing his cock. "Let's test it out."

She dropped to her knees, set her glasses on a nearby table and went to it with such zeal and skill he nearly came the first five minutes.

He wanted to come so much. It felt so good with her right then. But he wanted it to last, too. He fought himself as she took him closer, her nails scoring down the backs of his legs and up again, then over the back of his balls which sent a hard slice of pleasure through him.

Right on the very edge, he stepped back, his hand at her shoulder. "Remember, I like to come in you

best. It's your turn now. Jesus, Tuesday, you're killing me."

She was. Still kneeling. Topless. Moonlight on her
skin. Her nipples drawn up into hard, dark beads. Her
luscious lips swollen and slick from sucking him off.

He stepped from his pants and sat on the low, wide
couch. "Come here."

He'd been up there just the night before and it had
occurred to him he should show Tuesday the loft and
if they got up there one thing could easily lead to another with them so he'd put a few condoms in a container on a side table.

He rolled the condom on, nearly choking when she
decided to obey his call to come to him by crawling on
hands and knees, juicy ass swaying from side to side.

When she reached the couch, she stood, discarded
her panties and climbed up onto him but he stopped
her from putting his cock inside.

"We need to make you ready. What sort of guy
would I be if I didn't make extra sure you were nice
and wet?"

He slid a fingertip through her pussy. She was hot
and slick. Both of them groaned as he fluttered over
her clit.

Her tortured plea broke over him like a wave of
sex. The fingers he'd had on her nipple tightened as
he tugged just a little harder.

She writhed. *"Yes."*

His cock was so hard right then it was as if every
pulse beat was a hammer.

On his lap she was fire wrapped in velvet.

He collared her throat as he squeezed her clit gently and she cried out, coming in a hot rush.

That's when he found her entrance and pressed into her body hard and deep, the heat of her, the embrace of muscles still twitching and contracting after a climax, welcomed him and sank its nails into his belly, dragging him right to the edge of climax yet again.

But he needed her to go again first. He wanted to make her feel so good every time they were together he'd be burned into her memory. His touch would obliterate anyone who came before. He yearned for more of that sound she made when he hit just the right spot deep inside.

She made it and his fingers at her hip tightened.

She made it again.

"I need you to come again. Selfishly, you feel really good around me when I come. But I also love to watch when you climax. Perfection. And I think you should do it because my hands are full." He nipped her bottom lip and she shivered.

And then slid her hand down her belly to the place they were joined.

His gaze followed and then he devoured every move she made, watching greedily as she drove herself into another orgasm, taking him along with her.

She slumped against him, her head on his shoulder. He kissed her neck, picking her up and cleaning himself off before snuggling with her again.

"I'm never going to read up here again without having to jerk off."

She laughed. "If you'd like, we can christen every room in your house this way."

"What I'd like to know is who *wouldn't* like that?" He kissed her again.

"There's a sound that I think might be a cat trying to climb up a ladder."

He didn't have time to answer before Peanut bounded over the edge and landed, chittering a greeting as she hopped up onto the back of the couch and curled around Ezra's head.

"Honestly, I can't have you to myself anywhere." Tuesday stood, pulling her panties back on. "Your other fans are not happy you've retreated." She peered below. "Goldfish is pissed off. Loopy, well, I'm pretty sure she'd have that same sweet face no matter what."

"Come on. We'll go back. I'll let you work awhile before we go for round two."

Even better, she didn't put her shirt back on the whole rest of the night.

ONE THING TUESDAY had discovered about Ezra was that he, too, seemed to have issues with insomnia, though his seemed less severe. On average she got about five hours a night. Sometimes she napped. Sometimes she tried not to nap to make herself tired.

She'd tried sleeping pills but they'd made the nightmares come back and she'd rather have insomnia than relive all the shittiest moments of her life over and over.

So she was up and working for several hours before the sun began to rise. She'd let Loopy out and she and the cats had come to an agreement that they'd be allowed in the room with her when she worked but only if they stayed away from her table. Most of the time they obeyed.

Ezra shuffled in at just before five. "How long have you been awake?"

"A little while."

She moved to him, loving the sleep-warm embrace he gave her. "Morning. How long has it been that you've had trouble sleeping?"

"On and off since the accident when I was a kid. And then after Eric got sick it came back in full force. I've lived on three hours a night. It's better now." With him she rested.

He looked at her carefully and then kissed her forehead. "What helps?"

"It's one of the reasons I like to be physically active. I sleep best after a really full day. Anyway, you don't sleep much, either."

He shook his head. "No. I spent a lot of time totally out of it. My chemistry is messed up even now. But like you, I sleep better after I've had a really hard workout. Which bodes well since a certain gorgeous woman has kept me very busy. Now, speaking of that, I owe you breakfast for several hours of incredibly fun playdate last night." He kissed her and she laughed.

"Ooh good. I'm hungry. And I need coffee. I did make some tea so there's hot water."

She followed him out of the office, closing the door to felines who wanted to test the mettle of her resolve to keep them out if they broke her rules.

"She's on to you," he told the cats as he opened the curtains off the kitchen to flood the room in morning light.

Tuesday made coffee while Ezra made a huge stack of blueberry pancakes.

It was easy, this rhythm. It fit into her life without feeling intrusive.

"I'll take you down to your gallery or to your

house. Whichever you need," he said after they'd cleaned up and were headed out to take her back to town.

"Home, please. I'll drop this stuff off."

"So, HERE'S WHAT I was thinking," he said as they parked in her driveway and he'd keyed the car off.

"Uh-oh."

He grinned. "Hush. What time do you have to be at your stall in Portland tomorrow?"

"Nine. I leave here at seven-fifteen or so. It gives me time to find a place to park and get my stuff set up. I think Natalie and Paddy are driving up after she gets finished at the library. You can catch a ride with them and I'll meet you at my parents' house."

"I was thinking I'd go with you in the morning. Help you set your stall up. I could stay if you needed it, but if you don't I've got a number of things I need to do in Portland. My accountant is there and I have to pick up a jacket that you probably don't even care about. Anyway, I have errands so I'll do those and come back when you're ready to go and head to your family's place."

"Is your accountant open on Saturday?"

"My accountant is open whenever I need him to be." He shrugged.

"When you get all arrogant like that? It makes my nipples rock-hard."

"Why do you tell me this stuff when my brother is standing on your porch and I have to get back to deal with alfalfa and alfalfa-related issues?"

She leaned over, kissing him soundly as she ignored Paddy, who was indeed on her porch. "Because

I'm a villain. Okay, you can come with me to Portland if you really want to. Thank you."

"It'll be easiest if you sleep at my place, don't you think? Then we can head out from there? How about I come over after work and we can load whatever you need into my truck? I'll have it in the garage all night so it'll be safe."

"It seems like a lot of work for you. And getting up really early."

"I'm a farmer. I'm up early every day." And it seemed he liked taking care of her, even if he didn't say it out loud. Oh, and the fact that he was a control freak and if she was at his house he'd have more control.

"Okay then. I'm not arguing. I'll see you tonight?"

"Yes. Call me when you lock up. I'll meet you here after that."

She nodded and he and Loopy both got out to walk her to the door. Paddy clutched a mug of coffee and tipped a chin at his brother and winked to Tuesday. "Morning. Tuesday, how you manage to look so good this early in the morning I don't know. But you made my day."

She laughed. "You Hurleys are so full of it. I like it."

She kissed Ezra and waved goodbye before heading inside.

Smiling.

Natalie came into the kitchen wearing a robe. "Hey."

"Hey, yourself. You look like someone who came a lot last night." Natalie smirked as she poured a cup of coffee.

"Takes one to know one. Not like it's a complaint. I have to run to work now. Ezra's taking me to Portland tomorrow morning and he's driving up with me when I close up so you two don't have to give him a ride."

"No kidding. Did you ever think Ezra was going to ride with us when you were going to be alone in another car? Are you new here?"

Tuesday ducked her head. "I like it, okay? I don't know if it's okay to like it, but I do, so there. I like that he wants to make things easier for me. He does it without weakening me. He respects my abilities."

No time to think about that stuff right then. "I have to run. I'm spending the night at his house so I may not see you until tomorrow at Easton central."

"I'll probably see you tonight then. Why don't we all do something? Mexican food and a movie?"

"Works for me. Have the menfolk figure out the details."

"We should also finish the conversation we started last night in your room. I'm sorry it made you upset right before you left. It was bad timing."

Tuesday had no plans to go back to that convo anytime soon. She needed to digest stuff for a while.

"Maybe. Anyway, no need to apologize for caring about me."

After one last hug, Tuesday put her stuff away and headed into town.

CHAPTER TWENTY-TWO

EZRA'S PHONE RANG once he'd dropped Tuesday off and helped her set up. She'd looked so fantastic he really hadn't wanted to leave. But his accountant had invited him over for breakfast so he'd given her one last kiss—in full view of that dude hawking funky wind chimes who'd been staring at Tuesday—and headed out to the suburbs.

He punched the button on his steering wheel to answer.

"Hey, Ez, it's Jeremy. Did I catch you at a bad time?" Jeremy had been the band's manager for nearly all their career. The successful parts, anyway, which was what counted.

"No. I'm in a Portland traffic snarl trying to get out to my accountant's house. He'll get those papers to you after I sign them today."

"Excellent. Not the traffic part, but as I'm sitting in traffic trying to get to the airport to come up to Seattle, I can commiserate. I wanted to see if you had some time coming up. Maybe we can head up to Vancouver for a few days. It's been a long time."

He and Jeremy had been close once. Like brothers. And then Jeremy had lost his child to a terrible tragedy and within a year afterward, his marriage had also died. And then there'd been drugs that had torn through Ezra's life.

Both of them had to dig out of a metric fuckton of pain and they'd grown apart.

But that friendship had never died.

He asked Ezra to do things all the time and Ezra usually shied away, though he did have Jeremy come stay at his house when he was up with his other north-west clients—notably Adrian Brown, mega superstar rock phenomenon who lived in Washington with his family.

Adrian had been another close friend once. Ezra hadn't had the courage to try and rebuild their previous closeness. Maybe he needed to change that.

"We're bringing the alfalfa in next week. When are you going to be able to get away?"

"I'm going to a high school graduation. Adrian's oldest, Miles. And then I'll be in Bainbridge Island for a week or so and then I'm coming down to you all. I'll stay in Portland. I want to meet with the band, talk about the tour. I just got a bundle of stuff I need to go over on the plane. But you broke some records this tour. Label is thrilled. They want to talk new material and some box-set proposals. Let's say two weeks or so from now. A week after your harvest."

Ezra heard the pleased note in Jeremy's tone. It had been too long since he'd hung out with anyone but his family and more recently Tuesday. That had been good. So good it reminded him there were other relationships that once had been good in his life. And to get something else to focus on to figure this thing out with Tuesday.

"All right then. It'll be quiet for a few weeks after

we bring the alfalfa in. Then my dad will take over and get it where it needs to go. You sure you want to hang out with me for two days in another country when I might bore you to death with farm talk and you don't have a drinking partner?"

Jeremy's startled laugh made Ezra grin.

"It's been way too long, Ez. I'm sure we can eat harder now that drinking hard isn't on our dance card. I'll call you next week to coordinate when I'll be down your way. Wrangle your brothers if you can, please."

They hung up and Ezra remembered he needed to call Vaughan, too. Maybe he'd check in after finishing up with the accountant. He could swing out to Gresham and still get back to Tuesday in time.

There'd been a need to remove himself to get better. But he'd still had shame at what he'd done back then. Who he'd been. And that had kept him estranged from a lot of people. All that seemed to be changing and it was good. It felt awesome to be reconnecting with parts of his life from before that were good and right.

Which scared him because it all came bundled up with the entirety of change in his life he tried to work through. Mainly the Tuesday part.

He had to pull over about three blocks from his accountant's house. Leaning his head against the steering wheel.

It had been right and necessary to apologize to people when he'd got clean.

He'd reconnected with many of his friends but rebuilding had taken a lot of energy. So he'd started at home, where it was necessary to concentrate. And now, after five years, he'd been able to regain the trust of his brothers and parents. He'd shown fans and the label that he was all about the music once more.

But there had been friendships like the one he'd shared with Jeremy that he'd been scared to face. What he'd done, who he'd been, haunted Ezra even to that very moment.

But then Tuesday had shown up and the way he'd wanted her had overruled any fear or discomfort at pursuing something more than a few sessions in the bedroom and boom out the door.

The way they'd slow danced toward where they stood at the moment had been a big part of why he hadn't kept her away from the start. But now, after the way he'd felt the day of her party, he knew there was no hiding from the intensity of what he felt for her. And after years when all his most intense feelings were negative, feeling so good made him panic. He didn't know how to judge if it was an okay sort of happy.

Baby steps. That's what he needed to do.

He looked in the mirror quickly, finger combing his hair and getting himself together. He was stronger than this. Better than this.

"I'm ferocious. I'm dark and broody and broken," he whispered as he pulled back into traffic.

SHE SAT IN the cab of his truck and hid her smile. That morning he'd nervously asked if he should have come back to the ranch to get his Porsche instead of taking the truck to her parents' house. He was so ridiculously sweet.

"I didn't expect to see Vaughan there today," Ezra spoke, interrupting her thoughts.

He'd come with Kelly about half an hour before Ezra showed up. Then when he'd gone off with Vaughan for a few minutes, she'd finally had the chance to speak to Kelly in private to ask her for an update.

And then it had got really busy and they'd ended up selling every last piece so Vaughan and Kelly went home when Tuesday and Ezra left and Tuesday had barely had three minutes to talk with Kelly alone to get an update on what was happening.

"Me, either. He looks good, though. Like he's maybe gained a few pounds. She always looks fantastic. Do you hope they reconcile?"

"Kelly and Vaughan are a good example of what happens when love isn't enough. She's two years younger than him, but really, until maybe three years or so ago, she was far more mature. When she got pregnant it was like some switch got thrown. You could see the difference. He didn't change. It was ugly and awful and it broke my heart because all these years she's been raising them every day. He's a spectator and sometime participant in his children's lives. And he made that choice. So now he's grown and matured and understands what he gave up. He can look at the entire situation and know he's got no one to blame but himself. He can't ever go back and undo it. That's a heavy load."

"There are second chances, you know."

"How can you be so sure?"

"I've given second chances. I've been given second chances. She's changed, too. She's not that twenty-three-year-old who didn't know if she could survive without him. She did. And she thrived. She's got a great life and Vaughan isn't the only man who loves her."

He was quiet a long time and then her phone rang. "Gotta take this—it's Di." She swiped a finger to answer the call. "Hey, Mom. I have the naan."

"Oh good." There was a lot of noise in the background.

"I take it the house is full already?"

"Lord above. Both your brothers are here. All the boys and Sadie, too." Sadie was her seven-year-old niece and the boys most likely meant GJ and his wife Alana's oldest, Darius, who was ten, and Shawn's twins, Alonzo and Adam, with his wife, Tisha.

"I'm bummed we didn't bring Ezra's dog. She'd be in heaven with all those kids." Loopy would love the big backyard and running around with all the laughing, playing kids would make her day.

"Next time. Did he bring his guitar?"

"Mom, we talked about this."

"What? Just talk to him about it. Did you talk to him about it yet? Just one song. Surely he wouldn't deny my request."

"Diana Robinson Easton, don't even try that with me." But Tuesday knew it was a lost cause. Her mother would be dead set now.

"GJ agreed to play the bass."

"Okay, well we'll be there in a few minutes. Ezra is getting off the freeway now. Do you need us to stop and get anything else? Do you have enough to drink?"

"We don't have any alcohol in the house."

She'd already spoken to her mother about the situation. Tuesday knew they'd find out easily about the heroin and rehab so she preempted all that by getting it all out in the open. She'd also told her mother Ezra wouldn't care if anyone had a beer, though they didn't drink much except for a glass of champagne at New Year's Eve and the occasional glass of wine from that box that'd been in the fridge at least five years, probably more.

But there was no use saying anything else about it. "Okay. I'm hanging up now so I can give Ezra directions. See you soon." Ezra had GPS of course, but her mother didn't need to know that.

He didn't say anything for a moment. Waiting.

"So when I was a kid growing up my family had a band. Nothing like what you guys have obviously."

"Why didn't you tell me before now?"

"It's a silly thing my family did on weekends for about a decade when I was growing up. When we all spend holidays together there's singing. But they don't have a piano—my mom plays the rhythm guitar."

"Did you think I'd mock it?" She'd hurt his feelings, damn it.

"No. Not like that at all." She turned to him. They didn't have much time because her dad was going to want to get judging Ezra right away. "I'm telling you now because this is the first time you're meeting them and my mother brought it up right now on the phone. I'd never think you would mock my family. That's my job anyway."

He nodded. "I think it's awesome. My dad loves *listening* to music but he isn't musical. My great-grandmother was a torch singer apparently. She and her sister and brother had a three-piece band and they played all over the South for like twenty years in bars and small theaters. But nothing else after that until our generation."

Aww, man those Hurleys were adorable. Good lord.

Still Tuesday winced as she told him the rest. "She's going to ask you to jam. I'm just warning you. I'm going to try to head her off, but, well you'll meet her."

Ezra's features lit with delight as he grinned. "Tuesday, I'd love to jam with your mom. You have no idea."

"She's going to make you play Alabama Shakes. It's her favorite right now."

"Works for me. What do you play then?"

"Do we have to? I'm really not very good."

"I beg to differ. You're very, very good."

When he dropped his guard and teased like that—intimate stuff he'd only say to her—it made her crazy for him. The way she needed him hit her hard, crawled over her skin until she itched to touch, to nibble, to be held down and loved the way he did it.

"You still have to tell me, though."

She sighed. It wasn't like he wouldn't figure it out when her mother herded them all into the garage and she got behind the drums.

"Drums. Turn left up here at the light."

He did and she kept looking at him. "A word of warning about Di Easton. She's sneaky. My dad is a typical dad. He's going to look you over and be scary for a few minutes. Are you sure you want to do this?"

"Stop being nervous. I won't fart or pick my nose in front of them. I promise."

She rolled her eyes. "She's a master. I'm just saying."

"Sounds like she and Sharon will get along just fine."

"Probably. They'd either love each other immediately or hate each other on sight. They're both women like that." She blew out a breath. "Up there on the left."

He whipped around and parked at the curb. "Doesn't look like Paddy and Nat are here yet."

"She said she wanted to stop in downtown for something first. Plus she'll want me to get all the attention and they haven't seen her in months."

He leaned over and kissed her quick. "You have good taste in friends."

"I really do. Paddy is very lucky Natalie loves him. Though he does seem to make her really happy, which is why I haven't maimed him for making her cry those few times."

"He was scared. But they'll get through it all. He loves her to his bones. He made mistakes and acted like a dick. But he figured it out and now that he's truly chosen her, he'll be about her happiness always. Once they fall for real, Hurleys don't play around."

They looked at one another in the dying light filtered through his windshield. He laid himself bare for her in that moment, even if he didn't know he'd done it. He was scared, too. Like Paddy had been.

Between Ezra and Tuesday lay a twisty, complicated road full of potential hazards. The two of them carried a lot of baggage. So much it would get in the way at times. If the other person was also having a rough time they'd butt heads when they were both vulnerable.

The power of that, the ability to either open your

heart a little more and dig a little deep for patience to ride something out and get to the other side stronger. Or the circumstances leaving you worn out and agitated at the worst possible point.

That's what a relationship was. An agreement to navigate all that twisty bullshit that could sink everything.

"This is going to be fine," he said, kissing her fingertips.

She had to hope so because she was in love with him. "It will. You'll like them. They'll like you."

And then her phone rang. She picked up, thinking it was her mother. "We're right at the curb. Jeez, let us get out before we can get to the front door."

But it wasn't Di, as Tuesday figured out as the screeching began and she realized it was Tina again.

"If you don't stop yelling, I'm going to hang up."

Tina didn't hear, or didn't care because she kept yelling about Tuesday changing her name.

"Hanging up now. I'll tell my mom you said hello."

Tuesday not only hung up, but she finally did what Natalie had urged her to and blocked the number.

She tried to get out but he made a sound and she slumped back into the seat.

"You want to tell me what the hell that was about?"

She actually didn't. But he asked her to share. She wanted him to, so if that was the case, she figured she needed to, as well.

"That was my former mother-in-law. She's upset I'm changing my name back to Easton."

He paused and she realized he wasn't that comfortable with it, either.

Hmm.

"I should probably explain some of this backstory. Eric wasn't close with his family, though he wanted to be. A lot."

She filled in the details about the original name change and why she was going back, trying to edit carefully around the parts where it was clear he'd had some part in her decision-making because she didn't want him to feel bad or guilty or even uncomfortable.

It was her life and she made the choice for lots of reasons and that was that.

"You blocked them, though? Just now? I don't like this woman acting this way to you. Who the hell does she think she is?"

"Yes, I blocked her number. She'll find another way to get in touch when she next decides to." She shrugged.

"Why didn't you tell me?"

She sighed, turning to face him. "Lots of reasons. One is, she's awful and who wants that in their life? I didn't want to bring that to you. Second? You seem a little nervous about me, about being in a relationship with me, so I kept it to myself. Because it's my choice, Ezra."

"I'm not nervous about you, Tuesday."

"Bullshit. You're scared of me and of this intensity between us. It's okay. I'm trying to give you the space to deal with it. But that doesn't include pretending it's not there."

He was quiet for some time, taking it in.

"We need to go inside. My parents know we're here. Please don't tell them about this mess with the Heywoods. Oh god, or the feed store debacle."

"This isn't over. I want to talk about it more. Why

can't I tell them? You haven't told them, either? Not about the feed store or your in-laws?"

Tuesday laughed. "Ezra Hurley, you're such a fibber. You do not want to talk about this more. But we will. Just not right now. And my mother and Tina are not friends. If I told them about this, it would only make them both upset and they can't do a thing to help. Same with the feed store. This is not a new experience for any of us. It would only upset them and they can't do a thing about that situation, either."

He kissed her hard. "Fine. But you should tell them yourself at some point. If these people hurt you again, I'm going to show them just how displeased I am. You get me?"

"Yeah."

HE RAN AROUND to open her door and her father, who'd been watching from their bedroom window on the second floor, would have put that in the plus column.

Ezra would be fine. He'd charm her mother and her mother would charm him. Her family would like him. Natalie would be there shortly to buffer anytime things got annoying. And at the end of the night she'd escape, jump Ezra a few times in a hotel room. It was good incentive to get this in motion.

Tuesday opened the storm door and knocked while she pushed into the house. "Hey, all, I'm home!"

Her mother came in with a big smile. She wore an apron Tuesday and April had made for a Mother's Day present what seemed like a million years ago. At her ears were the delicate tree-of-life dangles she'd given her mother for Christmas the year before.

Her hair had been pulled into twists and the similarity between them was sort of scary for just a second.

And then it was just…wonderful. This was what her family was underneath all the stuff that made her crazy.

"Baby girl! Come over here and hug me."

Tuesday did as she was told, smiling behind her mom's back to her brother Shawn, who stood in the hall.

"Well, come on in here and meet the boy." Tuesday waved a hand at Ezra, who grinned and looked ridiculously handsome.

"Ezra Hurley, this is my mother, Diana Easton."

Ezra took her hand in both of his. "It's a pleasure to meet you, Mrs. Easton. Thanks for inviting me tonight."

Di looked to her daughter. "You're right. This is the single finest beard I've ever beheld."

"Don't be jealous, now, that you don't have a mother who blurts things like that." Greg Jr. came in. He hugged Tuesday and held out a hand for Ezra to shake.

Ezra chuckled. "Ezra Hurley, nice to meet you. I do actually have a mother who is a lot like yours."

"Ezra, this is my brother Greg, but everyone calls him GJ." Shawn came in. "And this is another brother, Shawn."

There was handshaking and looking over and they went through to the kitchen where her mother put the flowers they'd brought in water.

More introductions were made to her sisters-in-law and then the kids. Tuesday got them both a glass of iced tea and then her father rolled in.

Greg Easton was a barrel-chested man. His hair, what little there was left, was gray at the temples. He was six feet tall and when she'd been a little girl her dad's hands had seemed big enough to battle monsters on her behalf.

He pulled her into a big hug. "Happy birthday, sweetie pie."

She hugged him back. "Thanks, Dad."

It was good to be there. That feeling would wear off as the night went on, but for that moment, she was glad to be there in the kitchen she'd grown up in, surrounded by people who cared about her, about to eat a seriously delicious dinner her mother most likely spent most of the day making.

"I'm Greg Easton." He held out a hand to Ezra, who took it, and they had some sort of shake that she hoped wasn't too loose or too tight or whatever her father deemed less than acceptable.

"Ezra Hurley. Thank you for having me in your home, sir."

"Our daughter wanted you here. Walk with me, son, and we'll talk about what that means."

"Dad. No. Come on. This is silly."

Ezra kissed her temple. "We'll be back."

"Mmm. Well now, that boy is a tasty bite." Her mother watched them walk away. "Ezra, too," her mother said with a wink when she turned back around.

"Nat will be here soon. She stopped at Radiance for her favorite shampoo. If you like that brother wait till you see her version. In my opinion, I have the superior model, but hers sure isn't a chore to look at."

"It's been way too long since you've been here."

Her mother's gaze narrowed, taking her daughter in. "Come along then." With a very Di flourish, she turned and headed to the stove where multiple things were bubbling and smelling really yummy.

Shawn snorted. "You look good, Tuesday. You're dating a rock star."

"He's a rancher mostly, but yeah, sometimes during the year he's also a rock star. They're all pretty normal, but you see them onstage and it's mind-blowing."

They walked in their mother's wake, not keeping her waiting once she'd delivered an edict that they follow her to the stove.

"He's white," Shawn said.

"Oh my god!" She paused, slapping a hand over her heart. "He is?"

Her mother chuckled.

Tuesday held a finger up. "I'll continue in a second but for this moment I need to smell stuff." She closed her eyes and sucked in a deep breath. "I am going to get a gold medal in eating my dinner tonight."

She looked back to Shawn. "Is that a problem? Ezra being white? Like your wife is white?"

He flipped her off out of their mother's line of sight. "So listen to me because I know what I'm talking about maybe? Such a brat."

She mouthed, *suck it,* and he rolled his eyes.

"I just want you to be careful. Our biggest challenge is how people might react at the kids' school or whatever. With you two? This guy is in the public eye. That means a lot of attention and some of it won't be pretty. I'm worried about you."

This moment only underlined why she hadn't mentioned the situation with the feed store and wanted to spare them the Heywood stuff. Though Tina might think to call Tuesday's siblings as she had before so maybe she should warn them off.

Tuesday would bring it up with Nat later to see what she thought.

"Thank you. I'm sorry I was bratty. You're right. We get a little attention. He doesn't notice because I think he's used to being looked at a lot anyway."

Her mother's knowing laugh broke the last bit of tension left in the room.

GJ handed her an envelope. Inside was a rather sizeble check.

"Um, I think you added a few zeros too many. I'll take your money, no lie, but not this much of it."

He whacked the back of her head. "You kidding me? I don't have that kind of cash to be giving you for your birthday. I got a kid with braces. *It's yours.* When Eric died you got a check from one of the policies he had. Remember? It was for a few thousand bucks. I took it and invested it. That's what it's all worth now."

This money in her hand would enable her to put in the new display cases for her pieces at the gallery. She could afford to play around with some of the stones she'd dreamed of for some more expensive pieces. And she could get her transmission fixed. Even after she paid off bills she'd have a little left to put back into savings.

She hugged him. "You're awesome. Thank you so much."

He grinned when she let him go, a little embarrassed at the edges. "It's my job as your big brother. That's all. Don't get tears on my shirt."

"Sure."

Shawn bumped her with his hip. "Tell us about this new gallery thing."

"Boys, watch that rice. I need to have a chat with Tuesday." Her mother waved a wooden spoon and GJ stepped in to take it. Alana and Tisha came in with the kids so there were more hugs and kisses before her mother just sort of steamrollered the two of them out of the kitchen and into the sunroom beyond.

"Oh hey, new curtains."

"Your father has decided he doesn't need to wear any pants on the weekends. It was a way to save the neighbors the sight of his boxers at three in the afternoon as they tried to barbecue."

After they'd stopped laughing, Di took her daughter by the upper arms and held her still while she examined Tuesday's face.

"Tell me about him."

"I don't think I'd have enough time even if I was staying until next week. He makes me feel again. In that romantic way. He's a good man."

"A heroin addict."

"Someone knows how to use the internet."

Her mother's brows flew up. "Don't you sass me."

"I'm sorry. I told you he was in rehab for heroin and alcohol. He went in—he did his time. He does his work to stay clean. He is solid."

"And his lifestyle?"

She laughed. "Mom, he takes in foster pigs, for goodness' sake! He doesn't have a wild lifestyle unless you count riding horses to look at trees and talk about bud cycles. He's up before dawn most days because he runs a ranch. A successful ranch. He made a mistake. That mistake stole years from him. Friendships. His career. He's spent his life since making things right. No one holds Ezra more responsible for what he did then than Ezra. Believe me. You think I have guilt issues? He makes me look like an amateur."

"I'm not sure I believe there are people who take on guilt for things they didn't even do more than you. I'll have to know Ezra a lot longer before I can agree with you. I don't have much longer before we get interrupted. Your father likes him."

"How can you tell?"

"I've been married to the man a long time. He has three basic settings. When he went off with Ezra he was smiling. He likes the boy."

"Smiling? He was doing a flinty-eyed not-smile!"

Her mother waved a hand. "He didn't mean it. It didn't reach his eyes. What did you do outside? He was watching probably. He's been lurking around peeking out the windows to see if you'd arrived yet."

"He was up in your bedroom when Ezra opened my door."

Her mother laughed and laughed. "Nice."

Back when her older sister, April, had been in high school she'd dated a boy who, upon dropping her off, did not walk her to the door, instead parking out front and then pulling away before she'd even got in the house. That boy was never allowed near April after that. Not that her sister would have stayed with a guy like him, but it was sort of family mythology at that point.

Her mother pressed a small box into her hands. "Happy birthday."

Tuesday tugged on the ribbon and pulled the lid

free, finding her great-grandmother's ruby brooch inside.

"I thought about giving this to you when you got married. But it wasn't the right time. And then I wondered if it might coax you back from that place you went after Eric died. There have been four other birthdays since then and I have had this box waiting. I wasn't even sure I was going to give this to you today until you spoke about Ezra just now. You're in love. Today is the right time. She'd want you to have it."

She swallowed hard and looked up at her mother. "Am I that obvious then?"

Her mother cupped one of Tuesday's cheeks briefly. "Only to me. You're scared?"

"Yes. Oh god, yes. I love him. I can't deny it. But it's so complicated and big and both of us are weird and messed up and I'm trying to take it day by day so I can deal."

"Not how love works, darling. But you know that." An elegant shrug Tuesday had been imitating for years but never got as perfect as her mother did. "You can't pretend love away. Love is a force capable of breaking through just about anything. Tell me a reason why you love him."

There were so many, Tuesday realized as she thought about it. "When I'm with him he gives me all his attention. It's rather overwhelming."

"But it makes you feel special."

"Dad does that? To you I mean."

Her mother nodded. "The first time I met him he looked at me like I was the only person in the room. If anyone else had looked at me like that I would have been uncomfortable. But it was all right because it felt

to me like he got to because he understood me. It's
not only important to be understood by your man, it's
integral. Eric never understood you."

It hit like a slap and Tuesday took two steps away.

Her mother waited for Tuesday to be ready to listen again before speaking. "I don't want to upset you.
I'm sorry to have to say all this but you need to hear
it. Eric didn't understand you. He loved you, lord
yes. And you loved him and it was right and good
that you two were together. This is different and I
expect you're panicking. Always feeling guilty over
things when you were little, too. Tell me honestly,
does Ezra understand you? Oh, he's a man so you'll
need to give him a shove in the right direction sometimes. Mostly, when you're with him do you feel like
he's there for you, for the real Tuesday you are with
me or with Natalie? Do you feel like he sees all your
cracks and breaks and accepts them? Because that's
what you should demand. You're worth that sort of
understanding. You get to move on. You have *every
right* to do that."

A loud hail of hellos meant Natalie had arrived.
Her mother took the brooch out and pinned it to Tuesday's blouse. "Aletha Howard was a strong woman
and the man who gave her this saved every single
spare penny he could until he could buy it. It took him
three years. And he came to her and asked her if he
could court her. He said this brooch was his pledge
that she was worth more than diamonds to him and
that he'd put her first for the rest of his life. He was
ninety-three when he died. Just three months after
she did. This magic is what you need."

One last kiss on her forehead and her mother swatted her butt. "Now get in there before your brothers corner Natalie's boy and give him too much big brother attention."

Still reeling from all her mother had said, Tuesday put a smile on her face and walked out to see her family.

"HAVE A SEAT." Greg pointed at a recliner chair, a twin of the one at its side. Both pointed at a pretty fantastic media setup.

Despite how Tuesday had described this space, it didn't seem grungy to Ezra at all. "How does that surround sound handle the acoustics in here?"

"We added special insulation. I told my wife it would make her music sound better when she practiced." Greg shrugged with a wink. "You're seeing my daughter and you have quite a checkered history. You probably understand why I'm concerned about you."

"I can respect that, yes, sir. I made mistakes. Big ones. I don't make those mistakes anymore. I've been clean since I left sober living and I have no plans to ever change that."

"My daughter is far too precious to me to be exposed to any of that filth. She's had a hard enough time in her life. You will not be allowed to bring her heartache."

Ezra realized that if he handled this wrong he'd have an excuse to break off with Tuesday. He didn't entirely know how to process all his feelings about that night's events. Or that she'd known him so fucking well and called him out on his hesitance at letting her get too close.

But he chose otherwise. "Sir."

Greg held up a hand. "Greg, please."

"Greg, as your daughter told me a few weeks ago, we're bound to bring one another heartache from time to time because that's how it works when you're in a relationship. I'm a novice at relationships—I admit it. But never in my life until the moment I met your daughter in September, have I felt such a pull toward someone."

"You're very different, you and my Tuesday."

"Yes. But where it counts we're alike. We've both got our share of past heartaches. I care about her. I want to protect her. But Tuesday is her own person. She's capable of making her own happy ending. I just try to keep up."

Greg paused, clearly thinking. "You're in love with my daughter."

Ezra sucked in a breath. "I know for sure no one captivates me the way she does. I admire her and respect her. I don't want to be her life—I want to be part of it. That's enough for right now."

Greg nodded, having understood what Ezra had just said. And what he hadn't.

"So this music business. It keeps your bills paid? Living like a college student is one thing when you're in college. But neither of you are."

Greg Easton and Michael Hurley were going to love each other.

"I still have a percentage in Sweet Hollow Ranch. I don't go out on the road so they split the tour revenue between themselves, but I write, record and produce each album. And I run the ranch, which runs at a profit, though a far more modest one than music makes. It's enough to keep the lights on and my animals fed."

"You're rich."

Ezra laughed. "Filthy. Wasn't always so. We came to Oregon from Kentucky when I was very young. We lived in a camper trailer at first while my parents worked the land and built the house. Over the years as we became successful we all chipped in and bought more land around our original plot and now all four of us live on the land in our own houses. Sweet Hollow Ranch is our home. That place we all return to over and over because in the end it's not the size of your bank account that makes you happiest. But it sure helps when you have the ability to replace broken things before you've received payment for a crop of pears."

"I know you don't drink, but one of my daughters-in-law brought me some cigars today. Want one? They're very good."

"I'd love a cigar, thanks."

And then the conversation shifted to farming and after about twenty minutes, it seemed the interview was over and as Greg hadn't punched him or kicked him out, Ezra thought maybe he might have passed the test.

CHAPTER TWENTY-THREE

"I THINK YOU passed the Easton test," Natalie said to Ezra as she plopped down next to him on the couch.

"Yeah? What makes you say so?"

"A few things. You wanted more tea and Di told you where the pitcher was. If she hadn't liked you, she'd have served it to you herself. We'd have had dinner in the big formal dining room instead of out here at the family table. They only eat in there at Christmas, Easter and Thanksgiving. She treated you like family. Once I saw her treat someone like a guest, the guy John—he's one of the younger twins—was serious about and brought him here. She was so *painstakingly* polite. That guy was gone within a year. Of course then he met Alan about four months after so I guess Di was right. They love *him*. Even made him help with the new deck they built out back."

He liked the Eastons. Liked the way Tuesday was with them. Respectful to her parents but affectionate. There was clearly a lot of love there and between her siblings and their families, as well.

But he could also see the tension building up in Tuesday's posture the longer they were there.

"Is it just me or is she stressed right now?"

"Not just you. She's telling them about the gallery and they're not sure about it."

"ALL I'M SAYING, Tuesday, is that you've built a brand with your framing shop. Why switch to a gallery? Art makes way less money than service providers, which you are now." GJ, bless his heart, just didn't seem capable of seeing this in any other way.

"Because this is more than about my bottom line financially. I can make a profit on art, too, you know. I'll still be framing. I already do most of the stuff I'll be doing when I call it Easton Galleries."

Things got very still for a moment. Her father nodded.

GJ groaned. "That's even worse. What if people think you're an entirely different business and you have to start over?"

"It's more than a change in business name, GJ." GJ's wife, Alana, sent him a warning look.

"You're too old to be flitting around with this art stuff."

"Do you know I sold not just one piece priced at over a thousand dollars this last month, but *three?* Two boutique clothing stores are carrying my stuff. I sold more in a few hours today in Portland than I could have all season long in Hood River. I don't need to make a million dollars. I need to finally admit what I do is art. And I am."

Suddenly Ezra was there, sliding an arm around her shoulders. "We talking about how gorgeous your jewelry is and how fantastic it is that you're starting your gallery?" He sent her brother an easy smile but he was backing her up. But after the day she'd had, it brought tears to the back of her throat.

"I was just cautioning her to keep her eye on what's stable and to stop getting sidetracked by pipe dreams."

"When did you get so jaded, GJ?" Natalie asked.

"It's not jaded to want my sister comfortable. She doesn't have a head for business. It's why she went to Evergreen instead of the UW. You go to a place with no letter grades and you can't tell me anyone will take that seriously."

"Yes, do let's talk about that because someone might be confused and think you hold my degree with any measure of respect."

GJ lifted one shoulder. "You make your own choices, Tuesday. You can't get mad when people make commonly held judgments about you because of them."

Tuesday rolled her eyes. "You know, I'm thirty-four years old. I have my own business. I can pay my debts. I don't need to give one tiny little fart in the wind what you or some dude down at the shoe store thinks about where I went to college. Get over it, GJ. I *run* a business. I do so have a head for it."

"Tuesday, did you tell Ezra about our little band?" her mother interrupted, and it took every bit of her willpower not to run for the door.

"I did. I also let him know you'd understand that he'd be really tired."

"And then I said, I'd love to jam with you. She said you were really into Alabama Shakes."

WHICH IS HOW they ended up heading out to the garage. On the way they hit the picture hall. The walls lining the path from the house out to the garage was full of pictures. Wedding pictures of Diana and Greg along with newer shots from GJ's, April's and Shawn's weddings.

Grade-school pictures of all six kids and seven grandkids.

Ezra paused at one of her and April sitting on the Easter Bunny's lap, but April had been stone-cold freaked by the costume and her face was contorted into a howl of terror.

"My favorite picture of April," Tuesday joked to Ezra. She pointed to one of her mother twenty-five years prior. "This is her first shop-steward training here and these three next to it are times she's won Shop Steward of the Year for her union. Those are of my dad and his brother. They lived in Amsterdam for a year back in the day."

Ezra peered at the shot of her dad and uncle. "Your uncle's hair is like four feet wide."

"I know! He's bald now so when they come to visit my dad takes this one down so he won't feel bad."

They passed through her dad's domain, where he could watch television as loud as he liked and no one cared, to where the instruments were kept.

Ezra spoke as they all stopped. "I don't have my guitar with me. Tuesday forgot to mention this until we'd already got halfway here."

Shawn shoved a guitar at Ezra. "You can use mine." He sent Tuesday a look that said he knew exactly what he was doing. Ugh, brothers.

"Tuesday, get moving." Her mother pointed at the drums. "Since Paddy is also here I'll let him play guitar so I can focus on vocals."

"Yes, ma'am." Paddy handed Diana one of her seemingly endless collection of shakers and other things that made noise. "I'll trade you."

"Perfect." Di smiled Nat's way. "Their mother did a good job teaching them manners."

Nat nodded. "She did. There are two more—they're equally polite."

Tuesday got behind the drums and sat on a stool she'd had since she was fourteen or so and gave a few practice runs. That's when she looked up to find Ezra watching her.

Even in her parents' garage, jamming to make her mom happy, he was a rock star. It was like something happened to him when he slung a guitar on.

Paddy winked her way, grinning and already having a good time.

Di got herself behind her mic. "Let's hope the neighbors don't call the cops." She nearly giggled and Tuesday was so glad Ezra was there.

"It's not rock and roll if they don't," Ezra said seriously and then grinned at Di, who liked that attention a whole lot.

"You're very right. Do you all know 'Hold On'?"

"Yes. *Boys and Girls* is one of my favorite albums." Ezra turned to Tuesday. "You know it?"

She nodded.

"Count us in then, beauty." One corner of his mouth hitched up and she ducked her head.

Tuesday started the drumbeat and then Ezra followed with those first guitar notes and her father's bass line came in as her mother started singing.

Her niece and nephews danced around and her brothers teased her a little when their mother wasn't looking. They'd got out of the jam session and she'd never hear the end of that.

But it was fun, playing music with Ezra and Paddy

and her parents, too. The drum parts were easy enough for her to play and not sound too terrible. Her mother had a great singing voice and she loved being the center of attention. Ezra and Paddy both flirted with her just right and Tuesday loved them both for it.

By the time they'd finished the song she'd been glad they'd done it. Her mother was glowing and be-cause she was, her father was mellow.

They managed to escape just before midnight after hugs and promises to be back for breakfast in the morning before they headed back home to Hood River.

"WHAT WAS HE LIKE?" Ezra asked from his place next to her in bed. She knew he meant Eric.

"He was tall and lean. Easygoing. Everyone liked him. He had absolutely no rhythm and hated fried food. Who hates fried food?" She laughed.

"Did you know you loved him right away?"

"I've thought about this a lot. So much that to be totally honest I'm not entirely sure at this point if I'm remembering right. I liked what I saw and things were very intense very fast. All of college was like that. There was so much happening all the time."

"But you married him right after graduation so you must have been in love by that point."

"Yes, absolutely. We had our bumps and fits and starts, but we had a future, a direction. We shared the same values. Had similar goals."

"Why are you changing your name then?"

She sucked in a breath. "Well, it all started when I found out about his affair just a few months out from our wedding."

She told him about finding the letter and confronting Eric about it. About the affair and getting past it.

"So like a month before the wedding I said I wanted a new start and a new name. I'd been planning on keeping Easton, but I suggested we combine our names and make a new one. Eastwood was born and it has fit me a long time."

"Not anymore?"

"Back when I took on Eastwood as a name, I did it for a new start. A clean slate. Taking good energy and using it to start on the next leg of my journey. I feel like it's the same right now. I'm not Eric's wife anymore. I'm choosing to close a door on an important chapter in my life that is closed. Taking Easton again feels like a new coat of paint in some ways."

"All right. That makes sense."

"What brought that on?"

"A picture of you two on the wall at your parents' house. You were a beautiful bride."

"Thanks. I totally was."

They both laughed.

"I'm sorry he cheated on you."

"Me, too. But he was twenty years old when that happened. Fourteen years ago now. He stuck his dick in someone else and that sucked. But he didn't love her. I could tell from the letter and then how he reacted. At that time I could get past something that had happened two years before and that as much as I could parcel out, had never happened again. If he'd have felt something for her things would have been different."

"You never regretted giving him a second chance?"

"The morning of the day he died I'd slept at the hospice. He'd been increasingly weak. They'd given up by that point. We knew it was coming. I remember it felt like trying to hold water in my palm. His life ran out between my fingers and there was nothing I could do. He was weak and refusing to eat but since they'd shifted to more of a comfort-the-end-of-life reaction instead of working to cure, they hadn't pushed. So he was weak and I had to accept he was dying when five months before that we'd talked about trying to get pregnant. And I looked at him in the bed, a shell of the healthy, vibrant man he was. He turned to me and he said I had been the best memory of his life and that being married to me was something that carried him past the pain to accept death. He'd had me, and love, while he was alive and he'd take the memory of that into whatever was next.

"No matter what, that moment, knowing I'd given him some comfort at the very end means I'll never regret that second chance. Because if it made him less afraid to let go and discard a body that brought him only pain, it was worth it. That's what love is, Ezra." She said the last bit through tears as the memories hit her again. But it was different with the telling this time. It hurt less and she believed it when she said to Ezra that she didn't regret that second chance.

"People make mistakes. They can be stupid and thoughtless and yet you can love them anyway. Because being human means making mistakes. And being in love means maybe sometimes you can forgive something utterly unforgivable."

He pulled her close. "I didn't mean to make you cry."

She hugged him. "It's okay. I can look back and not have any regrets. If you get sick and don't go to the doctor, though, prepare for a full-stage freak-out. I am hard-core serious about that. Also, if you fucked some rando, I'd burn your house to the ground. After I made sure your animals were safe, of course. Just so you understand where you and I are."

"So you'd give me less of a chance?"

"I don't think I could get past the idea of you with anyone else now that you've been mine." Which filled her with guilt. "You think you could just write it off if I slept with someone else?"

He rolled on top of her. "But you could with him?"

"He was different. I was different. I couldn't get the image out of my head. You're mine, Ezra. And if you can't promise that you won't be fucking other people, we can't be together. And if I slept with someone else? Hmm?"

He kissed her so hard she forgot what they'd been talking about for a few minutes.

"You're mine, Tuesday. I don't share. Neither do I have any inclination to seek any other bed but the one I'm in right now."

It had been the most definitive declaration he'd ever given her. He branded her with it.

Claimed her.

He kissed her again. Slow. Teasing. "I'm a shitty bet—you know that, right?"

She snorted. "Stop. Are you hinting that you need a compliment? Do you need me to say how much I think about you on a daily basis?"

"Yes. I do."

"I think about you all day long. I think about you in the morning when I wake up. I'm in bed and you're not there. I wonder what you're doing. Think about you in your boxer shorts as you move around your house. You're talking to the cats because they're bouncing off the walls that you're finally awake and paying attention to them after daring to be unconscious for eight hours. Later, as I get to work, I think about you on horseback. You look really good in the saddle. All super at ease on a giant animal you ride over your lands. In my fantasies I might Viking you up a little, but just go with me here."

He laughed. "A Viking?"

"Yes. You're so big and brawny. And you definitely know your pillaging and conquering."

He leaned down to nip her bottom lip.

"Sorry, that Viking thing was a total tangent. Maybe we can revisit it at some point in the future. Like say, while you're dressed as a Viking. We can work out the details later on."

"Roger that. Will you dress as a wench?"

God, he made her happy. Just so full of happy it felt as if she might burst. "Is that your thing?"

"I might have entertained the vision of you in a white shirt, shoulders bared, cleavage high, serving me things. Maybe."

She laughed, hugging him.

"What did you do? Before me?" he asked.

She could have played coy and asked him what he meant. But she knew. "When Eric died I sort of...I don't know...it was like parts of me froze or withered away. It took me three years before I could even entertain the idea of having sex again. It came back eventually."

She loved sex and once that need had come back, she'd eventually allowed it into her life. So casual dating to get to decent sex for a few weeks before she broke things off and moved on. Four or six months later she'd do it again.

"Mainly I'd see someone for a few weeks. We'd meet in hotels, have sex. I'd shower at my gym and go home. After a while it petered out and we both moved on. I never fucked in anyone's house. I never learned their kids' names or what their favorite color was. It took nearly five years before I could consider having real feelings for anyone again."

That hung between them awhile.

Then he brushed his lips over hers. Over each one of her closed eyelids.

"Mmm. Do you know what it does to me that you respond so openly and honestly?" He kissed along her jaw. "You tear me apart just by being you."

There was something magical about that moment. So much energy had built up. All the *what-could-be* hung in the air. But like every important moment, it could go wrong, too, and she knew they both understood that.

"I do?"

"You really do."

"What did you do? Before I came along? Wait. I'm not sure I actually want to know."

"Before you, I waited until I needed to fuck or I'd blow up and then I'd go to see a woman I knew well enough to fuck and didn't care that I was *the* Ezra Hurley. But when I kissed you that first time you dug in. Your taste shoved out everything else.

"There was you. All lush curves and strong lines. I wanted a taste and then you kissed me back and there was *nothing* else I wanted."

She held on tight, breathing him in. "Thank goodness. Other than the woman in Portland, even before the drugs you never had anyone?"

"I never had the time. And then I don't think I ever met the right person. Or maybe I wasn't the right person. Then I was *definitely* not the right person. Since then I've spent my time trying to get everything else in my life back on track."

Tuesday understood that. "Which seems pretty fair when you think about it. The only way I could keep going each day was to break stuff into small parts. Take that piece, deal with it and move to the next thing. Sometimes it was just brushing my teeth. But you get over it. You realize scar tissue is tough and it hurts a little less as the days and weeks and months go by."

WHAT IF YOU had to look at your mistakes every day? What if he felt like he'd done so much harm to his family through his addiction that he'd never get past it?

It haunted him.

And maybe, he felt he deserved to be haunted.

It stood between them and he honestly didn't feel like he could truly open himself up until he learned how to live with it or how to get around it.

He needed to add her name change and all this stuff she'd revealed to the list of things to deal with and think about.

He knew for sure he wasn't worth that sort of intensity of emotion, but what did that matter? Did it at all?

She deserved better than he could ever give her. Deserved more than a guy who was afraid of actually being in love with her because it felt too much like something he hadn't done in five years.

Even when maybe it didn't.

He rolled again, settling her against his side, her head on his biceps, and put it away. There'd be time later but right now he wanted her to feel better. "Are you all right? You looked a little stressed at the end tonight."

"It's just family. You know? I love them. They're always there for me. But they can get to me in ways no one else possibly could. They want the best for me. GJ feels like he's in charge of all the siblings. He's a dingus, but it's from his heart. He just can't see why I make the choices I do. And sometimes he comes off as totally dismissive of my accomplishments. It's always the same. Which is actually sort of comforting. For a while no one got in my business for any other reason but cancer, dying, death and then how I was recovering, or not, from that. It felt like I was reduced to a place where all I was was someone to fix, you know?"

"Can't imagine the answers to those questions varied too much. Not for a while. I mean, I assume you were happy before he got sick, given the way you talk."

"I loved him. I was happy. He was good for me. I was good for him. We had a good life and then he got sick and died and then I lost my way. Or maybe I just sort of chose a different way for those eighteen months. Whatever. I'm good now."

She was quiet but he knew she was working something out and so he waited, enjoying the weight of her against him and the scent of sex still in the air.

"Who I am will always be part of what I had with Eric. But I realized after you and I started up that I can have those memories and still enjoy this. But I don't know how you feel. You said once you didn't think it was weird. Do you want to know about it or not at all? Do I make you feel bad when I talk about my life before?"

"It's not the fact that you loved someone before I came along. I can deal with that. But I can't compete with a ghost."

"You don't have to. It isn't a competition."

He snorted. "Of course it is. He'll always be frozen in time for you. He'll always be better than me because he never had the chance to fuck up and I'm a dick for thinking that."

"You're not a dick. But he's not better than you."

There was a catch in her voice as she pushed from the bed to stand.

"What is it, Tuesday?" He turned on the bedside light before piling pillows at his back.

She was agitated, clearly upset about something more than her argument with her brother or any of the feelings stuff they'd just exposed.

"You don't have to compete because he *never* made me feel what you do."

They both went still as the words echoed between them and then soaked into Ezra's brain.

"I was with Eric for a little over nine years. We had a great sex life. He and I fit well. But you? You touch me and everything else fades into the background. You fill me with so much raw yearning I can barely breathe. When it's you and me, skin to skin, it's raw and beautiful and all encompassing. It nearly hurts, you make me feel so good. That scares me and it makes me feel guilty. Like I'm betraying him. And I don't care. I want you more than any guilt I might feel. I've never wanted anything or anyone the way I want you."

It was exactly that combination of words he'd been waiting to hear. He hadn't known it until she'd said them and he'd heard them. He *had* been struggling with how to feel about this man she'd loved, exactly as he'd told her.

The longer he'd known her and the more he'd allowed himself to feel about her, the more he'd wanted to mark her in some sense. To feel like what they had was special and good and that she wouldn't trade it. Was that petty? If Eric had been alive he would feel that way about his wife, right? So why should Ezra feel bad that he finally believed she'd choose him.

He wasn't a man who could live in the shadow of another. But she'd just told him that wasn't the case. He was relieved. And a little uncertain he deserved it.

"How can this be a betrayal of a man who died over four years before we met? And if he was as good of a guy as you say, do you really think he'd be down with you existing by stringing together a few visits to hotel rooms here and there just to keep from losing your shit? Is that what you want instead? Never belonging to anyone so you never have to risk feeling again? Because Eric doesn't care. He's dead. You aren't. It's a waste of the life you're blessed with to choose an empty existence over something that makes you *feel,* because what you and I have is different than what you had with someone else. Big deal. Ezra and Tuesday *should* be different."

She stood there, just a few feet away and for the first time since they'd started sleeping together he didn't wonder if she was wishing on some level that he was another man.

And then she came to him, sliding in between the sheets.

"Okay," she said quietly.

CHAPTER TWENTY-FOUR

"Yes, yes, yes. That one." Kelly looked Tuesday up and down. "That looks gorgeous on you."

She'd come to Portland to one of Kelly's boutiques to find a new dress for her gallery launch in just a few days.

Tuesday looked over her shoulder at the mirror behind her. The dress had pretty much no back at all, leaving a lot of exposed skin to the waist. "This back, though, I don't know if I can carry it off."

Kelly rolled her eyes. "That dress has been hanging in the display for a month. Five women have tried it on when I've been in. Not one looked right in it."

The bodice was fitted in bronze metallic and led to a skirt of feathers in a fiery hue that worked perfectly with the bodice.

Feathers.

She'd come in to try a few little black dresses and Kelly had brought out one funky dress for every classic LBD she presented to Tuesday in the dressing room.

"Mere mortals can choose a dress that's flattering and fits well. Every woman should have clothes that make her feel beautiful and special, even if it's jeans. It's so rare when something funky and eclectic works perfectly on someone. You carry it. You're a bigger than life personality. Your beauty is bold and I think you'd be so wasted in that dress." Kelly pointed to the pretty black cocktail dress on the hanger. "Which I should point out costs two hundred dollars more than the one you have on. That one you're in now is on sale. Plus you get a discount."

Tuesday smirked at Kelly. "Discount? And why is that?"

"You're a contractor of ours. It comes with a fifteen percent discount. Plus it's been here in the shop for five months and hasn't moved and I had just decided to mark it down twenty-five percent. It's forty percent off. It's perfect for you."

Tuesday had just recently finished a piece that was all fire, in varying shades of red, orange and amber. A bracelet that wrapped up the forearm. Daring. A piece meant to be worn with something like the dress she had on.

"Your butt. Tuesday, look at it. Ezra needs to see that."

"You're supposed to be making me buy the more expensive one, not giving me price breaks until I have no other choice but to say yes and buy this dress."

"Is that what I'm doing?"

"Don't try that blonde *I'm so innocent* thing on me, sister. I've had a pretty blonde best friend for over a decade. I'm immune to it. But not this dress."

"You're relaunching yourself into the future. This is your gallery opening. You need to look like this. Because I'm thinking the finished product with lipstick and high heels will be a total knockout. The bodice is fitted and even has a place for your boobs to go because that's not a bra-friendly back and you're not going to get away with braless with your rack."

"Rack? Is that a term you learned at model school?"

"That one is courtesy of a thing called life. Oh, and my eight-year-old, who asked me why her teacher would have a rack and was she going to display things on it. I told her to ask her dad."

Tuesday laughed as Kelly helped her get free from the dress so she didn't rip it before she'd even left the store.

"All kidding aside. You need that dress. I know it might be sticker shock, but it's a piece of art and it makes *you* look like a piece of art."

"I'm buying it already. Sheesh."

Kelly beamed and looked even prettier.

"So...are you guys coming?"

"The girls and I will stop by with Vaughan, on our way home from *all* having dinner with Sharon and Michael." Kelly pasted on an expression that was more panicked than pleased.

"Wow, that's some smile. My mom calls that her *I'm in church so the Lord says I can't call you out but you need it. I'll pray for you* face."

"Ha! Good one. Sharon and I have never really got along. I know everyone thinks she's fantastic and maybe she is if she doesn't hate you but it took me two years in therapy not to hate her."

Sharon was protective of her family. Tuesday could only guess how painful it would be for the woman to decide you were a threat.

"Is Vaughan ever going to tell her the whole story? Why things broke?"

"That's between Vaughan and Sharon. The only

way I can envision this second chance working is for him to make sure he will always be between us because I'm not going to tolerate any shit from her this time around."

"So, you're back on again? You're together?"

Kelly sighed. "It's complicated. I know you have an opening to deal with on Wednesday night but maybe we could go out Saturday after your stall closes for a drink? I know Jeremy and Ezra are going up to Vancouver for the weekend so I'm not edging into his weekend time."

He was? Nice of him to tell her.

He'd been very sweet to her that weekend. He'd even told her about Jeremy's call. But not a freaking word about going away.

They'd both been superbusy, though, and only connected for brief phone calls and texts as she'd readied for her gallery launch and he'd been dealing with the harvest.

"Sounds perfect. We can grab a late lunch and a beer and you can tell me what the heck is going on."

"Only if you do the same."

"Sure. If I figure it out before then, I'll be happy to share."

EZRA HADN'T EXPECTED to be so damned busy that week, but they'd brought in the alfalfa, which looked to be a damned good crop that season. So pretty much all his life had focused down to was getting up, going out, dealing with alfalfa and alfalfa-related stuff for twelve to fifteen hours, calling Tuesday to hear her voice and crashing only to start over again the following morning.

He missed Tuesday fiercely. It had been over a week since he'd seen her last. Touched her last.

He looked at the satin pillowcase on the pillow she slept on—oh who was he kidding—on *her* pillow.

They'd had a breakthrough of sorts the night they'd gone to her parents' house. But there'd been so much between them that night he'd ended up in a panic when they returned and it had been a contest of sorts for him to see how long he could go with not seeing her. As if he could prove to himself that he could kick Tuesday if he had to.

Goldfish came to stand on his chest and Peanut decided to lie over his face.

"We're past passive-aggressive scratching my couch to attempted suffocation?" he asked as he moved her to the side. She gave him a look and kneaded his forearm with a little too much claw.

"She'll be back soon. Harvest is over and her grand opening is tomorrow night. I have plans for her after that so don't get any ideas about hogging her when I bring her back."

He sat up, sending animals scampering in all directions. Talking to his cats. He, the guy who'd filled tens of thousands of seats in arenas on a regular basis, was now a crazy cat lady.

If he got out there now and worked a solid four or five hours he had the time to run into town to pick up his beauty and spend some quality time with her.

It wasn't until he was out in the middle of an empty field that it hit him. He used to make deals like that at the beginning with heroin. If he just did these four things he had to do he'd get high as a reward.

And then it was three things. And two. And, *hey*

I'll get high first so I'm not thinking about getting high while I'm trying to get stuff done. And then he'd just got high and done nothing.

Everything in his life had been about getting heroin, doing heroin, thinking about how to get more and being unconscious. Opiate highs had been his favorite so he'd simply considered himself a *connoisseur* instead of a junkie until it was far too late.

He'd sort of been feeling that this thing with Tuesday was substituting one addiction with another but now, the corollaries seemed inescapable. She'd be the one craving that would slowly take over his entire life until he'd forgotten everything else.

The need for her crawled over his skin and he was going to reward it. Need? He didn't need her, he craved her. *Craved.*

Loopy head butted him and he reached down absently to pet her as he reeled. He *hadn't* been so needy for something since heroin.

Violet grunted at him.

"Yes, yes, let's keep moving." He continued on, pretty much on autopilot as he tried to figure out how to think about the issue.

Two hours later and the muscles in his arms burned as he struggled through pull-up after pull-up. He'd already jumped rope for so long his legs still twitched.

"What are you doing to yourself, Ezra?"

He opened his eyes. His mother stood a few feet away, glaring at him.

"Exercise, Mom."

"Try again."

He dropped down and hoped he covered that little bit of a wobble before his mother saw it.

"So you think working out until you can barely stand is exercise? Do you need to work on the concept of moderation again, boy?"

He groaned as he headed to the fridge to get some water. He was going to be sore as hell in the morning. But first he had to deal with Sharon Hurley, who was on the scent of something. She didn't know what it was, but she would stop at nothing until she figured it out or broke him open to get a confession.

"Mom, I work out pretty much every day. I don't know what you're upset about."

She leaned back against the wall, crossing her arms over her chest. One of her brows slid up ever so slowly as she dared him to keep it up. How she could even know he was troubled he didn't know.

"Well, you told me at six this morning that you were going to head down to grab Tuesday to see if she wanted to come to dinner. And yet, an hour ago when I retrieved your pig, who ate my carnations again I might add, and brought her back here, you were jumping rope and listening to music so loud I didn't want to bother you. And I come back to check in, to let Tuesday know your dad and I are so excited about her opening tomorrow night and I find you *still* working out and looking so tense and miserable there's no way I'm going to believe you when you say there's nothing wrong."

"It's just something I'm trying to work through. It'll be fine."

"Let me guess—you realized how happy you were and decided you weren't worthy. You're going to go off and do something stupid. Don't you break up with that girl—she's so, so strong, but you'll break her into a million pieces if you're careless and you don't handle your own fear first."

He dug deep for patience.

"I'm not breaking up with Tuesday."

Right? Because that would be stupid. He just needed to keep some space between them as he worked through how he could see her without craving her. Being with a woman was one thing; replacing one addiction with another wasn't a road he could survive.

"So you're going to bring her back here tonight then? Shouldn't you be on your way to her now?"

"Jeremy'll be here tomorrow morning. There's a band meeting and I have a lot to do. She'd just get bored up here and I can't really pay her any attention until her opening. She has things to focus on right now. I'll see her tomorrow night at the gallery."

"Ezra…"

"Mom, back off. I'm not kidding. I need some space. I'm a grown man."

"Whatever. You still make the same pouty face you did when you were three."

"I'm very charming. It clearly came to me very early on."

She tried to stifle a smile but failed. And that made him smile, too.

"You get your modesty from your father's side of the family. You can tell him I said so. Work it out. She loves you. It's written all over her. Which is good because you love her, too."

"She's my girlfriend so yes, I care about her. Too early for love."

"Oh, sweetheart." His mother tipped her head to the side. "You can't tell yourself when it's acceptable to love and not love. You simply love or you don't."

She hopped up onto a stool and he groaned inwardly. Sharon was making herself comfortable, which meant a lecture was imminent.

"Your problem is that you have spent every moment since you got home from sober living proving you're worthy of a second chance. So much time and energy that you can't even see we've given you that second chance long, long ago and you proved us right to have done so. When are *you* going to accept that you're worthy? You're the only skeptic left. So what is it? Your entire life can't continue to be one long prison sentence of guilt and shame. This isn't purgatory and you long since served your sentence."

"I'm going to my house. I'm going to eat something, take a shower and I'll be sleeping by nine. Go see Mary. She was having contractions earlier."

Sharon pursed her lips. "Look at you shoving your mother out the door and throwing your sister-in-law under the bus. Someone's defensive. Those were practice contractions. Our Damien, he's going to be a daddy. He's grown so much. Love does that."

He should have known his mother would be back to him.

"I was beginning to wonder if he'd ever settle down. My little charmer. But he has and he's grown. He's starting a family with a woman he took a chance on. Was vulnerable to. Maybe if you shared whatever it was with Tuesday? Sometimes once you say the scary stuff out loud it's not that scary anymore. Are you worried that your racial differences are going to be an issue?"

He laughed because she wasn't going to let go, like a bulldog with a Southern accent.

"No. I mean, it's there. There's no denying some people react negatively. Mostly people look twice because she's beautiful and has all that gorgeous hair." She always carried herself like a queen. "But that's outside stuff. Between us, that's not an issue. With our friends and family it's not an issue."

"I didn't think so. Is it that she was married before?"

He kissed her cheek as he passed her to head out and back to the house. "I'll see you tomorrow night at the gallery."

She hopped down and followed him, Loopy trotting along.

He paused at his back door. "Thanks for not making Violet into Sunday dinner. I'll plant you some new carnations next week when I'm back from Vancouver."

His mother waltzed right in through the door he'd opened for himself. He groaned, just very quietly.

"Make me some tea, please. I'm coming down with a sore throat. I want to feel better before the baby comes."

He put on a kettle for her and pulled out some tea and mugs. It was warm outside but his kitchen was shaded by the big pine trees in the yard so it was nice and cool inside.

"Do you feel like maybe she's still pining for her dead husband?"

"And she's back."

"Well, that's what he is. Dead. He's not coming back to claim her."

And even if he had been, Ezra wondered if he would have. From where Ezra stood, the man had done her wrong. Tuesday might have given him a second chance but Ezra didn't have to be forgiving. Ezra didn't have to have a very high opinion of anyone who'd cheat on Tuesday and he didn't think much of Eric as a man.

He'd never say so to Tuesday, of course. Or even out loud to his mother.

He ached to shoo her off toward Vaughan and Kelly to be free of this interference but Vaughan would kick Ezra's ass for it and given how delicate things were between his baby brother and his ex-wife, a visit from Sharon might just send the whole thing over a cliff in flames and he didn't want that at all.

"You're okay, right? Not struggling with sobriety?"

He put his face in his hands. "Mom. I'm fine. Have some tea. I'm going to shower. I've been up since four and this is the first time I've had a pause of longer than ten minutes all day long."

"You go on ahead. I have to make some calls. I'll finish the tea and make us some sandwiches if you're not just going to go to Tuesday's."

"Dad would appreciate that more than I would."

"Your father doesn't need it. You do, though."

"I'm fine! How many times do I have to tell you that before you leave me the hell alone?"

Though he'd yelled it loud enough to send the cats running from the room, his mother just looked at him.

"If you think this is going to drive me away you're dumber than I thought."

He turned and stalked from the room, slamming his bedroom door, which didn't make him feel any better and probably made his mother laugh.

CHAPTER TWENTY-FIVE

"HOLY WOW." NATALIE walked around Tuesday in a slow circle. "You were not kidding about that dress. You look so hot I'd totally bang you and yet, you also look like a person who runs a fantastically successful art gallery."

"Look at you with your compliments."

Tuesday gave herself a critical look in the full-length mirror in her room. "I can't believe the built-in bra part of the bodice actually works. We all know shelf bras and the like are pipe dreams." They never worked and the weight of her boobs would slowly begin to pull the front of the tank top or whatever down until her areolae were popping out.

"Totally presents the cleavage in a gravity-defying and yet superhot way. Jeez. You and I need to go to Kelly's boutique so I can find stuff that makes me look as smoldering as you."

"Don't worry. I transferred my half of the mortgage to your account three days ago."

Natalie laughed.

Tuesday had got her hair done that morning and her stylist had put in just a small hint of shimmer spray so when Tuesday was in the right light it would show.

"I want this necklace to fit backward. Can you help hold it while I fasten it?"

They fit it just perfectly to drape down her spine, a tail of amber at the center of the design keeping it in place. She'd hoped to wear the bracelet instead, but she'd sold it just a few hours after she bought the dress.

She had plenty of jewelry. Sales were even better.

The front of the dress was simple with her cleavage as the star. Even with the pretty feathers on the skirt.

The back was all her skin and the stones of the necklace. The bronze glinted in one way and the stones would another.

"You're like a four hundred and thirty on a scale of one-to-ten hot. Seriously. You're working every single angle tonight like a fabulous trifecta. I know this is your night and we're all *woo gallery* and I'm your very biggest woo-er. But if you, say, cared what a certain taciturn alpha male with powerful thighs and a great ass thought, you're thunderbirds go on that."

"His ass is remarkable, isn't it? Also his wrists and forearms. His hands. Shoulders. Piercings. Tattoos. The dick is my favorite. You don't get to comment on that."

Natalie saluted.

"So if I wanted to be the hottest woman he'd ever laid eyes on the whole of his life, I'd be in that territory tonight?"

"Since you just added that lipstick and those heels, what are they five inches? Jeez. Anyway, you're bull's-eye hottest woman."

Tuesday looked down her legs, which looked about a foot longer between the short skirt and the delicate, strappy stiletto heels.

"Well, get your glamazon on because you are fierce

and fabulous and absolutely gorgeous and he's going to fall over when he catches sight of you. But let's be honest here, he already does that. He's gone for you."

"It's mutual." She dabbed some perfume on her pulse points and looked to Natalie, who wore a cocktail dress with a spill of pink wild roses silkscreened over it. Tuesday had flat-ironed Nat's hair so it was in a Louise Brooks–style bob. Sleek and perfect for Natalie's features.

"Talk about pretty. You're like one of those Northern European fairy-tale princesses."

"Let's face it." Natalie handed Tuesday the little bag her tube of lipstick and phone fit in. Barely. They linked arms. "We're just awesome. Those Hurleys don't even know what hit them when we came into their lives."

Tuesday laughed. "I think that might be true and I'm not entirely sure if it's a good thing in every way."

"Love is good, Tuesday."

Yeah, but love also opened you up to the bad, as well.

"You ready to go?" Natalie asked.

"Yep. Ezra texted to say he and Paddy would meet us over there in about half an hour. I need to get back to check on the food. They were setting up as I left. Lara is there keeping an eye on things." Lara was Tuesday's part-time employee. She was smart and would keep everyone in line and on track. But nobody could be as scary as Tuesday when it came to her events so she needed to get down there.

"You used to be an event planner. Your opening is going to be great because you planned it and you're good at it." Natalie faced her. "I'm so excited for you.

You're not the old Tuesday. You won't be and that's okay. This Tuesday is living the hell out of her life again. I'm proud of how brave and smart and talented you are."

"Not allowed to make me cry. My makeup is perfect. Stop it now." She gave Nat a mock stern look and then blew her friend a kiss. "Thanks. Now let's go open my gallery, shall we?"

JILL SCOTT'S "SHAME" was playing as Ezra and Paddy walked into Easton Gallery. He paused, stunned at the change in the space. He hadn't been by in two weeks, as the harvest had sucked up most of his life and then Jeremy had come in so he'd been busy on band business, too.

And he'd been testing himself to see how long he could stay away. Needing to know.

And craving her even then as he took in the new cases she'd had installed for her jewelry. The fine art had been displayed a little and she'd spruced up the counter at the back where she handled the framing business.

This was a gallery. It was classy and sexy. She didn't fill every bit of the space with things and instead, let the space frame the pieces she did have.

Doors weren't open to the public yet so there weren't too many people inside. He smiled as Jill Scott faded and was replaced by Yeah Yeah Yeahs' "Maps."

And then she came around the corner and he exhaled hard and fast. Paddy whistled.

Her attention had been on the woman walking

along next to her but at Paddy's whistle she turned their way.

Christ, she was beautiful. Warmth and pleasure at the sight of her rushed through him and his muscles, which had felt locked for weeks, finally eased. Ten days without seeing her had made him hungry for the sight of those curls and the upward tilt of her mouth.

Her tits. Rude or not, he couldn't stop looking at the glory of them showcased at the front of her dress. Her very short dress exposing miles of gorgeous leg.

Tuesday looked to Paddy. "Your adulation has been appreciated and duly noted. Your girlfriend is around the corner."

Paddy kissed her cheek on his way past and then she was all about Ezra.

She looked him up and down, pleasure on her features enough to make him preen a little. He took her hand, turning it to kiss her wrist, breathing her in.

Then he tugged and she came into his arms like he'd been thinking about her pretty much nonstop since the last time they'd been together.

"Hi there, Ezra Hurley. You're quite handsome this evening." She smoothed a hand down the front of his shirt and tie.

"Beauty, I don't have the words to do justice to how you look. Sexy. Gorgeous. Juicy. Curvy. Strong. Smart."

"And that's just the front." She turned, exposing the line of her back before facing him again.

All the spit in his mouth had dried up and she knew it. Joy surged through him as she smiled, clearly happy.

"You don't even need words with that expression."

"Later on, I'm going to lay back on my bed and watch you strip out of this pretty little dress. You can keep the necklace on. And the shoes."

"It's been ten days since you've made me come. Well, in person."

He groaned. How could he have thought it was possible to resist this pull between them? Moving very close, he pressed his mouth to her ear. "Are you saying what I think you're saying?"

"That I masturbated thinking of you?"

He swallowed hard and dragged the edge of his teeth over the shell of her ear before he stood back. "I need to think about gelatin salad with raisins and carrots or I'm going to walk around with an erection and everyone will think I'm a creep."

"They'd all be jealous it was all mine." She indicated the gallery. "Want a tour?"

"Yes."

She'd shown him around the space and he'd got himself a plateful of appetizers when there was a commotion at the doors, which she'd locked after he and Paddy had arrived.

Tuesday came out toward the front doors. "We'll be opened in about—"

Her voice cut off so abruptly he turned, alarmed.

The people just outside continued to pound, yelling.

"What on earth?" Natalie came out. "Oh shit. Tuesday, don't open it."

Ezra had already moved to put himself between Tuesday and the front doors but those words from Natalie only underlined his resolve.

"Who are those people? Do we need to be calling the cops? Is there someone I need to punch?"

"It's Eric's parents," she said quietly. "I can't risk them making a scene closer to the time we open."

"There are ways I can make that a reality."

They pounded on the glass so loud he worried they'd break it. He turned quickly, very close to the glass. "Back off or I'm calling the police." He already hated these people for upsetting her so much. He only had so much patience and it was gone.

The man pulled his hand back as if he'd been scalded but the woman looked him straight on and pounded with her rings.

"Let's deal with this right now." Paddy moved toward the doors, ready to aid Ezra in protecting Tuesday from the people out front, who obviously had anger issues.

"I'm unlocking."

Natalie touched Tuesday's arm. "Don't let them in here. You don't know what she'll do."

"This is bound to be wrapped up in my changing my name back to Easton. I've had multiple incidents with them recently. No, not since I blocked her number so get that look off your face."

"I'll have any look I like, Tuesday Marie Easton. I told you they were awful and poisonous. Call the cops. You don't owe them anything."

Ezra had never seen Tuesday and Natalie arguing. He didn't want them to be upset, but since he was in his head and all, he hoped they kissed and made up.

"Open up, you whore!" Tina Heywood screamed.

Natalie's eyes widened and then her expression went very hard. "She did *not* just say that."

"Enough." Tuesday stood taller. "I'll talk to them outside. Call the cops only as a last resort."

Ezra put an arm around her shoulders. "Nope. *We'll* talk to them outside. And if that woman calls you a whore again we're going to have an issue, her husband and I."

"They lost a son."

Natalie reached past Tuesday and banged on the door right as the woman had, sending Tina scrambling back. Natalie's normally sweet voice was flinty. "You touch that glass again and I'll punch you in the throat—you hear me, Mrs. Heywood?" She turned back to Tuesday. "You lost a husband. Tragedy doesn't give you a blank check to be awful. You loved him more than they ever did. They don't get to call you a whore because Eric got cancer. *Fuck her.* If they care so much why do they only contact you to hurt you? You don't owe them anything. They're nothing to do with you anymore."

"I don't, no. But I loved their son and I can't call the cops on them, not unless I have no other choice. Now let's do this because I have a party to throw."

Ezra kept at her side, relieved she hadn't tried to send him away.

She unlocked and they started to come inside but Ezra shook his head. "Outside and any more of that type of talk from you, ma'am, and this will end."

"I don't take orders."

Ezra curled his lip. "I don't care what you take. I'm *telling* you that if you push me, I will call the police and have you escorted away. Now, state your business."

The woman looked to Tuesday. "You're going to let him talk to me that way?"

"You just screamed that I was a whore through the doors of my place of business. So I don't think you have any room to point fingers. I already explained to you why I'm going back to Easton. You never even liked the idea of me and Eric changing our names to Eastwood to start with."

"Before I wasn't sure what to think, but now I see why you're doing this." The man looked over to Ezra, with his lip curled.

"You think I'm opening up an art gallery and using my maiden name because of him?" Tuesday gestured to Ezra. "And even if I was, why would you care? Five years have passed since he died. Every time you contact me it's to be cruel. Your son called me several interesting racial epithets at Eric's memorial. You never liked me. You barely tolerated your son while he was alive.

"You don't have to like me. But my days of giving you slack because you lost your child are over. We have nothing to do with each other anymore. Which means you're being crazy, violent random people on a public street. What name I use or don't use isn't your business."

"You used Eric just like you're using him. Look at you!" The man waved a hand at her. "You should be ashamed of yourself for that outfit."

"Maybe I should adopt it and make it feel bad for being bronze instead of cream, like you did. How'd that work out for your nonwhite kids, Tina? How's Sam?"

"He never should have married you. When you

got cold feet before the wedding I told him to run and run fast. That you'd be the end of him. I hate that it was true."

The words hit Tuesday like a slap and she flinched. Ezra shifted to stand between them. Ezra addressed the husband because clearly the wife was beyond reason. "Take your wife and leave. We're done here. You've come all the way down here to ruin her evening. Well done. I'm sure your son would have been proud. I, on, the other hand, don't have any feelings for you at all other than loathing and a barely leashed urge to punch you in the face and throw your wife in the car and send you both crawling away."

While Ezra had been waiting for the wife to lose her shit, it was the man who actually leaped at Tuesday.

Ezra didn't want to fistfight in the middle of the sidewalk outside Tuesday's place of business, but he had absolutely no plans to let any more harm come to Tuesday at the hands, or mouths, of these people.

He caught the man by the shoulders and shoved him back hard enough that he connected with the car at his back.

Ezra wanted to hurt this man so much his hands shook. The hinted pleasure at the bloodlust he could indulge by bloodying the guy's nose pooled at the base of his brain. Urging.

Through clenched teeth Ezra snarled. *"I said no."*

Behind him, he knew she was upset. The waves of her emotion beat at him. He needed to protect her. Now that the man had actually tried to touch her, things were different.

He fisted and unfisted his hands.

"Just go!" Tuesday urged from behind Ezra. "Can't you see this is about to turn violent? You said what you wanted to say. Get the hell away from here now."

"Charlie Heywood, you back away from my baby right now or you and I are going to have a problem."

Greg and Diana Easton came hurrying over.

"They were just leaving," Ezra told Greg.

Up until that moment, Ezra had figured it would be Di who'd jump out there with threats of violence, but it was Greg who continued to speak. "They best. Because I have wanted to slap Tina Heywood's face for years now and I have an excuse. Her husband is a fool, but she's a nasty harridan. I will slap a woman who is trying to harm my child. Believe it, Charlie. And then I will slap you into next week."

Ezra didn't turn around. She'd seen and heard enough and he wanted her away from the Heywoods immediately.

"Beauty, why don't you go inside with your mom? I know Natalie was asking about her just a few minutes ago and if I'm right, Paddy is having to hold her back to keep her from coming out here to throw down to protect her best friend. Your father and I have this handled."

"That sounds like a good idea. I need something to eat. We drove straight here and I'm starving," Ezra heard Di say as she opened the door at their back. He heard Paddy speaking soothingly to Natalie and it made Ezra smile knowing her friend was in there having to be held back.

"Hey now, there a problem here?" Sharon and Michael Hurley came down the sidewalk toward them.

"These people were just leaving," Greg answered.

"She's shaming my son's memory and for what?" Tina gestured at Ezra. "For that?"

"*It's not your business.* You're not part of her life anymore. It's for the best because you spent a decade making her miserable as she tried to make you like her. We're all done with you. You've made my daughter upset for the last time."

Greg then got right in the man's face. "You hear me? I have had enough of you people. Haunting her like vultures. You got your punches in. No wonder that boy wanted the hell away from you. The both of you are horrible people."

The woman flinched, but Greg wasn't done and he wasn't letting up. He straightened, pulling his dignity back around him as he spoke to people it was clear he despised. "I wish to God you were flinching because you realize you drove your son away and you've tortured my daughter, whose only crime was to love him with all her heart. But you're a self-centered bitch who'd rather tear apart my Tuesday because you were an utter failure at parenting. I've held my tongue for years. Dealing with your pretentious bullshit at the holidays because my child begged us to look past your personalities. I loved your son. He was a decent boy with a good heart. But you had no part in that. I will do more than shove you, Charlie. Go ahead, because I can already taste how good it's going to feel when I break your nose. I've dreamed of it."

"I see you around her or this gallery again I'll call the cops," Ezra said, meaning every word. "You had your sick fun. That's over now. You need to find a new target. You understand me?"

Michael came to stand at Greg's other side and the

Heywoods finally took the hint, hurrying away and getting into a car half a block up the street, tearing away from the curb.

"So, Dad, this is Greg Easton, Tuesday's father. Mr. Easton, this is my father, Michael Hurley."

They shook hands.

"Can I do anything to help?" his father asked them both.

"The Heywoods are her former in-laws. Their son was a good kid. We liked him. But they're horrible people. Pretentious. Unbearable in social situations. The mother would spend an entire holiday picking and pecking and tearing at her children and husband. We'd do our best to talk around it, but one Thanksgiving Di threw a drink in Tina's face. She'd said something to Tuesday, Di won't say what and neither will Tuesday so it's bad enough they're not telling me to keep me out of jail, if you know what I mean. Then Di punched her square in the nose and pulled her hair off."

Horrified, all three men were silent a moment and then all started to laugh.

Ezra cleared his throat. "I would give money to have seen that."

"Not only was it the best Thanksgiving I've had my entire life, it also was a way to never have to spend a holiday with them again. When Eric got sick and we had to be around them more, Di just looked right through Tina. Like she didn't exist. They hated that she and Eric made up their own name. They hated Tuesday from the start. Hell, they didn't even partic- ularly like Eric. Those crocodile tears they just shed for a boy who shared my table more than theirs for a decade are bullshit. They're the slap to his memory.

They don't care about him. Or his memory. It's just a way to get worked up and take it out on my child and that will not happen. Thank you, Ezra, for protecting her."

Ezra nodded. "Yes, sir. Of course. Let's go in. They're gone and she's going to be upset. If we can calm her some before the official opening, that'd be good."

CHAPTER TWENTY-SIX

HER MOTHER HUSTLED her into the back and Natalie joined them. Diana stood in front of Tuesday to get her attention. "You will not let them steal this night from you. Do you hear me, Tuesday? The Heywoods are awful people. They were before you came along and they are now. You have a wonderful night all planned out to celebrate this wonderful new stage in your life. And, darling, you look so amazing you can't possibly waste it. This is one of those top-ten outfits over your lifetime sort of situations."

"Totally," Natalie agreed. "To all that. Boo to Tina. I'm just over here imagining what it must have looked like when you punched her and then yanked her hair."

Leave it to Di and Nat to make her feel better even at a time like that. Tuesday hugged her mother. "Thanks, Mom." She mouthed *love you* to Nat, who blew her a kiss.

"I didn't know her ponytail was fake. I just wanted to pull her hair and make her hurt. They dragged me out before I could do any real harm."

"After the thrown drink. And the punch."

Her mother sniffed like it hadn't been a big deal. "Those are minor details. She's lucky I didn't kick her face instead. The way she talks to people like she's so much better. What? Tell me what is and isn't classy to serve or eat or wear like I need advice from her raggedy ass."

Tuesday laughed so hard she had to dot her eyes over and over with a tissue for fear of the tears making her mascara run.

"I'm not going to lie that it is a little thrill when I move too fast and she flinches. I am a little sorry not to be watching your dad mix it up out there. He's sexy when he gets all het up."

Tuesday thought of the way Ezra had shoved Mr. Heywood in her defense. How he'd put himself in between them and protected her.

"She said I disrespected Eric's memory. Do you think that?"

Her mother shook her head. "Heck no. She's crazy! You can't listen to crazy people. Honey, what is it you think you need to do? Hide away for the rest of your life because your husband died young? Turn away a chance to love and be loved by a man like Ezra, who adores you? Will that bring Eric back? It won't. It changes nothing when it comes to whether or not that boy is dead. Five years. I've been patient. Daddy's been patient. Well, no because Daddy has no patience, but we've done our best to let you find your way back. This gallery is your next step. It's your future and you don't owe anyone an apology much less that bitter old bitch Tina Heywood."

"You're the best mom ever."

Her mother handed her one of the mini cupcakes from the cupcake trees near the door they'd come through. "I smuggled you one."

Tuesday took it. "I love Ezra. I haven't seen him in ten days. It was awful. I threw myself into all the

details of this party so at least I could keep busy. I've
only been sleeping three or four hours a night. I've
been making a lot more inventory with the extra hours
so that's good. When he came in today it was like
all my exhaustion faded away and I was recharged.
Eric never made me feel that. I felt guilty." She said
it really fast, barely taking a breath, just to get it out.

"Feel better? Baby, you can tell me and you'll feel
better. Don't you know that yet? Don't waste your energy on guilt. What does it change? Even if Ezra is
better on every level than Eric ever was or would have
been, so what? Do you want Eric back so you can see
if he'd fit you better now that you've gone through all
this hardship? Eric was a lovely man, but he was soft.
The Tuesday you are today wouldn't fit him. Surviv-
ing changes you right down to your soul. You are a
hundred times the woman now than you were before
Eric died. Because you had to make the choice every
day to keep going. Because you kept getting better
even if it was way too slow for my comfort. You did
it. You are hard, yes, but like a diamond is hard. You
take my meaning?"

Tuesday nodded.

"Your guilt won't make anything better. It won't
change who you are now. Be glad he makes you feel
so wonderful. I'm glad for you."

"You're just glad to have a handsome man to jam
with."

Her mother laughed. "Men! It's plural because I'm
claiming Paddy, as well."

"I'm not sure Dad is going to be down with that."

"I know I'm not." Natalie hugged Di. "You can

have a kidney but not Paddy. Look all you like, though. Heaven knows I do."

Sharon came back, calling Tuesday's name.

"Just a second." Tuesday reapplied her lipstick and opened the door.

"Sharon Hurley, this is my mother, Diana Easton. Mom, this is Sharon Hurley."

Sharon hugged Di. "So nice to meet you. Ezra and Paddy have been making me jealous with all this talk of how wonderful you are."

"What a fine job you've done with those boys of yours."

Sharon laughed. "If you only knew. But they're all okay now—that's what counts."

Ezra came in and his gaze flicked around the space until he finally found her. It was like the snap of a rubber band, their connection. They moved toward one another, meeting up halfway through the room.

He took her hands, kissing her knuckles. "Are you all right?"

"Are *you* all right? I'm so sorry about that whole mess."

He frowned. "We sent them packing. Your dad is badass. I think I've also been upgraded to a name every time. No more of that *boy* stuff."

"Great, you two can get matching jailhouse tattoos." She grinned and then sobered a little. "Thank you for defending me."

"All that stuff they said was wrong."

She shrugged. Even if it hadn't been, she didn't want to give them any more of her energy. "Doesn't matter. Come on with me to unlock the doors. It's nearly time."

HE LOOKED UP at her as she stood at the foot of his bed. Naked but for that necklace and the shoes.

"This is even better than I imagined it would be. Come up here."

She did and he reached out lightning quick and pulled her under him, kissing her senseless, loving the way she opened to him immediately.

"Do you know how many times tonight a guy looked at your tits?" He kissed her ear, down her neck. "Every time I turned around. Even my brothers. They're so spectacular I guess I shouldn't blame them. But I wanted to punch a lot of people tonight."

She laughed, digging her nails into his shoulders, urging him on. "You said it yourself—they're spectacular."

He nipped her neck and then down to her nipples. "They're also mine."

She hummed. "Yes. All right, that, too."

He licked over the curve at the side of her left breast and continued down to settle between her thighs. "It's been ten days since I've been here."

"I know."

But he didn't elaborate. Those ten days had seemed so important and yet he still wanted her so much.

He took a lick. "Damn, you taste so good." She did. She felt right, like sitting down in your favorite chair after a long day. He felt *received* by her.

He kept her spread wide as he took his time and when she came, he kept at it, pushing her into a smaller series of follow-up orgasms.

He crawled up to his knees, pausing to roll on a condom.

She nodded and that urgency ramped up between

them. He was in her then. Sliding into that hot wet embrace that he seemed to feel all the way down his spine.

"Gorgeous. Perfect. My beauty."

"Yours."

Then there was the slide of skin on skin, a sheen of sweat easing the way. The side of her neck was salty as he licked her there, body bent over as he kept to his knees, thrusting deep, lingering and then pulling nearly all the way out before pressing in again. Over and over until it felt like a magic spell binding them together.

One hand held her wrists captive. By this point between them it was just as much to feel her struggle against him, writhing around his cock. The other held her, fingers digging into her ass and thigh hard enough to leave a mark and he loved that idea.

More, he knew she loved it, too, and that's what made it so potent between them. He loved it hard, but so did she. Though he wondered at times after rehab if it was acceptable that he did. Whether or not he'd broken something and sought darker stuff because everyday sex couldn't get him off.

He had no such problem right then as orgasm tore through him, shredding him until he could only fall to the bed next to her and draw her close as he caught his breath and could deal with the condom.

"So, ALL KIDDING aside and the first round of reunion sex in the bag, tonight had a lot of stuff in it. Do you want to talk about it?" he asked as they settled in their respective places in his bed.

When he'd opened the door to go out to get some

water, he'd come back to find all three animals in bed with her. Peanut looked at him like she was going to poop in a shoe if he kept Tuesday away from them any more periods this long.

Loopy moved down to the tile floor, sprawling on her belly to get all the cool she could.

The cats burrowed between Ezra and Tuesday, purring like little jet engines as she scratched behind ears.

"My favorite part of the night was seeing you when you first got there. I kept telling myself it wasn't a big deal that I hadn't seen you in so long. We'd talked on the phone and texted, you had a harvest and I had all this work stuff but I missed you so much. And when I looked up and saw your face it was like every good thing I'd missed from not being with you for that time hit me all at once and made me just sort of drown in happy. The part with you going down on me and making me come for like eight minutes is also a high point. A full house at my opening. Selling so many pieces. Getting new contacts. All of those also hit the highlight reel. My sister and one of my brothers coming in from California was really amazing. I'll go up to my parents' house this weekend to hang out with them. Natalie will most likely come along because she and April get along well. I'm happy they got to meet you and your parents, too. I was thinking we could go out to dinner on Saturday so you can get to know them a little better."

It was then he realized not only that he'd forgotten to mention his trip with Jeremy, but that she knew it anyway.

"Of course, if I knew you were going to be away

with your friend this weekend I'd just plan around you. Were you afraid I'd be upset or something?"

"No. I honestly forgot. I'd mean to tell you and then I'd hear your voice and forget everything but you." He frowned.

She watched him carefully, waiting for him to elaborate and when he didn't she shrugged. "Have a good time. Bring me back chocolate."

That she *knew* he hadn't told her and that she *knew* he was holding back and was acting like she wasn't mad pushed him to finally speak.

"Two things. I had this epiphany that Saturday we went up to your parents' for your birthday. Jeremy called and we had a real conversation. He and I used to be pretty tight and he suggested he and I head to Vancouver for a few days to have good food and catch up. It was like an underline to this feeling I've had that I needed to make more of an effort to reconnect with my friends."

"I'm so glad to hear that. I think you do, too. I imagine some of your friends have really been hoping you'd reach out again."

"The second thing is that I don't want to go because I want to be with you. I want to snatch you up and take you to the mountains for the weekend, where it's just you and me."

"We can go up again at another time. I have my stall in the morning and then I'm going to Olympia for the weekend. You'll go to Vancouver and see Jeremy and when you get back to town I'll be here."

He pushed himself out of bed and began to pace. "Is it that easy for you?"

"What?"

"This week I needed to see you so much it nearly made me ache."

She turned to face him, reaching to turn the lamp on. "I know. I mean, I know you've been holding yourself away from me. Avoiding me."

"It's not avoiding you."

She got a sour look. "What is it then? I'm sitting here naked in your bed and I'm telling you the fucking truth. How dare you stand there and act like the truth isn't the truth and I can't see it. Fuck you, Ezra."

Wow. He'd never seen her like this. Not directed at him.

"See, Ezra, you could have come to me. At any time in the ten days since that weekend at my parents' and today. I'd have come to you. I will *always* come to you."

"I don't know how to want you and for it to be okay!"

She pulled on a robe and he was annoyed at the loss of all that pretty skin bared to his view.

"Stop yelling. You get the dog all upset and then she'll sleep between us. I'm right here. I can hear you just fine."

"How can you be so calm? I'm a goddamn junkie who is afraid of love because he doesn't know how to healthily need someone."

"I'm not confused." She shrugged. "See, that's the thing about tonight. I stood there and the Heywoods said all sorts of stuff and *you* got between them and me and absorbed all that hate. You defended me. For a long while it felt like anything good that made me happy was an insult to Eric. Tonight I told my mother I feel for you with an intensity I never had with anyone before, even Eric, and she said so what. And she's got a point. I can feel guilty about the feelings of a dead man or I can be thankful you were thrown in my path when I was ready for you. It's not right or wrong. It just is. You make me feel like no one ever has. And it freaks me out and I have moments when I wonder if I can really do it and be what you need. If I can be what *I* need. But the truth of it is the same either way. You can keep on with this talk about how you're a junkie and this and that. But you're not and that's silly so I'm telling you up front that *you* are the only one who sees Ezra that way. The rest of us clearly know you better."

"You deserve more than me. I don't want to disappoint you," he said quietly.

"I'm sure you're going to disappoint me. I know I'll disappoint you. Most of the time I won't mean it. I'll let you down. I'll piss you off. I'll hurt your feelings. I'm bitchy. I have a life. I don't need you to complete it. I'm complete already. I don't need a boyfriend."

She took a deep breath. "But I need *you*. Do you understand what I'm saying? It's not the office you fill in my life. It's you. Despite the reality that two people will inevitably annoy each other in some way, I like you in my life. I want you to take a chance. Be willing to need me. Why not? This is not the same as craving drugs or alcohol."

"But the feelings are the same. I'm a bad bet. We talked about this already. I am broken and you deserve way more than I can give you."

"Are they? I'm not where you are, so this is a real question, Ezra. If you compare what I am to you with what heroin was to you, do you really truly think it's

the same? If it is, I don't honestly know where to go
from there."

She got up and he watched as she put her clothes
back on.

"I'll still be in love with you when you get back
from Vancouver. I've never been much for other people deciding what I needed. I need you."

He paced, needing the rhythm of it. "After I got
clean I had to figure out what things that made me feel
good were acceptable and what ones weren't. It means
I spent more time focused inward than I had before
and looking at some hard truths. So while I could definitely say things like drugs and alcohol were definite
noes for me, I had to struggle with exercise and eating right. And sex."

She nodded.

"I tended to exercise too much, for instance. So I
had to be mindful about it for a while until it became
routine and not obsession. Sometimes when something feels good I panic."

"You cleaned up and you turned your life around
and you're indispensible to your family. And me.
Can't you see that? When are you going to accept
that it's okay to feel good? Not everything is shoving
a needle in your arm."

"You have no idea what I was like."

"Yeah? You think I'd be shocked? I imagine you
stole some money. You let people down. I saw the
fight you had with your brother onstage. Get online
and you can find ten different angles of him punching
you and your head slamming into the speaker. Would
that help? To watch rock bottom over and over? I bet

you have anyway because goddamn it you love to wallow in your mistakes."

She didn't know anything about it.

"What's that going to solve? How do you use that to move on and have a life? Because you can't possibly spend the rest of your life freaked out by everything that makes you enjoy it enough to want it more than once. Hell, what about pecan-praline ice cream?"

"Don't downplay it." He heard the anger in his voice and so did she.

But she pushed on. "I'm not downplaying it. I'm asking you a real question. How much is enough? When will you feel like you've finally made your reparations and that it's okay to want to see a gorgeous woman who loves to get naked with you? A woman who loves *you*, Ezra. Who *trusts* you. Like Paddy trusts you. Like Vaughan trusts you. Like Mary and Damien. Like your pigs and your chickens and three goats all named Marshmallow. Like your dog and your cats and your parents. All the people who know you best, we all trust you. When do *you* trust you?"

"After the fight I had onstage, they took me to the hospital to stitch up my head. But there were drugs there and all the shame I'd been starting to feel was gone in the face of all those painkillers. I filled my prescription and left when no one was looking. I hadn't been arrested or anything. So I walked out. My dealer picked me up, handed over a huge amount of heroin and dropped me off at a by-the-hour motel. I hid there for a few days until they found me. I was little more than an animal by that point. I used every single thing I knew to get them to leave. I said things that can't be taken back."

The memories of it, the shame seemed to coat his skin like dirt stuck to sweat. He wanted to run away. To clap his hands over his ears and pretend she didn't make so much sense he wanted to scream.

"You don't have to take them back, Ezra. You said them and then you sincerely owned it and made yourself into a better person. You can't constantly hold out the lowest point in your life as the norm. Unless you like feeling like shit. It might have been normal for *that* Ezra but it hasn't been for a long time. The only person who can't forgive you is you. The rest of us know better."

"My mother locked herself in the room with me. She was crying. In all the time growing up when we fucked up she never cried. Oh, she got pissed and we made her sad. But my mom doesn't cry like that. She was crying, begging me to get help. She was worried I was going to die. I probably would have but I didn't care. I started to get sick. I needed to get high and she wouldn't leave. Then she took my rig and touched the needle to her arm, pressing so I could see a bead of blood. I'd been in there with her for several hours and I needed it. I'd started cramping up. She said she would give me the heroin back if I really wanted it, but that she would use first. Use with me."

Tuesday didn't speak; she just watched him from where she stood, leaning against the corner of his writing desk, listening as she petted both cats, who'd moved to be sure she could reach them.

"I've never told this story to anyone." He threw a hand over his eyes and she did move then, coming to face him, taking his hand and looking him dead-on.

"I don't want you to hide your eyes. I'll close my eyes if you want. If it would make it easier to say."

"It shouldn't be easy."

But when he moved his arm, she'd closed her eyes. She took his hand, holding it in hers, not letting go. And he loved her and hated her. He needed her and she was *there* with his hands in hers and her eyes closed so he could finish his story.

She wrecked him right down to his foundations and he didn't know if he could survive. Not with her and not without her, either.

"You don't know what it's like. To need something so bad your entire body just revolts until you get it. Being drug sick is the worst. Your whole body hurts. Your muscles cramp. You can't keep anything down. So there I was in that dirty little hovel, subhuman, backed into a corner. I needed that heroin so much I could taste it. I thought about letting her do it just so she'd pass out and then I could make a run for it. But it was heroin-addict strength, you get me? And it was my mother with a dirty needle poised at her arm. She was going to do it. She was using everything she could to reach that part of me that remembered what it was not to be chained by addiction."

"You didn't make her do it, did you?"

"No I didn't. She opened the door and the treatment people came in and whisked me off. But I *considered* it." He could still feel it, that part of him that wanted to do it, no matter the cost. "What kind of person does that make me?

"You're going to feel guilty about *thoughts* in that situation? Really? What's your endgame then, Ezra? How do you get to the point where you can let yourself be loved by me and not panic that loving me back is as bad as being addicted to drugs?"

"I nearly lost who I was. It took *years* to live a normal life again. Yes, I'm afraid of falling back into that."

"I'm not belittling your struggle or how far you've come. I admire you a great deal. You're incredibly strong. You've rebuilt yourself. So you thought a bad thing five years ago. So you thought a bad thing five minutes ago. They're thoughts. Some of them are bad if we're talking serial killer–type thoughts. But we aren't. And you're not a cornered animal. You're Ezra Michael Hurley. You've written twenty-two hit singles, twelve of them since you got out of rehab and stopped touring. Your family sees it, your fans see it, I see it. Why can't you? What's holding you back?"

So few people spoke to him that honestly. That she would do it, that she paid enough attention and cared deeply…

"You said you loved me."

"Yeah, I did. Three times I think. I'm pretending it's no big that you haven't responded in any way."

He straightened, reeling once again. And once again she was the source. "You can't love me."

She nodded. "I totally can so love you. You're not the boss of me just because I let you hold me down while you fuck me. That night we came back to my house and Paddy and Nat were there? I figured it out during a whispered conversation with Natalie in my room while you were down with Paddy. I'm scared, but I'm at the point where I'm more scared to walk away than to stay. You better love me back, Ezra, because I am a fantastic catch. I will not tolerate your bullshit. But I respect your space and I'm supercute."

"What if I'm replacing one addiction with another?"

"I can't say. You have to decide. I'm obviously not a physical addiction. I'm not going to mess with your internal organs. I'm way easier on your bank account. I make your cock hard instead of, um, not. So you crave me. So you want to be with me. I want to be with you. You're supposed to want to be with people you like. You're definitely supposed to want to be around people you love. What's bad there? Tell me the horrible outcome of you craving what I've got right here?" She cupped her pussy and he had to cough to clear his throat. She pointed to her head. "Or here?" And her heart. "Or here?"

"We're both broken in multiple ways. And yet we found one another. My broken pieces fit with yours. I want you to crave me. I crave you. I want you with me. I want to fall asleep listening to the sound of your breathing. It's okay to be a little broken. I'll help you hold your pieces together. When you get tired and you just don't know if you can do it, I'll be right there."

"I'm freaked the hell out. I can't do this until I have it straight."

She looked so very, very sad. "All right." She went to the closet and came away with her dress on a hanger. She came back from the bathroom with her toiletries kit and he moved quickly to stop her.

"Wait. You're leaving? I'm not breaking up with you. Are you breaking up with me?"

"You need to figure stuff out first, Ezra. I can't be something you relegate to a resentful addiction.

Something you are powerless against. I'm not heroin. I'm not a bad thing at all and I can't be with anyone who thinks that."

She finished packing her things.

"Don't leave."

She turned, cupping his cheek.

"Yeah?"

He wanted to say the words she needed. But he knew she'd see right through anything but the truth and he didn't have the words she needed. Not right then.

She nodded. "Yes, I'm going home. Have a safe trip this weekend with your friend. Remember to let yourself have a good time."

"I tried to stay away. Tried to deny how much I needed you to prove to myself I could. But I hated it and I missed you."

She cocked her head. "I liked some of those words. Next time you think about doing something silly, how about you aim at doing things that don't punish us both. If you don't want me anymore you better say so right now. I'll go and this will be done. I don't want to be something you have to argue with yourself to want. I want to be with you. I want you to binge on me until you get your fill. Binge and binge until you realize you don't have to because I'm here waiting to give you whatever you ask for."

"Is that what love is?"

She shrugged. "In this case it is. From me to you, always, yes."

"And you love me even though I have a crazy family and three goats named Marshmallow? Even though I failed everyone in my life so badly I had to go away for nine months just to get to a place where I'd then spend years making right?"

She nodded. "Yes. Not *even though*. *Because of*. You're so much stronger than you know. You can need me. You can crave me. I'm here. I'm all yours. It's me and you and it's okay. You said Ezra and Tuesday were supposed to be different—you remember that?"

"And you'll be here when I get back from Vancouver?"

"Ezra, I told you. I will always be here when you get back from wherever you go. If you need to be alone, that's okay. If you need to be with me but in quiet, that's all right, too. I want you to rebuild your friendship with Jeremy. I know you have to harvest things and plant things and do that farmer stuff. And all of that comes with who you are. It's part of who *we* are. I need to be alone sometimes, too. But I love you. I can't hide it. I can't minimize it. I want you to love me back and you're not ready. So, I'm going home. You know the way once you get your shit straight."

CHAPTER TWENTY-SEVEN

TUESDAY SET HER glass down on the table and looked across at Natalie.

"So I told him that until he finds a way to accept needing me, I mean really accept it, we won't work." They'd stopped for breakfast on their way up to Olympia to hang out with Tuesday's sister for the day.

Tuesday'd shifted her lunch date with Kelly to the following week, but hopefully both women would have happy news. Kelly and Vaughan had stopped in to the gallery opening but they'd had the girls and after a bit they'd all headed out to dinner with Michael and Sharon.

She and Kelly had spoken about it on the phone the day before but they needed a long session with cocktails to update one another on what had been going on.

"Paddy said he was super grumpy and withdrawn at their meeting with Jeremy. He says good luck. Paddy, I mean, not Jeremy. For what it's worth, I think you made the right decision. He needs to accept how he feels for you. Not just for you, but for himself."

"I don't want to sound mean or unfeeling. I understand he's freaked by needing and craving anything. I get it. He never wants to be that guy again. I can get behind that totally. I don't want it, either. I can accept his broody darkness. His wounds and flaws. I love him. But I can't do it on my own. I can't face needing someone that much and him not allowing himself to do the same. It's uneven. I'd start resenting him."

"You deserve to be adored and craved and desired. I don't think you're wrong for needing him to really understand what it means to accept what he feels about you. All of it. So, does he tie you up or use handcuffs?"

"See, this is the drawback to sharing sex details with you. No it's not like that. He's rough, but not to hurt. Like he needs it so bad he has to take it. It's—I can't even believe I'm discussing this—it's all encompassing when he and I start up. He likes to be in control, but it's not whips and chains. I'd totally let him use whips and chains if it flipped his switch. If anyone could get me to like it a lot, he could. But it's just…he likes to be in control. He likes to set the pace. I'm fine with that. He's not telling me how to vote or how to spend my money—if he wants to hold my wrists while he fucks me I'm all for it. He works it. It's unbelievably hot."

"Sounds hot. I mean, all you have to do is look at him and know he has something happening in sexy-town."

Tuesday laughed. "It's the number one tourist destination voted for by me, that's for sure. But I don't want to be a visitor. I want us to be together. I want him to be all right with it. Before Ezra I was meeting men I barely knew in hotel rooms to have sex. I knew it was empty, but I needed something. I let it in as far as I could. You know? Like all right, I don't have to know these jokers that well. You go out on a

date, see if you have any click and if you do and he's
not a freak you might accept the second date invite
but middinner just say hey let's get to it. I'd do it for a
while and then break it off. I figured maybe one day
I'd be able to take the next step. But Ezra isn't a small
step—he's a trip to Neptune away from random fucks
in midpriced chain hotels."

They paid for their food and got back in the car,
heading north once more.

It was easier to say while she drove, her gaze on
the road ahead. Knowing Natalie would never judge
her helped as always. But she'd never said some of
this out loud. Speaking it gave it a whole different
sort of reality.

"Ezra isn't random or generic. He's not bland.
There's nothing mild about him. There's no *just one
bite* with him. It's the most intense thing I've ever
felt. Even when I first saw him it was like all the air
got sucked from the room. I guess for a while I was
so overwhelmed with sensation I was wary of it. And
then it lasted. I still feel that way every time he's near.
And I realized this was a vastly different sort of thing
than I'd had with Eric. You know, I talked with you
about it. Anyway, I've been struggling with it. Up
until Ezra got in between me and the Heywoods."

"Di spilled some truth in that room."

"Well, you've said a lot of the same stuff, so don't
think I haven't heard. But it was really her saying you
know what? Who cares? Who cares if I love Ezra less
or a million times more than I ever did Eric? The only
person who would have cared was Eric. I'd been hanging on to all that guilt and maybe I used it to protect
myself as long as I could. I closed the door on my

marriage with Eric. It's a memory. It's part of who I am now and who I'll continue to be. But whatever this is, I accept it. Ezra has brought so much into my life. As improbable as it seems, he and I are broken and jagged but when you put us together, our broken pieces fit. I am feeling so totally Zen about this right now. It's been a really long time since I've been so one hundred percent okay with where I was and who was in my life. If he can't love me back it will suck. But I will survive. I know I'm capable of this for someone else and that means a lot. I wasn't sure I could feel this way again."

"He'll come around. He's grumpy and emo, yes, but smart. You're the smartest option he has. He'll realize it. I promise. Anyway, I'm glad you love Ezra. Ezra is wonderful and handsome and smart and sexy and he loves animals. He has two pigs—how can you not just want to boop his nose sometimes?"

Tuesday guffawed at the very thought. "I'll give you twenty dollars if you do it."

Natalie's laugh deepened and went bawdy. This person who'd been with her through so many highs and lows. "So hey. I love you, Natalie. Thank you for being my sister and my friend and my lighthouse. You never let me get too lost."

"You're going to make me cry. I love you, too. I honestly wouldn't be here today without you."

That's what she'd told Ezra she needed. He needed to accept living every damned day. With her. He had to pick her and life and a future where they were open to all the other came along with.

"No more living in blacks and grays. Loving Ezra has left me broken open. I can't pull myself back together if he walks away. He's my missing piece. Don't get me wrong—if he comes back and says he can't give me what I need, I'll survive. That's how life goes. But I want to move forward with him."

"I want that for you, too. You deserve it. Let's buy stuff today. Let's get some new shoes and some cute outfits and go out in one tonight."

"You're on."

"DO YOU WANT me to drop you off at Paddy's?" Tuesday asked Natalie as she got off the highway after a fun day with her sister and brother the day before. They'd gone up to Seattle and spent the night at a swanky boutique hotel and had gone to dinner and had drinks and even went dancing in the new outfits they'd bought. That morning they'd got up, had a nice brunch and she'd dropped both her siblings off at SeaTac on their way back to Hood River.

It had been a long day with a lot of driving so it really wouldn't be that big a deal to just take Nat up to the ranch if she didn't want to drive up herself. Plus she could look at Ezra's house and go say hello to the pigs. But mainly she was going to say she was just being a good friend to drop Nat off at her boyfriend's place.

"That's okay. I'm going to take a long shower and then read and go to bed early. I have a lot on my to-do list at work in the morning." To underline that, Natalie actually had to pause to yawn in the middle of the sentence.

It was probably just as well she didn't go up there. She had to keep hope and yet not torture herself with it. He'd be back and come to her. If he didn't, he wasn't worthy of her.

Once home, Tuesday made them some soup before both women headed up to their respective sides of the house.

The plumbing was good, but the house was big and so she let Nat take the first round and then showered later. Since she had the time she chose a new color for her nails and toes and then deep-conditioned her hair. There was all sorts of moisturizing and trimming and plucking and several hours later she washed off the mask goop and gave herself a look in the mirror. Smooth and soft. Her nails and toes shiny in a summery coral shade.

She pulled out a navy blue dress to wear to the gallery the next day and realized the sandals she'd want to wear with them weren't in her closet.

Grabbing a robe, she headed downstairs through the kitchen to see if she'd left them at the back door. If not, they might be in her trunk but she didn't think so.

She looked around under the bench at the entry and finally realized the tapping she'd been hearing wasn't Natalie doing something upstairs, it was at the door.

Clutching her robe tighter, she went to look out the peephole and then wrenched the door open to find Ezra standing there.

She didn't have words, all her Zen gone. Now she worried he'd say no thanks and she'd have to live without him. If he did, though, she'd have so much hot revenge dating around town!

They looked at one another for long, silent moments. Finally, he stepped into the house and pulled her to his body, burying his face in her neck.

Joy rained through her, soaking into her cells until she was saturated and trying not to cry. "You're here."

"You promised. And here you are." He said it with a little edge of wonder in his tone. Like she'd planned to be down here right then when he got to her door.

She took his face in her hands. "I told you I would be. Still don't trust me? Why are you at my door at eleven-thirty on a Sunday night? I thought you were coming back tomorrow afternoon. "

He put his hands over hers, drawing them into his, kissing her fingertips. "Beauty, can we talk?"

She wanted to say, *only if you're here to tell me you love me.* But she didn't. "Yes. Come in. Let me lock up." She reached around him and took care of that, catching sight of her sandals tucked under the ottoman. She bent to snatch them up. "Ha!"

He followed her upstairs and into her room.

"Jeremy's plane leaves for LAX at six tomorrow morning. I was going to fly back to Portland and then drive here but I didn't want to waste time. I wanted to see you. So he and I had dinner and I took a private plane. A friend of Damien's is a pilot. He brought me back here. He brought me back here so I could tell you something. Well, a lot of somethings."

She hung her robe on the hook and sat on the love seat at the foot of her bed, tucking her feet beneath her.

"I'm in love with you. I may be crappy at it. You can find a million men better for you than me. But I don't care because you're mine."

She nodded sharply. "I'm glad we can agree on this. As a start goes, this is really good."

He flashed her a grin and she knew to her toes that everything was going to be okay.

"There's more."

"Hit me."

"All my life I've felt deeply about stuff. I've craved that depth of emotion. Adrenaline, lust, fear, pleasure, whatever, I wanted it and I wanted it in heaping quantities. And then that bit me in the ass." He sat with her, taking her hands. "So I had to wipe it all out and figure out what was okay to find pleasure in. I had to relearn what it meant to feel good. For a while I felt nothing but intense guilt. It was like the drugs had fucked up my brain. Like I was beyond being moved by normal, everyday things that make people happy. I couldn't connect. And then it came back slowly. I tried to live and take care of all the stuff my system needed without getting obsessive and so I had my animals and my family and sometimes meaningless sex to keep from exploding.

"And then you. You came into my view and I was no longer choosing what to feel deeply over, easy things usually. You made me feel no matter what I did or didn't want. Everything was bright and loud and I touched you and things quieted. When I'm with you, everything is manageable. You know me, ugly skeletons in the closet and all, but you see through it. You see right to my heart and I can't do anything else but tell you I love you. I crave you and over many, many hours of talking to Jeremy and staying up late watching black-and-white movies while writing songs about you, I can say it and be okay with that."

"Well, okay then. This is getting better and better." He leaned in to kiss her quick and hard before speaking again. "Missed your taste. You let me be when I need it and you shake my life up and show me what I've been missing. I'm a mess—you know that already. But I'm your mess if that's cool with you."

She hugged him, climbing into his lap, raining kisses all over his face. "I think I could probably be all right with that. I love you. I'm glad you're here."

"You trusted me to work through it."

"And you trusted me enough to know I'd be here when you did. I think we're pretty awesome and also both of us look great naked. And speaking of that, I just realized that standing mirror is perfect." She kissed him and then got up to aim the mirror a little better so they could watch.

SHE NEVER CEASED to amaze him. He took in the sight of the cheeks peeking from her panties as she made it possible for them to look at themselves as they had sex. Delightfully and perfectly sexy.

He'd got up to Vancouver and then he and Jeremy had gone out for a ride in Stanley Park and to dinner and back to the apartment they were staying in, talking pretty much all night long about life for both men since their friendship had started to fade.

Jeremy had been nursing guilt, feeling as if it were his fault. Like he'd dropped their friendship and of course Ezra had the same guilt. It had been stupid and once they'd starting talking it was like the old days. Only better because each of them had weathered personal storms and came out the other side better off.

"I knew going up there on the plane that I'd be coming back to you. I just had to find my way there."

She whipped off her tank top and stepped free from her panties and he grinned. "Hot damn."

She pointed. "You, too. I want to see you."

He stood and got naked and she looked him over. "You look good, Hurley. Good enough to be in my bed." She grinned at the tease and he grabbed her quick, sitting with her in his lap. "I'd have been here tomorrow, too, you know. But I sure am glad you're here right now."

He cupped her breasts as he nuzzled her throat. "Me, too. It startles me sometimes, how deeply you make me feel. How much more of it I want from you. I'm greedy. I was stupid to fear any sort of comparison."

"Yes, you were. But I understand. And if you tell me when you're having a hard time and I tell you when I am, we can probably do this thing."

"Okay. I'm in."

"Ooh! Wait a sec." She got up and hurried around to the table on the side of the bed he normally slept on. Holding aloft the little foil square, she headed back to him.

She settled again in his lap and he watched her, content to just be for those few seconds before his cock reminded him it had places to be deep inside her. Inside Ezra's woman.

He'd turned the concept over and then the words all the way back to her. And found that she'd known she was his before he'd been able to accept the very idea.

He snatched the condom from her fingers and got it on.

"Hey! I have plans."

His amusement sharpened. "So do I. I need to be

in you." He craved that connection they shared, especially now that they'd both bared their souls to one another.

She kissed him, her fingers dug into his hair, tugging him as she nipped at his lips and licked the sting away.

He slid a palm from her shoulder down her side to her hip while he angled his cock and pulled her down onto him.

She opened her eyes once he'd got all the way inside. "Yes," she murmured, her eyes on his.

"I love you."

She smiled at him so pretty. "You better." She circled her hips and he *tsked*.

He tightened his hand at her hip and levered them to her rug. "Now I'm going to fuck you so hard you'll find out how you like rug burns on your ass as well as your knees."

She moaned and he made that sound he knew she loved. She pleased him so much. So sexy and beautiful.

He got to his knees as she lay flat on her back, her thighs wide so he had a perfect view. He watched himself disappear into her body over and over, watched her nipples darken. She urged him in, rolling her hips to meet his thrusts.

There was sex, which he'd had plenty of to compare with what he did with Tuesday, which was sex times a million. He wanted to be in her as deep as he could. Wanted her to wrap around him like a cat.

He wanted to do things to her that left her begging for more, that left his touch burned into her heart and soul. Knew, too, that she'd already marked him that deeply.

Tuesday sheltered his battered heart. She was his safe place to be.

He sped up, pulling out to roll her to her side and slide back in.

Her answering gasp of surprised pleasure told him this angle was one he'd be trying again.

"I need you to come around me. I need that so bad right now," he nearly snarled as she writhed, tightening her inner muscles around him.

Her hand burrowed between her legs and soon after came the slick brush of her fingertips as she got herself wet. Then the slow ebb and flow of rolling waves of her inner muscles as she drew closer to climax.

Her body was a siren call around his. She smelled good. Partly the light citrus of her body lotion teased with the earthy, rich scent of their sex.

She came then on a whisper of his name and he was so close behind her he couldn't remember if he'd waited or they ended up coming that close together. Whatever the case, he continued to thrust until it felt like his knees were going to give out and he finally ended up on his back, gasping for air.

After they'd got up, they'd tossed on some clothes and headed downstairs to get something to eat and power them through two more rounds before they fell asleep.

Right as he was nearly unconscious, Ezra kissed the shoulder nearest his mouth. "Thank you for giving yourself to me the way you do."

"I'm yours. You're mine. That's how it works," she answered sleepily. "You were born to be mine. That's what my mother said. She also said you'd be way too much for any normal woman to handle so that's why I came along."

He snorted, hugging her a little tighter. "That's probably true. I should confess to you, though, that in my rush to get back to you, I left the chocolates I bought for you at the place we were staying. They're going to mail the box here."

"I suppose I can let you off with a warning this one time." She pushed her butt into his crotch as she wiggled to get closer.

"Playing with fire," he warned her,

"I just did three times. Surely even *you* can't go… well now," she nearly purred as he ground his fully revived cock into that sweet ass.

"Don't worry. I'll save it for when we wake up in a few hours."

She hummed. "You're on my approved-vendor list for all time. I love you, Ezra Hurley, rock star rancher with a heart of gold and a very large cock."

"I love you, too, Tuesday Easton, woman of my dreams, artist, my beauty."

"Yeah, that's nice." She sighed happily and when he fell asleep again, he knew he'd always have a place to return to.

* * * * *

ACKNOWLEDGMENTS

When I was eighteen years old, I met a boy with long hair, holes in his jeans and a muscle car. That was nearly three decades ago, and that boy and I moved 1200 miles away from home and started a life and a family in the northwest. That boy is now a man, with gray in his beard, who spends his life wrangling the wild spawn we've created together and being my heart. I love you, Ray.

Angela James, you are magic. Thank you for being as amazing as you are.

Thank you so *much* to the Harlequin art department for the covers for this series. I do believe the beard on the model for *Broken Open* is the finest cover beard in all the land. And you got Tuesday so perfect.

I'd be absolutely awful without the support and love of my tribe—my writerly community whom I routinely turn to for information, help, a shoulder, expertise, a rant and sometimes a kick in the pants. Thank you all for being my people.